*He had nearly hit her.*
Terror filled her. Why? Why was he after her?

Then she was running, zigzagging through the woods, fighting her way through undergrowth and close-spaced tree trunks where the snowmobile would have a hard time getting through. The snow was nearly three feet deep, and she struggled along, making a terrific effort. But she was so *slow*!

The motor suddenly roared. The snowmobile had left the trail. It was in the trees, eating up the distance between them.

She was trapped. She wanted to scream. She wanted to go home.

She wanted her mother.

# JULIA GRICE

## TENDER PREY

A TOM DOHERTY ASSOCIATES BOOK
NEW YORK

TENDER PREY

A Tor Book
Published by Tom Doherty Associates, Inc.
49 West 24th Street
New York, N.Y. 10010

ISBN: 0-812-51826-8

First edition: August 1990

Printed in the United States of America

0 9 8 7 6 5 4 3 2 1

*For my parents, Jean and Will Haughey,*
*in loving thanks*

Readers should note that the villages of Hartwick, Ossineke Lake, etc., are fictitious, as are all the characters in the book. Since the subject matter is sensitive, I want to make it very clear that these characters are based on no real-life person or persons. Any similarity of names is pure and simple coincidence, and not to be construed as deliberate. Although child pornography certainly does exist, the name of RAM Productions is a figment of my imagination.

I would like to thank Al Zuckerman, of Writer's House, for his good cheer and many kindnesses; and Melissa Ann Singer, my editor at Tor Books, for her expertise. Special thanks should go to Mr. and Mrs. Lester Grice, who, many years ago, introduced me to the world of northern Michigan.

# PROLOGUE

In northern Michigan, when the heat of a July afternoon reaches about eighty-six, an odor is released by the pines. It is created by softened pine pitch, mixed with an undertone of dead pine needles and gray tree fungus. It is pungent and musky, almost sexually intense.

Ray Innis, thirty-two years old with a head of black hair and a sharp, handsome face, breathed in that arresting aroma. He released his breath in a nervous push of air. He paced, his shoes scraping up tufts of old pine needles laid down by years of summers. Shit, he was scared. But then, he was always scared beforehand, his nerves built up to a sharp, anxious peak.

She was late.

The girl had said noon, and it was nearly 1:30 now.

*Jesus*, he thought, dry-swallowing. He heard his

tongue smack against his palate. He had to urinate again, too, the fourth time in an hour.

He took care of the need, listening to his water patter on the spreading fronds of a woods fern, glistens of yellow moisture catching the sun. He zipped up. This was crazy, he thought, this whole thing. It was dangerous, he should have his head examined for what he was about to do.

If someone were to see them . . .

Around him the woods were alive with bird noises, insect hums, and the lapping songs of the current from the Au Sable River that wandered across half of Upper Michigan. He felt safe here. A canoe livery was located a quarter mile downstream, but this property was posted and tourists seldom came here.

He glanced at a wide, scooped depression in the earth, overgrown now with a stand of weedy birches. The scar dated back to the 1880s, when lumbermen had dragged logs out of the river.

He had lectured about the lumberjack days in the science class he taught at Hartwick Junior High School, explaining the history of "the cut" at Higgins Lake, trying to fire the imaginations of twelve-year-olds who would rather giggle or scrawl notes.

He wasn't one of those few gifted ones to whom teaching came easily. His first year of teaching had been like his fifth, wearying and tense. He was too impatient, he expected too much, was too prone to disappointment. And he had his fatal flaw, the preoccupation that spiced his days with almost unbearable excitement.

The danger.

It was addictive, much worse than any cocaine or heroin.

He had tried, but he could not stop.

For the hundredth time he glanced at his watch, and even brought it up to his ear to make certain it was still running. She *had* said noon. But maybe she wasn't coming. It had happened to him before; girls of that age were notoriously changeable and fickle.

But today he did feel a reasonable expectation of hope. The Smith girl had a crush on him, and had bombarded him the entire school year with anonymous notes, lavish with big *X*s that stood for kisses. He knew he looked like a thinner Eddie Fisher, and this phenomenon—the notes—always amazed and delighted him. Girls created romantic daydreams and searched for a man to put in their fantasies, one who would be safe for them to adore.

Even adult women gravitated toward him, and he was having trouble right now with a red-haired beautician in town, Alma Henssen, who had twice showed up at the Dietz home where he rented a room, demanding that he take her to Grayling for a movie.

At least that was the way he saw it, *demanding*. Grown women caused him to feel an inner curl of revulsion. Their skin showed pores, there were too many hairs on their bodies, and the curves of their shapes were disgustingly full, their breasts sagging bags of flesh.

A bird began a high, thin, sweet call. Maybe it was the rare Kirtland warbler that lived around here in a few stands of jack-pine forest, this its only habitat in the entire world. He had lectured his classes on the warbler. Sherry Smith had brought in a copy of *National Geographic*, gazing at him with melting blue eyes, her skin without pore or flaw. She was the prettiest girl he had ever seen.

He expelled his breath, beginning to be angry now that she hadn't shown up.

He was gambling a lot being here—but of course if anyone saw him walking by the river, there wasn't anything wrong with that, was there? It was only when Sherry arrived that he'd be at risk. He had prepared for that, though. He was going to sug-

gest they go down the river a few hundred feet, to
a tiny sandy beach he'd discovered, shielded from
view by overhanging trees that had fallen half into
the water.

A few feet away was the duffel bag he'd brought
with him, containing a quilt, two towels, and his
bathing suit. He also had carried in a small picnic
cooler and a paper sack stuffed with snacks. In his
pocket was the trinket. He'd spent a whole Saturday shopping in Traverse City for just the right gift
for her.

He always gave gifts.

He started to sweat just thinking about it, and
that was when he heard the giggles drift from over
the hill, near the trail. High, trilling girl giggles,
*from more than one girl.*

Holy shit. She'd brought some friends with her.

His heart thudded as three twelve-year-old girls
came rushing down the twisting path that led from
the road, clad in brief shorts and tight little T-shirts
that revealed soft breast buds.

"Hi! Hi, Mr. Innis! We got lost!" Laughing, chattering, full of adventure, they skidded down the hill,
one girl stopping to tug at a thong sandal that had
come loose. He recognized Sherry Smith. With her
were Judy Sjoholm and Carole Hamner, her best
friends. The "giggle three" as he'd mentally dubbed
them.

He hurried to meet them, smiling to cover the
bad shock this had given to his nerves. What was
he to do now? He hated wasting the day, all the
planning. He would not waste it. He made the decision instantaneously.

"I see you brought your buddies," he greeted
Sherry, the tallest and prettiest. He gave her his
warm smile and turned to include the other two.

"Oh, yes, they wanted to come swimming too and
I wanted them to see your secret beach!"

"It won't be secret if everyone knows about it."

"Well, nobody's going to be able to find it; you said right near town but we had to walk and walk, and that path you said, the path back from the road, it's almost *all covered up* with trees; you must have come here when there weren't any leaves on the trees!"

The girl was smart; he had. He looked more closely, noticing that Sherry was hyper with the excitement of doing something forbidden. She was slightly more mature than the other two, her shirt stretched tight over what would be, in six months or so, perky new breasts. Her eyes shone eagerly.

Oh, God, he'd have to be so careful. Girls were skittish, and often not as innocent as they might appear. If he showed his real feelings, he'd spook them.

"It's okay, Sherry," he soothed. "You got here, didn't you? And we're going to have a great picnic. I brought us a cooler full of punch, and some brownies, and some potato chips for us to munch on."

"Oh, what kind, what kind?"

"What kind do you like? I've got two kinds."

The girls crowded around the cooler, prying open the lid to peek inside, rummaging inside the big I.G.A. sack that contained the chips, making free with everything. When Sherry bent over, Ray glimpsed the pink pucker-cotton of her panties.

"*I* want to carry the chips 'n' stuff," announced Carole, a stocky little blonde. She was the class coquette, always fighting, punching, or teasing the boys. Someday she'd be a grown-up flirt, and probably fat, like Ray's mother, exactly the type of woman Ray hated most. But for now she was very sensuous, with an amazingly rounded ass.

"All right, you can carry it—"

"No, me!" begged Judy Sjoholm. She had a pug nose and waif eyes, the adoring follower who willingly joined whatever mischief Sherry and Carole thought up. Ray thought her insipid, but her body was incredibly dainty, her waist easily encircleable with his hands.

Oh, God, God, the risk!

But he had taken risks before, hadn't he? He was no stranger to this, and today he was so psyched, he hadn't slept all night thinking of it.

"You can all carry stuff, there's plenty for everyone," he said, laughing. "But first, are you ready to get your feet wet?"

They chorused, "Sure, we brought our bathing suits—"

"Good. Well, we have to get to the beach first. It's just up the riverbank a little bit, but we'll have to climb around some branches. We're going to my secret spot. Nobody knows about it but me—and now, you. I come here and fish, so you've got to promise not to tell anyone because I don't want anyone coming here and stealing all my good fish!"

They nodded, agreeing. Living in a resort area, they knew all about fishermen and their jealous guarding of sites.

He added, "And no talking about our picnic either—anyone who talks doesn't get to graduate to eighth grade, because students are not supposed to fraternize with teachers."

Again they nodded, looking a little scared this time.

"You sure?" he questioned them. "No blabbing? We can turn back right now. I can send you home."

They didn't want that, of course. To them this was an adventure, being off alone with the handsome science teacher, and they felt safe in numbers. Their solemn faces told him what he wanted to know.

"Okay," he conceded. "But remember, I warned you." He took a deep breath. "Now, come on—I put ice in the cooler but I've been waiting here a long

time and it's going to melt in this heat if we don't
hurry."

He led the way down the slope to the bank, the
girls following him. Carole squealed when she
slipped on a root. Their laughter and chatter reminded him of the calls of beautiful tropical birds.

He forced himself to relax.

It would be okay.

He would make this work. He might even get
some of the girls to come back later, separately,
alone.

Didn't he have nearly a pint of vodka mixed in
with the Hawaiian Punch in the cooler? And in the
brownies, he'd baked some marijuana, purchased
in Ann Arbor four months ago and waiting for this
day.

The sun baked overhead, heating the pine pitch
in the trees and coaxing out its sensuous fecund
odor.

# CHAPTER 1

Sherry Vincent drew cold January air into her lungs, tasting its bite, and started down the snow-covered trail toward her rural mailbox.

She glanced back over her shoulder at the redwood-sided house with its shake-shingle roof, barely visible through the ranks of snow-blanketed red pines, jack pines, and young birch. Every payment on it was an adventure. So far she'd made them all, but November had been a bitch, since it hadn't snowed until December 2, and revenues from the small ski resort she owned hadn't started to come in yet.

Frowning, she wondered if she should sell the house on its gorgeous, high-priced lake frontage, take the money, buy a back-lot cabin someplace, and hang on by the skin of her teeth as so many people in northern Michigan had to do.

*No*, she told herself. *No way*. She had been divorced one month now. One wonderful, lonely,

heartbreaking, scary month. Didn't they say that
you should wait at least a year before you made
any major decisions? Even her therapist said so.

She scuffed at a snowmobile tread mark, her
mood darkening. More tracks this year than ever
before, and she didn't like it. It made her feel un-
private, as if the pureness of the woods had been
violated by something noisy and mechanical.

She reached the row of metal boxes bolted to a
long, solid redwood plank that jutted up out of a
snowbank. Her box, number 6, was jumbo rural,
big enough to hold three or four book-club boxes,
and still leave enough room for magazines.

The big house had been Dick's idea, the big mailbox hers. Sherry pulled down the front metal flap
and peered inside. No book-club selections today.
Just one fat brown eight-by-ten envelope that had
been folded over double and secured with strapping tape. And some bills, of course—what else?

Yes, the Citibank Visa was here. *Damn*, Sherry
thought. She knew this one payment would be over
$150, with all the stuff she'd bought for Christmas.
New skis and boots for Kady, and a beautiful blue
ski outfit that matched her daughter's eyes, plus
the same for herself. It had all cost a fortune
and she'd still be paying for Kady's jacket when
there were rope-tow burns and chair-lift grease all
over it.

But she wasn't sorry. They'd needed an emotional lift, both of them, so Sherry had seen to it.
She was *not* going to let this divorce make mince-
meat out of their souls. Let Dick stay holed up in
his A-frame cabin. Let him drink and brood, or
chase women, whatever he did. Sherry would go on
running the ski resort she'd been awarded in the
decree. She felt that she was a survivor.

She took out the bills and slid out the brown envelope. It was addressed, she noticed in puzzle-
ment, to her twelve-year-old daughter, Kady.

Had Kady ordered a book from somewhere? Curiously she examined the envelope, noting the crooked printing, postmarked in nearby Grayling, with no return address. Oddly, for she hadn't been cold before, she felt a light shiver ripple her skin beneath the jacket she wore. And then a prickly feeling penetrated the center of her back as if someone were staring. Actually, as if eyes were *boring* into her.

She turned and looked around sharply. Nothing but trees, road, lake, animal and snowmobile tracks. Higgins Lake itself was a blinding expanse of frozen white that made her eyes water.

Sherry gave her surroundings one more look, and gradually the being-watched feeling subsided. She'd been working too many eighteen-hour days, she needed a day off, that was her trouble. She turned and started back toward the house.

She stamped her way into the foyer and bent down to take off her boots. She yanked at their laces, squirmed her stockinged feet out, and deposited the five-year-old boots on what she and Kady called the "boot rug." This was a four-by-five segment of leftover carpeting, its purpose to collect the clutter of snow-dripping boots and muddy outdoor shoes.

Down the hall from the direction of the den she could hear the rapid switching of TV channels, followed by an exaggerated sigh of disgust.

"Mom? Mom, there's nothing to do, and the news is so *boring*, and Phil Donahue has got men who dress up in women's clothes, ugh. I'm going to call Maura. Maybe her mother will take us skiing, since you won't."

"Listen, monster, I told you I'd take you skiing about one. I do have housework, you know—*we* have housework. Did you think the bathroom gets cleaned by accident? Or the dishes fly to the dishwasher? The snow will be there this afternoon."

"But it won't be *powder*." Kady padded out, clad in her uniform of jeans and wool sweater. She was a leggy twelve, the tallest one in her class, a young Brooke Shields with impossibly clear skin, a wide rosebud of a mouth, and eyes that were pools of cerulean blue. Sherry was used to her, but sometimes in town, tourists would turn to stare at her beautiful daughter.

"Oh, you." Sherry laughed fondly. "It'll be nice and soft and groomed, though, and you get to ski on powder quite a bit, young lady. You've had more than your full share of powder this winter already, so don't get greedy."

Kady grinned. "I'm a powder pig."

"I guess you are."

"Oh, Mom, did any good mail come? Is there anything from Kelly and Larry?" Kelly and Larry were cousins from whom they heard every year at Christmas, and this year's largess had included four baby Pound Puppies and a subscription to *Seventeen*.

"No, honey, nothing from Kelly and Larry, what did you expect? Did you write them their thank-you letter yet?"

"Nope," mumbled her daughter.

"Well, I think that's a very good project for today, don't you? *After* you clean your room."

"Oh, ugh," Kady said. "I saw a pad of paper in the drugstore. It had these little blanks, you know? Thank you for the—whatever—and you could just fill in the blank. I could write all my thank-you letters in ten minutes that way."

"And be considered rude and crass? No, thank you, my Kadydid, you are going to do it the old-fashioned, polite way. One page on nice stationery, and spell everything right, please. Oh, hey, I almost forgot," Sherry said, unzipping her jacket and producing the stack of mail. "Something came for you, honeybug. Looks like a book."

"A book?"

"Well, something. Open it."

Kady loped forward to take the brown envelope, eagerly pulling at its corner to rip it apart in strips, several of which fluttered to the floor.

"Don't make a mess," Sherry said automatically.

Kady took something out. "Hey."

"Well, what is it?" Sherry called, busy hanging up her jacket in the closet that bulged with ski, snowmobile, fishing, and rain gear.

"It's not a book, it's a videotape. Some tape for the VCR, Mom! Did you send for something?"

"What?" Sherry emerged from the closet. "It's a tape?"

"Yeah! Hey, this is cool, can we play it? What do you think it is, *Beverly Hills Cop*? *Rambo*?" Kady turned the black case over in her hands. "Maybe a ski tape? On hotdogging or something? RAM Productions," she read aloud. "What's that?"

"Isn't there any label? Let me see that," Sherry said.

"But, Mom—"

Sherry took the videotape from her daughter and turned it over, examining the cheap black cardboard slipcase in which it was packaged. Odd. The movies they usually rented from Video Junction were packaged in bright wrappers that hyped the movie. This one had nothing but the words *RAM Productions*, and a rather fuzzy logo that might be, by a stretch of the imagination, a male sheep.

No further label or explanation, except for a number in the lower right corner: 855.

Frowning, Sherry pulled the tape out of the slipcase. The tape itself was an ordinary VHS tape, again cryptically labeled RAM Productions, with the number 855.

"Let's play it!" Kady suggested.

Some unease stirred in Sherry, a pricking sensation that suggested all was not right. It was the same feeling she'd had out at the mailbox.

"I don't know." She reached for the crumpled scraps of the brown envelope and pulled out the torn halves of the mailing label. "I wish you hadn't ripped it apart so much, Kady. Who sent you this, anyway? Did one of your friends send it to you?"

Kady was puzzled. "I don't know. Maybe Maura? But Maura doesn't have a VCR. I'm the only one with a VCR. Hey, can't we look at it? Let's go and see what it is. Maybe it's from Kelly and Larry, maybe they sent us something on skiing. All the way from Vancouver."

"It's postmarked Grayling," Sherry said. She kept the tape, its surface cool beneath her fingers. The unease was building in her. The odd, choky feeling that this tape held something very bad.

"Mom—gimme. It came to *me*—"

"*I'll* play it first," Sherry decided, dancing out of the way of her daughter's teasing, finger-wiggling grab.

"Mom . . ."

"You go and get started on that thank-you letter. One page, minimum, and say *nice things*, Kady, and tell them how the snow is here. Tell them we got a good big snowfall right after Thanksgiving and we've got two and a half feet of base."

"Aw . . ."

"Go," Sherry urged, with a pat on her daughter's narrow, young-girl rump.

As soon as Kady had left, Sherry went down the hall to the small den that held their television set and the VCR that she had kept in the settlement. The room's other main item of furniture was a long, wheat-colored couch piled with pillows on which she and Kady lounged, ate, read, played Pictionary, and watched TV.

She closed the door behind her and padded in her

stocking feet over to the set, her heart pounding a little. She supposed she was being silly, a mother hen. Still, the black videotape gave her a definite sensation of unease.

She pushed the buttons to activate the VCR, and then slid in the video. The machine sucked it in with a hissing noise.

Sherry punched the play button. There was a crackling, staticky noise, the familiar sound of the machine beginning the tape, and then the screen filled with another logo of the Ram.

Sherry waited.

No introductory music. Just more hissing, crude tape noise, some snow, and then a black-and-white title that appeared starkly on the screen, the letters so large that they almost bled off the edge.

## TENDER PREY

# CHAPTER 2

**W**inter prickled at the windows of Dr. Nanette
Frey's office over the garage of their house on Hartwick Road, tiny ice bits tapping the glass as if trying to get in.

The psychologist leaned back in her swivel chair,
her elegantly shod feet planted up on the desktop.
She had been daydreaming about a cruise in the
Caribbean. Sun. The rippling, bejeweled curl of the
ship's wake.

The sound of her office bell, situated downstairs
by the separate entrance, pulled her back to January doldrums in Hartwick. Nanette swung her feet
down, automatically glancing around her for any
open case records.

When she spotted two, she quickly skid them into
a bottom drawer. She was meticulous about that.
After all, this wasn't New York, where patients
lived totally separate lives. Hartwick's population
was less than 4,000, and it was a hotbed of gossip,

intrigue, and interlocking lives. In fact, Nanette happened to be the only practicing psychologist in the village. If people wanted another choice other than herself, they had to drive to Grayling, Midland, Saginaw, Traverse City, or Cadillac.

She had once been intrigued by the dollhouse smallness of this world, now she found it oppressive. If only Bob, her husband, didn't like the village so much. Oh, well, no time to brood about that now. She had exactly twenty seconds to push at her hair, check to see that her "crying tissues" were in their box within easy reach, and that the sofa cushions looked plumped and inviting.

Right on schedule, the door opened and Sherry Vincent, Nanette's eleven o'clock appointment, entered the room.

Nanette rose, smiling, calm, welcoming, professional.

"Hello, Sherry."

Sherry Vincent. Age thirty-six, a new divorcée, the type of beautiful that causes stares in restaurants. Sherry had grappled with her looks for years, finally rejecting them by wearing no makeup and living most of her life in jeans and boots. It still did not dim her glow.

Today, however, Sherry looked paler than usual, her fair skin almost pasty-looking. She looked like a woman who has seen the unspeakable, Nanette observed uneasily.

"Hello. I drove right over, I left Kady at her friend's. Oh, Dr. Frey, the mail, the mail today! Something came, it was addressed to my daughter, to Kady, and it was the most awful—"

"Come in first, Sherry, and take off your jacket. Take off your things," Nanette repeated, seeing that her patient was still standing there.

"Oh—sorry."

"How are the roads?" Nanette said to calm her.

"Oh, fine. Plowed. Kady is raring to go skiing today, I promised to take her afterward." Sherry's voice was wound up wire-tight.

She plucked at the zipper of her blue ski jacket, pulling at the scarf around her neck as if it choked her. She slung both over the coat rack Nanette kept near the door, divesting herself of boots, wool hat. As she took off the hat, a mane of black hair tumbled out, glossy with healthy highlights.

*Damn*, Nanette thought to herself. Even in all that loathsome winter paraphernalia Sherry Vincent was a knockout. She had a fine-grained complexion that was perfect enough to go in a magazine ad. High cheekbones, a short nose, full lips, and wideset blue eyes took her far past "pretty."

Sherry had been Miss Michigan in the early seventies. It still seemed incredible to Nanette, almost amusing, that she should be giving once-a-week therapy to a former beauty queen. Weren't beauty queens supposed to have everything? Plastic lives firmly in place, no problems, only wide, white smiles?

Sherry walked tightly into the sitting area and took her usual chair, a peach-upholstered lounger whose arms were beginning to be worn from patients plucking at them. She was wearing her usual jeans and a blue wool sweater knit across the shoulders with rows of leaping deer. She sat staring blankly at a pair of vanilla-scented candles Nanette burned sometimes at night.

"Dr. Frey—something awful came in the mail today. I have to talk to you about it."

Nanette had wanted to go more deeply into the nightmares again today, and the anxiety attacks that had begun six months ago and were Sherry's main complaint, the reason she had sought counseling. But usually patients resisted examining painful issues, preferring to take up time with things that were more comfortable. She sighed. "What's awful?"

"Well, I went out to the mailbox today and there was this envelope—it had a videotape in it, addressed to my Kady . . ." Sherry stopped, making an obvious effort to get control of herself. Her lips shook, and her hands were trembling.

"Yes?" Nanette prompted.

Sherry focused her eyes past Nanette's shoulder to the window, where nothing much could be seen but the road that led to the village, and a stand of pine trees. "I played the video," she said. "I started to, anyway. I've never seen anything like it; I didn't even know they could make things so . . ."

She was almost gagging. "Little girls, Dr. Frey, *little girls*. Tied up and raped, or being raped with—with objects. Things I've never even . . . anal rape. Dildos. And in one scene there was a dog . . ." Her hands moved in disgust. "I couldn't believe it! How people could—these were *children*, Dr. Frey, most of them barely had breasts or pubic hair, they were *babies*." She swallowed. "And this was sent to us. *To my Kady*."

"I see," Nanette said.

Sherry's voice rose. "Why would they send such filth to my little girl? What has Kady done, why would anyone want to send her anything like that?"

"Pornography," Nanette began.

"No. Oh, no, it was a lot worse than just that. This was *violent*, it was just so evil."

Nanette was thinking that pornography, violent or not, would affect Sherry more than the average person. There'd been a controlling, repressive mother, an incident in the seventh grade that left repercussions that were still surfacing. It was no accident that Sherry's nightmares had begun just about the time her daughter turned twelve.

"I can well understand. Do you have any idea who might have sent it?"

"No . . ." And Sherry buried her face in her hands,

her body quivering with paroxysms of movement that might have been sobs, or just shudders.

Nanette waited, knowing that it would be a mistake to get up and touch this woman, put her arm around her. Some crying patients she could hug, but others, like Sherry, erected barriers. Sherry Vincent was a very private person, who worked fiercely to protect her vulnerability.

"I didn't let Kady see the tape." Sherry lifted her head, her eyes dry and burned-looking. "She wanted to, she begged to, but I told her I'd look at it myself. I threw it in the garbage. I never want her to see anything like that. I don't even want her to know that such things *exist*."

"Don't you think you ought to save the tape, rather than throw it out? In case you want to report it to the police?" Nanette questioned patiently.

Sherry looked surprised. "Oh."

"Sherry, you've received obscenity through the mails. That's a felony, isn't it? Anyway, a punishable offense. You should report it to the police. Those people should be prosecuted."

Sherry stared at Nanette. "I just tossed it out. It was a gut reaction. I didn't even think."

"Well, you ought to report it. But I would say," Nanette added briskly, "that it was probably just a freaky kind of thing, a sick joke being played on you by someone. Or maybe even an accident, your daughter receiving material that was supposed to have been sent to someone else."

"Her name was on the envelope."

"Still, it could have been the wrong mailing label. Computers make mistakes all the time, don't they, it's the hallmark of our modern age. Come on, Sherry, let's talk about your dreams again today. Have you had any more? Any more nightmares?"

Slowly the glazed, horrified look left Sherry's eyes. "I guess so. Yes, last night."

"What was it about? Tell me."

Sherry sat tensely. "Well, the usual. This man's voice whispering to me, saying the most terrible, dirty, intimate things ... And I feel him, I know he's touching me between the—"

Sherry shuddered. She had a hard time using words like *vagina* and *vulva*, or even *pussy*.

"And then what happened?"

"Just like always. I woke up with my heart pounding, I was sitting bolt upright in bed." Sherry's fingers played with the side seam of her Levi's. "We've been over and over this a hundred times."

"Get it out, Sherry. Get it out in the open."

Sherry looked up, her eyes filling with tears. She looked much younger than thirty-six. "It's the same old thing," she burst out. "The same old dream, me being touched by that man. I hate him! Why did he have to dirty my life? I'm so tired of it! I've had these nightmares—what? For six months now, since last summer. They don't stop, they don't change, they don't go away. I want to get rid of them!"

"You will," Nanette said.

"But I've talked about them and talked about them. I'm spending my own money on these sessions, you know. I don't have Blue Cross; this is all coming out of my own pocket. I don't know how much longer I can afford it."

"Are you having money troubles, then?"

"A few," Sherry admitted. "Thank God we've had a good snowfall so far this year, so there's money coming in at Timberline, but Dick left me with so many debts. He hasn't paid any child support; he keeps promising but he hasn't. I might have to take him to court. And I spent a lot on Christmas for Kady. I had to give her a good Christmas. After all she's been through."

"You've been through a lot, too," Nanette said.

Sherry nodded. "I guess I wanted to give myself

a good Christmas, too. So now money is tight. And now this, this filth in the mail."

"It was probably just a mistake, a computer mistake of some kind," Nanette soothed. "It probably won't happen again, Sherry, I don't think you need to worry about that. It's highly unlikely."

Sherry seemed to relax, some of her color returning. "I hope not."

"And now," Nanette suggested, "let's try something different today. Just an experiment. I have a folder here, and it's got some inkblot drawings in it. They are really just blobs, but you can see pictures in them if you try."

"We did this at Michigan State," Sherry offered. "Freshman year. Psych 101."

"Then you know about Rorschachs."

"Oh, yes." Sherry brightened. "That would be interesting to try. Anything, Dr. Frey. Between those dreams and that horrible videotape, I feel like I've been wrung dry."

# CHAPTER 3

Sherry descended the stairs to the separate exit by the garage door and walked in the snow to her car, parked in a small area set aside for Dr. Frey's patients. She felt drained, but better. These sessions tapped unknown parts of herself that apparently had festered for years.

*Shoot, I'm a mess*, Sherry told herself as she slid into her old blue Toyota and started it. The interior of the car had lost heat while she was in Dr. Frey's, and she could see her own breath, pluming out like steam from her mouth.

A mess? Not really. As Dr. Frey had pointed out, many of the people in Hartwick were in a lot worse shape than she was, but they refused to do anything about it. It took courage to try to help yourself.

She drove west toward town. The sun had gone and it was snowing again, little swirly drifts of white that wouldn't deposit more than an inch or so, Sherry judged. When you ran a ski area, you loved snow. You didn't gripe about bad roads, either, not unless they were so bad the skiers couldn't get to the slopes.

Since it was a school conference day, she had left Kady at her best friend Maura's house. She planned to pick up a few things at the A & P, then run into the shoe-repair shop and claim her hiking boots.

Mondays were Sherry's "catch-up" days after the harried weekend, when school buses crammed with ski clubs from Midland, Mount Pleasant, and other Michigan towns converged on the parking lot at Timberline, discharging several hundred novice skiers. Yesterday, Sunday, they had carted off five people to the emergency room at the Grayling Hospital with assorted sprains and breaks.

For years Sherry had harped on ski safety. She had signs plastered all over the area. She offered one free lesson to each rental customer, she screamed at shop repairmen to double-check all rental equipment, she ejected skiers who carried flasks. Step-in ski bindings were much better now than they had been ten years ago, but still the accidents happened, mostly to beginners. It drove her crazy. Mondays were an oasis, and going to the shoe repair a haven.

Hartwick's main street consisted of two long blocks and one blinker light. Most of the storefronts dated from the 1880s, when lumbermen hauling logs out of the county had settled the town. Actually, Hartwick had once roared with saloons and whorehouses, a major supplier to fifty lumber camps. Now the old cribs had been torn down or converted to boutiques.

Sherry found a place to park right in front of Litwin's Shoes and Saddlery. A path was chopped through the four-foot-high snow pile left by the county plow, so shoppers could reach the sidewalk.

She walked in.

"Lots of good snow, eh, Sherry?" said Les Litwin, the retired policeman who ran the shoe shop, and, in the interconnected way of many Hartwick relationships, had once been in love with Margaret Smith, Sherry's mother.

"The more the better," she told him cheerfully.

"I did the best I could with these boots, but you ripped the suede itself and I had to add a patch. It isn't going to look like brand-new, but it'll hold. These are damn nice boots."

She took the time to admire the stitchwork, which was painstaking, of a quality that Sherry knew she could never get down around Detroit.

"Been shopping recently?" Les asked her, his eyes glinting as he sucked on his pipe.

"Not since December. It's the busy time, Les. You know that. I haven't even been in town."

"Well, you ought to, Sherry. A couple doors down, you'd see something. Maybe you ought to go and look. It's been out a couple days now. Interesting."

What was he talking about? Some item in the window he thought she ought to buy? These people—they oversaw your every move, offered their opinion whether you asked for it or not. That was small-town life; on a good day it seemed friendly, on a bad day smothering.

She exchanged a few more pleasantries with the old man, then left the repair shop. The videotape, she had decided, *had* been a mistake, not meant for Kady at all. RAM Productions. A play on words with other meanings she didn't even want to think about. Today was Monday, her day. Kady was safe at Maura's and in a minute Sherry was going to pick her up and take both girls skiing. She would put the ugly video out of her mind and not think of it again.

She ambled down the walk, automatically glancing in the familiar windows of the shops. Karpen's, specializing in women's sportswear. The D. & C. Variety Store. Mary's Fudge Shop. Herbertson's Men's Wear.

She stopped, puzzled. The fly-specked men's sweaters and rugby shirts that usually decorated Herbertson's were missing. The windows themselves had been remodeled, too, framed in brass and made smaller, like elegant pictures. Inside the first window was a swirled drape of dark green velvet, upon which had been placed an elaborately gold-lettered sign that said simply: *Dietz's. Photography*.

Dietz's? Sherry froze.

That must be what Les had meant. Everyone in town knew she'd been engaged to Glen Dietz years ago when they were both twenty, before she married Dick. Shaking a little—she hadn't seen Glen in *years*—she examined the display. A row of color portraits had been arranged on the velvet. All of them were of beautiful people with New York haircuts and big-city expressions on their faces. The quality had a certain hardness, a slickness rarely seen here in Hartwick.

She drew in her breath and let it out quickly. Glen. Grade-school notes. A snowball down her neck. Wild afternoons waterskiing on Higgins Lake. Drinking beer at Charley's, necking in the backseat of Glen's old VW Beetle, kisses and teasing, and silly pranks. But Glen had backed off after he'd given her the ring, scared at the seriousness, rethinking it. They both had rethought. She didn't remember now who had jilted whom. But afterward Glen had cut a swathe through town, seducing every girl in Hartwick over sixteen and under thirty, as if trying to prove something.

She walked on. There was another display window on the other side of the recessed shop door. It, too, was draped in velvet, deep red on this side.

Sherry's eyes automatically traveled over the pictures.

She saw her own daughter's face.

*Kady's eyes enhanced with makeup, languorous and full of sexuality. Her mouth, pouty and knowing. Her lanky, loose-limbed, perfect young body.*

*Not Kady!* was Sherry's first thought, as she fought shock and stepped closer. Someone who looked like her, maybe. But with another long look, there could be no doubt. It *was* Kady, staring back at her out of Glen Dietz's new studio window.

She felt her heart begin to thump. There were five of the photographs, showing Kady, dressed in torn jeans and a lace camisole, sprawled on what looked like a white fur rug, and sitting in a chair in various abandoned, spread-legged poses. Pictures that made her daughter look like a sultry young stranger, with sensuous eyes that almost made love to the camera. *Vogue* magazine type of photos, almost insolent in their blatancy.

Sherry found she was having trouble breathing properly. Where on earth? How could this be Kady? When could they have been taken? Why hadn't she known about it?

She turned and strode into the shop, pulling at the new oak door so hard that its attached bell set up a wild jangling.

Inside, redecorations had occurred, too. New partitions, carpeting, custom furniture, brass mirrors, displays of more oil portraits of people who did not live in Hartwick.

"Yes?" A woman of sixty or so was seated at a desk, going through a stack of photograph albums, and she looked up questioningly. Sherry recognized her as a Grayling woman who used to work in the public library.

"Is Glen here? Where's Glen? What are those pictures of my daughter doing in your window? Did he take them?"

The woman laid down the album and stared at Sherry, blinking. She had gray hair that had been rinsed with Silk and Silver, and was wearing a mint green pantsuit of a style popular with local retirees. "I beg your pardon."

"What is my daughter's picture doing in the window of your store? When did you take pictures of her? When?"

"I think you'd better talk to Mr. Dietz."

"Oh, yes, I think I'd better. And while you're at it, please take those pictures out of that window."

The woman stared at her, startled and confused. "But, Mr. Dietz, he put the pictures there—"

"Then he can take them out."

The clerk half rose in her chair, one hand fluttering anxiously to her silver-blue hair. "Why, I really don't think—"

"Take them out or I'll do it." Sherry turned and started toward the back side of the display windows, which were secured by glass slide-bars with padlocks. She gripped their handles, shaking them until the glass rattled. "How do you get in here? Do you need a key?"

"Please . . . Mr. Dietz . . . He's in the back, in the darkroom. I'll get him . . ." The woman scurried off, and Sherry stopped rattling the window display, feeling out of control. Glen's shop. *Glen.* What was happening here? Child pornography, and now this, her child in these pictures. Her sweet, natural, tomboy, twelve-year-old Kady.

She waited, feeling a chill pass along her arms and legs, turning her fingers icy cold. These pictures, *that* was what Les had been trying to tell her. They'd been on display here for several days apparently. Only she'd been working her head off at Timberline, Kady had been on the slopes, too, and no one had bothered to call them up and tell them. How dare Glen Dietz do this to her?

He was keeping her waiting. Sherry paced back

and forth. Calm down, she told herself. Surely there was a good explanation. Three women tourists in expensive skiwear walked past the shop, pausing to look at the window display just as Sherry had done.

After about ten minutes, the door to the back opened and a tall, good-looking man emerged. He stopped, stared at her, and then laughed.

"Sherry Smith. My God. Sherry."

"Sherry Vincent," she corrected him automatically. She stared at him, feeling her throat squeeze with the residue of old emotions.

*Glen.*

He was nearly six-two, with a full head of wavy brown hair beginning to silver attractively at his temples. Since she'd last seen him, Glen had added about twenty pounds, but it had only matured him, given him a more solid look. He wore a silver-gray pullover and gray, pleated slacks—elegant dress for Hartwick.

"Please take those pictures of Kady out of your window," she began.

"Oh?"

"I want them *out*. And I want to know when you took them, and how you managed to do it without my knowledge or permission," she went on, her tone icy. Her heartbeat had begun to normalize; good, she thought. She felt sure he didn't realize the effect he'd had on her, and she wanted to keep it that way.

"That's simple enough. Your mother brought her in about three weeks ago. Right after Christmas. You were working, she said, you were busy, and you wanted the work done. She signed for them and paid with her Visa."

Sherry stared; her breath caught in her throat and stuck there. "My *mother* wanted those pictures taken? My mother brought Kady in? She did this?"

"Well, I did the pictures. It's a composite, Sherry, a modeling portfolio. It's damn good work, too, if I do say so. There are girls in New York who would kill for that kind of quality, and I gave it to your mother for a fraction of what it would have cost her in New York. A fraction.''

"My God," Sherry breathed.

"You really didn't know about it?"

"No, I didn't."

"And, I take it, you don't approve of the pictures either.''

"No, I don't. They're—they're *sexy*, Glen!"

He grinned at her. In the silver-gray outfit he looked suave, professional, and very big-city. Had she ever really let him touch her breasts, neck with her until they were both frantic with need? It all seemed a thousand years ago now.

"Good," he said. "They're supposed to be sexy. Look, Sherry, you live here in Hartwick, and people here don't exactly subscribe to *Vogue* magazine and *W*. But take my word for it, these pictures are going to be dynamite out there in the world where it counts, and your little girl has got something. The pictures aren't sexy because of anything that I did. They're sexy because of her. She radiated it.''

"She did nothing of the kind!" Sherry's throat was choking up again. "She is a *little girl*, Glen Dietz, and you had no right to do anything like that, to pose her in that way." Firmly she extended her hand. "I want those pictures."

"Hey, the negatives are my property. I gave your mother her prints, and if you want to order some I'll be glad to accommodate you. At a nice discount.''

She stepped back, bewildered by the explosive melange of feelings that had welled up in her. First the video, now this. She tried to conceal her trembling anger. Shoppers were out on the sidewalk; the silver-haired clerk was lurking back in the darkroom area; this was Hartwick, where everyone local knew everyone else local.

"At least take them out of the window then," she managed to say.

"Well, I'll do that, no problem. If you really want me to." Glen gave her one of his famous appealing smiles. He had had a chipped front tooth repaired, she noticed. That tooth had been his one flaw as a young man—oh, he'd been devastating then, at least to her.

"I want you to."

Shrugging, Glen took a key out of his pocket and unlocked the display case. She noticed his hands, smooth and well cared for, with curls of dark hair dusting the fingers. One by one he extracted the pictures, putting them in a stack.

"These are yours. You can take them home. Hey, come on, kid. We go way back, we've known each other forever. Look, these pictures embarrassed you, you didn't want to think about Kady in those terms, so I won't display them again, as far as I'm concerned they're finished, *finis*. I had no idea you'd react so strongly, how could I know that? And Kady loved posing."

Sherry, who had started to relax at this apology, felt the color flood to her cheeks. "She *didn't*."

"She did, Sherry, she's a natural ham. Hey, what's wrong with that? *Hey*." He came toward her, started to reach toward her, then apparently thought better of touching her. "Friends, Sherry, that's what I want us to be. You and I. I've been going to call you ever since I got back here last month."

"I've been working pretty hard," she said stiffly. "Apparently so hard that no one even phoned to say you were in town. Even my own mother."

His eyes probed her, a changeable hazel color that at twenty she had found very alluring. The texture of his skin was ruddy and hinted at shaven whiskers. "Well, you can't work all the time. I was going to see if you'd come out to dinner with me.

Maybe the Holiday Inn in Grayling, or we could drive down to Midland. What do you say, Sherry? I know Hartwick hasn't got much, but we ought to be able to get some good seafood somewhere."

Something thrilled in her, something she'd thought long dead, killed by unhappiness and loneliness. Forcibly she pushed it back.

"Sorry," she said.

"What?"

"I said no, Glen. I don't want to have dinner with you. I guess I'd rather stay in Hartwick. It hasn't got much but I like it. And if I ever see one of those pictures out in your window again, I—I'll sue you."

"My, we are feisty, aren't we? You always were. Sherry—"

Sherry turned and marched out of the shop, hearing the jangle of the bells as the door shut behind her.

# CHAPTER 4

Margaret Smith freely admitted she had arranged for the photos and then sent copies to six modeling agencies in New York. Glen had neglected to mention making the copies, a fact that further annoyed her at him.

"It was time," Sherry's mother had responded calmly, not showing the least bit of dismay that Sherry had found out. "Kady is a natural for modeling and you know it, Sherry. She's five feet seven already, and only twelve and a half. She's going to be real tall, like her father, and a lot prettier than Brooke Shields."

The sheer bullheadedness of her mother's obsession always stunned Sherry. "I have absolutely no intention that she model, Mother. I've never wanted it, and you know it. You did this behind my back. You made Kady keep your secret; you forced her into your duplicity. Dammit, she's just an ordinary little girl!"

Margaret Smith carefully knotted a thread in the embroidery project she had been working on when Sherry arrived. "Kady is anything but ordinary. You know people stare at her on the street, just as they used to stare at you. If I'd had any sense I would have taken you to New York when you were her age, got you started in the business then. You could have made a hundred thousand a year, they would have worshipped you the way they did Margaux Hemingway and Candice Bergen and Cheryl Tiegs."

"I never wanted to be worshipped, Mom, I never wanted that life. I tried it and I hated it."

"One month," her mother said.

"It was enough! Please don't undermine me with Kady, especially now, after the divorce."

Margaret looked injured. "You know I'd never undermine anything you do, I never wanted to undermine you."

"What's arranging pictures behind my back, then?" Sherry inquired sharply. "And not telling me Glen was in town? You deliberately didn't tell me, because you wanted him to take those pictures!"

Her mother's answer was definitive: "I didn't tell you because I knew you'd get like this."

Sherry finally left, feeling angry and thwarted, as she always did after these encounters with Margaret. Her sweet, obsessed mother.

Now, as she drove past a row of old Victorian homes built by the lumber barons, her stomach felt clenched, a tight, acidy feeling swirling in its center.

At a stop sign, she forced her muscles to relax, using a technique Dr. Frey had taught her. In fact, Dr. Frey had helped her to see it *all* more clearly. The incident in seventh grade . . . three twelve-year-old girls molested by their science teacher, who'd been forced to leave town because of the scandal.

Luckily, there'd been no rape, just touching and fondling.

That was plenty, though. Afterward had come the guilt, the whispers, the "blaming of the victim" syndrome that the psychologist had explained so carefully. It was common enough in cases of rape or molestation, all of it traumatic, wounding, scarring.

Sherry's nightmares and anxiety attacks had begun shortly after her daughter's twelfth birthday, when Kady reached the same age Sherry had been when the "incident" occurred.

Of course, she couldn't let her own emotions affect Kady. She'd worked hard to protect her child from anxiety—Kady had enough on her plate right now with the divorce and Dick's sporadic efforts at visitation.

Sherry drove to Maura's house in the village to pick up the two girls to take them skiing. Maura's father, Del Camrack, was the town surveyor, and in winter he ran a snowmobile sales and rental business. Theirs was a typical, unpretentious, Hartwick-style home. There were no books and no magazines, except for *Time* and *TV Guide*. The furniture was beige, and the large painting over the living-room couch depicted a ten-pronged buck done in Day-Glo colors.

Still, it was a home in which there had been no divorce. Del and Susan Camrack were happily married, were even occasionally seen in town holding hands. Sherry pushed back a pang.

The smell of microwave popcorn permeated the house. One of the Camracks' two big male Labrador retrievers came to the door with the girls, and insistently nosed his muzzle toward Sherry's crotch.

Sherry kneed the dog away and gave him a swat on his shiny black rump. "Down, Fred. Go somewhere and scratch your fleas. Are you girls ready?

I thought you'd be waiting for me with your ski boots on."

The two girls wore look-alike rose-colored sweaters, both in identical stone-washed jeans. If Kady was the most beautiful twelve-year-old in Hartwick, then surely Maura was in second place, with her mop of tightly curled blond hair and her fresh roses-and-milk complexion.

"We were but then we got hungry. I thought you were *never* going to get here," Kady burst out, her beautiful face animated with childish impatience. "All the good snow is going to be skied off if we don't hurry, and we'll have nothing left but crud."

"Don't use that word, it's vulgar."

"And school buses," Maura echoed.

"Yeah, and all those school buses full of turkeys," Kady added with a giggle. "All those beginners who can't even do a snowplow."

"How many times do I have to tell you, Kady, you're not to use the word *turkey*. It's reverse snobbery and it's unpleasant and rude. We depend on those people for our income. Without those so-called turkeys, where do you think we'd be? Who do you think would pay our bills?"

"Oh," Kady mumbled, quenched.

"Besides which, as I recall, some of those 'turkeys' can ski pretty well. Wasn't there a boy from West Bloomfield last week, whipping down the bowl at a pretty good speed? Seems to me I remember him going off the jump you guys made. Fast."

"Yeah, he was different," Kady mumbled.

"Get your boots," Sherry snapped, knowing that her anger wasn't at the word *turkey* at all.

"I wanted to see the World Trade Center and the skyscrapers, and get tickets to the David Letterman show," Kady explained that night. "Besides, Grandma asked me not to tell you."

It was eight-thirty. The grilled peanut-butter

sandwiches Kady had insisted on had been browned in the electric fry pan and consumed. Melted by heat, the gloppy, runny peanut butter had stuck to the roof of Sherry's mouth, and made her wonder what teenagers saw in such stickiness.

Was it only twenty-four years ago that Sherry herself had been twelve, "best friends" with Carole Hamner and Judy Sjoholm? Grilled cheese and banana sandwiches had been their special treat. Sherry grimaced. Her mother had thought the concoction every bit as gruesome as she did her daughter's favorite.

"But didn't you think that I might want to *know*, honey? I mean, the whole thing is so ridiculous." Sherry felt tired and drained by the long, disturbing day. "How could you possibly get a contract to go to some modeling agency in New York City without me finding out about it first? And those pictures Glen Dietz took—"

"Oh, it wasn't anything," Kady said airily.

" 'Wasn't anything'! Kady, those pictures were very adult, in case you didn't know."

Kady popped a leftover sandwich quarter from Sherry's plate into her own mouth. She chewed stickily. "I mean, Grandma wanted the pictures and I didn't want to hurt her feelings, Mom. She said it was going to be a surprise for you. We were going to tell you later, when we got a contract, and you'd be all excited and happy because it would mean lots more money for us. Because I'd be making a salary, too, not just you. I could earn money like Brooke Shields did when she was my age."

Sherry stared at her daughter, nonplussed.

"Well, you *said* we had a lot of Visa debts," Kady explained. "You said Daddy doesn't pay child support, and you have salaries to pay at work and I thought . . . Grandma said . . ." At Sherry's disapproval, Kady's eyes slowly filled with tears.

"Oh, honey." Sherry reached out and grabbed her

daughter, pulling Kady to her, hugging the slim body that smelled beguilingly of wool, pink lipstick, and peanut butter. "Oh, honey, you don't have to support us! My God. Baby, baby . . ."

"But I thought . . . Grandma said . . ."

"Grandma is such a manipulator!" Sherry burst out. "Oh, honeybug, she told you some things that aren't really true. We're not having money troubles—not that bad anyway. You don't have to get a job to take care of us. The ski area is pulling in good money now, Kady. And your dad is going to start sending the support money soon, he promised, as soon as he gets his sporting goods store started. It's going to be all right."

"Is it?"

"Yes, honey, oh, yes. I promise. And you won't even have to think about those pictures again. It's finished, and Glen Dietz has given me the copies and I've put them away, and that's the last of it. Maybe this spring you and I will take a trip to New York City. Would you like that? We'll see some TV shows. We'll go to Radio City Music Hall, and to the top of the Empire State Building. You're not going to miss New York, I promise."

# CHAPTER 5

Outdoors, the temperature had sunk to ten above zero. Kady was in bed, asleep, and now the only sounds in the house were the ticking taps of snowflakes hitting Sherry's bedroom window, and the distant, snow-muffled roar of a couple of snowmobiles out on the frozen lake.

For once, Sherry wished their home weren't the only occupied one in the subdivision. The other owners were all summer people, who occasionally came up for winter weekends.

She flipped a page in the new Susan Isaacs novel she was trying to read, damning herself for her insomnia. But all she could see, instead of print, was her child's face looking up at her from a fashion photograph.

Sherry decided to take another look at the photos. Maybe, after that horrible videotape, she'd overreacted, maybe they weren't as bad as she'd first thought. She pushed aside the bedcovers and slid out of bed, padding over to her dresser. Her long, brushed-cotton nightgown stuck to her legs from static electricity.

Earlier today she had shoved the album in the bottom of a drawer, beneath a stack of old long johns and turtlenecks. Now she retrieved it and began leafing through the photographs, seeing more details this time. The expert way liner had been applied to Kady's eyes, artfully smudged to make them look larger and more wide-set. Had her mother applied the makeup? No doubt. Contrary to what Glen supposed, Margaret subscribed to all the New York magazines and possessed a whole library of makeup books written by celebrities.

Sherry stared at the photos. Margaret had drawn along Kady's lips with a lipstick pencil, deepening and widening the line of the girl's already full lips. The effect was to give the young girl a willful, pouty, petulant look, like Princess Caroline about to go on a rampage.

The ringing of the telephone interrupted her inspection. Sherry picked up the receiver.

"Hello?"

"God, maybe I'd better hang up and start over again," Glen said, laughing. "You sound as grumpy as a subway conductor."

"Oh," she said, her mood not lightening. "Well, maybe that's because it's midnight, Glen. Most people around here are in bed by ten."

"And you're not?"

"I had an upsetting day."

"Ah, and I was part of it. Look, Sherry, I really didn't do anything wrong. You act like I tried to abduct the poor child."

"Very funny."

"Say," he began. "I'm a photographer by trade. I got sick of New York so I came back home, and I did a job of work for your mother. At her request.

I don't deserve to be treated like I committed the crime of the half century."

Silence spun over the phone wire, interrupted by some dim crackling on the line. The snowmobiles on the lake were getting louder.

Sherry drew a deep breath. "Well, I'm sitting here looking at a picture of my little girl, and she's sitting in a chair in those awful, torn jeans, with her legs spread, and she looks about twenty-five years old and like she belongs to the jet set."

"Sherry."

"She's got makeup smeared all over her face and her eyelashes have been curled, Glen. Her mouth has been drawn too wide and there's glop all over her cheeks and she looks like hell."

"She did not look like hell, she looked beautiful, and blame your mother for that. *She* brought her to the sitting. *She* made her up, *she* did her hair, *she* dressed her, dammit, Sherry—"

"Okay," she said finally. She had started to shiver; she should have worn a robe. "Sorry. It's just that my mother pushes so much. I hate that part of her. I rebelled against it years ago and now she's doing it to my daughter, behind my back."

She heard Glen's rueful laugh. "I remember your mother. She could be quite a fireball when she wanted to."

"Yeah."

"Sherry, I called because I thought you might want to reconsider dinner tomorrow."

"No, I don't think so."

"You are divorced, aren't you? I mean, your divorce *is* final."

"Yes, it was final a month ago; I'm sure local gossip has caught you up on that, Glen. And you've probably also heard that I don't date, I don't want to date anyone right now. I'm not ready, it's much too—"

"Bullshit," Glen said.

"What?"

"You're afraid, Sherry. That's your trouble. There was a lot between us and you're afraid it might get stirred up again. That's why you're so edgy to me and it's why you got so mad when you saw those pictures."

"Oh, stop," she told him. "Really. Thanks for asking, but I have to work tomorrow night, we've got night skiing and I have to be there."

"You do eat dinner, though."

"Right. From the cafeteria line, Glen, I usually have a sandwich. Look, I'm really about ready to go to bed. I'm sorry ... This isn't a rejection, it's just reality."

She said good-bye and hung up, thinking that she had handled that with all the finesse of a St. Bernard in a dollhouse. Sixteen years, she thought. What had Glen been doing all that time, had he been married, divorced too? She supposed she could tap the local grapevine, find out those things if she wanted to. She wasn't sure she did.

*Dammit, I didn't lie, I really am not ready for all this.*

The snowmobiles on the wide-open space of the lake were racing on the ice, revving back and forth. Impulsively Sherry reached for the phone again, deciding to call her friend Carole to get her feedback on Glen.

She dialed, getting Carole's tape. *"Hi, there, this is Carole, but you knew that, didn't you? Wait for the beep ..."* Then Carole's voice interrupted sleepily. "Hello? Hello?"

"Carole? Did I wake you up? I never know what your schedule is anymore."

"My schedule is sleeping tonight."

"Sorry—the weirdest things have been happening ..."

Carole immediately perked up. "Weird things? Like what?"

It was good to hear Carole's familiar raspy, cig-
aretty voice, and the two launched into one of their
too-rare sessions. Their friendship had withstood
Sherry's being chosen Miss Michigan and Carole's
two messy divorces. Carole had lived in Dearborn
for two years with husband number two, but now
she was back, working the swing shift at the Grayling Hospital in pediatrics. Weeks went by when
the friends missed contact with each other, simply
because their work hours interfered.

Carole was disgusted at the idea of the videotape, but told Sherry that she agreed with Dr.
Frey—somehow, by some fluke, Kady's name had
appeared on someone's junk mailing list. Or else
someone in town had played a practical joke on
her.

"But why?" Sherry wanted to know.

"Who knows? Maybe like you said, they saw
those pictures of Kady at Dietz's, maybe that gave
them ideas. Some prude or other, trying to get back
at you. Or you've got that ski resort. There're lots
of people up here without jobs in the wintertime,
living on unemployment. Maybe they think you're
pulling in bags of money at Timberline."

"If only."

"Or maybe someone is jealous for other reasons.
You were Miss Michigan once—that brings out
emotions in people."

"Great."

"Forget it, Sherry. It's just the new modern-day
version of the obscene phone call. Ugly but harmless. There're a lot of kooks and weirdos out there,
you'd be amazed at what we see over at the hospital."

Sherry nodded, bringing up the subject of Glen
Dietz.

"I think Glen wants to start something back up,"
was Carole's opinion. "That's what *I* think."

"Oh, come *on*," Sherry said. She swallowed, won-

dering how she felt at that idea. Damn Glen anyway. She wished he'd stayed away.

"Well, you know that mother of his still lives
here and she probably told him you were getting
a divorce, and I don't think it's any coincidence
that he arrived back in town just about the time
you and Dick made it final. Why else would he
come here? Everyone's been wondering. I mean,
he made a lot of money in New York. He was a
well-known photographer there. He had a lot of
shows and things and his mother says he won quite
a few prizes."

"He said he got sick of New York."

"I don't believe that. Those people think the sun
rises and sets in New York. They think everybody
in the world would live in their city if they could,"
Carole insisted. "Why would he get sick of New
York? It was where he was successful. People don't
turn their backs on something like that."

"Glen did. But who cares?" Sherry heard herself
add. "He wants to take me out to dinner but I'm
not going to go, not yet."

"Not *yet*? Why, Sherry, does that mean you're
considering it?" Carole teased at Sherry's slip of
the tongue.

Sherry set her straight. "No, I'm not. I've got too
much to do, and I'm still too mad at Dick. You know
what he did to me. I'm too messed up from my divorce, Carole. I've made up my mind that it'll be at
least six months before I go out with anyone, even
casually."

"Oh, you'll be out with Glen Dietz within two
weeks."

"I will not."

"You will, Sherry. You're excited about this,
aren't you? I haven't heard you sound this excited
in months. And there isn't anything wrong with
Glen Dietz. Hell, I'd go out with him if you don't

want him. But as I recall, he doesn't like chubby
blondes.''

Carole had always been sensitive about her
weight, and it was the one area you did not discuss
with her. "I've got to get to bed," Sherry finally
closed the conversation.

After she hung up, Sherry brushed her teeth and
switched out the light, hoping she could sleep this
time. Darkness surrounded her. Night in northern
Michigan could be profound, with no city lights or
streetlights to dilute it. She stared at the shadows
cast by the necessary hall night light.

She drifted off to sleep, to a dream of hands
touching her body, sliding up her calves to her
knees and then down the silken inside skin of her
thighs.

With a cry she woke up, snapping bolt upright
with a wrench of her back. Her heart was slamming wildly. One of the snowmobiles she'd heard
earlier was buzzing the house, its motor sounds filling the air with the roar she'd half heard in her
dream.

The machine whined past the house, so loud that
it had to be six or eight feet away from her window.
Its motor sounded like miniature machine guns fir-
ing. Why would he come so close to her window?
Teenaged macho arrogance, coupled with too many
beers? This was a part of north-woods living that
Sherry disliked intensely. She herself owned several Arctic Cats that she kept at Timberline, and
she'd never deliberately bothered others, waking
them in the middle of the night.

The driver made another pass under her bedroom window, sounding as if he were almost *in* her
bedroom.

She rolled out of bed and stumbled to the window, dragging aside the curtain. But she had not
turned the yard lights on, and the shape of snow-

mobile and rider was already pulling away into the pooled shadows of the night, a flash of yellow headlights marking its passage.

Sherry let the curtain drop and crawled back to bed, where she pulled the comforter well up over her shivering body. She might as well give up hope of sleep now. Whether she liked it or not, she'd be awake till morning.

# CHAPTER 6

In her office at Timberline, Sherry sat bent over an application she was making to the Grayling State Bank for a loan for snow-making equipment. It was already late Wednesday afternoon, the sky a flat, matte white that promised more snow.

But snow could never be depended upon, and if it didn't fall during the holidays, traditionally "the" week for ski areas to make money, profits for the entire season could be adversely affected.

Forty other Michigan ski areas already made snow, ranging in size from tiny Mt. Holiday, in Traverse City, to big and commercial Boyne Mountain, in Boyne Falls. However, the former owner of Timberline had never installed the expensive equipment, and now it was going to cost more than $50,000 to put in even the first stage, which included a new well, water lines, and snow guns.

She was also investigating the possibility of using Snomax, a natural snow enhancer derived from grass and plants. This additive, mixed with water in the snow guns, would produce fluffier snow at higher temperatures while using less water and energy. Some areas had reported getting one-third more snow.

She rubbed her temples, looking up from the estimates provided by several contractors as her ticket-seller, Becky Trimble, burst into her office.

"Sherry! Sherry, we have a ski theft."

"Oh, no."

"Yeah, this kid says he had a pair of Rossignols and he left them on the rack right in front of the lodge, and they're gone now."

"Did he lock them?"

"He says yes."

Sherry sighed and put away the papers, following her cashier out to the lodge, where a fifteen-year-old boy in a black ski jacket and red, high-topped ski boots paced back and forth.

"This place sucks!" the teenager burst out as soon as Sherry approached to ask what the trouble was. "I mean, I left my skis right there, right in front of the lodge, and somebody came along and ripped 'em off! Took my lock and everything."

"Okay," she said, smiling. "Let's take it from the top now. What's your name?"

"Brian. Brian Leach."

"And who are you skiing with today?"

"My brother and a bunch of his friends, we drove up from Rochester."

Sherry nodded. Rochester was a suburb of Detroit about three hours' drive south.

"You say you used a ski lock?"

"Yeah."

"And you looped the lock around the skis *and* the rack?"

"Sure, yeah."

His eyes glazed a little with moisture, and Sherry sensed the effort of a teenager not to break down in front of strange adults. She felt a stab of sympathy. Skis were expensive, she knew, even for middle-class families, and the loss might mean no more skiing for the rest of the season, or even permanently.

Sherry gazed thoughtfully at the boy. His ski jacket bore a number of old tags from Mt. Holly, a ski area near Detroit. Obviously he was no novice skier—and knew enough to lock his skis properly. What had happened?

"Brian," she probed. "You don't think you might accidentally have locked the *wrong* pair of skis, do you?"

"No." He was definite.

Instinct, born of years of experience, led her to the next question. "Well, let me ask you just one more question. Is your brother older or younger?"

"My brother . . . ? Why, he's two years older, he's the one who drove us, he—" Comprehension was spreading across the teenager's face. His expression changed from frantic worry to sheepish grin. "Oh, God, I bet he—"

"He knows your combination, doesn't he?" Sherry smiled in relief that this had been settled so easily. Ski thefts were a distressing by-product of any ski resort. "I think you'd better go have a few words with your brother, Brian. I think he's done a little teasing on you."

The teenager clumped in his heavy boots outdoors to find his brother, and Sherry and Becky looked at each other.

"Well, I called that one right," Sherry said.

"I don't see how you knew."

Sherry grinned. "Becky, most of the people who come to a ski resort are under twenty-five, and believe me, they have more jokes and tricks and pranks up the sleeves of their ski jackets than a chocolate doughnut has sprinkles."

Becky giggled.

"Besides," Sherry added. "My friend Carole pulled that on me once, when we were about seventeen. I was so scared, I thought my mother would kill me for losing my brand-new skis. I was ready to strangle her when she finally showed me my skis, buried in a snowbank."

After school was the most boring time of the day. Outside it was already dark and had begun to snow again. Big snowflakes drifted past the window, as chubby as fat, white caterpillars. Kady watched them tumble down, wondering how many would fall on their own property alone. A million? Two million? A billion? They were learning in math class about large numbers, the biggest number being a googol. Kady figured there must be at least a googol of snowflakes in Hartwick right now.

She released an enormous sigh that shook her whole body, thinking how bored she was. Either Maura or her mother was on the telephone; the Camracks' phone line had been busy for the past fifty-five minutes. Kady had exhausted her entire repertoire of interesting after-school activities.

Get the mail. Make microwave popcorn. Reread another of the Sweet Valley High books she was addicted to. Watch a couple of hours of TV. Wait for her mother to get home.

Wait! That was all she seemed to do in ski season. Sometimes her mother would pick her up and take her to Timberline to ski the rest of the afternoon, but other days her mother was too busy. Kady was a latchkey kid, sometimes independent, other days rebellious, or even a bit depressed. That's why she watched so much TV—for company. She had it on now. An old King Kong movie.

She prowled through the house like an FBI agent, looking in the closets for any bags that might contain M & M candy or leftover Christmas mints. The only booty she unearthed was a half stick of gum in one of Sherry's old flannel shirts. It was so brittle it broke into pieces when she chewed down on it.

Kady chewed energetically. She did have some math homework, but she wasn't in the mood for it yet. Nor did she feel like reading the chapter in her history book on Indians. Kady somehow enjoyed homework more when she waited until the very last possible moment.

She paced the house, wishing she were at Grandma's and could do some experimenting with the huge bag of makeup Grandma kept under the guest-room bed. There were a zillion shades of eye shadow, lipstick, blush, lip gloss, and translucent powder that poofed all over the room when you opened the lid. Kady remembered the last time she'd used that makeup—when she got her picture taken by Mr. Dietz.

He'd played rock music while he snapped picture after picture, talking to her all the time, as if she were really grown-up. It had been the most adult day of Kady's life, even if Grandma was sitting right there.

She sighed, thinking it was probably the only time she'd ever model. Grandma and Mom had been at each other's throats about that for months. To Grandma, if a girl was beautiful, she used it; and to Mom, if she was beautiful, she hid it.

Grown-ups were funny. Kady thought maybe when she grew up she'd be a ski racer and try out for the Olympics. Then when she'd won a medal or two, she'd enroll in medical school and study to be a children's doctor. Probably Mom and Grandma would argue about that, too.

She found herself pacing past the hall table, where the day's stack of mail waited. Kady was under strict orders not to open the mail, but she couldn't help noticing there was another envelope like the one she'd gotten on Monday. The one that contained the video her mother had not let her see.

Kady wondered what was in the video that was so bad her mother did not want her to play it. Probably it was a movie with nude love scenes, she'd bet, rated R. Kady had been to several R-rated movies like *Rambo* and *The Terminator* and she knew all about them. R movies were bloodier, the actors said the *F* word a lot, and sometimes you saw the women in bed without any clothes on.

She shuffled through the stack, examining the bills, which looked very boring, and the envelope, which looked very interesting. There was even her name, in rather sloppy printing: *Kady Vincent*. Kady hefted the envelope in her hands, shaking it a little. It definitely was another videotape.

The wrapping tape had begun to unpeel at one end of the package anyway, so Kady slid in her quick, slim fingers and just helped it a little, sliding out the black tape as smooth as butter. It looked exactly like the other one, but with a different number, 902. Kady decided that it wouldn't hurt anything to play it just once, and she could slide it right back into the envelope and just press the edges of the tape down tight.

Kady loved secrets, and she didn't consider this wrong. It *was* addressed to her.

Feeling much more cheerful, she sauntered down the hallway to the TV room and walked in. The little clock on the VCR said 6:45. On the TV set, King Kong was dying, his hairy, ugly face wrinkled pathetically, his lips moving like a human being's.

Kady watched him for a few minutes, and then she pushed the power button for the VCR and slid in the tape. She flopped down on the couch to watch.

Sherry pulled into the drive about seven, feeling her usual spasm of guilt that she'd left Kady for so long. But the ski season was so short, and their entire livelihood depended on it, and she felt she had little choice but to leave her daughter. A babysitter was impractical, and her mother was only a phone call away.

She checked the mailbox on her way in, finding it empty. She drove in, planning what she would do tonight. She'd been taping old episodes of *L.A. Law* and now had a collection of five, none of which she had seen yet. That sounded great . . . good mindless TV and a couple of microwave dinners. Just what she needed to get her psyche back on track.

In the small foyer, she noted that Kady had left her snowboots sprawled half off the boot rug, so that salt and melting snow had pooled on the tile, drying in a white crust.

"Kady," she called. "How many times have I told you to leave your boots *on* the rug?" She kicked off her own boots and made it a point to line them up side by side as an example.

There was no response, but she heard music coming from the den, where the television set was running. Sherry frowned. Homework was supposed to be the first evening priority.

"Kady," she called again, hanging up her jacket. She walked in her stocking feet down the hallway to the TV room. "I hope you've finished your homework, because if you haven't, there isn't going to be any TV tonight, not even the *L.A. Law* that I taped—"

She pulled open the door. Kady was seated on the corduroy couch, her lanky, beautiful body curled as close as a five-foot-seven girl could manage to a fetal position. Her hands clasped her knees so tightly that the knuckles of her hands showed white. Kady's eyes were fastened on the TV set with a fixed, blank, terrified expression.

A spurt of premonitory fear curled in Sherry's chest.

"Kady?" she questioned. "Kady, what are you—"

Her puzzled gaze swiveled to the TV screen, where the camera was focusing on an image of bare legs and thighs and a dog's muzzle. This was television? Sherry felt a flash of surprise that quickly ripened into horror. "Kady? What show is this? Kady?"

Her daughter didn't answer. Kady was focused on the TV screen with total concentration.

Sherry gasped. On screen, the camera had pulled away to show the dog, a German shepherd, licking the girl between her spread thighs, while the pitifully young, thin body vibrated and shook with trembling spasms that couldn't possibly be sexual pleasure, but had to be fear and horror. A man stood behind the girl, totally naked, his erect penis gargantuan. He was holding the child down, his hands digging into frail arms.

Sherry lunged forward and snapped the TV set off. The picture swallowed itself in a pinpoint of light. Then she reached down and grabbed Kady by the shoulders and hauled her daughter to her feet. Kady's eyes were still wide and blank, but tears had begun to well in them, spilling down her cheeks in wet, huge dollops.

"Mom," Kady managed to say.

"Kady! *That tape, where did you get it?*"

"Mom . . ."

Sherry shook her daughter, aware for the first time that Kady was almost as big as she was, and within fifteen pounds of her own weight. "Kady! Tell me! Did it come in the mail? Oh, Jesus, did it?" Sherry dropped her daughter's shoulders, and Kady fell back on the couch again, sinking onto the cushions with a fluid flop, as if she had no bones in her body.

Sherry turned and scrabbled around on top of the TV set until she'd found the casing for the videotape, the same black format as the other one, with the same logo of a faintly blurred figure that could pass for a male sheep.

A ram.

Symbol of fertility, of sexual excess.

She stood holding it, tasting her own nausea.

*"Kady, why did you play that tape?"*

The girl had started to cry now, flinging herself onto her side, half buried in the deepness of the corduroy cushions on which they'd played so many games of chess, eaten so many TV dinners, watched so many innocent *Bill Cosby* shows.

"Mom . . ." The voice came out choked, childish, horrified. "There were girls . . . girls like me . . ."

"Oh, *Kady*. Oh, God." Sherry didn't know what to do. The world—the ugly, real, horrible, vicious world—had crashed in on Kady without warning or preparation, and she'd had to face it alone. Why hadn't she listened?

Kady's voice shook. "I hated it . . . I wanted to turn it off . . . there were horrible things . . . they had some of them tied up . . ."

"Stop," Sherry said. "Stop talking about it. Stop thinking about it."

"There were men, Mom. Men with their things hanging out. Men—"

"It's over now. It's all over, Kady. I'll take the tape and throw it away and we'll never have to look at it again. It was pornography, honey. Horrible, bad. Some crazy person sent it. You weren't supposed to see it. Oh, why, why, why did you have to look?"

Somehow she'd started crying, and she flung herself on the couch and sat with her arms around her child, feeling the vulnerable wings of Kady's shoulder blades, her young-girl bones.

"I thought . . . I thought Kelly and Larry sent it. It had my name on it."

"But I told you, Christmas is over, Kady, why would they send presents now? Oh, baby, baby."

Kady went on in a monotone. "I stopped and got the mail and I c-couldn't find any snacks except for some old gum about a year old ... and Maura's phone was b-busy ..." Kady collapsed in sobs again.

"Damn," Sherry said over and over. "Oh, damn, damn." She hugged her child, crooning to her, saying anything that came into her head, not knowing whether it was right or wrong, only that she had to say something. "It was dirty and bad, Kady; it was terrible stuff meant for terrible men to look at ... It wasn't for girls to see ... not for us ... I want you to forget you ever saw it. Forget it. Don't think about it, not ever, ever again."

Odd, how familiar those words sounded, almost as if they came from a tape in her own brain, some tape that had been recorded years ago for the first time and was now being played back, almost verbatim.

"You have to put this out of your mind, Kady. Never think about it again. Never even dream about it. Because it didn't happen."

"But, Mom ..."

"*Don't think about it ever again,*" Sherry told her daughter fiercely.

Kady was finally in bed, where Sherry had tucked her in as if she were a five-year-old, and brushed the soft, lustrous, dark hair back from her daughter's forehead. She ached with a love for her child that was so intense she could weep.

"Kadydid, from now on, I don't want you going out to the mailbox at all. *I'm* going to bring in the mail, is that understood?"

"Okay, Mom."

"I mean it. And I don't want you running any tapes on the VCR either without my looking at them first."

"Okay." Then Kady's eyes filled with tears again. "Mom . . ."

"What, Kady?"

"Those girls on the tape. They looked so scared."

"Don't think about it, Kady."

"But I can't help it."

"Try, honey. Think happy things tonight. Think about all the good snow we got in this latest storm. I told Larry not to groom the bowl so we'll have some good powder there, and tomorrow is night skiing, I'll take you over."

Kady hesitated. "Okay."

"Now, close your eyes, Kady."

"I am, Mom. I'm not a baby, you know. Anyway, those things on that tape, I've seen stuff like that before."

"You have?"

"Yeah, over at Maura's. Her dad gets these magazines, he hides them in a drawer. Maura and I looked at the pictures one time. All those naked ladies. Is that pornography, too, Mom?"

Sherry moistened her lips, wondering what to say. "I think it is, honey. But at least the ladies were grown-up and knew what they were doing when they posed for the pictures, so it's . . . it's a little bit different. Please close your eyes, Kady. It's late, it's after eleven, and you know the school bus comes early. Get some sleep."

"Okay, Mom."

Sherry left her daughter's room, feeling the vise-like pangs of a throbbing headache, and the conviction she'd handled it all wrong. She knew she'd transmitted her own fear and tension to Kady. What she'd said had seemed to come from some deep inside part of her, already there, already rehearsed. But what *did* you say? What was reasonable? How did you explain evil to a twelve-year-old, especially when that evil had touched her?

Oh, God, where had those tapes come from?

It could hardly be an accident, not after receiving two. Who had sent them? And why? Sherry went around double- and triple-checking all the locks, even the sliding glass doorwalls that had metal stop-bars and were now blocked with snow, and hadn't been opened since October.

Anyone could be outside. That snowmobiler—

Outdoors, the wind had picked up and went howling across the front deck, whipping around the snow fencing and through the jack pines. Somewhere across the lake snowmobiles roared, sounding faint but menacing. Sherry pictured faceless drivers in black goggles and suits, hunched over throttles.

Finally she walked back into the den and went to the television set, where she looked for remains of the mailing envelope, the wrapper that the videotape had come in. Yes, there it was, on the floor. Her heart pounding, Sherry picked up the envelope, which Kady had opened carefully but then apparently dropped onto the floor.

Sherry fumbled in the bottom drawer of the nearby small desk, until she'd found an old, folded store bag. Carefully she stored the pieces of the envelope in the sack. Then she looked again at the blank screen of the TV set. The tape was still in the player, the red lights of the VCR glowing like miniature eyes.

*Evil*, Sherry thought.

Right here in her home, a touch away, the reach of a hand, no farther than the pushing of a button. Evil of a kind she had never dreamed existed.

The tape rewound with a clacking sound. Sherry's hands and feet felt clammy, and although she wore a wool sweater and cotton turtleneck, she was shivering.

But she wanted to face this. She wasn't a physical coward; she could canoe rapids, ski expert slopes, and she had even done some scuba diving. She believed she was tough and strong in the ways that counted. She wanted to see exactly what they were facing. She could help Kady better if she knew.

As before, there was the whirring hiss of dead space, and then the crude title flashed on the screen. *Young Meat* was the title of this one, and at the sight Sherry almost jumped up and pushed the stop button. *Young Meat*! How could they have chosen a title so . . . so vile and crude and suggestive and cruel?

But that, of course, was the whole point of pornography. It was manufactured so that men—the likes of whom Sherry couldn't even imagine or visualize—could masturbate while they watched it. Sherry believed the real purpose of movies such as this one was to give sexual pleasure to twisted and perverted minds that couldn't respond to sex normally, but had to be stimulated in sick and unusual ways.

She forced herself to sit there while the first scene came on the screen. A dark-skinned young girl about Kady's age, possibly Mexican, wearing a brief little white playsuit, walked across a dry field, scattered with unfamiliar, brittle-looking bushes. Once the girl glanced back at the camera, apparently for instructions, then went on. She was not a particularly pretty child, her features round, blurred with plumpness, her expression vacuous.

Or was it simply that they had drugged her, so that she'd be more willing to do whatever horrible things they would require of her?

She forced herself to keep watching. Another little girl appeared on the screen. Dirty blond hair, a waif look. Her bikini bathing suit was so minuscule that it hid none of her skinny, young ribs or the board-flatness of her immature stomach. What, fifth grade? Sherry wondered, sickened. Or fourth? This was a child who should be playing with Cabbage Patch dolls.

A man entered the picture. He looked like a terrorist, Sherry thought, with his shock of oily black hair, cruel features, and half-smiling lips. He wore leather pants and a black, armless T-shirt, with ropes of chains around his neck and waist.

Arrogantly he approached the little girl. Some music had begun to play in the background, but there wasn't any voice track, and Sherry hoped that there wouldn't be. She didn't want to hear these girls crying, pleading, or moaning.

The two girls began to take off their clothes, the man gesturing commandingly. Sherry watched, fascinated and repelled. The girls were quiet and scared. The man pulled the younger one close to him, bracing her against the tree trunk and pushing her thighs apart with his hand. She struggled weakly, her eyes glazed. Maybe she had been drugged, Sherry hoped. Maybe she wasn't fully there, didn't fully comprchcnd . . .

The camera pulled in closer. The man tugged at his leather pants, pulling open a flap from which protruded his enormous penis, thick and blue-veined. It looked unreal, like a big dildo, huge in size, especially in relation to the petite girl. Fluid gleamed on its tip.

The man entered the child roughly. The girl's face twisted in pain, her mouth forming an ugly O. Terror transfixed her as the man continued to thrust, each lunge lifting her body and slamming it against the tree.

Sherry had seen enough. She doubled over, retching, and finally managed to twist forward and punch the VCR's stop button. She sat breathing shallowly, trying to make her thoughts rational. How crude the tape was. Crude and sick.

How could people do that to children? And how could others watch? She'd read about kiddie porn, of course, but it had always been far away, concerning other children in other cities like Des Moines, or Pittsburgh, or New York. Not really real, just some newspaper story.

Now it was real, all right. She felt raw, as if *she'd* been the one raped against that tree. Or Kady. Dear God, if anyone ever touched her Kady like that— She was trembling uncontrollably. This tape, this vicious, exploitative tape . . . *it had been sent to her Kady*. It wasn't abstract anymore; it had struck at the very heart of their lives.

# CHAPTER 7

By morning Sherry had calmed down a little, enough to point out to herself that she could not allow her daughter to see her scared, or shaking. Kady's reaction to all of this depended on her own. If Sherry showed her fear, Kady would feel fear, too.

Kady appeared late for breakfast, her eyes puffy with sleep.

"Hi, Kadydid. You've still got a few sleepies in the corners of your eyes, kid."

"I know." Kady grinned tiredly and rubbed at her eyes. "I'm not hungry this morning."

"Sure you're hungry. Want some pancakes? A stack of nice blueberry pancakes would sure give us some energy."

"Blueberries? I didn't know we had any."

"Remember all those berries we picked last summer? I've still got four quarts in the freezer, and that's one good thing about frozen blueberries—

they go straight from freezer to griddle. All you have to do is say the word."

" 'The word,' " Kady responded, in their game that dated from when she was five.

"Okey-dokey." Sherry busied herself mixing up pancake batter and adding the tiny, hard, wild berries that were four times tarter than any commercial blueberry and twice as delicious.

"I want to pour the batter," Kady insisted.

"Okay—just remember, not too big or we won't be able to turn the pancakes."

They stood together at the stove, and Sherry poured little "extra" dabs of dough onto one of the pancakes to make a smiling face, nose and mouth, that would show up darker when the griddle cake was fried.

"You don't have to cheer me up, Mom," Kady said finally.

"Sorry. Have I been too cheerful?"

"A little bit."

Sherry hesitated, and then she pulled her daughter to her for a long hug. "Kadydid, I guess you're a lot more grown up than I give you credit for. I'm sorry for what happened last night—I never wanted anything bad to come in and upset you like that. I'd have given anything if you didn't have to see that."

"I know." And then it was Kady who reached out to Sherry and pulled her tight. "Mom . . . don't worry, Mom. I'm not that upset. Honest I'm not. I read an article in the Sunday magazine about stuff like that one time. Porno—"

"Pornography."

"Yeah. Anyway, looking at things can't really hurt you. It just gives you bad thoughts, that's all. But it doesn't really hurt *you*."

At her childlike reasoning, Sherry felt a pang that she carefully hid as she used the pancake turner to pick up the last of the pancakes they had made. "Now come on, let's sit down and have a feast, huh?

I want my beautiful girl to have plenty of roses in her cheeks. Do you want the syrup with the red or yellow top?''

"Red,'' specified Kady, choosing the high-sugar variety.

"Well, I think I'll have the yellow. And, Kady?''

"Mmm?'' Her daughter was already munching pancakes.

"Nothing,'' Sherry finally said. "It's just that . . . I really love you, Kadydid. You're the best thing in my life, and I mean that.''

Kady gave her a sweet grin that was full of blue-berries.

Two hours later, Sherry sat in a cluttered office in the Crawford County Sheriff's Department, in Grayling, staring around her at a room that looked as if she had seen it on a hundred made-for-TV movies. Four desks were jammed close together, and six ancient filing cabinets looked as if they had been through a war. A quartz heater whirred uncertainly. There were even Wanted posters tacked to the wall.

She studied the posters. The faces looked to her like men she'd seen working at car washes or gas stations. Sleazy, shifty, tired, sullen. *Scuzz-balls*, as her ex-husband, Dick, used to say. And now here she was in a place that dealt with people like that, and such a person had intruded on her life, and that of her daughter.

"Mrs. Vincent? I'm Detective Mike Arrington. They told me you were waiting—sorry, I had a long-distance call.''

The detective loped through the opened door, almost immediately making the little office seem even more cramped than it was. He was about thirty, six feet two in height, the kind of lanky, outdoorsy man who would be most comfortable standing in a trout stream. His white shirt seemed too tight for him, his tie loosened at the neck, which had the kind of tendoned thickness you saw in college athletes. Dark blond hair spilled over his forehead, and his windburned face was seamed with lines more appropriate in a man of forty.

"It's okay." She managed a smile. Her nervousness had receded a little. She knew Mike Arrington. Oh, not that she knew *him* specifically, but he was the type of man that northern Michigan bred or attracted. He probably drove one of the several Blazers parked outside. He lived somewhere outside of town on a lot big enough to have acreage; he fished, hunted, snowmobiled, owned a couple of dirt bikes.

"They said you'd gotten some porn in the mail." Gray eyes assessed her with a look men used so often around her. A twinge of sexuality filled the air, like smoke. Sherry looked away from him.

"Two of them," she said. "Two tapes." She realized that she was clutching the plastic sack so tightly that her fingers were perspiring. Consciously she made an effort to relax her fingers.

"The contents?"

She flushed. "It's—young girls, men . . . very . . . very obscene. I can't— They are bad. Take my word for it."

"They depict sexual intercourse?"

"Yes."

She dropped the sack onto the nearest desk, and Arrington sank into the chair that belonged to the desk, reaching for the bag. He rummaged through matter-of-factly. Sherry was struck by how innocuous the tapes looked. They could have been Jane Fonda videos, or copies of *E.T.* For an instant, she wondered if he would think she was lying.

"I see you saved the mailing wrappers."

"Yes, I thought there might be clues. They were both mailed from Grayling. And the printing looks like a child's, I thought it might be disguised. There's no return address," she pointed out.

She waited while Arrington examined the two black slipcases. His hands, she noticed, were large and callused, the nails clipped short and very clean.

"This looks like pretty standard catalog porn—the type you can order in the back pages of *Penthouse*, for instance. They even have them for rent now in some video stores—not at the counter but in a back room. People are interested in tapes like this; they'll rent them to watch at home in private."

"Not tapes like these." Sherry crossed her arms over her chest, setting her jawline.

Arrington expelled his breath. "Are you married, Mrs. Vincent? I didn't see a ring."

She hesitated. "No, I'm divorced. It's been final a month."

"Congratulations." His tone was dry. "Look, how long has it been since your husband moved out?"

"Five months." Her throat tightened. "What do you mean? You don't think that *Dick* sent these, do you? To his own daughter? You have to be kidding!"

"No, he might not have sent them, but he might have ordered them. Stranger things have happened, Mrs. Vincent," Arrington said as Sherry's mouth fell open. "People go through a divorce, maybe the sex life falls apart, the man has urges, he goes out and buys some flesh magazines, *Penthouse*, *Hustler*, or maybe he sends for a few things."

She snapped, "These came to Kady, my daughter, not to Dick!"

"Still, it is a possibility."

Sherry felt hot and cold waves of clamminess sweep over the surface of her skin. Arrington had touched on a very raw note. Her marriage had broken up when Dick's periodic womanizing had finally resulted in Sherry's being transmitted a case of gonorrhea. For Kady's sake, she had stuck in the marriage, but that she just could not tolerate. Penicillin had cured her venereal disease, and filing for divorce had seemed the only answer.

She thought. Dick *had* read magazines like that. Not often, but she'd found a few copies around the house, they'd even had arguments about them. His position was that men were attracted by the visual—there did not need to be feelings, sex could be a mechanical act on occasion.

But Dick's dirty magazines had been the standard issue, featuring young women over twenty-one years of age. She looked at Detective Mike Arrington, irritated by his assumption that this was something all men did, a natural function.

"My husband bought his own magazines at the drugstore, he didn't send for them, and he didn't order kiddie porn. That's what this is, child pornography, and whatever else Dick did, he wasn't interested in little girls."

Professional eyes studied her. "You don't know it for a fact, though, do you?"

"I do know it. I was married to him for fourteen years. I know him." She flushed. "He was normal in his orientation."

Arrington shrugged. "Okay. Well, since the tapes were mailed in Grayling, it might mean that they were sent as a practical joke then."

"A *joke?*" Sherry swallowed.

"A sick joke. Look, there are a lot of people out there who are, well, running a quart low. Their engines are just not running right. Now, you run that ski resort over there near the state forest, don't you? Timberline?"

"Yes, but—"

"People in a village like this, people are funny. They want everyone else to fit in, they don't like other people who stick out, who act a little different. Here you are, you've gotten a divorce. You run what some people think is a pretty fancy ski area. Maybe you've got a disgruntled employee. Maybe you turned down someone for a job who thought he ought to get one. Or maybe you kicked someone out because they were carrying a flask. I heard you're pretty tough on liquor over there."

"It's a family resort," she retorted.

"There, you see?" Arrington rose from the desk, towering over her. He shoved the videos back into the bag and stood balancing the shopping bag, staring down at it. "You have any enemies?"

This was the joke, she thought. This interview.

"No, I don't have any enemies. I owe a few creditors, but I'm only a month or so late with the payments and I really don't think that Visa is going to get all excited and send me pornographic videos through the mail. I'm really sorry I bothered you with this." She jumped to her feet, not troubling to hide the sarcasm in her tone. "*God*," she finished. "This all sounds just like some TV detective show. You're not going to do anything, are you? There isn't anything you *can* do, is there?"

He eyed her, then dropped the bag into a bottom desk drawer. "Actually, the procedure when you get porno in the mail is to go to the post office and fill out a form."

"You have to be kidding."

He shook his head wryly. "I'll keep these for the U.S. Postal Service, but porn is real hard to get a conviction on, Mrs. Vincent. If another one comes, we might get fingerprints, but I doubt it. It's a lot harder than you think to take a really good print. And even then what good will prints do if we don't have people on file? It doesn't do any good then at all."

At least he had spent time talking to her, she realized, unlike a big-city police department that would just tell her to go fill out the form.

"And what should I do in the meanwhile?" she asked. "Just wait until another one comes in the mail?"

"It probably won't. Videotapes are too expensive.
But if one does come, save it, and don't open it this
time, just leave everything the way it is."

"And my daughter? My twelve-year-old? What am
I supposed to tell her?"

"Keep her out of the mail. And by the way, maybe
it's one of her friends who's playing the joke. What
kind of kids does she run with? Are there any older
ones—any kids that are into punk rock, that sort of
thing?"

Sherry edged toward the door. "No," she
snapped. "My daughter is *twelve* and *innocent*."


Instead of driving back to Timberline, Sherry
found herself turning onto M-72 and the road to
Lake Ossineke, where Dick lived. The road had been
salted and was clear, and she allowed her speed to
creep up past seventy mph. She would confront
him, she decided, get it all out in the open, while
she still had her anger to fuel her.

Dense secondary forest flashed past on either side
of the highway, skinny jack pines and birches
crusted with white. Huge rotten stumps were visible here and there among the undergrowth, relics
from the days when lumberjacks had raped the
woods. She fussed with the radio dial, switching
from Frank Sinatra to Bon Jovi to an ad for the
Dairy Bar in Manton. Static crackled, and impatiently she flicked off the set.

She could not believe Dick would send such filth
to his own child. He had sinned plenty, but it had
been with adult women, usually blondes, usually
fully built, women with jobs like ski instructor or
waitress.

As for enemies, Sherry had always had those, but
not the type the detective had suggested. Even when
she'd been twelve, there had been townspeople who
thought that *those three girls* had somehow been at
fault in the seventh grade incident.

*Things like that don't just happen, those three girls must have done something.*

*Didn't Sherry Smith have a crush on Ray Innis anyway? Wasn't she caught writing love notes to him?*

*Maybe those girls weren't quite as innocent as everyone made out.*

She clamped off the memories, tightening her hands on the steering wheel. Enemies: little old ladies who thought that Sherry's divorce from Dick Vincent vindicated what they'd "known all along." But what little old lady would send Kady a dirty video? None she knew of.

She drove, thinking. She *had* fired several people from Timberline, though. Bun Starkie last winter for drinking on the job. But Bun was working now for the DNR, the Department of Natural Resources, and was probably getting paid a lot better, so why would he be resentful?

She'd had to fire Angelina McNaughton out of the kitchen last month, too. Sherry had discovered her one day, piling dozens of hamburger patties in a paper bag to take home, with more stuffed down her voluminous bosom. But Angelina, one of the county's chronic poor, owned no VCR, probably had never looked at a pornographic video, or any video, in her entire thirty-three years. Besides, she was female. Sherry just didn't think that a woman, any woman, would send a child a filthy tape like the ones Kady had received.

Anyway, maybe there wouldn't be any more. Even porn tapes had to cost money, Sherry told herself. How much? $40, $70, $150? Sherry had no idea how much pornography cost, but Hartwick wasn't a rich village and here $150 meant something, a week's pay for some people. Sooner or later their persecutor would have to give up, simply because it was too expensive to continue.

Dick lived in a tacky little A-frame development

near the lake that somehow had never proved profitable to the developers. Now, in winter, the cottages were closed for the season, driveways
unplowed so that it looked as if the A-frames rose
directly up out of the white. The only sign of life
was a plume of chimney smoke that rose from one
of the homes.

Sherry drove her Toyota down the access road.
She parked behind Dick's Mercury Cougar—
champagne-colored and only one year old. A new
Ski-Doo snowmobile was parked behind that, covered by a tarp. She got out and trudged through
the snow, a tight constriction beginning in her
chest, as it always did when she had occasion to
talk to Dick.

Angry because Sherry had been awarded the ski
area, he had paid no child support since the sepa-
ration, and he'd only telephoned Kady three times.
His Christmas presents to his daughter had been
wildly extravagant, far too many for a twelve-year-
old, and fussily gift-wrapped by a female hand, with
touches a store wrapping service could not provide. Rumors circulated around town about Dick's
girlfriends. A ski instructor at Boyne Mountain. A
waitress at the Holiday Inn.

Sherry hated the rumors and tried not to listen
to them, but people kept bringing the subject up,
even Carole, who was supposed to be her best
friend. Didn't people realize that it hurt to hear of
his carryings-on? Both of the men in her life had
done that to her, she reflected as she tramped up a
narrow shoveled path. Glen Dietz, years ago. Then
Dick. Flaunting their sexuality in her face as if to
tell her, *You might have been Miss Michigan once
but you aren't worth anything to me now.*

She banged on the door.

His car was there, so he had to be, and by leaning
forward she could hear the sounds of a TV set, running an afternoon movie. Something violent.

"Dick!"

Finally there was a sound on the other side of the door, and then it was being pulled open, and her ex-husband stood looking down at her.

He was very tall, nearly six feet five—Kady got her height from him. He had a big, wide build that had started to go to beef, but still looked held in, like Roger Moore in his last James Bond movie. In fact, Dick looked like Moore. He had brown eyes and in recent years had grown a full beard that he kept neatly trimmed and soft to the touch, almost pettable. Women had always responded to Dick. Doing the laundry Sherry had found little scraps of paper with phone numbers in his pockets, and once a motel room key with a note attached: *Jill—I'm here tonight and tomorrow.*

"Sherry," he greeted her. His eyes were wary.

"Can I come in? I need to talk to you."

He stepped aside and ushered her in, making a little-boy, sleepy gesture toward his eyes that stopped just short of a knuckling. So he had been asleep in front of the TV. Sherry felt a spurt of contempt. Since the divorce he'd talked of starting up a sporting goods store, but she suspected it was more talk than action. Dick was coasting on a recent inheritance from his father who had made a fortune selling discount tires.

Car wheels squealed from the TV set—cars were crashing and rolling in a chase scene.

"Yeah? Well, sure, we can talk. Just watching the afternoon flick. Nick Nolte. You like Nick Nolte?"

Sherry didn't bother to answer. She stood looking around the cluttered A-frame living area, crammed with the detritus of bachelor living. A new stereo, a compact disc player with about 250 discs scattered on the floor. A wine rack containing one bottle. A leather couch piled with dirty clothes, books, newspapers, and mail. And beer cans, lined up in rows along tabletops and along the wall, like trophies.

"Those beer cans are ten cents each," she couldn't help remarking. "You could turn them in and get money for them."

"I know that. I'm saving them for the big push. Forty bucks at one time."

She laughed bitterly. "I can't believe this place. My God, Dick, what do the women say when you bring them here?"

"They want to clean it up for me," he told her, grinning down at her. "Hey. How's the Skeezer? How's she doing? She miss me?"

"You know darn well she misses you."

"She wearing that new outfit I got her, the layered outfit, whatever you call it? I picked it out down in Midland, they said all the girls were wearing them."

"You know Kady. You know how she likes jeans. It's her uniform."

"She hasn't worn it?"

"Well, she did once. They had something over at the junior high, a class party."

"Oh."

Dick sank onto the couch, which creaked under his weight, and Sherry sat down on a La-Z-Boy upholstered in tobacco brown. She caught her breath, expelling it in a long, slow pressing-out of air. "Dick. I need to know if you placed an order for any videotapes recently. Any tapes that might have come to the house."

He stared at her. "No."

She gazed into the chestnut brown eyes, trying to detect a lie there. He had told her enough lies over the years, all about women.

"Are you sure, Dick? This is important."

"Hey. Of course I'm sure! I know what I've ordered and what I haven't ordered. I've been getting compact discs. Anyway, you kept the VCR so what would I want videotapes for?" Their eyes locked. "Why do you want to know, Sherry? What kind of tapes?"

"Well, they're filthy, they're—"

"You mean, el porno? Sexy stuff? Hot bikinis and all that?" Dick grinned. "Poor baby, you never did like that, did you? You hated my *Penthouse*s. It always drove you freaky. It was only fantasy, Sherry, but you never could see it."

"*These* tapes aren't fantasy!" she burst out. "And they aren't hot bikinis either. They're horrible, they're kiddie porn, they're of little girls, and I don't think it's so funny. Two tapes came in the mail to *Kady*. To our daughter."

"Hey, come on."

"They came to our child."

Dick shifted uneasily, his eyes going from Sherry to the TV set and then back again. "What do you think I am, some kind of asshole that would order dirty tapes and push them off on my kid?"

"I really wouldn't know."

"Jesus Christ. Look, I didn't order any tapes, and if I did, they'd come here. I've got the other room full of shit I ordered for the store . . . I've got Parcel Post coming here every other day. When I get the stock in I'm going to open in time for spring; I already signed a lease in Grayling—"

He was talking about his sporting goods store, leading her away from the question; was it deliberate or was it just the way Dick always was, sliding away from important issues? She was so glad she was divorced from him. If not for Kady, she would never see him again.

"Dick—"

He scowled. "You're really serious, aren't you? You really think I'd— Well, Christ. What is this, your idea of a new way to harass me? To get me to play the role of bad guy, the heavy that doesn't visit his kid often enough, doesn't pay out his money when the court says he should? You want to take me to court, Sherry? You want to haul me in front of the judge and force me to pay on demand? Like some kind of a criminal, being punished because you decided you wanted a divorce?"

"*You* wanted the divorce, too," she cried, jumping up. "Otherwise, why did you give me gonorrhea? So don't tell me I was the one who wanted it. And you're damn glad to be single again, too. You wallow in it, you love having beer cans all over your living room and getting your girlfriends to come here and wrap our daughter's Christmas presents!"

On her way out, she slammed the front door so hard that a row of beer cans scattered across the floor.

# CHAPTER 8

That night Sherry's nightmare came again, the hands insistently caressing, pushing in between her thighs, a finger inserting itself into her most private place.

*You like this, don't you?*

*I can tell, I know. You're so pretty ... Such a pretty girl, so soft ...*

She tossed and turned, tangling herself in the bedcovers, kicking at them as if they were ropes, tying her down.

*I just want to make you happy,* crooned the dream voice. *You're the prettiest girl in Hartwick, in the whole wide world ...*

She sat bolt upright, her body drenched with sweat, her heart hammering. Her mouth had a sick taste. She looked around the room, trying to orient herself, to pull reality around her again. Across the room the light on the digital clock glowed red. It said 5:32:43.

*Jesus*, she thought. Five-thirty in the morning.

Outdoors wind whistled through the pine branches, banging something against a tree trunk. A hollow, lonely sound. It wasn't even dawn yet.

She reached for the comforter that had slid off her body as she struggled, and pulled its downy heaviness up around her chin. According to Dr. Frey, all these years she'd repressed things, pushed them deep into some safeguarded part of her mind where they couldn't bother her. She had actually forgotten Ray Innis—or thought she had.

But Kady's turning twelve had unlocked memories inside her, like turning a key. Triggering these nightmares.

Dr. Frey had explained it all. At age twelve, when the molestation had occurred, Sherry had been at a very vulnerable stage in her sexual development. She had been at an age where she had been experimenting with herself and her feelings. Part of her had actually liked what happened, had been seduced in fact. Part hadn't. This caused the guilt that bothered her now.

*Tell the truth*, a voice taunted inside of her. *You were in puppy love with him. You thought he was handsome; you wrote him love letters; you wrote his name all over your notebooks. You organized that picnic; you made Carole and Judy go.*

Sherry grabbed her knees and sat huddled, hearing her ragged breath gradually smooth itself, her pulse rate slow. The damn dreams. How she hated that voice, so soft and calm, and yet pleading, too, with a thin line of dirtiness to it, the combination one that made Sherry's skin crawl. *He* had been an adult; he knew what he was doing; he had used them. A teacher, with children entrusted to him.

There was still a half hour before she had to get up. She forced her mind to think about the day that lay ahead. Mundane details. She had to make sure that Kady didn't sleep through her alarm again.

Make sure her daughter ate something for breakfast other than warmed-over pizza. She wanted to see her accountant today, and there were repairs to the number one chair lift, for which she needed to consult with Bob Nisinby, her new chair operator. She'd imported him from Aspen, now let him earn the big dollars she paid him . . .

She must have drowsed off, for she was awakened by the trill of her clock alarm. In her flannel nightgown she walked out to the hall to turn the thermostat up. Padding past Kady's room, she could hear her daughter's clock radio playing Michael Jackson's "Man in the Mirror."

"Kady?" She peered into the room. Her daughter's bed was a tangle of bedcovers, Sweet Valley High books, Pound Puppies, and a mop of black, curly hair. "Kadydid! Don't push the snooze button; you've got to get up on time this morning; I don't want to have to drive you to school today."

Kady mumbled something and dug herself farther into the mattress.

"I mean it," Sherry said.

Kady moaned and turned over.

"Five more minutes!"

Sherry sighed and returned to the master bedroom to begin dressing. She felt drained from the night before, her muscles aching, as if she had clenched her body all night. Stripping off the nightgown, she went into the small bathroom and stepped into the shower stall. Goose bumps on her body anticipated the first spray of warm water.

She twisted on the faucet and stepped underneath.

*There was something wrong*, she thought. And it wasn't only the dirty videos they'd received, or the fact that her mother had manipulated Kady into posing for a model's portfolio.

No, the wrongness went deeper than that.

The dream she'd had last night, the nightmare—

It had something to do with that. Yes, somehow the dream, that horribly soft and insinuating male voice, was part of what was wrong.

*Don't be crazy*, she told herself. *Don't be imaginative. Let it go, just forget about it.*

But she couldn't. Water sprayed around her, sending up a fine mist of droplets that she breathed and tasted. She reached for the soap and lathered herself, thinking about the wrongness. Or maybe wrongness wasn't the right word. Maybe it was similarities.

Yes, that was it. There were so many similarities.

In 1965, when the Ray Innis thing had happened, when the scandal had erupted in Hartwick, Sherry had been twelve years old. Now Kady was twelve. Back then, Sherry had been the "prettiest girl in Hartwick." Now Kady was.

And the videotape, that first awful video. There had been a river in its background, Sherry was sure of it, she could remember seeing a flash of water through the trees. A river something like the Au Sable that ran past the outskirts of Hartwick.

And there had been young girls in the video, the same age as Sherry, Judy, and Carole had been when—

Sherry stood stock still, water splashing unheeded over her skin. *There was a connection.* She finished her shower and stepped out to dry herself, a knot in her stomach like a tight fist.

Twenty-four years, she thought, beginning to dress for work, was an entire generation. People had been born in Hartwick, grown up, got married, and moved away in that space of time. It had been scandalous, yes, a teacher molesting three of his pupils, but no real harm had been done to any of them. They had not been raped, after all, just touched and fondled. Ray Innis had been forced out of town, and now the incident was no more than a colorful part of local history. Old, dead gossip.

She went into the hall, called Kady for the third time, then returned to make the bed, pulling up the striped comforter that had once been a wedding gift.

*No*, she thought.

It was not possible. It was ridiculous to suppose that Innis would decide to take revenge after all these years. If he'd wanted to do something, he would have done it right away, not a generation later. And, Sherry thought ruefully, he probably would have unleashed his anger on the three mothers involved, Margaret Smith, Eleanor Hamner, and Linda Sjoholm. They were the ones who had formed the vendetta, who had hounded him out of town.

Her stomach twisted again, and she knew she wasn't going to be able to eat breakfast.

"If you miss the bus today, Kady Ann, you are going to walk to school, and I mean it this time. I cannot afford to drive you around and be late every day."

"Mom . . . it's a four-mile walk."

"You have good boots and good legs."

"Not that good," her daughter groaned.

A typical morning conversation with both of them slightly edgy. "Kadydid, you could walk from here to Traverse City and not even breathe hard. I wish I had half your energy."

Kady looked balky and fractious this morning, but her skin was as fresh as camelia petals, her sweep of dark hair making her look like one of the models in *Seventeen*. The thought was an unpleasant pinprick.

"Eat your cereal."

"Ugh!" Kady said. "I *hate* Shredded Wheat. Is this all we have? Can't we have pancakes again?"

"Pancakes are for when you get up early. We haven't got time today," Sherry said. "Now, hurry.

You've got ten minutes until the bus hits the road end, and you know it won't wait."

Sherry drove to Timberline with the car radio tuned to Anne Murray, allowing her favorite singer's warm, mellow tones to "air lock" her for the pressures that waited her at work. The revelation she'd had in the shower—about the two incidents being similar—had shaken her. But she had to put it out of her mind now. Running a business was all she could think about during work hours . . . if she wanted to keep on running it, that is.

Profits had jumped forty-three percent since she'd taken over ownership, but could easily slip back if she wasn't vigilant.

Sherry pulled into the upper parking lot at Timberline, and inspected the long, one-story, redwood-sided lodge with pride. Five years ago, when she and Dick had bought the ski area, the place had been nearly defunct, the lodge a cinder-block structure that looked more like an A & P than a ski resort. Sherry and Dick had sunk thousands into remodeling. Now they still weren't Michigan's best-known resort, but they boasted two chair lifts, five rope tows, eighteen runs, lessons, night skiing, a spring carnival, and a rental shop that could service 300.

Sherry strode inside, breathing in the yeasty odor of freshly deep-fried cinnamon and chocolate doughnuts, a specialty she had added last year, with profitable results. She greeted several of her staff members.

"We just got these posters about Silver Streak Week," said Becky Trimble, looking sleepy. "Do you want me to put them up?"

Silver Streak Week was a promotion many ski areas were participating in, that would let skiers age fifty-five and older ski free.

"We did decide to participate in that, didn't we?" Sherry frowned. "The only trouble is, some people over fifty-five aren't physically very flexible . . . I don't want them getting hurt. How about if we also offer free *lessons* to skiers over fifty-five? That way, at least they'll be under supervision.''

"Do you discriminate against senior citizens?" Becky teased.

"I discriminate against accidents," Sherry said. She walked over to greet several skiers who were lounging at one of the tables, waiting for the chair lift to start.

"I just wanted to say there was ice on the Bunny Hill yesterday," one woman complained. "Especially under the rope tow. My son slipped and fell about eight times."

Sherry smiled. "We groom the slopes every morning, especially the Bunny Hill. So it should be fine today. I'll tell you what, though. I'll give your son a slip for a free half-hour lesson on using the rope tows—that should really help him with falling."

She wrote out the slip and accepted the woman's thanks. She got a lot of repeat business here; she wanted people to feel that this was a club, not just a place where you spent fifteen dollars on a lift ticket and no one knew you. Besides, she had increased their profits on lessons by twenty percent by offering free samples.

Bob Nisinby, the new chair-lift operator, came into the lodge, felt-lined snowmobile boots making squashing noises on the carpet. He was about fifty-five, bearded, his skin reddened and roughened from years of outdoor exposure. In his army surplus coverall, he looked like an oil pipeline worker. However, he was supposed to be excellent at chair-lift management and was able to make most repairs himself. This alone made him invaluable.

"Hi, Bob," she greeted him.

"I wanted to ask you," he said. "I saw a couple of guys on Sunday, a couple guys with flasks. They

were drinking out of 'em right on the chair lift just
as plain as day. Getting drunk."

Sherry felt a spurt of annoyance. "Why didn't you
say anything on Sunday, then? You were there for
orientation, you remember what our policy is. No
flasks, period."

"Sorry," the man mumbled.

"Bob, I know you came here from Colorado, and
that's the best—in this country anyway. Lots of
wide spaces that give skiers plenty of room so they
can fall without hitting anyone. Or ski around people who *have* fallen. But here it's different. Our runs
are narrow, and we funnel a lot of people in a close
space. We can't afford to have skiers who are out
of control."

"Right."

"We *have* had a very smooth chair operation
since you've come, though," Sherry added, wanting
to assuage the man's ego. She went into her office
and closed the door. In five minutes, the lifts would
start up, and their day would be officially under
way.

At 9:30 her private phone rang. Busy on the loan
application again, Sherry snatched it up. "Timberline, Sherry speaking."

The other voice drawled, "This is the Internal
Revenue Service, calling to arrange an audit. You
owe one hundred thousand dollars in back taxes."

For an instant panic clutched her—her experience with the I.R.S. had taught her this was all too
possible. Then, "Oh," Sherry said, sagging into her
chair. "Carole."

"God, aren't you the cheerful one this morning,"
her friend teased. "And I was going to come over
and make you go skiing with me, put a little north-
country red in my cheeks. I'm so damn unhealthy-
looking, I don't even remember what it feels like to
have a day off."

"You have a day off?" Sherry repeated stupidly.

"Three days, as a matter of fact. And I've already got my ski stuff on, so you'd better not flake out on me. I don't like riding up chair lifts by myself."

Sherry grinned, twirling her chair around on its pedestal, feeling relaxed for the first time today. "Well—"

"I'll be over in half an hour," Carole announced.

Overhead, the morning's gray cloud cover had begun to clear, and a watery sun lit up the red pine and jack pines that covered most of the resort with a thick blanket of greenery, except for where the runs had been cut.

"Gorgeous!" sighed Carole, the crumb of a chocolate doughnut clinging to her upper lip. "Oh, God, Sherry, to think that you can work in a place like this instead of a stinky hospital where you have to stick needles in little kids and wash their rear ends and wipe up blood."

"Yeah, I've got paradise," Sherry said.

"Well, you do." In her canary yellow ski outfit, Carole Hamner looked like a plump winter melon, her blond hair stuffed under a matching yellow hat. Carole had always been chubby, and two divorces and uncountable failed love affairs had added weight. Now she was easily forty pounds too heavy, and the ski pants were stretched sausage-tight. But men seemed to adore Carole's full curves and she seldom lacked for company on her erratic nights off.

"Have you gone out with Glen Dietz yet?" Carole wanted to know as they skied forward to board the oncoming chair. "I heard a couple of the nurses at the hospital talking—the little twenty-two-year-olds think he's gorgeous."

"I believe it," Sherry said. They boarded the lift.

"A new man in town always does that—turns the females ferocious. You'd better be careful, Sherry, or some honey pie who looks good in a white uniform is going to get her hooks into him."

"Let her."

"Hey, he's not that bad. He's good-looking, Sherry, he's—"

"So? I've told you, Carole, I don't want to date anyone, and I especially don't want to date Glen Dietz. He makes me feel funny."

"Aha!" Carole said.

"Not that way."

"But he does make you feel funny?"

"Oh, lay off, Carole, I don't even want to think about Glen. I've got worse things to think about."

The chair neared the top, and the two women straightened their skis and skied down the small incline. They stood looking over the resort, a vista of white slopes, in places still marked by the cross-hatching of the grooming machines. Laughing skiers sped past them, with the characteristic sliding squeak of metal edges cutting snow. There was something exhilarating about standing at the top of a hill looking down. Sherry never tired of it.

"What worse things?" Carole demanded.

Sherry punched the tip of her pole into the snow. "It's those videos. I've been thinking about them. I think they have something to do with . . . you know. What happened when we were kids."

Carole stared at her. "Come on, Sherry."

"Well, I think I'm right. I know I'm right. Whoever sent me those videos has something to do with *that*."

Both of them were staring at Sherry's ski pole as if it were some prehistoric Indian artifact they had just unearthed. Sherry had never been able to talk about *it*, and she could tell that Carole was the same. Things happened when you were children, and you didn't want to discuss them later, they made you too uncomfortable. You tacitly agreed not to bring them up. She hadn't discussed this with Carole in ten years, she'd bet. Maybe longer.

At last Carole let out her breath in a short puff of steam that drifted whitely from her lips. "Okay, Sherry, I see what you mean. You get a dirty video in the mail and immediately you think of something dirty that happened a long time ago. I can understand how you might make the connection. But it's just coincidence, that's all. I mean, what happened . . . it was when we were *kids*."

"I know."

"Hell, we were *babies*."

"I know that!" But she bit off the sharp retort, jabbing the pole over and over into the snow. "Sorry."

"Hey, don't let it get to you," Carole said. "It's just some stupid prank, like an obscene phone call."

Despite the beauty of the day, Sherry was suddenly near tears. "I hate obscene phone calls! I hate tricks being played on me. This is all *connected*, Carole. I know it is. I feel it. I can feel it deep inside me."

Carole began adjusting her ski hat, tucking her hair under the wool. "Will you stop worrying? It's just some weirdo's idea of a practical joke, that's all. Throw those videos out. Trash them. Never look at them. That's all you have to do. Nobody said you had to *look*."

"Fine. I'll do that. And I won't worry that someone picked out my little girl from all the possible people in the world he could have sent the damn things to. I won't worry about that at all."

Carole gave an embarrassed laugh. "Well, whatever you say, there's no connection," she said shortly. "You've got that on your mind so you think everyone else does too. Well, they don't. Nobody is thinking about what happened in seventh grade except you. Come on, let's ski. I didn't come here to stand at the top of the hill and talk."

With that, Carole gave a kick turn and pushed off, skiing down the hill in a wide blur of yellow.

# CHAPTER 9

They skied for two hours, Sherry finally ending it by pleading she had to get back to her desk work. Could she really blame Carole for not wanting to talk about what happened in seventh grade? If Sherry herself had repressed it all these years, could she fault Carole for doing the same thing? For not wanting to be reminded of sexual molestation and helplessness?

They had parted as if the mention of it had never happened. "I've still got a couple days off," Carole remarked as she was leaving, skis slung over her shoulder, boot bag in her hand. "Maybe you can get away, come and have dinner with me, or at least a drink. We'll drive over to Traverse City, check out the night spots, go on a pub crawl."

Sherry couldn't help laughing. "Pub crawl? At our age?"

"Sure—we'll lush up the town, we'll dance on tables and toss our brassieres out to the wildly cheering crowd."

"You are crazy. You really are."

"Well, hey, you've been divorced a month, girl, and you haven't even celebrated yet, have you? Nobody's properly divorced until they've gotten themselves shit-faced and come dragging home with their panty hose down around their knees."

"Carole— Really—"

"Sorry. Okay. Look, you give me a call today or tomorrow and we'll see what kind of mischief we can get up to."

Sherry nodded and smiled, not really agreeing, and watched as Carole pulled out of the lot in her blue Camaro. In a way she wished she had Carole's defiant sense of humor. If Carole had received the videos, she probably would have given a party and awarded prizes to those with the most original idea for trashing them.

She went back into the lodge and stowed her skis and boots in the locker she had had built for them in her office. It bulged with extra jackets, wind shirts, goggles, gloves, ski masks, extra pole baskets, even a cowgirl costume she wore every year for spring carnival.

She was just reaching for a proposal from Ossineke Plumbing Contractors when her private line rang.

"Timberline, Sherry speaking," she answered automatically.

Kady's eager voice. "Mom? Is it all right if I take the bus home with Maura and sleep over with her tonight? I'll ride the bus to school tomorrow with her, and she can loan me a nightie and stuff like that. Please? Huh? Please?"

"Tonight, Kady?" Sherry was dismayed. After her daughter's reaction to the videos, and the slight edginess they'd had this morning, she'd counted on a nice long evening with her child. They would pop popcorn, maybe play Pictionary, watch some TV, pretend nothing had happened, that their lives were normal and simple.

"We have to write this report for Mr. Alberto's class and it's due tomorrow and Maura's mother's got a typewriter. She said she'd help us type it. *Please?*"

"I was going to buy us a pizza tonight," Sherry hedged.

"Can't we get pizza tomorrow or something? Maura's mother is going to make us tacos."

"Oh, well, tacos! That beats pizza any day, doesn't it?" She tried to speak lightly, over the lump of disappointment that filled her throat. "All right, Kadydid, if you promise you and Maura will really work on that homework report and won't stay up too late. It's a school night and—"

"Mom," Kady responded with dignity. "Maura's mother always makes Maura go to bed by nine-thirty on a school night. She's even stricter than you are."

Sherry said good-bye and hung up, feeling rebuffed somehow. She had wanted to minister to Kady's need, to comfort her, offer closeness—and apparently her daughter didn't need that. She had obviously pushed the videos from RAM Productions out of her mind. Maybe girls were tougher today than they'd been when Sherry was twelve; had prolonged TV watching and violent movies blunted them?

*Well, good*, Sherry told herself firmly. She didn't want Kady haunted by obscenity; she should be happy her daughter wanted to be with her friend.

Which left her the evening to spend alone. And not with Carole either.

By the time Sherry left Timberline it was dark, the sky a dramatic sweep of pewter and silver clouds massed against an icy winter moon. A bitter wind blew from the north, tasting of arctic ice floes and pine needles. The temperature had already dropped to fifteen, and by morning it would be zero. Skiers would have to wear masks or risk frostbite. In the distance snowmobile motors buzzed, spoiling the clear silence of the air.

She drove straight to Grayling, slowing twice to avoid deer that ran across the road in front of her, their fleeting silhouettes fragile, so beautiful in the headlights that she thought of unicorns. To her the deer were magic, a symbol of all that was right with the north country. She hated seeing their bodies strapped to the top of hunters' cars and vans, all the magic turned into a matted bloody corpse.

The outskirts of Grayling sped past her, shacky little log cabins that now sold souvenirs, a muffler shop, a farmhouse, a truck-rental company, a newly built mini-storage place. Outside one house a pickup truck sat in the driveway, its motor running, white vapor from its exhaust surrounding it like a cloud.

She passed a convoy of snowmobiles, joyriding along the shoulder of the highway toward town and the local bars. The lead machine swerved back and forth, kicking up a rooster tail of white. All the riders were swathed in dark, anonymous snowmobile suits, their faces hidden by goggles and masks.

Just as she came abreast of them, the driver in the last machine turned and glanced back at her, her headlights flashing off his opaque lenses. Sherry gave a shiver, tightening her grip on the steering wheel.

Much as she enjoyed driving her own machines, there was something about the sport that set her on edge. Suited up, the riders were faceless, all alike, figures from a child's Dungeons and Dragons game. Anyone could be behind one of those masks.

Forcing the thought out of her mind, she drove to the Sheriff's Department again. Probably Arrington had already gone home, she told herself as she pulled into the nearly empty parking lot. Arc lights cast brilliantly black shadows across the snowbanks left when the lot had been plowed. She should have phoned first to say she was coming, she realized. She had wasted time and gas driving here.

But just as she was about to pull out of the lot, she recognized a tall figure loping out of the main entrance, wearing a navy blue ski jacket with old ski tags from Boyne Mountain dangling from the zipper.

He hadn't noticed her, turning toward an Aerostar van parked at the end of the lot. She jumped out of her car and hurried forward, calling out to him.

"Detective!" That didn't sound right. How should she address him? "Mr. Arrington! Please—"

He turned and saw her, pausing with his car keys in hand, his look preoccupied, as if he had been thinking of something else and she was an interruption.

"Please—it's Sherry Vincent—we talked yesterday about the videotapes—" She felt awkward, stopping him in the parking lot when it was obvious he was headed home and didn't want to be bothered.

"I remember you. You didn't get another one, did you?"

"I'm going to fill out a postal form. But I don't feel they're going to do anything. I—I need to talk to you. Something's come up."

He hesitated, glancing toward the police post, then toward his own car. Finally he gave her a half smile that crinkled around his eyes briefly. He looked tired, and there was a tension about his mouth that suggested he had had a bad day. "I suppose we could get a drink. The Holiday Inn. You follow me in your car. You know where it is, don't you?"

It was a question that would never be asked by a native.

She followed him through town, noticing that he was a scrupulous driver, using signals at every turn, driving at exactly the speed limit. He even slowed up so she could make the traffic lights at the same time he did.

Ten minutes later they were being seated in the bar at the Holiday Inn. The bartender, Eddie Jackovitch, who had been two years behind Sherry in school, greeted them as they entered, giving Sherry a wink.

She smiled nervously and nodded at several others: May and Frank Kelpine, who ran a little trailer park on the edge of Hartwick and had skied at Timberline long before Sherry and Dick had bought it. And Maida Thomas, her mother's best friend, out with Augusta McClurg, who ran the town's only nursery school. She felt a twinge of dismay. Everyone here would be eyeing them, wondering what new man Sherry Vincent was having a drink with. She should never have agreed to such a public conversation. But it was too late now.

"You seem to know everyone," Arrington said as they divested themselves of their ski jackets and laid them along the vinyl banquette.

"Well, not everyone, not the tourists." Sherry indicated several tables full of boisterous men, ice fishermen by the look of their windburned faces. "But I do know quite a few. I grew up here. And there's no such thing as a private meeting in the north country," she blurted. "I mean, people can't even have affairs around here without about fifty people knowing."

She flushed bright red. Why had she said that? He would think she was an idiot.

He laughed. "I gathered as much. I grew up in

East Detroit, moved up here two years ago. Detroit's a different world from this, I'll tell you. When they opened up a crack house on my street—two houses down from me—that's when I decided to move."

The waitress came to take their orders, white wine for Sherry, a beer for Arrington. As soon as her wine came, Sherry took a big, stinging gulp. This was going to be more difficult than she'd thought. It would be like stripping naked a part of herself.

Maybe she didn't have to tell him. Maybe she could pretend she'd only wanted an update on what he was doing, or had some questions on laws or procedures.

"All right," he began. "What is it? What's happened?"

"It's not so much that something's happened," she hedged. "It's just that I think I know what this is connected with. There was this big scandal in town when I was in the seventh grade. A science teacher at the junior high was run out of town for molesting three of the girls."

"Oh." His eyes studied her; they were the gray of Higgins Lake in April, just after the ice had melted. "You were one of the girls, I take it."

Blood pounded in her cheeks. "Yes, I was. There wasn't—nothing really bad was done. It was just— you know, touching and exposure and he—" She reached for her drink, the wine suddenly tasting bitter.

He waited patiently for her to continue. She lowered her voice, although the room was noisy and no one at an adjoining table could possibly hear her. "We were down by the river, near Carole's father's canoe livery—there was an old trail through the woods. We were supposed to be at Judy's house playing Monopoly, but we weren't."

He nodded.

"Someone must have been canoeing and seen us, because the mothers got up in arms and went to Mr. Powers, the principal, and had the man fired. They talked pretty wild, they talked about slashing his tires, about castrating him. You know. Small-town scandal, but it was pretty awful."

"What happened to the guy?"

"Oh, he left town—he'd been boarding at Mrs. Dietz's, and she locked her doors to him."

"He was never officially charged?"

"Oh, no, he'd left town by then, and my mother said it might affect our lives later, we'd be in the papers. I might not be able to enter any beauty contests or anything."

"Beauty contests?" Arrington frowned as if trying to make the connection.

She was annoyed at herself for blurting that out. "I was Miss Michigan. That doesn't have anything to do with any of this."

She saw his eyes widen, then he looked at her again, as she'd known he would, shaking his head.

"You were Miss Michigan?" He laughed. "I'm sitting here with Miss Michigan?"

"I told you, it was a while back. We don't go around with crowns on our head, you know, and a big bouquet of roses. It was years ago," she said.

"Hey, I wasn't saying that you weren't—you still look like you could win a contest. It's just that I was a little startled, I guess, sitting here with a beauty-contest winner. No, that doesn't sound right. You just don't—you don't have that plastic look," he finished lamely.

Why did she have to go through this with men she met? Exchanges like this always made Sherry feel uncomfortable. People expected you still to be Barbie Doll gorgeous, wearing an inch of lip gloss. She hated being judged on the basis of a stereotype.

"Anyway," she steered the conversation away, "back to Ray Innis. I think the video Kady got is related to him—to what happened. I know it is. I just feel it. My instincts feel it."

Arrington studied her. "What year did you say all this happened?"

"In 1965. But—"

He grinned. "1965 is a *long* time ago."

"I know it is!" she snapped. "I've told it to myself over and over, and I've had it pointed out to me." She toyed with her drink napkin, folding it into pleats. "Anyway," she added, "there's one more thing. Glen Dietz is back in town—I grew up with him, I was engaged to him once—and he took some model portfolio pictures of my daughter, pictures that were very sexy."

"Sexy?"

"*Vogue* magazine type of sexy. I don't suppose you've ever read a high-fashion magazine, have you? Well, fashion photographs capitalize on decadent sex. Young, rebellious-looking girls sitting with their legs apart, or lying all twined up with some scowling boy, and both of their faces are in heavy shadow. It's all very arty. They take young people and pose them as if they were sullen and angry, sexy dolls. Yes, I think that's it."

"I see, but what does that have to do with your daughter?"

Sherry was embarrassed at spilling out so many personal things to this stranger, in a public place with people she knew observing them. "My mother used to be obsessed with me and beauty contests. Now she's obsessed with making my daughter into a fashion model."

Arrington grinned. "If she's as pretty as you are, I can see why."

"That's not the point! The point is that my daughter's pictures in those sexy poses have been displayed in the window of Dietz's photography studio and anyone in town could have seen them. Maybe someone . . ." Her throat closed involuntarily. "Maybe someone saw them and . . ."

"Okay," he said. "You say your mother commissioned them?"

"Yes."

"It wasn't Dietz's idea, his suggestion, he didn't see the girl on the street and tell your mother he'd give her a good deal, a good price, if she'd bring your daughter in?"

"No, nothing like that."

"Well . . . this isn't our jurisdiction."

"It isn't?" Her eyes stung. "Dammit, if you could have seen the things those men were doing—they were committing *rape*, Detective Arrington, they were committing things I don't even know the words for. *Crimes*, Detective Arrington."

"Mrs. Vincent—"

"Maybe more crimes are going to be committed," she said angrily. "Maybe someone wants Kady. Don't you think it's a little *unusual* that someone would send videos like that to a twelve-year-old girl? Don't you think it's—"

"All right," he said. "I'll check it out. But if he had anything to do with the videos, I'd be surprised. Your ex-husband is a more likely candidate. Can you give me his name and address?"

"I told you—" Then Sherry sighed and reached into her purse for a pen. She scribbled Dick's address on a scrap of paper.

# Chapter 10

It was ten P.M. by the time Sherry pulled into her driveway. She frowned as her headlights picked out the cross-hatched tread marks of a snowmobile. The tracks angled out of the woods and down the drive toward the house, superimposed on her own tire marks from this morning.

Someone had obviously been joyriding on her property again, and Sherry didn't like it.

She had some extra snow fencing stored in rolls at the back of the garage, and she went and dragged two out. The fencing consisted of rickety-looking, narrow wooden slats bound with wire; their purpose was to block wind in order to prevent drifting of snow. However, local residents also used the fencing to prevent trespass of snowmobiles. The fencing could be knocked down, yes, but joyriders usually didn't take the trouble and went elsewhere.

The woods were quiet now, filled with the deep, chill hush of winter. She unrolled the fencing, wiring it to trees to provide support, and then tied rags to the top of the slats and along the wires, as a safety warning.

She stood staring at her handiwork. Why should she have to spoil the pristine beauty of her own woods with the claptrap fencing that had a shantytown look to it? Some vacationers up here believed the very fact that they owned a snowmobile gave them the right to trespass anywhere on it: to them the whole north was their playground, and private property existed for their amusement.

She went inside and made herself a cup of hot cocoa in the microwave. She sat down at the kitchen table, sipping it and thinking about what Arrington had told her. Okay. Glen Dietz was a very long shot. There was still a remote possibility that the videos had been legitimately ordered by her ex-husband, who was ashamed to admit he'd done so.

Arrington had finished their session by giving her advice she could have given herself: keep an eye on her daughter, keep her out of the mail, and not allow Kady to go anywhere alone.

She stirred the cocoa where a lump of mix hadn't dissolved. She wondered how Kady was doing, and thought of calling Maura's just for a minute. But she knew she shouldn't. In the first place, it was nearly eleven and both girls would be in bed. Maura's parents were probably in bed, too. She'd alarm them for nothing. She sat cradling the warm cup, pushing back her anxiety. *Was* it true, what Carole had said, that she was making too much of what had happened when they were children? That everyone else had forgotten about it except for her?

Well, she was too tired to think about it tonight. Exhaustion had begun to drag at her, and she rinsed her cup, put it in the dishwasher, and trudged down the hall and into her bedroom, where she pulled on an oversized T-shirt Carole had given her once, its emblem, *If Men Are God's Gift To Women ... Then God Must Really Love Gag Gifts!*

She crawled into bed. The sheets were icy, and she dragged up the comforter, curling herself into a ball until the bed warmed up.

Maybe she'd buy an electric blanket, she told herself as she drifted off. Beds were chilly when you slept in them alone ...

She was awakened sometime later by the whining roar of a snowmobile motor. It was a repeat of the other night. She jumped out of bed, banging her knee against the end table. She reached the window in time to see the shape of the machine, its headlights splitting apart the darkness. Her attempts at snow fencing had been useless; he had simply gone around them.

Sherry ran barefoot through the house to the kitchen, where the switches that controlled the yard lights were. She smacked them all on at once. Lights flooded the yard.

The lights vanquished him.

The snowmobile—she hadn't seen what make—roared up the driveway, its cacophony fading. Angrily Sherry began to dial the Sheriff's office. He had no right to wake her in the middle of the night! Then she stopped dialing and put down the receiver.

What was the use?

Hartwick didn't have a village police force, as some towns did. This wasn't the big city where emergency help was only minutes away. It would take a patrol car between twenty-five and forty-five minutes to get here. And when he arrived, what would she tell him? All she had seen was a shape, headlights. The track marks would tell little.

But again, so what? A violator could not be fined unless he was seen and caught.

Sherry paced through the house, double-checking all the locks and leaving the floodlights on, even though running them was expensive. She felt weak with the aftermath of her surge of adrenaline. She'd had enough of this. She was going to go out tomorrow and buy a chain to put across her driveway itself, she decided.

The next day at work, Sherry's eyes burned with the exhaustion of getting only three hours' sleep. A young reporter from the *Hartwick Eye*, the local weekly newspaper, had chosen this day to do a write-up on Sherry as "Business Person of the Week."

"I guess I'm kind of shy about publicity," Sherry told the girl regretfully. "I mean—everybody in town knows me, so what new material would there be?"

The reporter, an eager twenty-one years old, would not be fobbed off. "I looked you up in the newspaper files, Mrs. Vincent—all your old beauty photographs. I just thought it would make a nice angle . . . and Timberline is such a popular ski place now. Lots of people are coming here now, instead of Shanty Creek or Boyne Mountain."

Sherry gave in. Publicity, even in the small local paper, was priceless. "I'd really prefer no beauty pictures. Just normal business shots. Can you promise me that?"

The girl, Melanie Simms, daughter of the postmaster, nodded.

"Well, if you keep the main focus on Timberline . . . What do you want to know?"

An hour later, Sherry had taken the girl on a complete tour of the facility, including the small, heated hut where Bob Nisinby was stationed, the shed where her snow-grooming machines were kept, and the small, but efficient, ski-repair shop.

"What's your philosophy in general?" the girl finally wanted to know, after she had drained Sherry on every question possible regarding ski-area operation and management. "I mean, your philosophy of life?"

Sherry couldn't help smiling at the naiveté of the question—and then its difficulty. Her philosophy? She hadn't thought about such things in years.

"I guess . . . doing your best," she finally said. "Doing more than your best. Giving one hundred ten percent. And loving the people in your life. That above all."

Just before lunch her mother called, with the news that the Wilhelmina Agency was very interested in Kady's portfolio and wanted her to come to New York for an interview and maybe more pictures.

Shock swamped Sherry. "You're kidding!"

"Oh, no, they called today, they said—"

Sherry stood gripping the telephone. "I don't care what they said. Mom, how could you do this? You know how I feel about Kady and modeling! I've never wanted her to model. I think it's an awful life. I don't want her growing up thinking that she's nothing unless her body is perfect. And what if she goes to New York and they don't want her? They interview hundreds of girls! What then? She'll be all built up that they're going to take her and she'll feel terrible if she's rejected."

"Now, dear," her mother said in the calm, sweet, reasonable tone that she had used to coerce Sherry into entering beauty contests. "Kady is beautiful, even you will admit that, and surely you don't want to hold her back. She'll always resent you for it."

"She won't resent me."

"She talks about it all the time; she gets books from the library on modeling, and she dog-ears my *Vogue* and *Seventeen*. This is her time, Sherry. Her skin right now is perfect, she hasn't a line, and she's got *the* look. *The* presence. All she needs is a little dental bonding, and I thought I'd take her down to Midland sometime next week and have that done."

"Dental bonding?" Sherry closed her eyes. "Mom, a twelve-year-old girl does not need dental bonding."

"But she's got a little discoloration on the front teeth and they can really help that, Sherry. It's not like when you were her age. Also, they can make the teeth a little whiter, it's really not that expensive a procedure and it makes all the difference in close-ups—"

"She's not going to be in close-ups. She's not going to New York. And she doesn't talk to *me* about wanting to go, it's only you she talks about it with, because she wants to please you and *you* want to talk about it. Will you drop it? Will you please drop it? You've already done enough harm, haven't you?"

Her mother's voice rose. "What harm? What harm have I done?"

"You let those pictures be plastered in the window of Dietz's! And we got—" But just in time Sherry bit off the rest of what she had been going to say. She didn't want her mother upset about the videos, or giving unwanted and inappropriate advice.

"Well," Margaret Smith said complacently. "She did look wonderful, didn't she? I was proud of her. You should be, too, Sherry; you should thank your stars you have a daughter like Kady."

"I do."

"Then let me call American Airlines and make a reservation for next week. I'll take her, if you're busy, I'd be happy to do it. I'll take her shopping for the clothes she'll need, and we'll go a couple days early so we can find a good makeup person—"

"*No,*" Sherry said. "*Don't you dare.*"

She hung up. Her own battle with her mother had been rejoined with Kady. But she had won then, and she would win now. She could not have her child growing up in a world where physical appearance was put at a premium, where women were Barbie Dolls and love was finding a Ken.

She spent her lunch hour driving into town to the hardware store to buy a chain length for her driveway. Afterward, she drove past Dietz's to be sure he had kept the pictures out of the window.

Kady's photograph had been replaced by an oil portrait of Ed Weibull, the mayor of Hartwick, his wife, Emmy, and their three blond daughters.

She left Timberline at 3:00, in order to be home when Kady arrived, and to be able to install the chain while an hour or so of daylight remained. When she pulled up at the mailboxes, there were more snowmobile tread marks, as if the driver had amused himself by making repeated passes at the row of rural boxes.

Who was in residence in the subdivision? Inspecting the boxes for signs of use, she pinpointed the Englesons', and the Tierneys'. Bob Engleson was an internist in Grosse Pointe, and Len Tierney a professional baseball player with the Detroit Tigers. She would telephone both families, she decided, both to ask if someone was snowmobiling near their house, and to warn that a chain now would block her drive.

Automatically she opened her own box to scoop out the day's quota of mail: four bills, a CouponPak, a Land's End catalog, the March issue of *Ski*. But reaching in, her hand touched a package that had somehow gotten shoved to the back of the box. Trembling, Sherry drew it out.

Another video. The third one.

Sherry stood looking at the package, feeling her gorge rise. She resisted the urge to fling the tape into the snow and kick more snow over it, bury it until spring. It seemed malevolent, so much more than just a prank. Every instinct screamed to her that there was danger, that this videotape was the nearest she had ever come in her thirty-six years to pure, rank, raw evil.

She heard the sound of a motor and saw a yellow flash through the trees and smelled engine exhaust; Kady's school bus was approaching. Instinctively she stuffed the video into the front of her ski jacket. Kady must not see it, must not even know it was in the house, in case she was tempted to watch it on the VCR.

*God*, she thought as she went forward to meet the bus. *How many more are we going to receive?*

Kady jumped down from the bus, her book bag slung over her shoulder, in her powder blue ski jacket looking fresh-faced and achingly pretty. She came trotting toward Sherry, her face alight. "We got the report done! We turned it in today and Maura's mother let us type part of it ourselves, and I typed, Mom, and I didn't hunt and peck, either, I used my whole hand just like a professional typist!"

"That's wonderful," Sherry said.

"Yeah, and I'm going to ask Dad for a typewriter for my birthday, one of those kinds with the little window where you can see all the letters you've typed."

"You're talking about an electronic typewriter, Kady. He's starting a new business, Kady, he's not going to have a lot of extras for a few years."

But her daughter was looking down at the snow, at the confusion of cross-hatched tread tracks that trampled the area near the mailboxes. "Who left all these tracks? Are the Tierneys up?"

"I don't know, honey, I'm going to go back to the house and call them and find out. And I'm putting up a chain across the drive—I want you to come and help me hook it around the trees. I think I'll have to hammer in some kind of a wooden cross-support for it."

Kady looked at her. "Nobody puts chains across their driveway. What are we going to do when we want to drive out? Are we going to be locked in here?"

"No, silly." Sherry forced a smile. "We'll just have to stop and unlock it, that's all. Come on. It's no big deal; it's just that I'm tired of these snowmobilers buzzing us in the middle of the night. You need your sleep and I don't like the noise."

Back at the house, while Kady was getting herself a snack, she stuffed the video inside an old barbecue mitt, and then jammed the mitt in a woodbox in the garage. Even touching the package made her feel soiled, as if she had touched something filthy, and she went into the hall powder room and scrubbed her hands with soap.

"Mom," Kady was saying around a mouthful of Doritos. "Maura is going to get her own phone when she's fifteen, so she can have all the calls she wants. Her dad promised."

"That's nice."

"*I* could pay for part of a phone out of my allowance, and Dad could get me the rest, don't you think that'd be neat? Then I wouldn't have to use your phone so much and you could get all your calls."

"All my calls, right. My many calls. I'm so popular." Sherry rummaged in a desk drawer until she had found the photocopied list of subdivision residents. All except for herself were summer people. *What? Spring Subdivision Meeting! When? Memorial Day Weekend!* was circled at the bottom of the sheet in yellow felt pen.

She started at the top of the list, getting six recorded messages that the numbers she had dialed were temporarily out of service—summer residents usually did this to save on bills during the winter. However, the Tierneys' telephone was picked up on the third ring.

"Jo? This is Sherry Vincent."

"Hi, Sherry, I was going to stop by and say 'hi,' but we were skiing at Sugar Loaf all week . . . sorry, but Len wanted to, and you know how he is. So I thought, since we planned to go to Timberline tomorrow, I'd do it then."

It was typical that people who skied at Boyne or Sugar Loaf felt apologetic around Sherry, as if they had somehow insulted her.

"You've been out skiing all week?"

"Yes . . . is anything wrong?"

"Well, nothing, really, it's just that we've had a lot of snowmobile traffic past the house and I was wondering if you'd brought guests—anyone with a machine."

"Why, no. I heard the motor last night but they didn't come near here."

"Sorry," Sherry apologized. "I'm getting a little antsy about it; he woke me up at three in the morning. I'm putting a chain across my drive—it'll be flagged with rags, of course. But I just wanted you to know."

After she hung up, she made a similar call to the Englesons, who said their machine stayed in their garage unless they were out with their SnowKat Club. Like the Tierneys, they hadn't been bothered either. Apparently Sherry had been the only one.

She stood leaning against the phone table for a moment before going to the kitchen to collect the cardboard carton that contained the length of chain she'd bought at DeWeese Hardware.

"Mom, this is really weird, us putting a chain up." Kady stood by the box, toying with the loose chain links, a frown furrowing the space between her brows. "Is it because of those awful videotapes we got? Is that why you're putting up a chain? Are you afraid?"

Sherry hesitated, afraid to say too much and scare her daughter. Yet something had to be said. And now Kady had at least brought up the topic of the videotapes, giving her an opening to talk about them.

"I'm not afraid, no, but I didn't like getting those tapes. And now I think we need to be more careful. Like not talking to strangers, not opening the door to anyone when I'm not here, things like that."

"Oh." Kady lifted a section of chain and let it slide through her hands into the box, where it landed with a metallic clink.

"Did any more of them come? Is that why you're acting funny, Mom? Is that why you want to put this chain up?"

"Now, Kady—"

"*Did* another one come?"

Sherry knew she'd let the little beat of silence go on too long. "Yes," she finally said.

"Oh, God!" Kady's wide-set eyes met hers, swimming in tears. "Why, Mom, why? Why are they doing this to us? Why would they think we'd want those awful tapes? We don't have to look at it, do we?"

"No, baby, we don't have to look at it." Sherry went to her daughter, who was nearly as tall as she was, and attempted to hold her in her arms, but Kady pulled away.

"I'm not a baby, Mom, you don't have to act like I'm going to fall apart or something."

Sherry said, "They can't keep on sending tapes forever, they're costing someone money."

Her daughter nodded, blue eyes focused out of the kitchen window at close-growing tree trunks and low shrub growth and an old bird feeder nailed to a tree.

"Mom?"

"Yes, Kadydid."

"Mom, what happened to those girls in the videotape? I mean, after the tape was all over with and they stopped running the camera?"

Sherry looked at Kady in all of her budding

beauty, her body lithe, so new and young and perfect. A painful spasm shivered her stomach, like broken glass. "I don't know, honey."

"But those men didn't just let them go home, did they? I mean, after ... after those terrible things they did."

"I don't know. Come on, Kady, don't fuss with that chain, help me carry it out to the drive and we can put it up before—"

Kady's voice continued inexorably. "Maybe those girls never went home."

"Kady—"

"That's the only thing that could have happened, Mom, because nobody sends a little girl home after they've done horrible things to her, because she might tell her parents, right?"

"Let's not think about it," Sherry said, struggling for an explanation that would not involve child murder. "Maybe those little girls were from a foreign country, maybe they made that videotape to get food for their families. Things like that happen in Third World countries. It's sad and it's awful; we're really lucky to be living in the United States where we have so much. Where nobody has to go hungry."

Kady nodded, seeming to accept her explanation. "You mean, countries like we see on TV? In Lebanon and places like that? Or Afghanistan?"

"Right," Sherry said. "Places like Afghanistan."

# CHAPTER 11

It was one of those blindingly bright winter mornings when sunlight exploded the white-packed snow into the glare effect of looking straight into a flash gun. The light seemed to arc into Nanette Frey's office, making torches of the vanilla candles she kept on top of her file cabinet.

She looked away from the light. Another Monday. And she was coming down with a cold. Even a one-second glance out the window made her eyes water, and she could feel a swollen, itchy sensation in her nostrils, the constant sense of being on the verge of a sneeze.

She and Bob never should have left New York, she thought. This place—it was incestuous, the way the patients interlinked their lives, and the weather . . .

"Excuse me, Sherry," she said, unable to wait longer, and reached for a tissue.

Sherry Vincent waited politely while Nanette
blew. She was wearing a blue wool sweater today
that pointed up the exquisite clearness of her skin
and made her look no older than twenty-six. She
could still get a modeling job if she wanted one,
Nanette reflected, burying a tiny stab of hostility.
Sherry had rejected all that, of course, but was having to face it all over again, thanks to that manip-
ulative stage mother of hers.

They continued with the session, Sherry's tale of
how her mother had arranged a modeling interview
behind her back.

"Why do you suppose your mother is so focused
on having your daughter live out her fantasies?"

Sherry shrugged. "It's a big circle, I guess. She
was brought up by my grandmother to be the
beauty of the county. My father was the most eligible bachelor around, and my mother snared him.
It was a big triumph for her."

"So your mother was brought up to see herself
needing her looks in order to get a man. And she
projected that onto you," Nanette said patiently.

"Oh, yes. She spent hours leafing through magazines, trying to absorb what were the most fashion-
able clothes, then copying the patterns on her
sewing machine for me. She had a series of dress
dummies built to my measurements. She fitted the
clothes on them, then made me stand still for hours
while she pinned the hems, making them profes-
sionally straight."

Resentment colored Sherry's tone and Nanette
sighed, knowing how long it could be, how ardu-
ous, to work through mother-daughter conflicts.
Some women never worked it through, fifty-six-
year-old women still angry over things that had
happened when they were six.

"And how did you feel standing there while she
pinned?"

"Mad, and yet wanting to please her, too. She

was always looking at me up-close, inspecting my nose, trying to figure out if my eyes were wide enough apart, if my shoulder blades didn't stick out too much, if I was going to be tall enough. She was absolutely fierce about blemishes. We drove all the way down to Midland to get prescription creams. She slapped me once for picking at a zit."

Sherry toyed with the fabric on the knees of her Levi's, that had probably seen 150 washings. "It took me years to conquer her. I modeled in New York for about a month. One day on a booking, this photographer started fondling my breasts while he was supposed to be adjusting my blouse for a take. I pushed him away, shoved his camera off the tripod, and ran out of there. I called my mother and told her that was the last time I'd ever do that. I had *had* it with beauty rituals and forty minutes to make up my face and sleazy men coming on to my body."

This was old territory, but Nanette asked the question anyway. "And what did she say?"

"Oh, she cried. She sobbed and sobbed, right over the phone wire, as if somebody had died, it was an incredible performance. Now she wants to take Kady to New York to be interviewed by a modeling agency. She never gives up. She'll hound Kady until she's thirty if I don't take another stand." Sherry's eyes grew opaque as if she were thinking of something else. "It all seems to be coming to a head, all of it, the videotapes, and what happened when I was a kid."

"Let me get this straight," Nanette said. "You are making a connection between the pornographic videos you received in the mail this week and what happened in seventh grade."

"Yes."

"But that was years ago."

"I know. But you've always told me to listen to

my feelings, try to hear what my body is telling me, and *I know there is a connection.*"

Sherry slumped down in the chair, her legs sprawled out. The fingers of her right hand drummed on the tabletop. "I've been thinking about this for four days, Dr. Frey, I've woken up every morning thinking about it."

"But, Sherry . . ." Nanette wondered how to express this. "This event—your molestation—has been an issue you've been trying to deal with for years, because it's all connected with another very central issue in your life, the fact that your mother programmed you to be a professional beauty. The mind is an intricate organism, Sherry. It keeps bringing up what we're working on, presenting material to us in different ways so that we can begin the work of confronting it."

Sherry's mouth was set. "You're saying that I'm so focused on the molestation that my mind brings it up and makes it part of something it has nothing to do with."

"Well, yes, something like that."

"I don't agree with you. I don't think my mind is doing that. I think there really is a connection."

"Such as what?"

Sherry said, "I just don't think it's an accident that the tapes are coming to Kady, who is the same age I was when—when *it* happened. And that their subject is child molestation, when I was molested as a child!"

"Maybe whoever sent them saw the pictures in the window of Dietz's," Nanette suggested. "That's a reasonable explanation. The world is full of strange people, even Hartwick has its share."

Sherry sighed. "Maybe. Maybe not. I don't know. That's the trouble. I don't *know.* And last night while I was lying there in bed, I got to thinking. I'm going to start asking questions."

Nanette eyed her patient with interest. It had

taken nearly two months of therapy before Sherry
Vincent had been able to discuss her sexual molestation at all. It had taken four more long and painful months before she could face her guilt and begin
the task of forgiving herself for being the one who
had had a crush on Innis, who had set up the whole
event.

"You know how hard that's going to be," Nanette
said gently. "Sherry, this is a village where people's
problems and lives are all interconnected and in-
terrelated. Most people don't want their past trau-
mas dredged up. You're not the only one who's
repressed it, you know. Repression is a very good
mechanism and that's why people use it, because it
works."

"I already know that. I mentioned it to Carole.
She was very distant with me, almost hostile."

"She was a participant and she doesn't want to
face her share in it. Sherry . . . are you sure you're
ready for this? You've only been coming to therapy
for six months, we still have a lot of work to do—"

"I have to find out," Sherry said.

Sherry hurried down the steps and went to her
car. So even Dr. Frey thought that it had all happened years ago and she'd only be clawing at her
own psychological wounds by investigating further.

But Dr. Frey did not have children or she
wouldn't be so casual, Sherry thought.

Outdoors, sunlight flashed around her, intensified by whiteness, the kind of day when skiers had
to wear goggles or risk snow blindness. Sherry
fumbled for her sunglasses, following the shoveled
path to the turnaround, where her car was parked.
She glanced backward. Upstairs, Dr. Frey was visible in the window, moving toward the row of file
cabinets she kept on one wall.

Sherry started her car, the tape she'd been playing on the way over, Paul Simon's *Graceland*, blasting out of the speakers again. She pushed the stop button, letting silence sift into the car's interior like snow.

All right, she thought.

She'd admit it. She was afraid. When she'd been ten, once she had seen a thread dangling from her hemline. Curious, she'd pulled it, and the thread just kept on pulling. Along with it had come the entire hem, flopped over and hanging unraveled.

She could go around Hartwick, ask questions, find a loose thread and pull it, and find herself unsewn like the hem. That was why Dr. Frey had sounded so doubtful, why she had warned her.

Her mother's house was a cream-colored Victorian four blocks from Main, its etched glass front door distinctive enough so that tourists occasionally paused to snap a photo of it. Like many Hartwick people, her mother rented out the top floor, to an inhalation therapist who worked at Grayling Hospital.

"I was wondering when you'd stop by," Margaret Smith said placidly as she answered the door. She leaned forward to give Sherry a perfunctory kiss on air. She smelled of talcum and tea.

"I was just driving past," Sherry said, kissing back.

She walked into the front room crowded with drop-leaf tables, three-tier tables, overstuffed chairs, and an enormous roan-colored buffet. Pictures of Sherry as Miss Michigan dominated the room. There was Sherry in her bathing suit, in an evening dress, with the first and second runners-up, smiling at the wheel of a new Ford. Even clippings from the *Detroit News* and *Free Press* had been framed, the newsprint yellowing now, rippled by years of summer humidity.

They regarded each other. Margaret Smith was sixty now, still slim, still pretty, her complexion softened by minute parchment wrinkles. She wore taupe pleated pants and a knit top in stripes of peach and taupe.

"Would you like some tea, dear? I just heated some water."

"All right, but I can't stay long, I have to get back to Timberline."

"I'll give you some of that nice herb tea I sent for; it doesn't have any caffeine and it's supposed to be extremely good for your skin. It's full of natural plants and vitamins. I use it constantly."

Sherry waited while her mother puttered with the tea, returning with two flowered Spode cups. They sat making conversation that carefully skirted the Wilhelmina Agency, focusing on trivialities. A test Kady had taken, a letter Sherry had received from an aunt.

"Mom," Sherry finally said.

"Another cup of tea, honey? I heard on the radio it's going to snow again, but I suppose you don't care, do you, you want all the snow you can get."

"Mom— Mom, I wanted to ask you, it's about—" Sherry heard herself sound as if she were still twelve. She started over again. "It's about what happened back in seventh grade."

"Seventh grade?"

"You know what I mean. Ray Innis. That."

Margaret's baby-doll eyes looked surprised, as if Sherry had begun talking about an exotic form of rain-forest insect. "Ray Innis? Why are you asking about that, Sherry? You were only a little girl. I thought you'd completely forgotten it."

Sherry got up and began to pace the living room, her body filled with sudden tremors. What was she doing, dredging up all of this again?

She said, "I haven't forgotten. What makes you think I'd forget?"

"You don't have to get aggressive about it, Sherry."

"I'm not being aggressive. I just wanted to know. I'm dealing with it in my therapy."

Margaret didn't bother to comment. She began to gather up the cups, for her the topic apparently finished. In a minute she would be in the kitchen rinsing them in the sink, asking if Sherry wanted to take home a loaf of banana nut bread.

"Please. I need to refresh my memory," Sherry said.

"Why would you want to think about that, I'm sure it's not healthy. Come out to the kitchen with me while I clear these up. I have a new recipe for turkey hash, Maida Thomas gave it to me. It's absolutely wonderful. It's got bread crumbs and fresh mushrooms and—" Her mother went on, listing the ingredients.

Sherry almost went along to the kitchen as asked; it would be so much easier than forcing her mother to talk. They'd already avoided the issue of Kady and the appointment in New York; she'd been here thirty minutes now and the subject had yet to come up.

"This is something I would really like to talk about," she said, sitting down again.

Her mother reluctantly sat down herself, on the edge of her seat this time. "After all this time?"

"It's important."

"I don't see why. Let sleeping dogs lie is an old-fashioned motto but I'd say it's a pretty good one. Why do you always want to know about things, Sherry? You always *dig* at things, don't you? You're never happy unless you're digging into something."

Sherry stared at her mother. Was this Margaret's view of her, as someone who "dug" unpleasantly? When had she "dug" into anything? She could not believe her mother really saw her like that.

"I guess I'm going to have to tell you then," she said. "Kady has received some pornography through the mail, some dirty videotapes. They're anonymous and they're pretty horrible and I had to take them to the Sheriff's office."

Her mother seemed to shrink visibly inside her striped top. "Pornography? You received pornography?"

"*Kady* received it," Sherry emphasized. "It came to her, to the twelve-year-old girl that you want to take to New York and introduce to the world of lecherous photographers and makeup men who might have AIDS or who knows what."

Margaret Smith jumped as if slapped. A flush of color rose to her cheeks. "I would do no such thing," she cried. "I would never let Kady be exposed to such things, how dare you say that I would. I would have gone with her on every booking she had, that's what mothers are for, in case you've forgotten."

"Grandmothers," Sherry corrected.

Margaret touched her face, fingers fluttering over the delicate lines grooved at the sides of her mouth. "I don't know why you do this, Sherry. Why you want to upset me like this. I didn't do anything. I never meant harm. Young girls are like flowers, you know. First they are buds and then they blossom and before you can turn around the petals are starting to get old and then it's over and you've wasted them, it's finished. By twenty-five years old a model is going downhill."

Sherry stared at her mother as if at a stranger. "You are the one who should have modeled. And you should have been Miss Michigan, too."

Margaret said nothing. She looked as wounded as if Sherry had poured the contents of the teacups over her head.

"I'm sorry," Sherry said at last. "I shouldn't

have said those things. At least not that way," she
added.

Margaret nodded.

Sherry's hands, clenched in her lap, were sweating. "Anyway, let's not talk about that," she forced
herself to say. "I just wanted to ask you about seventh grade, what happened then, what you remember. I *need* to know it, Mom."

Margaret flicked a piece of lint off the deeply
polished surface of her coffee table and wiped her
hand nervously on her slacks. "Then you've come
to the wrong person because I don't have a good
memory for things like that. I don't like to remember unpleasant things. I push them from my mind,
it's best to do that, I think."

"But you were a grown woman then. You were,
what? My age. You were my age when it happened!
If something like that happened to Kady you can
be damned sure I'd remember it, every detail, for
the rest of my life."

Margaret shifted uneasily. "You can say that,
Sherry, but you haven't been through it. It was
terrible, yes, but it passed and no real harm was
done. I told you to forget it, I helped you to forget
it, and then I forgot it, too. That is not the kind of
thing you want a young girl to remember. You
don't want it spoiling things for her, not when she
had such a bright future ahead of her the way you
did. Even at twelve you were such a beauty, you
know."

God, to her mother a bright future was being a
slick and plastic beauty queen and model.

Sherry said, "Do you remember what he did or
said? What other people did? Any details?"

Margaret's face reddened. "I did what was necessary, we all did; we got rid of the man and we
wrote letters; we made sure he could never teach
again. I kept you in the house the rest of the summer. But it all died down after a while and things

went back to normal. Now a lot of the people who were in town then are dead, or moved away, or they don't remember anymore, Sherry. Nobody remembers now.''

Her mother was an ostrich with her head in the sand, convinced that if she could blank her own mind out, others could and had done so.

"Of course people remember!" Sherry snapped. "What about Judy's mother and Carole's mother? And Judy and Carole? Mrs. Dietz? And—what was the principal's name, the one who did the hatchet job on Mr. Innis—?"

"Elton Powers," her mother said. "Good Lord, he's been retired for fifteen years now. Down in Florida someplace, I think. Maybe Naples, or is it St. Petersburg? Anyway, I imagine he's getting on, what would he be now, eighty?"

"I'd like to talk to him," Sherry said.

"Sherry, it's so long ago."

"Do you know his address? Do you exchange Christmas cards with him or anything, or know anyone who does? Do you think the school board would know?"

Instead of replying, Margaret gathered up the remaining cup and started definitively toward the kitchen, her body language announcing that this time she was finished with this unpleasant conversation.

"Who knows where these teachers go when they retire?" she threw back over her shoulder. "But I'll tell you one thing, Sherry, and you'd better think about this before you ask any more questions. After it happened, people *talked*. Some of the things they said were cruel and they had to do with all those love notes you wrote to Ray Innis. Do you really want to bring all that up again, now that Kady is growing up? Make them talk about *her*? Because they will, if they find out she's been getting pornography in the mail. They'll say it all runs in the family."

As Sherry sat stunned, her mother delivered her final message. "Now you want to go digging up things, but let me tell you this. You might get more than you bargained for. Yes, you just might."

# CHAPTER 12

By evening the day's brilliance of sunlight was gone, replaced by banked gray clouds coming in from the west, bleak-looking with the promise of new snow. The announcer on WGRY was full of a snowstorm that had hit the Denver area, stranding thousands of motorists and closing the passes. Predictions were that the snow would hit Michigan by the following morning.

Sherry felt a sudden lift of her spirits. She loved snowstorms. Fresh powder was the exhilarating acme of skiing, and in a storm people flocked to ski areas, risking icy roads to be first on the slopes. It'd be bedlam tomorrow, crowds of skiers and a constant series of snow-connected crises.

She made arrangements for extra plowing services and locked up her office at 2:45, deciding to drive to school to pick Kady up after her classes. Her daughter needed a haircut and Sherry herself could use one, too, she decided.

She drove to the junior high school, pulling up behind a row of yellow buses that belched steam. The junior high, dating from the early sixties, looked as if it had arrived in a time capsule from that era, its front windows embellished with panels of weather-pitted turquoise.

She was five minutes early. She switched off her motor and sat gazing at the building. In one classroom window, papers had been taped to the glass, in another a boy was silhouetted, scowling at a book. In a third classroom she saw a man walking back and forth, gesturing broadly as he lectured. Almost every windowsill held rows of books, or stacks of boxes or other junk. It made Sherry think of a huge, scruffy apartment building.

Funny, how you could be familiarized with a building to the point where you no longer really saw it. How long had it been since she had really looked at this school? Maybe she had never looked at it.

She focused her eyes on the lecturing teacher. Was that the science room, the room where she, Judy, and Carole had sat in the third row gazing with moonstruck eyes at their handsome science instructor? Or was it the next room, the one where the papers were taped?

She let her eyes travel along the front of the building. Strange, she couldn't remember which room it was anymore. Was that what Dr. Frey meant by repression? All the rooms looked alike now, homogenized into generic schoolrooms. *That* room, *that* teacher, no longer existed. Even her mind had erased them.

*Because it's more comfortable that way*, she told herself, feeling her forehead tighten with tension. There were things in life that you didn't relive, you couldn't, so you put them aside and your life formed a smooth surface over them, and you didn't look beneath the surface anymore.

Even thinking about Innis made her stomach muscles clench.

Was it possible—was it remotely possible—that somehow he had come back to Hartwick and was, in a twisted way, trying to take revenge on Sherry through Kady?

She closed her eyes, pressing her lips together, pulling in a thin breath of air.

*What if he was here in Hartwick?*

It was a fantastic thought. He'd be older now, he'd be—what? In his fifties? Early sixties? Maybe he had come to town as part of the crowd of ice fishermen and snowmobilers who filled the motels this time of year. There were so many of them—*turkeys*, as Kady and Maura called them. Thousands of them every winter. Or *fudgeys*, those were the summer people who bought slabs of fudge from the fudge shops.

She expelled her breath, forcing her tense musculature to relax. Was there a way that Innis could be traced? She would have to ask Arrington about that. What had the man been doing all these years? It had never occurred to her, until now, even to think about it. And she was sure that no one else in Hartwick thought about it either.

A side door popped open, and a leggy boy exploded from it, ski jacket half on, a red book bag dangling from his shoulder. A two-second pause and then two more boys leaped through the exit, followed by a pushing crowd that now contained several girls. Laughing, chattering, pushing, yelling, the youngsters scattered for the waiting buses.

Suddenly there were hundreds of kids pouring out from all the exits, and Sherry leaned forward, straining to see Kady's pale blue ski jacket. If she missed her, Kady would get on the bus and then Sherry would have to drive home and pick her up there before proceeding to the beauty shop.

Then three girls came bursting through the side door. Kady, Maura, and Heather Wycoff, leader of their little clique. Kady, seven inches taller than either of the others, was laughing to Heather, her face expressive. They were probably talking about boys.

Sherry banged her horn, waved frantically.

She honked again and this time all three girls looked up and she managed to catch Kady's eye. Her daughter came running over to the car, Maura and Heather behind her.

"Mom! I didn't know you were coming, can you give us a ride home, all of us? Maura and Heather too? Can they come over? We want to talk about a party Heather's giving."

A party with boys, Sherry gathered. Kady's face was alight with enthusiasm, and Sherry felt like an ogre as she said, "Oh, honey, I made us an appointment at Alma's to get our hair done, we have to be there in twenty minutes."

"A *haircut*? Today? Now?" You would have thought Sherry had suggested they go home and clean the garage.

"Yes, Kadydid, today, now. Tell your friends you'll see them tomorrow and they'd better hurry if they're going to get on the bus. Hop in, Kady, Alma worked us both in."

Kady sighed and said good-bye to the others, then bounced into the front seat beside Sherry. "I want to get a root perm," she announced, slamming the car door shut.

"A perm? Kady, you don't need a perm, you have perfectly good curls already."

"But it's unmanageable," her daughter retorted. "Even when I use the blow dryer it comes out funny, and I never can get it to curl right."

"Your hair looks very nice."

"No, it doesn't, Grandma says it's my weak point; it's hard to style and it gets all tight in humidity."

"Well, we haven't got any humidity right now, it's the middle of winter."

They drove back into town to the small shop, Alma's Beauté Nook, to which Sherry had been taking her daughter for cuts and trims since Kady was two.

As they parked and walked inside, a wall of odors hit them: perm solution, shampoo, conditioner, hair spray, and cigarette smoke. A dim memory of humiliation shivered over Sherry. It had been another shop, another day, that she'd heard the women talking.

"Well, long time no *see*," Alma Henssen greeted them, looking up from the tiny reception desk where she was writing something in a book. She was in her seventies, with henna-dyed hair that made her a Lucille Ball look-alike. "I thought you folks'd forgotten all about me, decided to let your hair grow down to your knees like Lady Godiva."

"Very funny." Sherry smiled; she had always liked Alma.

Kady grinned at Alma and sauntered over to the shampoo chair where she seated herself with the air of one who is perfectly at home.

"No kidding," Alma said to Sherry. "Even hair like yours has to be thinned and trimmed a little, you get the wild woman look when you don't pay attention. Unless that's what you want. I've got a couple new style books with far-out cuts—"

"No way," said Sherry.

"You sure?" Alma teased.

"I don't think I'm the type. We both need the works, if you don't mind. Kady can go first."

"I think she already decided that."

As the beautician shampooed Kady, Sherry waited with a magazine, her thoughts flowing back to the seventh grade incident. Alma Henssen had been in town then—in fact, she had bought this shop the year after it all had happened. Breezy, gossipy, talky Alma who probably heard most of the dirt that silted through Hartwick, and passed on some of it, too.

While Kady was under the dryer, leafing through a copy of *Teen*, Sherry settled into the shampoo chair for her own turn, shivering as the cool water permeated the warm skin of her scalp.

"I suppose you saw those pictures of Kady in the window of Dietz's," she began.

"Sure, who didn't? I did her hair you know."

"Oh?"

"Yeah, your mother came in here all excited about it. She had some pictures from *Vogue*, and she stood over me the whole time. It was unreal, fussing with a twelve-year-old like that. Reminded me of a beauty convention, those models sitting around all day being worked on."

Alma kneaded Sherry's scalp with professional rigorousness. "There, hold still while I rinse, and then I'll comb you out and we'll figure out just what I need to trim here. You always let yourself go too long."

"I was thinking," Sherry said as soon as she could sit up. "You hear a lot, don't you, Alma? I mean, you've owned this shop for years. You know everybody's secrets."

Alma removed the soggy towel from the back of Sherry's neck. "Sure, people say things. Hell, I hear all about everything, people's marriages and divorces and sex lives and what they have for dinner. But I try to let it run in one ear and out the other, honey. See, this is a small town and I can't depend on the tourists, I need the repeat business. I have customers I've been cutting for twenty years. I've got to be loyal to those customers if I want them to be loyal to me."

They walked over to Alma's station, the mirror pasted with hundreds of wallet-sized baby, school, and graduation pictures of all the children whose hair Alma had cut. Kady's was among them.

"I need to know about something," Sherry began. "For—for personal reasons."

"Yeah?"

"That thing years ago, the teacher, Ray Innis, the—the molestation." Her voice cracked on the last word and she felt a flush sting her cheeks.

Alma stopped working on Sherry's hair, drawing in her breath. "That?" There was a two-second pause. "Good grief, that was the year I came here. That same spring."

"But you remember it, don't you?"

Alma laughed roughly. "I don't let stuff like that stick in my mind, honey, I just let it all slide through."

"But this was hard to forget."

"Like I said."

"Do you remember *anything*?" Sherry persisted. "Like what Innis might have done or said? Did he talk to anyone, did he make any threats, anything like that?"

"If he did, what would it matter now?" Alma said, turning Sherry's head critically in front of the mirror. "Sure, I suppose he threatened people. He hated your mother, Sherry; she was the ringleader; she was the one who went to the principal and got everyone up in arms."

Sherry bit her lip, remembering her mother's talk about gossip ruining a career. Why hadn't she worked to hush things up rather than escalating the incident into a full-scale scandal? Or had she just been so enraged she hadn't thought rationally?

Alma went on after a minute as if Sherry's questioning had turned some key in her.

"He was a good-looking man and I guess that

really freaked people out, because a guy like that, a molester, people except him to be a dirty old man, you know? Old and nasty-looking." Alma gathered Sherry's bangs into plastic clips. "How much do you want taken off?"

Sherry measured a distance with her thumb and forefinger. "Then what you're saying is that my mother forced the man out of town?"

"Your mother started it, yes, but it didn't take much. No one wanted him. This is a good town, clean, we have good people here, good children." The hairdresser gestured toward her gallery of pictures. "He was a pervert, Sherry. That's the bottom line. This isn't Detroit where they have crack houses and convenience store killings and all kinds of murders and violence, even in the suburbs. The man didn't belong here and we didn't want him and good riddance to him." Vehemence had risen in the woman's voice, coloring it.

"Where do you suppose he might have gone?"

"Who knows? People like that, scum like that, they go somewhere else and they do the same thing again, that's what happens to them. They don't quit. A pervert is a pervert for life. But at least he didn't do it here."

*A pervert is a pervert for life.* Sherry shivered, thinking about an angry, lifelong child molester, who might be thinking about her daughter even now, this very minute. What kind of thoughts would such a man be having? Sick ones. Ugly ones, unspeakable, like the acts on those tapes.

They finished the hair-cutting session in silence, and then Alma combed Kady out, posing her in front of the mirror. "How does she look, eh? Beautiful, huh? This is one pretty kid."

She was. Sherry could not take her eyes off her perfect child. She felt such a powerful wave of mother emotion that it dizzied her.

This beautiful child was her daughter, her flesh, *hers*.

She would protect her if she had to question every individual in Hartwick, if she had to stir up every old hornet's nest of gossip that there was.

# CHAPTER 13

Kady peered out of the window as the swaying school bus jolted to the left, lumbering onto Lake End Road. Snow already covered the road in a smooth blanket of white.

All around her kids yelled and laughed, talking of what they were going to do, and how long the storm would last. School had been dismissed at 12:30, and it looked as if they might get at least two snow days.

Usually the bus dropped Kady off at the mailboxes, near the road end, making its turnaround in the wide space left by the county plow, but today the snow was too heavy, so she and two others were being dropped off a third of a mile away, where an intersection allowed maneuvering space.

Kady slumped in her seat, sighing disconsolately. Here it was a snow day, and she'd be stuck at home alone in the *boring* house, with nothing but the TV, the telephone, the microwave, and the refrigerator. Again.

The bus pulled to a stop, air brakes whooshing. Kady, Robert Dix and Tracy Allen, both ninth graders, crowded to the door, bumping into one another with their book bags and the clarinet case carried by Robert.

"You all be careful now," called Mrs. Francetti, the bus driver.

They climbed down, standing there a minute in surprise as windy air blew wet snow onto their faces, big flakes the size of pennies. Without speaking to Kady, as befitted their status as ninth graders, Robert and Tracy turned and started up the road toward a pair of log homes built in a grove of pines. One house had a sign in front: *Rabbits. Bunnies and Lops.*

Enviously, Kady eyed the sign. She'd always wanted a rabbit, especially a cute lop-eared one, and Robert Dix got to have about fifty of them. But her mother had told her that the Dixes ate the rabbits they raised, which killed her envy a little. She knew she could never eat a rabbit.

Snow-filled wind buffeted her, spraying cold flakes onto her cheeks as Kady started south toward the road end. Beyond was the flat, white expanse of snow-covered ice that was Higgins Lake. Somewhere a snowmobile buzzed, its sound hollow and insectile.

She trudged forward, face bent into the wind, blinking as snowflakes hit her eyes, dozens of them, hundreds, a whole universe of white dots. When she glanced back the way she'd come, Robert and Tracy were no longer visible—they must have gone inside.

It was a lonely feeling. The plow hadn't been down the road yet, and from this point on there were no more houses. Just stretches of woods on either side, red pines and jack pines, and tangled undergrowth where, in summer, Kady loved to come and pick wild blueberries.

But it was another world now.

Cold. White. Even in the minutes since she'd left the bus, the snow had thickened. The pines looked spray-gunned with snow, the little ones bent and drooping from the weight. In one of her *Little House on the Prairie* books, Kady had read about a blizzard where the farmers had to string a rope between their house and barn, or they'd get lost in the white and freeze to death. Today the idea seemed believable.

But that wasn't going to happen to her, of course. This was just snow, that's all. To prove it, Kady licked out her tongue and tasted one of the white crystals. It tasted watery and full of minerals, as snow always did.

Kady guessed she was just feeling creepy lately, because of those horrible tapes they'd gotten in the mail. She hadn't told her mother, but they bothered her a lot.

Those poor, naked girls, her own age.

Just thinking of those girls made a horrid tightness grow between her legs, and her stomach knot painfully. She was just glad they'd filmed the video in a foreign country. That didn't make it seem as real. She didn't want it to be real. She wanted it to be fake-pretend, like *Friday the 13th Part VII*, all actors and cameramen and makeup.

Anyway, it was too scary to think about that here on the deserted road. She sucked in another couple of snowflakes, letting them melt on her tongue, forcing her thoughts away from the video.

The snowmobile noise, louder now, caught her attention. First it buzzed loud, then soft, then loud again, as the driver posted over hills or bumps. Riding on the ice was a favorite pastime of snowmobilers, who went crazy on all that open white space, acting like it was Indy Raceway, as her mother often said.

Kady remembered the guy who had been buzzing their house, and pulled in her breath. Hey, it was probably just some kid out hotdogging in the new powder, racing around like crazy in the storm and probably taking awful chances.

It was dangerous snowmobiling if you couldn't see barriers or things like wires strung across the path, her mother had told her. That was why you always had to put rags or flags up on any wires you strung, or snow fences, because a snowmobiler could be speeding along some trail, not see a wire, and get beheaded by it.

Kady shivered inside her new ski jacket, wishing she hadn't thought of that. Unconsciously she hurried her steps, each swing of her boots tunneling through the white. It was like walking in fluff. When she got home, she decided, the first thing she would do would be warm herself a cup of hot cocoa in the microwave. Then she would bake a package of brownies. She would add a package of chocolate chips to the mix, making them double-chocolate.

The chocolate would make the house smell delicious, and then she would sit down in front of the TV and watch *Santa Barbara* and eat the brownies while they were all soft and gooey.

The thought warmed her. In about ten minutes, she'd be home.

She walked as fast as she could, nearly slipping several times on patches of ice that lurked beneath the snow blanket. Just a little way now, and she'd be at the mailboxes, and then it was only about a third of a mile, down the subdivision drive that everyone called "the trail." That was the part she walked every day and she knew almost every tree, every fallen log, every squirrel's nest and outgrowth of fungus on a tree trunk. She even knew the animal prints she'd see there, tiny, delicate bird tracks and three-toed hoof marks of deer, once in a while a dog's happy lope.

All this time the snowmobile motor had been whining, first louder, then faint, as its driver joy-rode in the storm. Now, as Kady approached the row of mailboxes, its sound grew louder.

She paused at the boxes. Gingerly she opened their own box, a big pile of snow falling off its lid as she did so. She pulled out two envelopes, one that said State Wide Real Estate, and the other one a Domino's Pizza ad.

No crudely wrapped package. Just some nice, friendly ads.

Kady actually liked to read ads.

It was as she was closing the latch that she heard the roar of a motor.

The snowmobile came bearing down on her, snow spraying behind it in a wild rooster tail. The driver wore a black coverall suit. His face was shielded with snow goggles and a yellow ski mask with black lines knit around the eye holes, and the slit where the mouth should be.

The machine nearly laid on its side as the driver spun out in a turn, snow flying toward her, spraying all over her. Kady stood paralyzed as the snowmobile missed her by about twelve inches.

She choked back a scream, squeezing herself underneath the redwood plank that held the mailboxes and scrambling up the bank of old, plowed snow that mounded behind it.

*He had nearly hit her.*

Was he doing it on purpose, or was he drunk or something, trying to show off?

She crouched beside the bank of snow, partly shielded by the plank that held the mailboxes, her heart drumming. The driver sped away, then circled back, again spraying her with a hard tail of snow. Gasoline fumes gagged her.

He *was* doing it on purpose! But why? What had she done? Terror filled her.

She hadn't done anything!

The driver circled away and this time when he made another pass, he buzzed the machine up behind the mailboxes at Kady's back, where she was unprotected. She felt him coming, the roar, the sensation of energy and speed, the hard, hurting spray of snow. He wanted to run her down, wanted to hurt her. And he could do it, he could just run her down and smash her.

Wildly she rolled back under the redwood plank again, scraping the top of her head on the wood with a painful, scalp-wrenching bruise. Her new ski hat fell off, tumbling in the snow. Then she was running, zigzagging through the woods, fighting her way through undergrowth and close-spaced tree trunks where a snowmobile would have a hard time getting through.

She struggled through deep snow, her boots sometimes sinking through a crust layer and sometimes staying on top. The snow was nearly three feet deep, layered by a succession of storms and melts, some of it crusty. You couldn't go fast, you had to hop and leap. It was a terrific effort, even for a twelve-year-old, and she gasped with stress.

She staggered along, sweating under her jacket. Pine needles whipped her face, bursts of snow exploding from them. She gasped in a breath and got a mouthful of snow.

From the "trail," the snowmobile roared but there was so much snow in the air and so many trees that she couldn't see him.

Maybe if she ran fast enough and into dense enough trees, he'd lose sight of her. Then she could lie down or something, roll herself in the snow, and he couldn't see her, and then maybe he'd go away.

The motor suddenly roared closer and she

smelled the whiff of fuel. Frantically Kady turned her head.

He wasn't on the drive anymore. He was in the trees. Zigzagging toward her. Taking the wider spaces, eating up the distance between them, aggressive.

She leaped and dodged, running blindly toward a tangle of birches and young, snow-bent pines. He couldn't possibly fit in there, there were too many tree trunks.

She turned again for another terrified look and tripped over a hidden fallen log. She fell forward, doing a belly flop in the snow. The rounded shape of the log hit her in the stomach and knocked the breath out of her.

For a minute Kady couldn't breathe. She raised her head and dry-gasped, panicked, like a goldfish out of its tank. Snow coated her face, it was in her nose and on her eyelids, all over her cheeks. Finally the air came, and she lay crying facedown in the snow, wetness pressing into her nose and mouth.

She was trapped.

She couldn't outrun him in this kind of woods, not with the snow so deep, it was too deep to run in. Machines could go almost anywhere, and if they couldn't, a man could walk. He could search her out on foot—

She gagged from fright, her heart jumping and skittering, making her sick.

Finally she realized she was near a tree, one of the medium-sized red pines, about five feet tall and festooned with white like a Christmas tree, its bottom branches sagging on the snow. Instinctively, she burrowed deeper into the white, squirming toward the overhang of a pine branch.

Some of the snow fell on her as she rolled under the tree. Maybe he wouldn't see her here. The snow was thick and getting thicker— Maybe the snowstorm would conceal her.

Hidden under the tree she waited. Minutes ticked by. The snow had changed all the sounds, making everything sound wet, hollow, and echoey. She could hear her own breath, even a gurgle from her stomach. She heard the motor, too, as it sped away from her, then back again, then away.

He was searching for her! First on the trail, then in the trees, she could tell by the changed motor sounds. She waited, shivering. Her head was bare, snow clung to her hair, she could feel it freezing next to her scalp. More snow had somehow fallen down the neck of her ski jacket and was now melting against her chest.

She lay crying without making a sound. Oh, she wanted to go home. She wanted to be in their own kitchen sipping hot cocoa with melted marshmallows, all warm and cuddly in her bunny slippers and fleecy flannel nightgown with red Santa bears on it that her dad had given her for Christmas.

How long could she stay out here, lying in the snow like some kind of an animal? She was already cold; she'd freeze if she had to stay out here very long, especially if she had to lie still and not move around. Kady had skied all her life, she knew about cold and what it could do.

She sobbed again, biting her lips to keep back the sound. With her head bare and her ears exposed, she could get frostbite. One of the guys on ski patrol at Timberline had lost part of an ear to frostbite, and his earlobe looked all gross and misshapen.

She cried because she didn't want to have gross ears, and she was afraid lying here in the woods, and she suddenly had to go to the bathroom. Her bladder felt so tight and painful that she was afraid she would wet herself.

She squeezed her inner muscles, trying to hold the urine back. But she was so cold and so exhausted that her muscles didn't work right, and suddenly there was a flow of hot liquid down her legs.

She was wetting herself.

Like a baby.

Oh, gross, horrible.

Kady smelled the ammoniac stink of her own urine, a bathroom smell that was totally alien here in the clean snow. Her jeans were soaked with it, and she'd probably made a yellow steaming puddle in the snow just like when a dog peed. She sobbed in humiliation, pressing back the sounds with her gloved fist.

Then she lifted her head, realizing something had changed. Was it her imagination or were the motor sounds growing fainter now?

Yes.

*He was going away.*

He had just been some kid, some big boy out on his dad's snowmobile, playing a trick on her, she realized with a gasp of relief. He'd buzzed her a couple of times and made her run, probably was laughing at her behind the ski mask, thinking what a baby she was, a twelve-year-old infant. She'd run off into the woods terrified and he would laugh all the way home at how dumb she was.

She had been such a dork. Running, hiding—

She waited a long time, until she couldn't hear any motor noise, until all she could hear was the whistle of the cold wind, blizzarding branches against one another. She waited so long that an inch of fast-falling snow coated her, and her wet jeans froze right on her. They were so stiff they hurt.

Shivering, she finally picked her way out of the woods and onto the trail. She walked unsteadily toward the mailboxes, her thighs burning from rubbing against ice. The letters were gone. The contents of her book bag were scattered all over the snow, books helter-skelter, one spiral notebook crushed beyond redemption. Her beautiful new ski hat had been run over repeatedly, its wool shredded into ratty tangles. Kady eyed it in horror.

She picked up the books, shaking off the snow as best she could, and stuffing them back in the bag, trying not to cry now, even though her math book had had its spine broken. Then she buried the hat in a drift under a tree. Nobody must ever know how babyish she'd been, how fearful and crying, or that she'd peed her pants like a baby in diapers.

Scraping snow on top of the mutilated hat, she noticed that snow was erasing the snowmobile tread marks, too. In an hour, they'd be gone, and her mother, driving home from Timberline, would never even notice.

She started toward the house, tears glazing to ice on her cheeks.

# CHAPTER 14

At Timberline, Sherry was plunged into the chaos that a blizzard usually brought. Stuck cars. Injuries. Breakdowns in equipment. Staff who could not make it in. At four o'clock she took a short break to dial home.

She sat listening to the telephone ring, eight, ten, fifteen times. She was just about to hang up when Kady picked up the phone and said "H'lo" in a muffled voice.

"Kady? Are you all right? Did the bus drop you off?"

"Yeah, it dropped us off down the road and I had to walk," her daughter said, her voice dragging.

Sherry knew a short hike was nothing for Kady's boundless energy. "Well, you're home now," she said comfortably. "What are you going to do? Don't forget your room, Kadydid—clean that up first and then if you could take that package of chicken breasts out of the fridge and thaw them—"

"I want to go skiing. It's a snow day. There's fresh powder."

Guilt and frustration flooded Sherry. "Oh, baby . . . You know I'd love to come and pick you up and bring you back. But I can't, honey, we've got a couple of cars spun in the ditch, and a couple of girls in the Ski Patrol hut with broken bones. You'll be all right at home just for this afternoon, won't you? If you have the day off I'll bring you to Timberline tomorrow, I promise."

"I don't like being here alone." Kady's voice sounded tense.

"I know, but you've locked all the doors, haven't you? And the Tierneys are up this week, so if you have any trouble you could always call them. Or call Grandma. I'm sorry, Kadydid, I was going to come home early today but this storm . . ."

"Mom," Kady pleaded.

"I have the responsibility of those girls and I can't leave. Dammit, I'm sorry, but I'll make it up to you tomorrow— Turn on the TV, why don't you? *Days of Our Lives* is on, isn't it? And *Guiding Light*?"

"I'd rather watch *Santa Barbara*."

"Then watch *Santa Barbara*. There's microwave popcorn, Kady, and I think a couple of bottles of Pepsi. And I put some cookie mix in the pantry."

"Brownie," Kady corrected.

"Okay. Just don't forget to thaw the chicken, and maybe you could take one of those loaves of French bread out of the freezer, too."

"All right," her daughter agreed dispiritedly.

"Has Jimmie Van been down the road yet?" Jimmie Van was the plowing service that the subdivision used, prorating costs among the residents. As permanent resident, Sherry paid a larger share.

"No . . . Nobody's been down."

"Well, he'll be coming soon, and when he does I want you to run outdoors and give him the key to the chain so he can plow the full length. Remember, Kady."

"Okay."

They hung up, and Sherry frowned as she replaced the receiver. Kady had sounded edgy and depressed, not her usual self. She pushed back her anxiety. Kady would be okay for one afternoon, she rationalized. In this storm most people wouldn't be on the roads anyway. It was only snow-crazed skiers who braved such conditions when they didn't have to.

Sherry's thoughts had come full circle, back to skiers again, and the stuck cars. She'd better go out and see how her maintenance crew was progressing with that. Jumping up, she shrugged into her ski jacket and pulled on her ski hat, adding a pair of yellow wraparound goggles to protect against snow glare.

It was after seven before Sherry finally felt she could take the opportunity to leave. It had been a whirlwind day. According to Becky, they'd sold 306 tickets, an excellent total for the middle of the week. Sherry rode to Grayling Hospital in the minivan with the two teenagers who'd been injured in falls, girls fifteen and sixteen years old. Both were novices, one on her first day of skiing—a typical story for injuries.

The other had been wearing borrowed equipment, a dangerous practice, since bindings could not be adjusted for the proper weight.

To her relief, one girl had only sprained her arm, not broken it, and the other had an uncomplicated broken ankle.

"Next time," Sherry counseled, "come to our rental department and get fitted right. We just bought a lot of new step-in bindings, and they're safe. It's a lot better than clumping around in a cast for six weeks."

She had bought a bunch of "toe caps" on a trip to Aspen once, knitted, mittenlike circles to warm bare toes that protruded from a cast. She got one from the glove compartment of the van and gave it to the girl with the broken ankle.

"Just to remember us by," she explained.

As she returned, tired from the long drive on slippery roads, Sherry's phone was ringing in her office. Hastily she picked it up, hoping that it wasn't another problem.

"Well, I see how much my getting some time off means to you," drawled Carole's husky voice. "We were going to go up to Traverse City and you didn't even call me."

"I didn't have time," Sherry excused herself. "It's been so busy here."

"*One* evening," Carole said. "One pub crawl, that can't hurt you. I don't have to work Friday night."

"I just haven't had time, Carole, and what would I do with Kady?"

"She's a big girl, let her have a sleepover with one of her girlfriends. Come on, Sherry, what do you say? Tomorrow night?"

"Well—"

"By tomorrow the roads'll be cleared. Come *on*, Sherry, you're *single* now, you can't sit in front of your TV forever! There aren't any eligible men inside the TV set."

Sherry couldn't help laughing. "I don't want an eligible man."

"Sure you do. All single women do. *Sherry*," Carole said warningly.

"All right," Sherry finally agreed, thinking that this would be a golden opportunity to ask Carole about what had happened when they were in seventh grade. Wasn't that part of her plan? Now she could make it all seem casual.

They made arrangements, and Sherry left it that

they'd go, *if* Kady could go to Maura's, and *if* there were no pressing problems at Timberline.

On the way out, she found a child's ski glove that had been dropped in the snow, and she picked it up for deposit in the Lost and Found. She looked at the glove, feeling a stab of remembrance for when Kady had been tiny enough to wear a mitten like this. They had started her at nineteen months, on toy plastic skis, letting her shuffle around on level ground. The following year she'd actually gone downhill with Sherry, her tiny skis braced securely between Sherry's big, "snowplowing" ones. By age six, she'd been riding the chair lift and doing a wide parallel turn, the turn with skis together that many adults had trouble mastering.

Sherry felt a wave of melancholy as she walked out to her car. Kady was on the verge of womanhood now; if her mother had her way, she was on the verge of becoming a professional model.

*At twelve.*

What had happened to childhood? Sherry wondered.

When she had been in seventh grade there had been no R-rated movies, and here in northern Michigan, few pressures to try drugs and sex. Now even here, society pushed little girls into adulthood, and the little girls themselves actively cooperated. Glen Dietz might have posed Kady for those model photographs, for instance, but Kady *had* cooperated. She had put her own body into those positions; it hadn't all been a passive act. And, as Glen had pointed out, she had even liked it.

Sherry frowned, made uneasy by the circuit into which her thoughts had fallen. The unease continued to nudge her as she drove home on slippery roads, once getting caught behind the county plow, salt particles spraying her car windshield like hailstones. The night was dense and dark, myriad snowflakes dancing in front of her headlights. They eddied and swirled, and if you tried to focus on any one dot, you'd get dizzy.

She stopped at the mailboxes, but the box was empty. Jimmie Van's pickup truck with plow attachment was just pulling out, and she waved at him, relieved that she wasn't going to get stuck on the trail. She hoped Kady had remembered the key to the chain.

Driving in, she saw that the entire driveway had been done, but Jimmie had solved the chain problem by knocking the entire chain over with his plow. Sherry grimaced. So much for that idea. It would have been very inconvenient anyway.

She parked in the garage and went in the house. The chocolaty smell of brownies greeted her, mingled with the odor of laundry soap. Voices came from the TV set in the den.

"Kady?" she called, taking off her boots and leaving them at the edge of the boot rug. "Kadydid, are you doing *laundry*?"

There was no response from the den, where a game-show audience was laughing hysterically.

In her stocking feet, Sherry trudged around the corner to the first-floor laundry room. Her yellow Sears dryer was vibrating with a small load that seemed to consist of one pair of jeans and a flash of something white that probably was underwear. When was the last time that Kady had willingly started a load of laundry?

She went into the den and found her daughter curled on the couch in her Christmas nightie, a red plaid wool blanket pulled over her legs. Kady's face seemed pinched, her eyes focused glassily on the flickering TV picture. A dinner plate loaded with brownie squares sat on the couch arm beside her, and by the looks, about eight of them had been consumed.

"Oh, Kady," Sherry groaned. "You've spoiled

your dinner. And I was going to make that chicken and rice dish you like so much."

"I'll eat it," Kady said, looking away from Vanna White.

"But you won't be hungry . . . And what are you drying in the dryer? If you were going to do a wash, why didn't you do a full load? It's wasteful to just dry one or two things, that all takes electricity—"

"I know, I *know*!" Kady screamed, jumping up from the couch, and hurling the blanket to the floor. Patchy red blotches stained her cheeks. "I fell in the snow, I got wet, I just wanted to dry my *favorite jeans*, is that a crime? You're always *late*! You're never home, you spend all day at Timberline, you never think about me, you just leave me here at home, you don't care!"

"Kady!" Sherry stared at her daughter, shocked by the outburst.

Kady sobbed, "I *hate* coming home on a snowstorm day and not being able to ski! Everyone else got to! I bet Timberline was jammed with people, wasn't it? But not me! *I* had to stay here alone! I fell down and you weren't even here! Those two girls with broken legs were more important than me!"

"Kady—"

But her daughter was already racing barefoot down the hallway toward her bedroom, and she ran inside, slamming the door behind her with so much force that the moldings shook.

Sherry remained in the hallway, feeling the beginning throb of headache. My God, she hadn't realized Kady had such violent feelings. She leaned against the wall, trying to calm herself. Usually Kady didn't mind a few hours at home alone.

Even from here she could hear Kady's wild weeping.

The sound created a surge of guilt in her. But, dammit, she *had* to work. Who was going to take care of them financially if she didn't? Not Dick. He hadn't paid child support, and he had no wages to garnishee. All of her resources were sunk in Timberline, and if it went bankrupt, so would she. If she failed here, they would have to move, probably to the Detroit area. Crowded suburbs, congestion. They'd both hate it.

"Kady," she called. "Honey?"

*"Go away!"*

Kady's sobs penetrated through the doorway, heartrendingly anguished, punctuated only by brief pauses for breath.

"Kady—"

More sobs. Sherry sighed and turned away. Kady didn't want her now, and it would be best if she waited until later before they talked.

She decided to make arrangements for Kady to go home with Maura on snow days, so this wouldn't happen again. It was so hard to think of everything. She'd been working such long hours, she didn't need this . . .

She wandered into the kitchen to discover that Kady hadn't thawed the chicken as requested. There were chocolate chip crumbs, nutmeat pieces, and dry brownie mix scattered all over the countertop, with an unrinsed mixing bowl sitting in the sink, broken egg shells carelessly tossed in the sink with it.

She cleaned up the mess, and then she heard the dryer buzzer and went in to take out the laundry. She'd been right—the entire load consisted of only one pair of jeans and a pair of panties. Sherry shook her head, wondering why she hadn't realized before.

Her daughter hadn't fallen at all, but had gotten "the curse" and was too ashamed to say so. Vividly Sherry remembered that particular humiliation from her own teen years. At this age girls were paranoid and embarrassed by the slightest mention

of bodily functions. You couldn't even say the
words *sanitary napkin* around them. She herself
had been exactly the same.

Poor Kady. This was only her second period, and
she'd obviously stained her clothes. Add to that the
obscene video; no wonder Kady had fallen apart.

Sherry went to the freezer and fished around until she found a package of frozen chicken. By tomorrow, she assured herself, glorying in sugary
slopes of white powder, Kady would forget all
about her anger. They would both get back to normal.

# CHAPTER 15

They ate a hurried and silent dinner in front of the TV, Kady staring toward the set, where the movie *Willow* showed an entire village of dwarves laughing and reveling. Snow rattled against the windows, wind blowing in gusts.

"Kady? Do you want more chicken?"

"No, thanks. I'm not very hungry."

Sherry bit back a remark about all the brownies Kady had eaten, and cleared away the plates. In the kitchen she loaded the dishwasher, waves of exhaustion sweeping over her. She glanced out the window at the ceaseless drift and swirl of snowflakes. Two or three more inches had fallen since she'd pulled in the driveway—Jimmie Van would make one more pass at six A.M. so she should be able to get out in the morning.

She trudged into her bedroom, wearily stripping off her sweater and jeans. It was as she was taking off her bra that she heard the *whump-whump* of snow tires in the driveway.

"Kady, get the door," she called.

By now the doorbell was chiming.

"I'm not *dressed*!" her daughter called over the sound of the TV.

"You're wearing a robe!"

"That's not *clothes*."

"All right, all right," Sherry muttered, pulling the sweater and jeans back on again, not bothering with underwear. Barefoot, she crossed the hallway while Kady modestly retreated back into the TV room, shutting the door.

The bell chimed again before Sherry could reach the door. She flicked on the yard lights, peering through the side panels to gasp with surprise. "Glen! Glen Dietz!"

She pulled open the door and stood looking up at the tall man dressed in a city-style dress leather jacket, snowflakes starred across the shoulders. More snow sifted onto his shock of brown hair, as if he wore a cap of ivory flakes. One crystal clung to an eyelash.

"Glen," she said again awkwardly.

"Can I come in? That driveway's filling up, I can't stay long."

She was standing here with her hair in a tangle, like some barefoot Daisy Mae, and she had no underwear on. She didn't hide her ambivalence. "I would imagine not. It's the middle of a snowstorm. Anyone with any sense is at home; do you have chains? How far do you have to drive anyway?"

He stepped inside her foyer, stamping snow off his boots, and shaking his head so that moisture sprayed from his soft hair. She could smell a faint whiff of whiskey, and tonight the famous appealing smile was missing.

"Look, I was at the Tip Inn, and I had to come home anyway and this wasn't that far out of the way. I didn't come here to make conversation; I've got a bone to pick with you. A nice big bone."

"What?" She stared up at him, feeling at a disadvantage. He had left puddles of snow, and her bare toe encountered one, the freezing water chilling her skin.

"You've been mentioning my name to the Sheriff's office, Sherry, accusing me of some rather nasty things. I don't like it. I'm not a creep, I'm not some damn child molester getting my jollies from sending dirty videotapes to little girls!"

"Shhhh!" Sherry hissed. "Kady's still up! She's in the TV room."

He scowled, leather creaking as he took a step into her foyer. "Let her hear if she wants to listen. You have made false accusations, Mrs. Vincent; you have dragged my name in the mud, and you had no basis for doing it, none whatsoever!"

"Hey, wait a minute. I . . . Glen, I . . ." Her mouth opened and closed. "Come in and sit down, will you? Come sit in the living room. We can't talk here."

She walked into the living room, leaving him no choice but to follow. However, when Sherry indicated a chair, Glen shook his head.

"I'll stand. You had no right to mention my name. He actually came and questioned me, some guy named Arrington." Blue eyes, warm when she last talked to him, now were as chilly as pack ice. "I resent it. I resent it a lot! I'm trying to start up a new business here in Hartwick. I don't need people placing me under suspicion by the police just because I took photographs of a child, pictures that were *legitimately commissioned* by the child's grandmother, who told me she had parental permission!"

Oh, brother, this was all she needed. One more crisis to make her day complete. But she couldn't blame him for being angry—she supposed she'd be, too.

"Glen. My child has been receiving obscene videotapes through the mail—kiddie porn, really bad stuff. I just—"

"You just thought I might have sent them, right? Your kid gets a filthy tape and right away you think of good old Glen, who's new in town and who wants to make his living taking *family portraits* of all the good people in Hartwick. So right away, naturally, I'm going to antagonize everyone in town by sending a twelve-year-old child dirty videos. Isn't that the way you reasoned? Huh?"

"I was scared, Glen. I went to the Sheriff. What was I supposed to do? Those tapes showed men torturing little girls!"

"And you connected me in your mind with that?"

"No!" she cried. "No, I didn't! But I was questioned. What was I to say? I said that you'd taken some sexy pictures of Kady— Well, you did," she added as Glen seemed about to raise his voice again.

She continued, "He asked me if you suggested doing the pictures on your own, and I said my mother asked you. He said you weren't really under suspicion, but I guess he must have decided to be thorough."

"Oh, he was thorough, all right! I'm lucky he didn't run a computer check on me—or maybe he did. Dammit, Sherry—" But some of the anger was seeping out of Glen, and finally he threw himself onto a couch, scowling at the window, where undrawn curtains revealed a white maelstrom of storm.

"I *am* sorry you got questioned," she apologized, her voice low.

He nodded. "I came back to Hartwick because I wanted some peace. I wanted small-town life; I wanted my work to mean something."

A wave of guilt flooded Sherry. Silence fell between them, full of static electricity as they waited to see whether they'd escalate the disagreement, or downsize it. Sherry suddenly remembered, as if a computer keyboard in her head had suddenly pulled up a file, that Ray Innis had boarded with Glen's family that year.

Another image popped up on that screen, Glen at twelve, short for his age, the class "shrimp," a Norman Rockwell kind of kid, all freckles and ears and cowlick. Glen used to throw spitballs in class with deadly accuracy.

She said, "Will you let it drop, Glen? Please? I swear I wasn't trying to harm your business. I was thinking of my daughter and she's a lot more important than your business—or mine."

"Okay, okay." Moodily Glen stretched out his feet, staring at his boots, which had leaked splotches of damp onto the plush carpet. They sat for a few minutes, the TV set still going in the den. By the sounds, it was the scene at the castle where the giant two-headed dragon was devouring warriors.

"What kind of tapes?" Glen finally said, his tone normal, as if their angry exchange had never occurred. "Have you got one around? Let me see it."

Sherry drew backward. "No, I haven't got one around," she lied. "I gave them all to Detective Arrington. And anyway, I wouldn't show it to anyone. Glen, it's filthy. I couldn't even watch the whole thing. It made me sick, it turned my stomach!"

"Why do you suppose they sent it to Kady?"

"I don't know why. I can't imagine why. Unless—" She leaned forward. "Unless it's some kind of revenge act, maybe for something that happened a long time ago."

Yes, she decided, she'd get his help. He'd lived in the same house with Innis—he had to have some memories. Even twelve-year-olds noticed things.

Glen's eyes flickered. "What are you talking about? Kady's just a kid. What could she have done that was so bad?"

"It wasn't she. It was me—and my mother."

"What?"

Sherry said it quickly. "Don't you remember? That big fuss when we were in seventh grade, the big scandal?"

"What big—you mean . . . the science teacher? Mr. Innis?"

Sherry nodded.

"God, Sherry, that was years ago! We were kids then, that's so long ago I'd almost forgotten about it!"

"Well, I hadn't." Sherry could not keep the coolness out of her tone. "Don't tell me you're going to scoff at me, too! That's what everyone says—it all happened so long ago. Well, there are too many factors in common for it all to be a coincidence."

Glen unfolded himself from the couch and began a restless prowl of the room, stopping to flip through old issues of *Ski* and *Ski Racing* Sherry kept on a teak bookshelf. He pulled out one magazine that showed a skier in red hurtling upside-down over a snowy cliff, teeth bared in a manic grin, snow scattering against an almost neon blue sky.

"Look at this guy, he's gotta be crazy. If I tried that, it'd kill me. You're really serious, aren't you, Sherry? That guy, that science teacher, Innis, he lit out of town and nobody ever saw him again. My God, he'd be an old man now, maybe even dead."

"He wasn't that old," she said stonily. "And he did live with your family that year, didn't he? I remember that."

"Yeah . . . It's all crazy . . . Why would he have waited all this time? This doesn't make sense. After what, twenty-five years? He's suddenly appeared out of nowhere sending videotapes to your little girl? Why doesn't he just come over to the house someday and"—Glen gave a mock lunge—"grab her?"

Sherry jumped. "That's not very funny," she said stiffly.

"Hey." Glen grinned as he dropped the magazine back on its pile. In his well-cut jacket that emphasized the line of his wide shoulders, he looked every inch what he was—a good-looking man who had kept his body well, and who had plenty of lusty appetites.

He added, "Let's change the subject, okay? I came over here mad as hell, now you're the one who's mad. What do you say we forget it, maybe talk about going out for dinner sometime? In Hartwick if you don't want to drive far. We'll go to Mama's Cafe," he added, winking. Mama's was a greasy spoon near the edge of town. "I hear they do a wonderful road-kill chili."

Sherry couldn't help laughing a little. Glen. He was something else. Somehow this discussion had gotten all out of control. "I told you, I'm not dating," she said with less reluctance than previously.

"This won't be a date. We'll talk business. I'll come and take pictures at your spring carnival, how'd you like that? I'll set up a concession. Give away a free family portrait. I could use the publicity."

"I don't know . . ."

"Are you afraid to go out with me?"

"No!"

"Are you afraid you can't handle me?"

"No!" she cried out, and then was embarrassed. "It's just that I—I don't want the whole town knowing my business; I don't want to be involved with a man right now; I have been too scarred by Dick Vincent and all his love affairs. I'm not sure I can ever trust another man again and I don't want to start trying, not right now. Besides . . . we didn't make it before, did we?"

Now his smile held a trace of sadness. "You don't have to trust me. Just come and eat a meal with me, Sherry. I promise I won't leap at you. I'll give you time."

Sherry finally agreed. She would talk to Glen, too, she decided, try to root around in the memories of a boy who had been twelve at the time. *All of us*, she thought suddenly. *We were all twelve, weren't we? Me, Glen, Carole, Judy, and now Kady too.*

After Glen left, Sherry went into the den to tell Kady to turn the TV set off as soon as *Willow* was over. She found her daughter lying on her stomach on the couch, bunny-slippered feet hanging over the arm.

"Why was he so mad at you? Mr. Dietz?" Kady mumbled, one long arm reaching out as she combed through the nap of the carpet with slender fingers, her attention as total as if she were grooming herself.

"Mad? He wasn't mad. We're going to have dinner on Saturday."

"He was mad, I heard him, I heard him saying stuff about dirty videos."

Sherry swallowed. She didn't want Kady involved in this any further, and she didn't want her to feel uneasy around strangers. Except that of course, Glen Dietz wasn't a stranger since he had taken Kady's portfolio photos.

"I was just telling him about the tapes we got in the mail," she said casually. "Kadydid, it's late, if you're not going to watch the rest of this movie, you'd better get to bed."

Kady still lay flopped on the couch. The hem of her bathrobe had ridden up so that Sherry glimpsed the reddened skin on the backs of her daughter's legs. "What happened to your legs?" she asked.

It took a few seconds for Kady to reply. "Oh . . . when I fell I got my pants wet." Kady stretched out and flicked off the TV, her eyes avoiding Sherry's.

Suddenly, without warning, Sherry was flooded with a sensation of impending loss so strong and profound that she felt herself rocked under its impact. Her chest and stomach seemed clenched, her throat ached, her eyes burned with tears. This beautiful child, her Kady. She would lose her. Already was losing her, to adulthood, to time and distance.

Just as her own mother had lost her.

" 'Night, Mom," Kady said, padding past her on lithe bare feet.

# CHAPTER 16

In the distance multiple snowmobile motors whined, the sound carrying on the clear night air. The sky was sharp black, stars glittering like mica. Snow lay everywhere, seeming almost to glow phosphorescently. A trail of footprints across a yard looked surreal.

Sherry drove down Meredith Street, which meandered in back of Hartwick's downtown area, and probably once had been a lumber-camp trail. Now it was a typical Hartwick street, slightly down-at-the-heels and lined with a variety of homes, from a few old Victorians that had been turned into bed-and-breakfasts, to shabby Cape Cods, to an occasional brick ranch with carport.

Carole Hamner lived in one of the ranches, and as she pulled into the drive, Sherry saw three snowmobiles parked under Carole's carport. She had inherited them from her father when he died last year.

She pulled in behind Carole's car, blocking it, which would be okay, since she intended to drive.

Carole came to the door in a cloud of Fabergé, round, pink, and flushed in a peach-colored satin quilted bathrobe.

"Jesus, I got on the phone and forgot the time—I'm just blow-drying my hair, I'll be done in a sec. Do you want to come in and talk? Put your jacket on the couch. What are you wearing? A black jumpsuit? Mmm, sexy. You're gonna wow 'em."

"It's old," Sherry said, glimpsing herself in Carole's hall mirror. She seemed a stranger to herself, lipstick and eyeliner making her face seem unfamiliar. She did not know why she had chosen to wear makeup: why had she rejected her usual self?

She explained, "I wore this one New Year's Eve ... My closet isn't exactly full of singles clothes, you know. I feel funny in it. The shoulder pads are too thick."

"If I could look like that— Come on, I'm in the john."

Sherry followed her friend into her cluttered bathroom. A black-and-gold dress hung on a hook over the door, size sixteen and with just the right suggestion of sleaziness for the "pub crawl" Carole insisted on. Every inch of vanity space was lined with jars, bottles, atomizers, hot rollers, potpourri jars, body lotions, cosmetics. Sherry didn't own a sixteenth as much. She eyed a curling iron, wondering if the thing would brand your scalp like a Texas steer.

"Well?" Carole demanded. "How many places are we going to hit? Shall we really do Traverse City?"

"How many places are there?" Sherry hedged. "I don't know. How about just one to start?" She laughed uncomfortably. "I sound real eager, don't I?"

"We'll get you going." Carole picked up the curling iron and squeezed its curved tongs over a hank

of her blond hair, expertly rolling the hair into a
corkscrew. She counted aloud, a warm smell of hair
adding to the perfumy odor already in the bathroom. "Thirty, thirty-five, forty . . ."

Was she really going to do this? Sherry leaned
against the tiled wall, fighting the tension that
tightened her shoulder muscles. Last night she'd
had another of the nightmares. The sly, soft, whispering male voice.

Afterward, she hadn't been able to fall asleep, but
had lain in bed, her mind obsessively worrying at
the few facts she knew about Ray Innis. She barely
remembered what he looked like. Black hair, yes,
she remembered that, but the rest of his features
had been faded by repression and time. He'd
seemed handsome—to a twelve-year-old—but what
did that mean?

Lying there, she'd racked her brain, dragging out
every fact she knew, and finally realizing that she
really knew very little. Where had Innis come
from? How long had he been in Hartwick? Where
did he go after he left? Had he a history of child
molestation? And—most nerve-wracking question
of all—how accurate were her memories of what
the man had actually done to herself, Judy, and
Carole?

These were some of the things she hoped to learn
tonight.

In the car on the way to Traverse City, Carole
kept up her chatter, bringing Sherry up-to-date on
hospital gossip. Carole could be an outrageously
detailed raconteur, and Sherry heard more than she
wanted to about a Detroit-area chiropractor who
had reported to the hospital emergency room with
sections of cucumber up his rectum.

She had to laugh. "God, Carole—!"

"Well, it's honest to God true, would I lie? He
had a regular vegetable salad up there."

Then Carole started on her latest admirer, a

sales engineer who, as it turned out, had been one of Timberline's "casualties," breaking a knee on Snowsnake Run. "He's kinda cute in a cast up to his wing-wang," Carole said, lighting up a cigarette. "He likes women with curves, and he likes them to be aggressive, he says. God, Sherry, do you suppose that means he wants me in leather and chains? I can really pick 'em, huh? My whole life. If a guy is really, really cute, then he has about six ex-wives, or he's afraid to commit, or he'd rather go to bed with a bottle of Jack Daniel's."

Carole had been talking like this about men for years. Speculating, complaining, telling outrageous stories. She was the quintessential tough, gutsy career woman who had gone through a pack of men and ended up alone.

Now for the first time Sherry wondered if the crowds of men were really an expression of unhappiness and anger. Neither of Carole's two marriages had lasted longer than two years, and often her relationships ended in as few as three months. "There's always another one down the pike" had been her friend's motto.

A motor home suddenly pulled out in front of them from a side road, lights on inside as men in lumberjack shirts stretched out at tables, playing cards. Sherry automatically put on her brakes to avoid rear-ending them.

She knew the incident in seventh grade had profoundly affected *her*. Could it have affected Carole too? Was Ray Innis the reason why Carole couldn't really relate to men?

Traverse City, in the center of cherry-growing country, was a postcard-pretty resort town that boasted several prime ski areas and championship golf courses. Situated at the base of Grand Traverse Bay, it was bifurcated by a fingerlike peninsula into two "arms." The bar that Carole chose was on the west arm of the bay, a Swiss chalet that could have been lifted bodily from Zermatt, Switzerland. Snow decorated its carved wooden rafters like vanilla frosting, and yellow windows glowed cozily.

"This is *the* place here, if you're over thirty anyway," Carole gloated as they walked in and were immediately assaulted by taped rock music. The combined smells of liquor, cigarette smoke, and barbecue sauce swirled around them. Well-dressed people clustered around a long, semicircular bar, their conversation drowning out the music. Several men eyed them predatorily as they waited to be seated.

They managed to get the last empty table, by the windows over which drapes had been drawn, to block out the chill winter view of the bay. They ordered peach margaritas. Sherry noticed that Carole's personality had subtly changed. Now she seemed nervously revved up, gesturing animatedly, her eyes glittering as she began giving a running commentary on the men.

"Look," she pointed out over the pounding rhythm of the music. "Those guys over there, they've got to be ski instructors, that tan looks practically precancerous. I wonder if they've got any brains at all. But I guess if you look as lean and mean as they do, you don't need brains, right?"

She giggled, and Sherry made an effort to smile back.

"Oh, and there's Ken Chavey, remember him? He was the one who had that party, remember? When we all got drunk and Leann Trimble fell off the dock and almost drowned? He works for the DNR now, he's— Oh, good Lord, Sherry, there's Dick."

"Oh, no. *Dick?*" Sherry's heart sank. She immediately turned in her chair so that her face wasn't visible to anyone standing at the bar. "What's he doing here? Who's he with? Oh, God, Carole . . ."

Carole giggled. "I don't think he's with anyone, but he'd like to be by the looks of him. He's sidling up to a little blonde with a pug nose, I think he's feeding her some kind of classy line. 'Haven't I met you somewhere before?' " she mimicked.

Sherry could picture it only too well. "I want to leave," she said, pushing away her drink and starting up.

"Hey." Carole pulled her down again. "You haven't finished your margarita."

"I can't sit here with *Dick* here," Sherry blurted. "My God, Carole, what if he sees me? What if he comes over here and talks to us? What if I see him pick up some woman? What if some man comes over and talks to *us*? This is so embarrassing—"

"Why? You have a right to be here. Come on, Sherry, don't be such a chicken. You're *divorced*. You can go to a bar if you want to."

Flushing, Sherry sank nervously into her chair and sipped at the margarita, which tasted strongly of peach and was already creating strange, rippling sensations up and down her arms.

She waited tensely for Dick to look up and notice her.

But Dick seemed very absorbed in the blonde, and after half an hour Sherry realized that he probably *had* noticed her but was pretending not to because he didn't want to spoil his chances with the blonde. *Sick*, she thought. *I think I feel sick. Or is it just disgusted?*

Sherry got up and edged her way toward the lobby, where there were a pair of pay phones. She dialed Kady at Maura's, suddenly longing for the sound of her daughter's voice.

"Hi, Kadydid," she said when Kady finally got on the line. With the noise coming from the bar she could barely hear and had to plug her left ear in order to make any sense of what was being said.

"Where are you, Mom? Who are all those loud voices?"

Sherry whitewashed the truth. "Oh, just people, we're in a restaurant in Traverse City. What're you doing, baby?"

"We're playing Pictionary," Kady said, sounding as if she'd like to get back to the game. "But Maura is drawing terrible pictures, she drew this thing, and I thought it was an airplane and it turned out to be the state of North Dakota! Maura is a horrible artist!"

"Well, you draw something good and show her how it's done," Sherry said, laughing.

"I can't draw anything but stick figures, my pictures suck too."

"Kady! We don't use words like that." But Sherry couldn't help it; Kady's voice sounded so fresh and sweet, she had a wild longing to be with her, to be sitting on the floor playing the game, too, the two of them safe together, wrapped up in the cocoon of family.

"Well, I gotta go now, we're having frostees, Maura's mother is making us these drinks in the blender, she's putting bananas and orange juice and Seven-Up in them—"

"Okay, baby. See you tomorrow."

"Sure, Mom," Kady said, hanging up with disconcerting alacrity.

Sherry threaded her way back to the table. In her absence, several men had stopped by their table, and Carole introduced her to Chris, who worked in X ray at Traverse City Osteopathic Hospital, and Ben, who was in ICU. Fresh from the innocence of Kady's voice, Sherry barely looked at them.

Finally, discouraged, they moved on.

"What's with you?" Carole leaned forward to say over the ruckus of Billy Ocean. "Don't you *want* to meet anyone? You didn't say one word to Ben and Chris."

"Why should I say a word to them? I don't know them, Carole. I'm not the kind of person who does things like this, and I feel weird sitting here with my ex-husband thirty feet away. I feel like I don't belong here."

Carole's voice took an edge. "Jeez, kid, how else are you going to meet guys if you won't talk to them? What are you going to do, put an ad in the paper?"

Were they quarreling, here in this hot, smoky, crowded room drenched with the sound of rock music? Sherry set down her margarita glass, which was slick with condensation. Its effects were already swirling in her insides, making her feel spacy, far away from her surroundings.

Carole—indeed the whole night—was slipping away from her, and she remembered she hadn't really come here to meet men anyway, she'd come here to talk to Carole.

Well . . . if she didn't mention it now she wasn't going to.

"What do you remember about Ray Innis?" she leaned forward to say into Carole's ear.

Carole turned, seeming both startled and annoyed.

"Ray *Innis*? God, are you talking about that again, Sherry? Jesus— Can't you just sit and enjoy a drink and some music without making a federal case about things?"

Sherry wished she hadn't had so much to drink, she'd be able to handle this better. "I'm sorry," she said placatingly. "It's just that Kady got those videos and I'm so worried, I'm just trying to—"

"Well, you're way off track." Carole tipped up her drink, drained it, and motioned to the barmaid, who was angling past them with a full tray. "Sherry, that's one of your faults, you think too much about things. You make yourself obnoxious sometimes. No, I don't think about Ray Innis anymore, why should I? He was just a weird guy who touched us a couple times and wanted to look at us without any clothes on. It was just one of those things that happen, and *I* don't want to think about it tonight or any other night!"

"Carole—"

"Look, if you can't sit here and be pleasant, then at least don't bring up old crap. I don't want to hear about the man, for God's sake! I want to have some fun. That's why *I'm* here!"

Every time she mentioned this, Carole had gotten angry. "I need to have some questions answered," Sherry began.

"Why? Why do you have to know? Sherry, you're being an ass. I was a kid. Some old guy had the hots for me. But it's over now, it was all over about a hundred years ago, and *I am sick and tired of thinking about it.*"

"Okay," Sherry said, defeated.

"Just drink your drink," Carole snapped. "We've got another one coming. And here comes hubby, I think he's going to speak to you."

Dick and the blonde were leaving the bar, threading their way through the crowd toward the exit. The blonde was too petite to look well with Dick's six-foot-five frame, and she was plainly inebriated, her walk wobbly, one high heel catching on a rough area in the carpeting. Solicitously, Dick caught her as she stumbled.

As the couple passed Sherry's table, Dick looked straight at Sherry. "Hi, cupcake."

"Hi, Romeo," she snapped back, letting some of her anger at Carole boomerang on him.

After Dick and the blonde had gone, Carole ex-

cused herself and went to cruise the bar, leaving
Sherry alone at the table. Sherry sat staring at the
tabletop, perspiration soaking her body underneath the black jumpsuit. Carole had gotten so angry, she was thinking.

If all it had been was touching—

Oh, God, what if it had been more?

Questions opened up other questions, each one of
them causing Sherry's heart to thump sickeningly.
Could her friend possibly have been *raped* all those
years ago? Was Carole a rape victim?

If that were true, it might explain Carole's long
and unhappy history with men, her anger when
Sherry had brought up the subject of Innis, her
touchiness over the years, the spirit of tough defi-
ance that often moved her friend.

Unwelcome pictures flooded her mind. Carole,
chubby twelve-year-old Carole, being forced into
sex—a man pushing her down, forcing her knees
wide, inserting his—

*His penis, long and thick and pink-red, with a
kind of pink bulb at the end, surrounded by thick,
curling hairs . . .*

Sherry gagged. Sour fluids flooded up from her
stomach, drenching the back of her throat, tasting
of liquor, and she jumped up and pushed her way
through the crowd at the bar, running into the ladies' room.

There were four booths, none occupied, thank
God, and she rushed into the first one and began
dry-heaving. She was able to force up only a small
amount of vomit, but the effort left her trembling
and weak, and she knelt beside the commode, her
whole body shaking.

These two events—the obscene tape and the Ray
Innis incident—just *had* to be related. She felt more
than ever sure now. This just could not be a coincidence.

Shudders rippled through her.

And Kady. Dear God, Kady . . . Kady involved in this, an innocent victim who'd merely happened to be born to a woman who'd been involved in the original event, but prey for some man's twisted fantasies.

# CHAPTER 17

At home, Sherry let herself in through the garage door at three A.M. The emptiness of the house, without Kady's presence, weighed on her hollowly.

She walked into the kitchen and poured herself a glass of milk. She stood by the refrigerator drinking it, the fresh dairy taste cleaning out some of the alcohol fumes. It had been an endless evening. Carole had made a connection with a man at the bar and spent the rest of the evening talking with him, or dancing on the tiny dance floor, behaving as if Sherry didn't exist. Sherry had been left to sit at the table by herself, fending off advances from interested men.

They had driven home in silence, Carole sleeping most of the way, leaving Sherry to her thoughts. As soon as she'd mentioned Ray Innis, Carole had changed. Were there facts about Innis that she wouldn't or couldn't discuss? Sherry bet there were. But she didn't see how she was going to find out those things, not from Carole anyway.

But there had been three girls involved, she reminded herself. There was still Judy Sjoholm. Tomorrow she'd call Judy, who now lived in West Branch, only a forty-minute drive away.

She wandered through the house checking locks, then took a quick shower, hanging up her jumpsuit in the bathroom to rid it of the stink of cigarette smoke that permeated every fiber. Finally she crawled into the haven of bed, too tired to give more than a token tug at the comforter before she fell asleep as if into a black pit.

Her dreams were restless, images of men who lined the edge of a sidewalk, waving and yelling at her while she ran the gauntlet between them, dodging out of the reach of their grasping hands. Then somehow she was in a bedroom in a great stone mansion, a dark Victorian room paneled with mahogany in which bright metal hooks had been set at ceiling level. A huge four-poster bed dominated the center of the room, and there were more hooks set halfway up each of the four support posts.

What did the hooks mean? Something sexual and dreadful. In the dream Sherry's heart began to fibrillate with panic, her throat quivering from the push of blood through her veins. Someone was shouting at her, his voice huge, roaring with menace . . .

She woke with a shock of adrenaline, finding herself already sitting on the edge of the bed, every muscle in her body tensed, her breath coming in gasps. A roar filled her bedroom, a sound she knew well.

The snowmobile.

It was in the yard again, racketing across the driveway, its lights caroming up against Sherry's windows like searchlights.

Four A.M.

Why? Why was he here? How could he be just an ordinary kid out joyriding, if he kept returning to her house again and again and always at the deepest hour of sleep, when he *knew* he'd wake her and Kady? She heard the roar again as the machine rammed through the trees near the drive. Then the sound intensified as he drove the vehicle directly beneath her window, less than four feet away from her, violating the very space she occupied.

Sherry had had enough.

She sprang off the bed and ran barefoot, her long T-shirt flapping, through the kitchen to the garage, where she jammed her feet into an old pair of boots that had been Dick's, grabbed up an old three-pronged hoe she used for gardening, and ran out of the side garage door into the night.

There was nothing but the dark, noise, and headlights, the snowmobile itself only a suggestion of dark shape and rider.

Sherry screamed out a curse word. She didn't feel the cold; she didn't feel anything except the savage anger that ignited her entire being. He had no right to terrify her like this!

The machine raced for the corner of the house, lying flat in a reckless turn that kicked up a long tail of snow. Sherry ran fiercely toward it, brandishing the long hoe handle. She was like a mother bear protecting cubs. Her mind had reverted to some atavistic, primitive level. She only wanted to get to him and swing the hoe, hit him, knock him off the machine!

It almost seemed as if the driver was grinning at her. The snowmobile finished its turn and aimed straight at her, spitting out snow as it tried to run her down.

Sherry screamed again and jumped backward, dropping the hoe. She only had time to glimpse the pale ski-mask slit with holes for eyes and mouth,

partially covered by a hood, before the vicious
tracks were pounding the snow within inches of her
own feet.

She lunged backward, falling across one of the
young pines that grew at the edge of the drive. Then
she was down in a welter of pine needles and snow,
cold wetness stinging her bare buttocks.

She lay tangled in branches, waiting to be
crushed, and then the motor noise changed, and she
realized with incredulity that the machine had
turned and was headed back out the driveway.

He was going away.

She put a hand over her mouth, and then her
body finally began to feel the freezing chill of the
snow. My God, she was sitting in it almost naked,
her flimsy sleep shirt already soaked.

She struggled up, noticing that she'd bent the
pine tree over double. *He had tormented her deliberately.* Might even have killed her—and laughed.

She'd gotten that feeling, that he really hated her,
that he was unbalanced and would do anything.

Or was that just what he wanted her to feel, was
that part of the terror?

She stumbled toward the garage, the loose rubber
boots squashing in the snow. The sounds of the machine had faded into the snowy woods, sounding
dim and harmless now. She dragged herself into
the house, her adrenaline all used up now, leaving
her weak.

Thank God Kady hadn't been here, that was all
she could think. She locked up all the doors again,
pulling an old dresser out of the laundry room to
put against the back door for added security. Finally she went into the bathroom and drew a hot
tub bath because she didn't think her knees would
take standing up in the shower.

She soaked in the tub for forty minutes, until
her heartbeat had slowed to almost normal. Her
backside was covered with welts from the pine

branches, and in the hot water her chilled flesh had turned beet red. Someone hated them. But who? And why?

She amazed herself by actually falling asleep again and was awakened by the alarm at 6:30. Groggily she lay there, the sound creating another sick burst of adrenaline in her. Finally she realized it was only the clock, and reached out to push the alarm button.

It was Saturday—which meant crowded slopes and another hectic day at Timberline. She had also promised Kady that she could invite Maura and Heather to ski today with her, on condition that she would have another overnight with her friends so that Sherry could have her date with Glen.

My God, she had farmed Kady out for two nights in a row. But it was necessary, she thought grimly, and her daughter would be safe, which was what counted.

She dressed quickly, pulling on the first sweater her hands encountered when she opened her dresser drawer, a ragg wool she'd bought several years ago from Land's End. She felt so so tired. Her eyelids burned, and she must have strained a muscle in her leg from running into that tree. She now felt she'd really overreacted. She'd had no business racing out into the night like that.

She drove into town to pick up the girls.

Even at 7:15 A.M., the girls were effervescent with giggles. Heather, the leader, talked nonstop about a party her mother was letting her give for her class. The girls teased Kady about a boy, Ryan Hill, who had phoned her the previous night. Apparently Ryan was a "babe," an accolade that meant exceptionally cute, and the girls expected that Ryan might be skiing today, too. The prospect caused them to go into spasms of twelve-year-old merriment.

Heading out of town toward the ski resort,

Sherry was seized with a wave of envy. She, Judy, and Carole had once been like this. Giggling, teasing, bound together since kindergarten, unable to imagine life without each other. They hadn't known then all the things that would happen to them. Sherry's Miss Michigan title, Carole's divorces, Judy's long-term, dull marriage.

And being molested by their science teacher.

At the ski area, the girls dawdled over doughnuts and hot cocoa, and Sherry went into her office. She chewed on a doughnut she'd brought with her, her mind picturing the blank mask of the aggressive snowmobiler. Dammit, who *was* he? And there was Carole, whose whole attitude and personality had changed as soon as Sherry mentioned Ray Innis.

Maybe she and Carole weren't really friends; the sudden thought electrified her. She'd taken friendship for granted because Carole had always been there, to her what Maura was to Kady. But was knowing someone since they were five "friendship"? Maybe not.

She stopped chewing, startled. She had never had a thought like this before; she had always assumed so much.

Troubled, she reached for the stack of ticket receipts, and began checking them off against the register total for Friday. But after only a few, she laid the stack down again. The third member of the triumvirate had been Judy. Judy Sjoholm. Well, what was she waiting for?

She rummaged in her desk drawer until she found the telephone book for West Branch, another old lumber town still located in the middle of tracts of state forest. Judy had married Ned Mageel a year out of high school and had moved to West Branch, where Ned owned Mageel's Bottle Gas and Fuel. To Sherry, the story was sad. Judy seldom traveled more than one hundred miles away from home and had only flown in an airplane once.

She located the number and dialed.

"H'lo?" The voice that answered the phone was male and going through the cracking phase of adolescence.

"Is your mother there?"

"Yeah . . . Mom! Maaaaaa!" Sherry waited, wondering which one of Judy's boys this was. She'd given birth to three in three years, giving them all names that started with *B*.

The phone rattled, there was a long wait, and then Judy's familiar voice came on the line, soft, warm, and breathy in pitch. "Hello? Brian, I told you, I can't give you a ride until your father gets b—"

"Hi," Sherry said.

A startled silence.

"It's Sherry. Sherry Smith. God, Judy, how long has it been? I'm embarrassed by all the time that's passed."

"*Sherry*," Judy said. "Oh, Lord, I must have sounded like a fool. But Brian's over at basketball practice and I'm here without a car until Ned gets back from making deliveries, and I can't reach Ned unless he calls in, which is a real pain. How *are* you, Sherry? How is Dick? Oh—I forgot—you're divorced."

"Oh, Dick's doing great, he's still got an eye for blondes," she said lightly. "The divorce was final last month." She went on, "Hey, I have to drive over to West Branch today to pick up some parts for our grill stove here at Timberline, so why don't I stop by and say 'hi'? You're right on my way."

"Today?"

"Unless you've got plans."

"Not until later, well, Ned's out, and I'm here alone until he gets back—well, except for Billy and Brad, but they're going to be out snowmobiling in the woods . . . Sherry? Could you stop by the I.G.A. store and bring back a couple of half gallons of milk before you come? And some of those Pepperidge

Farm cookies with the big chocolate chunks? I have a real craving for them, and Ned doesn't like us to buy stuff like that. I'll pay you when you get here."

"You don't have to pay me, Jude."

"But I want to. I can't let you buy our groceries."

"Cookies aren't groceries. I want to do it. It'll be my treat."

They made arrangements and Sherry hung up, her heart hammering a little. If she left now she could run over to West Branch and back while Kady was still skiing, and she'd have Becky Trimble keep an eye on the girls.

West Branch, although in Ogemaw County, had similar roots to Hartwick. Until 1871 the county had been wilderness. The Jackson, Lansing & Saginaw Railroad had opened it to lumbering. Now all the big trees were gone, but secondary growth was abundant, some of it maturing now, the woods scattered with the stumps of giants.

The Mageels lived on forty acres in the woods, their home an old deer hunting lodge that Ned had remodeled. Deer flocked to the Mageels' backyard every winter to eat the sugar-beet cullings that Ned threw down for them. Judy had to get a deer license every year so that Ned could shoot her quota as well as his own.

The driveway was a third of a mile long, lined with jack and red pines. As she avoided ruts of snow, Sherry wondered how Judy stood the isolation, especially if they had only one car. But Ned Mageel didn't believe in his wife working; in fact, Judy seldom drove the car at all, and then only on two-lane roads.

The two women embraced on the doorstep, Judy laughing nervously as she took the grocery sack. "Oh, *cookies*. I love cookies, they're going to make me fat as a pig someday. Come on in. The boys are out in the woods, and Ned just called, he won't be back till six, so we can just pig out if we want to."

Despite her love of sweets, Judy Sjoholm Mageel was still a trim size eight, and once had possessed a perky prettiness that had won her a place on the Homecoming Queen court along with Sherry. However, the perkiness was gone now, leaving Judy a tired housewife who wore loose blue pull-on polyester pants and an old Higgins Lake sweatshirt.

Sherry felt a spasm of guilt as she followed her former classmate inside. She'd really let her friendship with Judy fade. Dick had thought her boring, and had called Ned a backwoods asshole, refusing to see them.

The small house still had plastic Christmas greenery on the mantel. They sat in the kitchen, which smelled of cooking odors. Judy's hobby was hand-decorating plaques, and dozens of them lined the walls: *Our Home Is Our Heart*, *Judy's Country Kitchen*, and others of similar sentiment.

But what else did Judy have to do? Sherry reflected. She had not worked since her marriage, and the plaques, sold to a local gift shop, were her source of pin money.

"Oh, it's been so *long*," Judy breathed, arranging cookies on a Dutch blue plate. From outdoors came the distant hum of snowmobiles. "Sherry, you look *just* the same. I can still remember when your mother had that party for you after you got crowned Miss Michigan, and we all got to try on your crown. Remember? And Carole went in the bedroom and wouldn't come out?"

"It was a long time ago," Sherry said, feeling guiltier than ever if this was the most recent and best memory that Judy could come up with. They chatted about people they had known in high school. Judy's oldest boy, Brian, showed talent in basketball and was being scouted by the University of Michigan.

"That's the only way Ned'll ever let him go to college, for the basketball." Judy sighed. "He says

what does the boy need college for if he's going to
help run the business? He's going to start Billy and
Brad on deliveries, too, as soon as they get their
driver's license.''

Sherry smiled politely. The whole atmosphere
here depressed her. No wonder she and Dick had
virtually dropped Judy and Ned. Slavery still existed in the twentieth century, and Judy might as
well have a metal bracelet around her ankle. In this
era of VCRs and microchips, Judy had never even
driven her car out on I-75 because Ben was afraid
she'd have an accident.

She worked the conversation around to Kady
and found herself explaining about the videotapes,
leaving out most of the details when Judy's face
became transfixed with horror.

"Oh . . . God . . . that's awful! Sherry, I can't believe they would send such horrible things to a little girl. Kady's just a baby! She's just a child!'' Judy
rose and began to clear away their plates and cups,
her hands shaking so badly that she had to set a
plate down. "Oh, it makes me *sick*. That anyone
would do that to a child!''

"She's twelve now, Judy, she's had her period already, she's thinking about her looks all the time,
she's no baby anymore.'' Sherry said it slowly,
wondering how to get into this. "Judy, I need to ask
you some things about when we were kids, because
I think maybe the two are connected.''

"Connected? What's connected? What are you
talking about?'' Nervously Judy fussed with the
dishes, her back to Sherry as she opened and closed
the refrigerator door.

Sherry drew in a breath of air and let it slowly
out. Judy's nervousness was infecting her, she
could feel her own stomach clenching. Judy was
going to be just like Carole, she could sense it.

"It's about what happened when we were in the
seventh grade,'' she started.

"I don't know what you mean."

Sherry wet her lips. "Mr. Innis. You remember him. All I need to know is a couple of things," she added quickly, as Judy turned, involuntarily throwing one hand up to her face, as if Sherry had threatened to hit her.

"What couple of things? What do you need to know? Sherry, Ned doesn't know anything about that and I don't want him to know, I can't have him know."

"I won't tell anyone. Judy, you can't know how important this is—"

"And *you* don't know how *he* is. You don't know how jealous he is! He doesn't want other men looking at me or talking to me; he hates it that I was on the Homecoming Court. He thinks all the guys in school were after me, and he hates them. He won't let me mention the name of any guy I ever went to school with."

"Judy. Judy, I know, and I won't tell him, I promise. But I have to protect my daughter. I have to know about this man, because I think he's the one who's been tormenting us. A snowmobiler has been running by the house, too, and he nearly ran me over last night."

Judy stood by the refrigerator, her hands clutched to her chest, fingers interlocked as if she were praying. "Oh, Sherry. Oh, God. I can't—I can't think about it, I can't talk about it! I can't take the risk. I don't want Ned all upset by this. He knows I wasn't a virgin when I married but he doesn't know w—"

She stopped, her eyes wide, one hand splayed across her mouth.

Sherry felt a surge of nausea, and a rocking sensation as if every memory in her head had been violently tilted and realigned, as if she had lived her whole life without knowing what she had really lived. "You mean you were raped, Judy? *Ray Innis raped you?*"

Judy's face had drained of color, making her look pasty and frightened. "Please, Sherry. Let's not talk about it."

"But, Judy! You have to talk about it! My God!" Sherry's eyes filled with tears. "I didn't know. All this time I thought it was just . . . you know, a man touching us, but that was all. That's all he ever did to me. And now you say that he did more. When? It couldn't have been on that picnic—"

Judy seemed almost to cower by the refrigerator. "I don't know when. And it wasn't—it was— It was penetration but it— Oh, *shit*," Judy burst out. "Why did you have to come here? It wasn't to see me, was it? You didn't want to see *me*. You wanted to ask these questions, that was why you really came here. Because you wanted to dig up old garbage!"

"Judy—"

"Well, I don't want to talk. I have a *husband*. I have *kids*. I have *three wonderful boys*. I live for my boys, Sherry, they are my life; they're the reason I stick with Ned because I know Ned is no bargain, and he's terribly jealous and possessive. But I put up with it because *I want to be with my boys and Ned will take them away from me if I get a divorce and I can't do anything to make him want to divorce me!*"

Judy was screaming now, and Sherry got up from the table, feeling sick. "I'm sorry," she said. "I'm so sorry, Judy."

"You're not a friend!" Judy screamed. "You're just a user, Sherry! You just wanted something from me, that's all, so get out of here. Just get out of here and go back to that stupid ski resort you own and stay in your own life and I'll stay in mine!"

"I'm sorry," Sherry repeated, backing out of the cluttered kitchen that smelled of venison burgers. "But I have to know, Judy. Did you receive any videotapes yourself? Did you get anything in the mail?"

"No!" Judy shouted.

"Do you know where Ray Innis might have gone or what happened to him after he left Hartwick?"

"Are you crazy?" Then Judy seemed to sag. "Why would *I* know that? I was only a little girl, for God's sake. Would you get out of here, Sherry? Will you just get out? Ned is coming home and I don't want you here!"

# CHAPTER 18

What had happened to the butterfly? That was the odd question that suddenly dropped into Sherry's mind as she turned onto the entrance ramp of I-75 back toward Hartwick, Judy's shouts still ringing in her ears.

The beautiful, iridescent, cloisonné butterfly pin that had glistened in the sunlight that day at the river, as if any minute its wings might move and lift it soaring away. A gift for one of them, Innis said, if they were "real good."

Sherry's fingers clenched the wheel. My God, she hadn't thought about the butterfly in years. Innis had shown it to them, but had never given it to any of them that day. As far as she knew, he had kept it in his shirt pocket, never using what had obviously been a bribe.

Now the intuition came to her in a blast of white heat, shocking her with its certainty. Ray Innis *had* given away that butterfly—but it hadn't been on the picnic that day with all three of them, it had been later, and it had been to Carole or Judy, not to her.

One of them, maybe both, had been raped. She was shaking, her skin clammy. She hadn't known, hadn't dreamed.

She had been friends with Judy and Carole for a lifetime. She had laughed with them, traded secrets, argued over boys, attended their weddings, quarreled and made up, drifted apart from them, but always they had been in her mind as her *friends*, part of her life, part of her.

How could Judy have kept a secret like that from her? How could she have borne it alone, like some sort of curse, so horrible you could not talk? *Why* had she borne it alone?

But as soon as Sherry asked herself that question, she knew the answer. Judy had been only twelve when it happened, a child. Twelve-year-olds didn't have mature judgment. Maybe Judy hadn't told *anyone*. Sherry felt her stomach heave and swallowed back the nausea. Twelve years old, and bearing all that.

Suddenly another memory came clicking back. It had been five or six months after Innis had left town, when her own breasts began to grow rapidly. She'd started forming stretch marks that radiated out from the nipple, red striations that she couldn't explain. Sherry had thought she had been stricken with a disease, that Ray Innis had given it to her because he had touched her there.

Terrified and guilty, she'd waited for the stretch marks to fan out from her breasts and appear on the rest of her body, eventually killing her. She hadn't told her mother. She hadn't told anyone. She'd just waited to die. But months passed and she didn't die, she felt as healthy as ever, and one day she'd noticed her mother coming out of the shower, with the same sort of marks on her stomach.

Thinking of it, Sherry felt tears moisten her eyes, and then they were streaming down her face, so that she had to wipe them away to see to drive. The sobs kept coming, shaking her. Finally she had to pull off onto the shoulder of the road. She sat bent over with her head in her hands, sobbing out as she hadn't cried in years.

She didn't know how long she sat there, trucks and campers whizzing past her, an air blast from each one shaking her car. She cried for Judy, for herself at twelve, for Carole, for her lost marriage to Dick that had never been a real marriage at all, and she wept for Kady who still had it all to face. She cried for her mother who was going to die someday, and from whom she was estranged. She cried for the little girls on the videotapes, who'd looked so drugged and scared, who'd been forced to perform such unspeakable acts.

But at last it was over, the sobs abating to sniffles. She fumbled with a trembling hand in her purse for a tissue. My God, what was the matter with her? She was falling apart. How many truck drivers, roaring past, had glanced down at her and snickered?

But somehow the crying had been therapeutic. She didn't feel quite so fragile anymore, so vulnerable to facts she might learn.

She broke the speed limit getting back to Timberline. Suddenly she had a feeling of urgency. There was so much to do, so much to find out, and she might not have much time.

Back at the ski resort, she quickly checked on Kady and her friends. Becky told her that the girls were skiing the west area, and were fine. Relieved, Sherry spot-checked the ticket office, visited the Ski

Patrol hut and maintenance, then locked herself in her office again.

First she dialed information for Naples, Florida, asking for an Elton Powers. The operator told her that there was no such person listed.

"But he's retired—I know he's living somewhere in Florida."

"Ma'am, Florida is a big state with three area codes. I don't have a listing for him in Naples, and if you don't have the city I can't help you."

Sherry hung up. Elton Powers had been the principal of the school the year she was twelve, a key figure in the drama as far as Sherry was concerned. She went to the file cabinet in her office where she kept a collection of old road maps, and sorted through them with their memories of old trips. She pounced on an AAA map of Florida. Tampa, St. Petersburg, Bradenton, Sarasota . . . Maybe if she just started dialing the main retirement communities she'd find him. She'd just have to pray he hadn't installed an unpublished number and wasn't dead.

Half an hour later, she hit pay dirt with a listing for an Elton F. Powers in Coral Springs. She sat shaking for a minute, remembering a balding man with strong features and a big nose, escorting a boy down the hallway toward his office, hands hooked in the boy's Windbreaker. The boy had been screaming the word *fuck* over and over.

"*Son, son,*" the principal had been saying.

That was all the memory that remained in her mind now—a snippet of an event. She could hardly imagine that strong man as a senior citizen, cashing his social-security check and playing shuffleboard in the sun.

She dialed the number, waiting while it rang. Eight times, nine. She was about to hang up, then remembered that older people sometimes had trouble getting around, what if Elton Powers now walked with a cane?

On the eleventh ring, the phone was picked up. "Hello?" The voice was male and old, with a phlegmy, walrus quality to it. Not a voice that Sherry remembered at all.

"Mr. Powers?"

"Speaking."

"This is Sherry Vincent—Sherry Smith," she explained hastily. "I was one of your students at Hartwick Junior High back in 1965, I was twelve years old when you were principal."

There was a lengthy pause. The old man hawked, clearing his throat. "Yes? I had a lot of students but I can't remember them all now."

"Please . . . try."

"I left Hartwick a couple years after that, I went down to Detroit. I was principal there for nine years and then I came down here to Florida and I taught adult ed for six more years until I got too old to do that. Now they've got me farmed out, I live in a trailer court and collect my check."

The man sounded ancient and bitter, and Sherry's heart sank. What of value could he remember now? But she had dialed him, and it felt too awkward to hang up, so she asked, "Mr. Powers, some things have come up and I need to know about Ray Innis, the science teacher. I was one of the girls he—" She forced the word out. "—molested."

Another pause so long that Sherry thought she had gotten a bad connection. Then the old man said, "You were the pretty one, weren't you? The one who wrote the notes. You were prettier than Shirley Temple, weren't you? Even the teachers remarked on it."

What was she supposed to say to that?

"Some things have been happening to my daughter; I need to know where Ray Innis might be now."

"Now? Oh, who would know that now? He left

under a cloud—I sent out letters, he wasn't going to get another job in Michigan, I sent out letters everywhere I could." Suddenly the old man cackled. "He got his house set afire, that's what happened to him! Singed him out of there without hardly a stitch to his back, that's what they did! Ran him out! The dirty child molester! Told him if he even came back for his clothes they'd get him— Oh, ho! That's what we did!"

"A fire? There was a fire?" Sherry said stupidly.

"There sure as hell was. Near burned the whole house down, too, whoever did it. Near burned that woman out—what was her name, Dietz? A widow, trying to make ends meet, a nice lady as I recall. Lucky she had insurance."

Sherry felt shock wash over her. Why hadn't she known about the fire? But her mother had kept her at home all summer long, until school started in the fall. Besides, hadn't she repressed it all? She hadn't wanted to remember any of this. She had wiped her mind clean of it.

She forced her lips around the question. "Have you any idea, any idea at all, where Ray Innis might have gone after he left Hartwick?"

"He had family in California. San Diego, San Mateo, someplace like that. Who knows where? I didn't pay attention. He was a pretty boy, for a while I thought he was queer but I guess he wasn't, was he? Maybe he went to the Vietnam war," the principal added suddenly. "He was always afraid of that. Maybe he got drafted and sent to 'Nam, maybe that's what happened to him. Maybe they put his name on that new War Memorial they're talking about now, that big long black fence in Washington, D.C., with all the names."

Sherry felt a shiver. "No," she said. "I don't think so. He's alive."

"Molesters, they never quit," the man remarked in his deep, phlegmy voice. "They move from city to city, they might get put in jail but then they move on again, they don't stop. They can be seventy-five years old and they don't stop. We should have tarred and feathered him that day. We should have got out a branding iron and stamped him in red right on the forehead.''

Sherry hung up, her hand pushing the receiver into the phone with a violent motion as if that might stop the sound of the grainy old voice with its warning.

Her heart looped and clenched. Ray Innis had been a young teacher then, in his early thirties. Which would make him in his early fifties now.

Fifty wasn't that old.

Fifty was still vigorous, and a man did not have to be that strong in order to overpower a twelve-year-old . . .

At home, dressing for her date with Glen Dietz, Sherry felt a tension headache begin to pound in her temples. She took three Tylenol, washing them down with tap water so chilly it nearly formed ice. She thought of calling Dr. Frey, to spill out all her anxiety and get a little comfort.

Then she rejected the idea. How could Dr. Frey help? By reminding Sherry that she had repressed a lot of the facts involved in the case?

Well, Sherry already knew that. She'd gotten more proof during her phone call with Elton Powers. But she was finding things out now, she was starting to learn what had really happened. Like the butterfly pin. She'd remembered that today, too. More details were going to come back, and she didn't need Nanette Frey to make that happen. What she did need was exposure to people who had been there during that time. That was what had triggered her memory of the butterfly—Judy's screams.

She rummaged in her closet, dismayed at the

choices it offered. All her clothes dated from her "married" era, holding memories of Dick locked in their threads like cigarette smoke. Finally she pulled out a black knit dress with a paisley jacket she had bought several years ago. She would wear a locket with it that once had belonged to her grandmother.

Glen was ten minutes early, catching Sherry still in her stocking feet, pawing through her small jewelry box, looking for a bracelet that might complement the locket. Hearing the doorbell made her heart jump, and she slammed the jewelry box shut so quickly that its lid pinched her fingertip.

Sucking her fingertip, she ran to her closet and frantically sorted through the clutter of boots and running shoes at the back.

The bell rang impatiently.

"All right, all right," she muttered. She jammed her feet into a pair of black pumps, realizing at the last minute that they were too tight. She hardly ever wore high heels; she supposed her feet had spread from too many years of ski boots. Why had she agreed to this? She felt about as glamorous as a contestant at a hog-calling competition.

The bell buzzed again, and she hurried to answer the door.

"You're scowling, Sherry. This is supposed to be a date. This is supposed to be fun," Glen said as he negotiated the "trail," his speed about twice what Sherry would have driven on the winding driveway. His headlights picked out ivory flakes glimmering on laden pine branches.

"Careful," Sherry said.

"I'm being careful, I've got front-wheel drive. And snow tires. And chains in the trunk if I need them. I believe in preparedness." But Glen said it affably. "You look gorgeous tonight," he added.

"In a three-year-old dress that I wore with my ex-husband?"

"You mean you didn't rush out and buy something new?"

"I buy from catalogs," she admitted. "And I hate high heels, these are so tight my feet feel like sausages."

Glen laughed, as if she'd said something witty. Sherry squirmed, wishing she hadn't been so blunt. This was her first date in fourteen years. You were supposed to patter along with small talk, drawing the man out with questions and making him feel important. Mentioning your feet was very low on the list of preferred topics.

Anyway, that was how dating had been when she was twenty-two, and she wondered if all the old rules still applied now that she was thirty-six. She forced herself to lean back against the headrest of Glen's blue Land Rover. She was so nervous she felt sick. And if he made a pass at her, she was going to refuse him, firmly and finally.

Glen chatted away, listing the three restaurants in town that were possibilities for dinner: the Holiday Inn, the Quality Inn, and Mario's, a little Italian bistro run by Joe Fox, the larger share of his business being the bar with giant-sized TV set. Sherry now wished she'd specified Midland or Traverse City, where most Hartwickians went for a night on the town.

"Which will it be?" Glen wanted to know. "Since you want to stay in town, I mean? Prime rib, prime rib, or spaghetti?"

He made her sound like a bumpkin. Sherry's nervous stomach clenched still tighter. This was a man who'd lived in New York, where fabulous restaurants were legion.

She said defiantly, "You decide. I guess we folks here in Hartwick don't have your New York gourmet tastes, but we don't charge one hundred dollars for a meal either."

"Hey, hey, I grew up here, too, remember? And I chose to come back. So give me a break, will you, and stop treating me as if I were some kind of jet-set jerk."

She made a sound of denial.

They were on the main road now, passing a few homes set back in the woods, nothing but squares of yellow light and a drift of chimney steam.

"Cold tonight," Glen said.

"Four above, I think," Sherry mumbled.

"Long-john weather, isn't it?"

"Right."

Then they drove for ten or fifteen minutes in silence, passing the homes of several people that Sherry knew, including that of Dr. Frey. As they went by, Sherry couldn't help glancing at the office window over the garage. It was lit, and Sherry could see candles flickering. She wondered if Dr. Frey was working late, or just listening to her stereo.

She realized that she was driving along with a stranger, really. No matter what he said, Glen wasn't a Hartwick man anymore, he was a sophisticated city person who'd only come back here to pursue some citified fantasy about getting back to "basics." Basics in Hartwick were economic survival, not woodsy idylls.

"Pretty, isn't it?" Glen said.

Startled, Sherry realized that they had just pulled over the rise that led into town. Hartwick lay spread before them, a carpet of twinkling lights, steam rising from chimneys, a magic, Chagall village of friendliness and happiness.

"Yes," she reluctantly agreed. "I see it so often—this road is the only way into town for me—I guess I forget how pretty it can be."

"It's God's country," Glen said.

Without asking her, he drove to the Holiday Inn and pulled into its parking lot, which was crowded with cars and vans. "I made reservations," he said.

"Here? But I thought you said—I thought we didn't know which restaurant we were going to."

"I gambled and made reservations here," Glen admitted. "I didn't want us to have to stand in line like peons. Besides—I wanted our date to be special."

She didn't know what to say.

"Are you surprised?" His eyes smiled into hers. "We have a few things to catch up on and I wanted to get started."

As she followed the hostess to their table, Glen behind her, Sherry felt like an impostor. Glen was saying all the right things, and he was certainly handsome enough; already several women in the room had turned their heads to assess him as they walked past. But to her he was too suave, too big-city, too confident in assuming that his sexual powers were working with her.

Or was it just that she was having a bad case of the jitters, both from it being a first date and the things she knew she was going to have to ask him?

By the time they were seated, and had ordered drinks, Sherry felt herself slip into a foul mood. She didn't want to be on a date with Glen. Now she was stuck the whole evening, and would have to banter with him, parry his romantic overtures, and at the same time quiz him on Ray Innis.

They ordered the Surf and Turf, and talked about New York and the various celebrities Glen had photographed: Tom Brokaw, Sam Shepard, Madonna, Janet Dailey, Carol Channing, models Paulina and Cindy Crawford.

Sherry pushed back her irritation. "Well, the biggest celebrity we've ever gotten here in Hartwick is a stunt man for Sly Stallone. His parents come from Rogers City and he stopped by once last year for a hamburger on his way north. They wrote it up in the *Hartwick Chronicle*, he took ketchup and a big slice of red onion."

"I'm sorry," Glen had the grace to say. "I guess I've been name-dropping."

She looked him in the eye. "We're just ordinary people here in Hartwick; I hope you won't find us too boring."

"Sherry, Sherry, will you just relax and try to enjoy this? You act like I'm the enemy instead of a man you almost married—what, is it twenty years ago?"

"Fifteen." She picked up her water glass and stared into its crystal depths. "It never would have worked with us."

"Why not? How can you be so sure? We were so damn young, that was all, and I was commitment phobic. But if I'd been able to get over that—we had a lot in common, Sherry."

She examined the glass minutely, the droplets of condensation running down its sides. "What? What did we have in common?"

"Why—we were smart and bright and full of the joy of life, Sherry, and we both liked the outdoors, and we both skied, and we liked sailing . . ."

"Attributes any two twenty-one-year-old kids can have together." She heard the sharp tone in her voice and wondered what it was about him that jarred her—sparks had flown between them from the moment they'd met again in Glen's photography studio. Or maybe it was just her own fear, she told herself.

"Okay, okay," he said, smiling. He reached across the table to lay his hand over hers. "We were two young kids who didn't know what we wanted—now is now. Let's spend some time together, enjoy doing some things. We can go skiing if you want. We'll drive over to Boyne Mountain, you can check out the competition. You do still ski, don't you?"

She had to laugh, unwilling as the moment of humor was. "Yes, I still ski. Glen, I'll go skiing with you on one condition. Will you talk about what happened with Ray Innis in the seventh grade? The man lived at your house. You saw him every day, not in school but in a home situation. I need to know what he was like. Where he might have gone afterward, what happened to him."

Glen let her hand drop. "Whew," he said.

"Please, Glen."

"I was only a twelve-year-old kid, I was a hell of a lot more interested in getting my mom to buy me a ten-speed bike than I was in some guy who rented a room from us."

"Still, you must have seen something—"

He shook his head. "My memories are poor. I don't have good recall, Sherry, never did. A few things, a camping trip I took in Boy Scouts, my grandmother's funeral—those are the kind of things I remember."

She was bitterly disappointed. "But he lived at your house."

"Upstairs," Glen said. "He lived on the third floor. He had a separate entrance. He never came in our part of the house except to pay his rent; my mother didn't give him kitchen privileges. She wanted to pretend we didn't have to do that. She kept all the roomers at a distance."

"Oh."

"I can show you the room if you want—my mother still has the house, you know. Of course, the room was plastered and painted after the fire and the furniture's not the same."

She felt her heart turn over. "Could I? Could I see?"

"There won't be anything to look at. Sherry, don't you think you're being kind of obsessive about this? I mean, it's ridiculous to start playing detective on something that happened when Elvis Presley was still alive."

"Now why would you say that?" she retorted angrily. "What does Elvis Presley have to do with it? I want to see the house, Glen. Please show me the house."

# CHAPTER 19

Glen's mother lived in another of the old mansions, the paint on its gingerbread trim amazingly intact. It had been painted several times, Sherry guessed. But always the same white. In fact, it looked just as it had in 1965. Lights burned in a first-floor apartment, behind Nottingham lace curtains.

"It's after midnight. Are you sure your mother won't mind talking to us at this hour?" Sherry questioned.

"She's an insomniac," Glen said.

"Is this where you live?"

"Me?" Glen's grin showed white in the darkness as he pulled into a narrow driveway and switched off his motor. "I'm renting a house out near the state forest. I do pay her taxes every year, though— her social-security check is pretty small, and you can't ask much for rooms here in Hartwick."

As Glen helped her out of the car, Sherry's high

heel skidded in the snow, and she had to clutch his arm to avoid falling. His forearm was muscular, bespeaking hours, no doubt, spent working out in some big-city gym or racquet club.

Ruth Dietz greeted them with a spate of nonstop chatter. "Well, Glen! And Sherry! How long has it been since I've seen you, Sherry? At least a year. Wherever are your boots, you're going to slip on my walk and break a bone. I don't know why women like those high spike heels, it seems plain suicidal to me. Of course, I have foot trouble so I have to wear Hush Puppies, with a plastic orthotic—"

"Mother," Glen said.

"Oh—" Mrs. Dietz seemed flustered. She was a small woman with wavy silver hair and the sad, sweet face of an aging Southern belle. She wore a sweatshirt that said *Hartwick Art Fest*, and loose blue jeans, her feet encased in corduroy slippers. "Come in, come in, won't you? I can give you some ginger ale. Or grape juice, I have frozen Welch's—"

They took seats in a sitting room filled with memorabilia and an extensive collection of Franklin Mint commemorative plates. A television set was showing a color-tinted movie, *Million Dollar Legs*, with Betty Grable.

"Oh, turn that thing down," Mrs. Dietz said, hurrying toward the kitchen, her movements those of a woman fifteen years younger. "Blare, blare, blare, I just keep it on so I won't have to listen to the sound of the wind. I've got a loose shutter in back and it's driving me cuckoo."

"Mother, Sherry wants to see the room that Ray Innis rented," Glen said as his mother returned with three ginger ales.

Ruth Dietz began handing out glasses. "Mind now, I think I filled them a bit too full. Ray Innis, goodness. I remember that fire, it could have ruined me. Thank God I had insurance and there wasn't any serious structural damage. Why would you want to see his room, honey?''

Sherry explained, seeing the way Glen looked impatient as she repeated her theory that the pornographic videos had something to do with the long-ago scandal.

"Oh, goodness," Mrs. Dietz said. "That was *so* long ago. I've kept that room rented, I don't know how many people have been in and out of it. All of the furniture is new since Ray, of course—it all got burned in the fire. There's nothing there. Except for the attic, of course. He did have some boxes stored up there, I let him have the storage space, and he never took them with him."

He had stored things in the attic.

Sherry felt her heart leap. Her eyes met Glen's in triumph. This whole evening was going to be worth it.

"Could we see the boxes?"

"If you don't mind spiderwebs."

Mrs. Dietz led the way up two flights of stairs to an attic that, she explained, still contained junk dating from 1949, when she and her husband bought the house from the original owners. It was a pack rat's paradise, filled with a mind-boggling array of boxes, bags, crates, old suitcases, and garbage bags. These last contained, Ruth explained, possessions of roomers that had been left.

"I label everything, I'm not going to be accused of being a thief, I've saved it all. There," she added. "At the end near the window, those cardboard boxes. Those were Ray's. You step down there and get them, Glen, I don't want to get dust all over me. You'll see that I've labeled them. He could come back today and find everything just as he left it."

The attic, lit by two hanging forty-watt bulbs, was cold, frost rimed on the insides of the row of windows that faced the street. There was a feeling of lost lives and decay. What if there was a clue here?

Sherry felt her throat close, and her stomach clenched with tension. Boxes that he had left!

Mrs. Dietz went back downstairs, and Sherry followed Glen down a narrow aisle that gave walking space between the junk.

There were three of the boxes, themselves curios now, time-worn cardboard that once had held Dreft soap. Each carton was marked with an old luggage tag carefully printed with a real fountain pen, not ballpoint. *Ray Innis, Teacher, July 17, 1965,* was what Glen's mother had written.

"My God," Sherry whispered. She stared at the boxes, feeling a sense of old time creep over her. It was like being in a graveyard, it was like exhuming a grave, she thought, swallowing. This wasn't exciting at all—it was somehow terrifying. In the dim light from the naked bulb overhead, the boxes looked menacing, as if they might actually open one and discover a desiccated hand, or grinning skulls.

"I think— Can we take them out into the hall? Into the light? It's lighter out there," Sherry suggested.

Glen eyed the boxes in distaste, kicking at a gray, trailing hank of spiderweb that looked exactly like a stage prop. "I'm allergic to dust. Don't you think you're being a little ridiculous, Sherry? What could possibly be in these boxes? Some guy's dirty undershorts, probably. My mother packs up everything, even the toothbrush, she's thorough."

"But she said he gave her the boxes to store. So anything could be in them." Sherry bent over, and, careless of her black dress, hefted up the first box, which, by the feel of it, held books. A pungent, sour smell of mold rose from the box. Its cardboard was gritty with dust, and more spiderwebs trailed nastily from it.

She lugged the box out through the path, trying not to breathe in its stench.

Glen stood and watched while she carried all three boxes into the landing that opened onto the attic. "Jesus," he said as she set down the last one, from which the rolled-up body of some dead insect dropped.

"Thanks for your help," Sherry said sarcastically, wiping the dust and some stray webs off her dress. She knelt down by the first one, pulling at the yellowed twine that still wrapped it. It came away in her fingers, fraying with rot, and she let out a small cry as one of the flaps of cardboard came popping up.

"Books," Glen said.

Inside were rows of old Book of the Month Club editions, biology and mathematics textbooks, many whitened at the edges with mildew. Sherry poked gingerly among them, discovering one book titled *Otto of the Silver Hand*.

"Open the other boxes," Glen ordered.

"In a minute—I want to see if there are any names or addresses inside the covers."

"There won't be. And if there are, they're going to be twenty-five years old. Come on, Sherry, you can go through these later, at home. My mother will let you take them if you promise to bring them back."

Sherry knelt by the second box, fumbling with its twine, which was less rotted and more difficult to break. This box contained clothing: woolen shirts now peppered with moth holes, a quilt stitched out of squares of Civil War–era satin and velvet, and what looked to be a World War I uniform, badly faded.

Sherry eyed the mementos, all obviously family treasures Innis had dragged along with him on his travels. It made the man seem human. Even vulnerable. And she realized as she shoved the box away and reached for the last one, she didn't want to think of him in that way. Because then she might begin to feel sorry for him.

As soon as she opened the last box, she knew she

had made a discovery. This one contained stacks of what appeared to be photo albums, children's school notebooks, and loose pieces of paper, many scribbled with the large, careful, loopy handwriting of the prepubescent girl.

"Glen." She sat back on her heels, her heart beginning to thud in swift knocks that slammed at her chest wall.

*Letters.*

Were any of them her own?

With a trembling hand she reached out and took one of the bits of notebook paper that had been folded childishly into eighths.

The brittle paper seemed almost glued together by mold and water stains. But at last she had the letter unfolded. *I like you. Nancy.*

"Love letters," Glen said, reading over her shoulder. "He probably collected them. He's probably got yours in there, Sherry; everyone said you wrote him letters, too. And I'll bet anything those albums have nudie pictures in them. This is the jackpot, all right. Only trouble is these things are a little old, aren't they?"

She turned to stare at Glen, at the careless expression on his face as he cut with his words at the fabric of her childhood, of her very life. Suddenly she was shaking, her whole body trembling, her throat raw with dust.

"Nudie pictures! How can you talk like that! You disgust me!" She reached for the box and slammed the cardboard flaps shut. "Help me carry these down to the car, will you? If it isn't too much for you, if you don't think you might get *spiderwebs* on your nice clothes."

"Sherry—"

But already she was sorry she had snapped at him. He was insensitive, but most men showed some insensitivity, and besides, she needed Glen. He had lived in the same house with Ray Innis,

there might be more clues he could unearth, she
would be calculating enough to use him.

She forced her tone into apology. "I'll go through
these boxes when I get home. Thank your mother
for me, will you? I'll return them to her when I'm
done."

As a further act of amends, she brushed off all
three boxes with a rag she found inside the attic
door, so they could carry them downstairs without
soiling their clothes.

After Glen had left, Sherry carried the third box
into her utility room and sat cross-legged on the
floor, trying to get up her nerve to open the box
again. Her radio was turned up, emulating Ruth
Dietz, to provide defense against the eerie hollow-
ness of a house on a winter night. It had to be after
2:00 and she knew she'd never get to sleep until she
had done this.

*Were* there really "nudie" pictures in here, as
Glen had suggested? My God, might she even see
pictures of Carole or Judy?

The thought chilled her, and even worse was the
prospect of discovering one of the letters she herself had written to the man. It would be like coming
upon a photograph of yourself taken inside a public rest-room stall. Not only a violation of your privacy, but also a revelation of an ugly part of
yourself, a part of which you felt ashamed.

*Go on*, she urged herself. *Isn't this box why you
really went out with Glen? And now that he isn't
here to act superior, you haven't any more guts.*

She decided to begin with the school notebooks,
and leafed through them, puzzled, finding books
that belonged to girls with fifties names like Diane,
Sandy, Debbie, and Kathy. Perfectly ordinary notebooks, as far as she could tell, containing seventh
and eighth grade essays on flowers, respiration, and
other similar topics. Had Ray Innis been so ob-

sessed with these girls that he had preserved their notebooks as mementos?

Then, turning to the back of one of the cardboard end covers, she discovered the penciled note in an obviously adult hand.

> *Just peaking, she has little hard breasts that excite my fingertips, the pink nobs so beautiful, I want her always as she is, I want to see her eyes glaze with lovely excitement as I open up her budding flower and taste its petals . . .*

Sickened, Sherry pushed the notebook away.

Was he talking about what she thought he was talking about? Oral sex? *Oral sex with an eleven- or twelve-year-old?*

She felt her insides heave. She sat rigid, forcing the sensation back. She could *not* get sick—not now, when this was so important. She could not fail Kady with her lack of courage.

She sat with her eyes shut, realizing that the radio was playing "Islands in the Stream" by Kenny Rogers. She'd been so absorbed in these horrible boxes she hadn't even heard it. She wished she could be on some island in the sun. Far, far away from all this horror and tension. She didn't want to face this. It cut too close to the crevasse at the center of her, the guilt.

But then Kady's face floated in front of her, and after a minute she reached for the box again. She had brought these boxes home, where was her courage? She could not help Kady if she could not bring herself to look at these things. Maybe there were names, an address book, some clue to a city Innis might have gone to live in.

Gingerly she picked up one of the albums, and, opening it, gasped with horror. It was pasted with dozens of grainy, black-and-white postcards that

showed naked little girls in a variety of poses. One
dark-skinned girl thrust out her bare buttocks in a
Betty Grable–type pose. Two girls licked each other's breasts. A chubby blond child sat with legs
spraddled wide, revealing the innocent, hairless
cleft. None of the girls could be more than twelve,
and there were several who seemed to be as young
as six.

Six years old. That was first grade.

She slumped down, defeated, tears stinging her
eyelids. This man—this man with vileness in his
brain, this monster of a man—was after *her* child.
She couldn't look through the box. This was terrible, she couldn't do it. Any of those girls on the
postcards could be Kady.

She stumbled to her feet and found a couple of
large Hefty lawn bags. She stuffed the cartons inside, strapping them shut with duct tape and stor-
ing them in the garage behind several bags of Weed
and Feed she had bought last fall. Whatever happened, Kady mustn't find these boxes.

And then, just as she was shoving the last box
behind the bag of fertilizer, she had an attack of
self-disgust.

Who was she to feel fear when it was *Kady* who
was twelve years old, target for this man. Prey for
him, tender prey, just as it had said in the title of
that first, horrible videotape. Sherry ripped apart
the garbage bag and reopened the carton again.

# CHAPTER 20

Sherry's dream was of the letters she had found in the box, on one of which Innis had written his own remarks. Now in the dream his voice whispered, over and over, *nipple buds ready to burst with life and joy . . . nipple buds ready to burst with . . .* Then she was clawing through the box, finding a wadded-up handkerchief that contained something like dried, yellowish glue. The glue came alive in her hands like semen, its smell so realistic that Sherry woke from her dream trembling and sick.

She lay under the covers, taking deep breaths, listening to the pounding of her heart. The worst part of the dreams was the feeling of total helplessness. No power, no *control* over something vile and sexual that was about to happen to her.

My God, what time was it? She sat up and gazed at her alarm clock in shock. One o'clock in the afternoon! She hadn't slept this late since she was a teenager. No wonder she felt enervated and out of sync. Half the day was done.

She sagged back down onto the pillow again, rubbing her temples where a headache throbbed. In only a few hours, she'd have to go and pick up Kady. She lay curled in a ball, narrowing herself to the warm hollow in the blankets heated by her body. Images of the girls on the postcards swirled in her mind.

Fifties porn.

Why, those postcards were probably collectibles now. Doubt shook her. Maybe Dr. Frey was, after all, right. Maybe her mind was playing tricks, projecting material from the past onto the present.

The telephone rang. Sherry extended an arm toward the bedside phone, noticing that she still wore her blouse from last night. She squirmed in self-disgust. She had even slept in her clothes.

"Hello?" She had to clear her throat to say the word.

"Did I wake you up?"

"Glen?" Suddenly the world came crashing back. "Oh, Lord—I've got to be at Timberline—I haven't even called them—and I have to pick up Kady at four!"

"You sound cute when you're sleepy."

"I'm grumpy when I'm sleepy."

Still holding the receiver, she slid out of the covers. The cold air of the room hit her skin, raising goose bumps. Stretching out the long phone cord, she managed to get to her dresser drawer. She held the receiver under her chin while she rummaged for a clean bra and panties.

Glen said, "Hey, it's Sunday. Call Timberline and tell them you're not coming in today. I'm going to take you over to Traverse City and we're going to have a decent lunch."

"Glen, I have to work."

"You work too much," Glen pronounced. "You've

got managers over there, people who could fill in.
Come on, there's a new Szechuan place, I've heard
it's pretty good."

"I'm not some kind of a socialite who can drop
everything and drive sixty miles away on a whim.
I have obligations."

"Okay." The disappointment in his voice sounded
real. "I do care about you, you know, Sherry."

"Do you?"

There was a pause. "You spent half the night
looking through those boxes, didn't you?"

"I did look at them."

"And you still think I might have had something
to do with those videotapes, don't you?"

"No."

"That's the trouble, isn't it? You don't trust me.
You were so tense last night—you think *I* might
have sent those filthy tapes to Kady."

"*No* . . . I— Really . . ."

Over the wire his voice came clear and crisp and
faintly hard. "I didn't send Kady those tapes. I'd
like to know who did it just as much as you would—
if not more so, since it's my reputation at stake,
too. I'll pledge my business to you, Sherry."

"What?"

"I'll pledge my whole goddamned business to you
if I'm the guilty one, my goddamned studio. Will
that satisfy you? I can't think of anything more to
pledge. I pulled up stakes in New York; I came here
to Hartwick because I want to earn my living here
and *I don't have any goddamned reason for sending
your daughter dirty videos.*"

"Glen." Sherry was embarrassed now.

"So will you lay off me, Sherry, and can we try
to be friends? We might have been married once,
you know. We could have been husband and wife.
We'd have been married, what, sixteen years? Kady
would have been *our* kid, not Dick Vincent's."

Uneasily Sherry clutched the small bundle of

clothes to herself. Surely Glen couldn't want her now, after all this time, and the diverging paths both of their lives had taken. He was now a sophisticated New Yorker, she a provincial north woods dweller. Neither of them were the same. And she no longer really trusted men, Dick had scarred her irrevocably.

"But we weren't married," she pointed out. "And I really do have to get in to Timberline. Look, Glen, I'm sorry you thought I might have thought—I mean—"

"It's okay," he said. "I left something for you on the hall table last night. For you and Kady."

"For us?"

"Just go and open it."

After she hung up, Sherry wrapped a bathrobe around herself and went barefoot out to the hallway. On the small mirror table rested two large envelopes, each printed with the logo of Dietz's. The address labels, she couldn't help noticing, were typed.

"Oh!" Kady said that night, running to the hall table. "What are these? Are these for us? Did these envelopes come in the mail?"

"Glen left them. They're valentines, I guess."

"But it's early, it isn't even Valentine's Day yet. Can I open mine?" Kady was already snatching at hers, like the twelve-year-old she was.

Sherry wished she had put the two envelopes away. "Oh, all right," she said reluctantly.

Kady tore hers open to find a black-and-white enlargement of herself, not a sexy photo this time but a portrait that showed her laughing, girlish and unguarded, hair tangled back from her fine, broad forehead.

"It's *me*," Kady squealed, and Sherry came over to examine the photograph, which must have been one of the rejects taken that day Kady had posed for the model portfolio. However, this was a natural picture, not posed, that captured the young zest of the girl, her smile lucent. It was an apology, she realized.

"It's a pretty picture," she conceded.

"And there's a valentine, too," Kady said, fumbling in the envelope again. She pulled out a card that was all sophistication and high gloss, a photo of a heart-shaped cake with one wedge cut out of it. *Sweetness* was the message inside and then Glen's scrawled signature.

Sherry frowned at the card, not liking it as well as she had the picture. She'd have felt more comfortable if he'd sent her daughter a card with kitties and heart candies and lace.

Kady had already lost interest in the card, and was after Sherry's envelope now. "Can I open yours?"

"I guess."

The picture had been placed inside a photo-mailer cardboard, and this inside a cardboard frame. Kady's agile fingers poked and pried at tape that bound the two together, and then the tape was free and the girl held up a black-and-white, smiling face.

"Who's that?"

"Let me see it."

"Is that you, Mom? You look like me," Kady said wonderingly. "We're like twins."

Sherry stared at the photograph, both entranced and frightened. It was herself at age eleven or twelve, the detail obviously enlarged from some group photograph, for she could see shapes of other children in the background, made grainy by the enlargement. There she was, with the same wide-spaced eyes and achingly young smile as Kady, the same tilt of chin and mass of untidy hair. And the eyes, shiny with innocence.

It was this girl who had written puppy-love letters to Ray Innis and been responsible for a riverside picnic that had changed four lives.

An attached card said, *Found this at my mother's house, thought you might like it. You and Kady are a matched pair. Glen.*

Sherry tossed the card into the wicker wastebasket near the desk.

"Mom? You threw that card away."

"There's no law that says I have to keep it."

"But the card has flowers and lace—"

"You have it then," Sherry said shortly. She turned to go into the kitchen, feelings roiling in her. Damn Glen anyway, she wasn't sure she wanted a romance with him. She wasn't ready, and even if she had been, she wondered if it was Glen she'd choose. Her tastes at twenty-one certainly weren't the ones she had now as a thirty-six-year-old adult.

She decided to call Dr. Frey as soon as Kady went in to watch TV.

Dr. Nanette Frey was expecting a patient, someone she had agreed to see on a Sunday because of a complicated work schedule, but the patient was now thirty minutes late, and was having ambivalence over treatment. Waiting, she busied herself putting some papers into the fireproof safe she kept near the entrance, putting several records, which needed case notes, into the in-basket she used for this purpose.

She returned to glance through a book she had just ordered, *Silent Screams and Hidden Cries: An Interpretation of Artwork by Children From Violent Homes.* Outside her window, snow dotted the night, blowing in lacy white vortexes. Car headlights flared yellow in the darkness, illuminating a dancing whirl of specks before it swept past and was gone. It was the first car that had come by in thirty minutes, Nanette realized.

She didn't think she would ever get used to the

vacantness up here, the vast tracts of land with nothing on them except forest, not the city kind of trees you might see in Central Park, but tangled secondary growth so thick in places that branches acted like barbed wire, actually blocking access.

And the cold, she would never accept that either, the bitter ten-degrees-below-zero mornings when you walked outside and breathed air that seared your nasal tissues like dry ice.

She moved restlessly, going over to the window and pulling the miniblinds down against the night. Once the idea of a village like Hartwick had been enchanting, a place where a therapist could really have an influence. To be the only practicing psychologist in a radius of thirty-five miles, to enjoy rural peace, birds singing outside her office window instead of taxi horns blaring.

Now they both were going to have to face it, she was not cut out for such isolation, and there was no decent library for hundreds of miles, even Detroit lacked the kind she had been used to in New York. As far as she was concerned, the pathetic little one-room collection of volumes that Hartwick called a library did not even count. She had decided to go back to New York. She wondered what Bob would say to her ultimatum and if her marriage would survive it. They had sold everything to come here, they had both agreed on it, and now she was the one chickening out.

The phone rang, and she picked it up on the second ring, wondering if it was her tardy patient.

"Hello?"

"It's me, Sherry Vincent. I'm sorry to interrupt you, Kady is watching TV now and I had some time— Dr. Frey, I'm confused about some things," Sherry Vincent began.

"I have time," Nanette said. "What is it, Sherry?"

She listened to Sherry's story of finding the boxes in the Dietz attic on Saturday night. "I see. And you're absolutely sure they belonged to Ray Innis?"

"Glen's mother labeled the boxes. Dr. Frey, am I crazy to be thinking these things? Glen, Carole, my mother, Detective Arrington, everyone has told me it all happened so long ago. And the boxes," Sherry's voice dropped. "They did look so old. And the postcards were practically antiques."

"Sherry, I can't tell you what to believe. Maybe your mind is connecting two matters that don't belong together. Or maybe it is telling you something else. You do know that the right side of our brain is a very complex mechanism that processes materials not available to our conscious mind. It examines all the evidence that comes before us, even evidence we might not consciously hear or see or remember."

The wire was silent while Sherry absorbed this. "I've felt so—so—" She seemed to struggle for the right word. "Like I wasn't being rational."

"Thought processes can't be readily cataloged," Nanette agreed. "And not all of them are rational, as we think of it. But that's okay. Hunches and intuition, that's what we call that looser kind of thinking."

"Oh—"

"We have to learn to trust, Sherry. Trust in our feelings and our instincts." Just then Nanette heard the ringing of the downstairs bell. "Sorry to interrupt, but I have a patient arriving. Call me again if you have any more problems to discuss. Otherwise I'll see you tomorrow for our regular appointment."

Nanette hung up, frowning as she made her usual clean sweep of her desk, putting case records away. Something about her conversation with Sherry had put her senses on edge, prickling her skin. The mind was so complex. People lived lifetimes without facing everything there was to know about themselves. She did not know anyone, including herself, who could face everything unblinkingly.

Something had alarmed her in her conversation with Sherry.

But what was it? Why did her stomach suddenly begin to tighten, a little pulse of warning beating in her neck?

She heard footsteps, then her office door opened. The patient who entered did so with a curiously tense gait, striding across her office to choose the peach-colored lounger, flopping into it, and then staring at her with moist eyes.

"I wasn't going to come tonight, and then I did. I—I've been so torn up, so depressed, I feel like I'm going to blow up."

Nanette's pulse quickened a little with anticipation. After several months of hard work, it looked like tonight might be a breakthrough.

"Mom?" Kady said as they were sitting in the kitchen waiting for microwave popcorn. "Mom, why are you acting funny?"

"Acting funny?"

"I heard you on the phone. You were asking someone if they thought you were crazy."

"Oh, Kadydid—"

Kady's eyes filled with tears. "I don't want you to be all worried, I don't want bad things to be happening, I don't like them."

Sherry reached forward and rubbed her daughter's young, pliant shoulder. "Nothing bad is going to happen, I promise."

"I don't like bad things," Kady repeated, staring down into her lap.

"Hey, pumpkin, the popcorn is done, listen to the pops, I'd say it's about finished. Are we going to melt butter?"

"Okay," Kady said, listlessly reaching for the microwave door.

"Kady, is something going on that I don't know about? Did something happen when you were over at Maura's?"

"No!" her daughter suddenly cried out, slamming the microwave door shut and leaving the puffed bag of popcorn still inside.

Alarmed, Sherry ran after her. "Kady! Kady, what's wrong?"

"Nothing! Nothing is wrong! You're always asking me! You're always tired or you're upset about something and you're always leaving me with Maura! You're acting like Maura's my babysitter, Mom. Don't you want me home anymore? Or do you just want to go out all the time?"

"*Kady,*" Sherry said, horrified.

Her daughter's face was red with rage. "Grandma says that you don't want me to have a modeling career because you're selfish! You don't want me to go to New York; you don't want me to have anything good, or to be prettier than you are!"

By now they were in the doorway that led to Kady's bedroom, Kady backed up against the door upon which had been taped a poster of Michael Jackson.

"I can't believe you really said that," Sherry said quietly.

"You don't want me to be pretty! Grandma said so!"

"Let me tell you something, Kady Ann Vincent." Sherry was angry, her voice low and vibrating. "I am your mother and I love you more than anyone or anything on this earth. I've made decisions on your behalf because I felt that the world of modeling in New York would steal away your girlhood. Kady, it would force you into behaving like a grown woman when you aren't even a teenager yet—you are only twelve years old. As for the rest, it doesn't matter whether or not *I* want you to be pretty. You are, you're more than that, you are a very beautiful

girl. But if you think that's all it takes to make it
in this world, you are very much mistaken. Sure,
people like a pretty person—for about five minutes.
But if she isn't nice inside, if she behaves in an ugly
way, if she hurts other people—they won't think
she's pretty for very long!"

Kady had begun to sag against the poster, tears
runneling down her cheeks.

"It's just the snowmobiler," she sobbed.

"What snowmobiler?"

"The man—the one who came chasing after me!
He—he chased me in the woods and made me wet
my pants! I was like a baby, he made me into a
baby." Kady turned and leaned into the door frame,
sobbing.

"Kady, oh, Kadydid." Sherry felt a stab of love
and horror, her knees weakening under her as if
someone had hit her in the back of her legs. "When
did this happen?"

Blue eyes, swimming in tears, accused her. "I
don't know, a couple days ago. You were busy,
Mom—you're always so busy—"

At the accusation, Sherry felt the blood leave her
skin, turning it white. My God, she had neglected
her daughter. All this time she had been trying to
deal with the nightmare of those videos, and Ray
Innis, and instead she had hurt Kady. Her child had
been scared and worried, and she had shipped her
off to Maura's.

Guilty, she was guilty, a mother who hadn't done
her job. But what was she supposed to do, how *was*
she supposed to handle this? She was only one person; she had a ski resort to run; she hadn't wanted
to scare Kady by dragging her into the Ray Innis
thing.

"Kady, if you ever see that snowmobiler again, I
want you to tell me. Call me up at Timberline if
you have to, or even call the Sheriff's office. The
number is on that decal right on the telephone."

"What if he comes when you're not *here*?"

"Then—" Sherry fought for control. But, my God, she couldn't panic, Kady would totally freak. What should she do, what could she? Timberline was a business burden she had taken on, its pressures would not go away simply because she had home problems. Without Timberline, they had no means of support.

"Then we'll take you over to Grandma's for a visit," Sherry decided. "You can take the bus to school from there, and Grandma'll be home all day, and it's right in the village, so you won't have to worry about snowmobilers. At least it's safe."

Kady wailed, "Mom ... Grandma doesn't have good *food*, she never buys stuff like popcorn, and she never has Pepsi, she always drinks tea, ugh! And she watches *60 Minutes* all the time, and she tries to make me do needlepointing— She makes me do this *project*—"

"You're going, Kady. It's only for a couple weeks. You can take Pepsi with you; you can take half the pantry if you want to."

"A couple *weeks*? I won't, Mom! I hate going with Grandma that long! It's desertion," Kady yelled. "You're just dumping me on her because you—"

Sherry raised her hand and realized she had almost slapped her daughter's face. She stopped in time, appalled.

"I'm doing it because I love you," she snapped. "It's time for bed, Kady, go brush your teeth. I'll drive you over tomorrow. And now I'm going to take a shower—I'm beat."

Kady's eyes flashed rebelliously, but something in Sherry's stance made her think twice, and meekly she did as she was told.

# CHAPTER 21

Snowflakes tapped on the window, and somewhere in the walls a joist snapped. Nanette Frey sank back in her desk chair, listening to the sounds on the stairs as her patient left. Yes, there was the ring of the bell she'd attached to the door, and the muffled slam. A motor started up in the parking lot, revved briefly, then began to fade away on the road.

Gone, thank God.

Despite the chill of the office, Nanette wiped away droplets of clammy perspiration that had begun to form on her forehead during the last thirty minutes of the session.

It had been a breakthrough, all right. She had let the session go on for almost ninety minutes as it all poured out—the stresses, anger, guilt.

She sat trying to calm herself, willing her rapid heartbeat back to normal. She had not suspected. The depression had seemed mild, although apparently of long standing. They had been working on childhood events; an alcoholic father and co-alcoholic mother, fairly routine material for most therapists, nothing remarkable.

Then suddenly a dream of the patient's had triggered the revelation. There had been not just psychic trauma, but actual . . . crimes.

She got up abruptly and began to pace the office. With shaking hands, she lit the vanilla candles, breathing in their calming aroma. She was furious at herself. She prided herself on her perception, and an almost psychic ability to grasp the "essence" of each patient. With this one, she should have known, should have guessed— Why hadn't she?

Because she was complacent, she castigated herself, because she was lax, and because she was used to practicing in New York, where people's problems didn't overlap, where her patients didn't all know one another, didn't possess lives so wrapped and woven, one into the other.

What was she going to do now?

She could still hear the ragged voice, sobbing out a story of hate and desire—

A story that affected others here in Hartwick.

God, she hated Hartwick! Because it was directly facing her with a problem of ethics, and a decision to make. A child involved—Kady Vincent. Oh, God, God! Nanette actually felt her eyes burn from tears of anger. It wasn't fair that she should be faced with a decision like this. She was too tired for it, she wasn't ready.

She almost started downstairs to go and talk this out with Bob, but the movement died even before it had begun. She didn't share her caseload with her husband. First, her patients' problems were private, it would have been a breach of ethics. But even if she had wanted to tonight, Bob was working late at his office, researching a case against the Department of Natural Resources.

Sherry Vincent's instincts had been accurate.

Somehow her mind had leaped over facts and come to the essential truth.

Nanette paced for a while, stopping to peer out of the curtains, then jerk them closed again, shutting out the winter night. She would make her case notes, she decided. Maybe the act of writing would allow her to catalog her thoughts and help with the decision.

It was after she had been writing for about forty minutes that Nanette first became aware of the snowmobile motor noise. It made a pass and was gone. It really did not impinge on her conscious awareness. Their neighbors on each side owned several machines; and they had grown accustomed to snowmobilers who used the shoulder of the road.

She closed the case record, pushed away her ballpoint pen, and sighed. She carried liability insurance, and she had recently added to her coverage. Before, she hadn't known the facts, but now she did, and either way she was in trouble. If she did *not* tell, harm could happen. But if she did, she might be liable for a lawsuit.

A lawsuit could wreck her.

*I'm tired*, she said to herself. *I'm tired of being a repository for other people's agony, because pain rubs off, and I absorb some of it, I take it into my brain and it hurts me, too.*

She reached out for her telephone and dialed Sherry Vincent's number. Kady answered, her voice pure and sweet and young.

Nanette found her voice. "Is your mother there?"

The girl sounded edgy, maybe she and her mother had been fighting about something. "She's in the shower."

"Oh . . . Well, could you tell her to call me right back? It's important. This is Dr. Frey—my number is 825–9611. I think your mother has it."

"Okay," the girl said.

"Have you got a pencil, can you write that down?"

"I can remember," Kady said, and then Nanette heard the click of the phone as the girl hung up. She sat listening to the dial tone.

Half an hour later, Sherry had not called back. Nanette had turned her stereo up to a compact disc she particularly liked, Mannheim Steamroller, trilling piano notes and water-droplet, grotto sounds. The music made her feel as if she had been transported away somewhere, soothing some of her anxiety.

She was lying on the patients' couch now, and had taken a bottle of Bailey's Irish Cream out of her bottom desk drawer. She wasn't a drinker but she did love Bailey's, and somehow it seemed to soothe the butterflies in her stomach, the apprehension that seemed to be building in her, growing logarithmically. As soon as Sherry called back, she decided, she was going to go downstairs and to bed.

Outdoors, she heard the snowmobile motor again. One motor, its whine insistent. In fact, it seemed to be right outside in their yard. A vague alarm pricked her. Hadn't Sherry complained of a snowmobiler buzzing their property?

Nanette got up and went to the stereo, where she fed in a new disc, and then she checked the lock on her office door, returning to enjoy more Steamroller, this time with monks singing a cappella, straight out of the twelfth century. She lay back down on the couch and took another sip of Bailey's.

She must have dozed off for a few minutes, for a sound awoke her. A popping sound, like potatoes exploding in the oven.

Uneasily she got up and walked across the room to her door, noting with surprise that the door handle was hot.

That was very odd. If there was one flaw her of-

fice had, located as it was over the garage, it was
that it was too cold. In fact, she had had to install
a quartz heater that she used sometimes when the
temperature got below zero.

She stared at it, wishing the Bailey's hadn't
fuzzed her mind. Why would her doorknob be hot?
Now that was a very good question. Nanette froze
as an answer came to her. Maybe there was a fire.

*Oh, but no*, she thought, beginning to be frightened. Surely she'd had too much to drink, or some
kind of a weird dream while she was dozing. Finally, to settle it, she reached for the handle and
pulled open the door.

She was met with a wall of flame.

Nanette stood paralyzed for a second, unable to
take it in or to realize that it was real. How could
it be? But then the heat pushed her back, and now
she could hear popping sounds down below as
fluids stored in the garage began to explode. The
heat was so intense that it was like leaning into an
oven set on broil—only worse, eight times worse
than that.

She backed inside the office, away from it.

It was real, all right . . . Jesus, the fire leaped after her like an animal, spilling into the room with
orange-blue, licking tongues.

"Bob!" she screamed for her husband, and staggered backward, falling against the couch and trip-
ping, but catching herself again. She ran to the far
side of the studio where a small window overlooked the parking area. The little vanilla candles
still burned, their flames flattened by the wind-force
of the larger blaze.

How could it all have happened so *fast*? She
watched, horrified, as the fire billowed after her,
almost alive in its ferocity. Almost before she could
scream again, it overran her oak file cabinets, her

bookcase, the couch, her desk, igniting papers like firecrackers, blowing others away.

She had read once about the way a fire could explode through a house in seconds, but it had never meant anything until now. She was going to have to try to escape through the window—it was her only exit, for the fire had blocked the other, larger pair of windows to her right.

Thank God, there was a straight chair beneath the window. She jumped on it and began yanking at the sliding casement. It resisted, frozen shut by grit, paint, and frozen moisture. This house had been eighteen years old when they bought it. Had the former owner ever opened this window, even in summer? She never had. And now it was her only way out.

She jerked at the metal slide, hammering at it desperately, the metal lock cutting her fingers. But the window would not give. Panic flooded her, and somewhere beneath it, amazement that this could be happening at all.

Only a minute ago she had been lying on the couch drinking Bailey's and listening to her stereo.

Behind her, the fire breathed red, its heat searing. She picked up a ceramic lamp and hammered at the window, finally breaking out one of the two panes. The ceramic broke and her fist went right through the glass, blood spraying.

*Bob*, she screamed.

The heat, the smoke . . .

She used the inner part of the lamp to pound out the glass; she didn't even feel it as broken glass lacerated her fingers, slicing off the little finger on her left hand at the second knuckle. When the glass was partially free she thrust herself into the space, jamming herself against the now red-hot metal edges of the casement. There was no air anymore, only heat that she sucked into her lungs.

Through a haze of alcohol and terror, she realized her fate. She was too large to fit through the window! Her shoulders were wedged in the narrow aperture, blocked by the metal edges of the sliding casement. Screaming, Nanette twisted herself, jamming her body farther into the frame. But shove as she might, she was a size-fourteen woman trying to fit into a size-three space.

She hung there, sobbing. The garage below her was on fire, and she heard more popping sounds, saw papers go flying into the night. Desperately she jammed herself into the window frame, unaware of the pain as she dislocated her right shoulder.

Still she would not fit.

Flames had found her, climbing up the chair legs, climbing up Nanette's good wool slacks. Heat sucked at her and she felt her hair crinkle alight. She breathed heat now, flames tore down her throat, searing her insides.

She screamed and screamed, stretching her arms through the jagged glass, toward the snow that could never cool her.

# CHAPTER 22

Sherry woke up the next morning with a headache already in full grip. The night had been full of snowmobile motors, or was that only her imagination? Whatever the sounds were, they hadn't come close to the house and she hadn't really wakened, sensing the sounds only on a subliminal level.

Still, she was feeling a tightness in her stomach, a fluttering unease as if something were about to happen.

She woke Kady and hurried around the house, getting her daughter ready to take over to her mother's. She had talked to Margaret last night; her mother had agreed to take Kady as long as was needed.

"Of course she might get bored living with an old fogey," Margaret had added. "I'll have to try to keep her busy."

"I'll come over and see her every night," Sherry had promised. "And she can go over to Maura's as often as she wants to, but Maura's mother has to be home, I don't want them there alone. And, Mom, no more talking about Kady modeling. I mean that. I want you to promise me."

"You know I don't pressure her," her mother had said aggrievedly.

"I don't want you brainwashing her; I mean it. She is *not* going to be a model. And I want you to stop telling her how pretty she is."

"All right, but I don't know what you're so upset about. She'd have to be blind not to know what she looks like. Are you going to pack her some decent clothes to wear? I might want to take her out to eat, and she'll need something besides those jeans she wears."

"Okay." Sherry had sighed, knowing she really had little choice right now. Maura's parents both worked and she could not park her daughter on another family for weeks on end, nice as the Camracks were.

Now she hurried through the house in winter darkness, urging Kady to get a move on, rummaging through her daughter's closet for a couple of outfits her mother would consider acceptable. She filled several grocery sacks with Kady's favorite snacks and the Pepsi she was addicted to.

"I don't want to go to Grandma's," Kady grumbled over a dish of cereal. There was a red blanket mark across her left cheek. Even so her beauty was breathtaking, the shape of her mouth a perfect pink pout. It sometimes scared Sherry to see her daughter objectively, the way others did.

"It's only for a while. And I'll come and take you skiing," Sherry promised.

"It's the middle of *powder* season, Mom, it's the best skiing time," her daughter griped. "Grandma hates skiing, she thinks I'll break something."

Sherry pushed back a stab of annoyance at the fickleness of twelve-year-olds, who saw all reality only as it related to their immediate needs. "Kady," she said. "Have you forgotten why we're doing this? It's because of that snowmobiler. And those dirty videotapes we received," Sherry added, deciding to be blunt. "It isn't any time to leave a young girl alone in the house. And I want you to be extra careful at Grandma's, too. Don't stay in the house alone, even for a couple of minutes."

"I'm not a *baby*," Kady protested.

"No, but that has nothing to do with it. Do what I tell you, Kady—and do what Grandma tells you, too. This isn't just a game we're playing."

"I know," her daughter said, sobered.

"Okay; now, I've got a weekend bag packed for you, plus a couple of dressier outfits so Grandma can take you out to dinner. If you want to take any books, or stuffed animals or anything, please get them. I want you to pick up after yourself, Kady, not just throw your clothes around your room the way you do here."

"I will."

"What's this?" Sherry added, noticing a scrap of paper lying near the telephone.

Kady was standing on tiptoe, rummaging through the kitchen cupboard in search of another box of cereal. "Oh, that's from the call last night. I wrote down the number."

"Dr. Frey called here? Why didn't you tell me last night?"

"You were in the shower and then I forgot. I guess it's important, she said. Mom . . . can we take some cereal over to Grandma's?"

"Kady . . ." But then Sherry decided not to scold her daughter about forgetting the message. "Oh, all right, you can bring cereal." Sherry made a mental note to call her therapist. "Hurry now, Kady, will you? I don't want to be late."

\* \* \*

They headed down the road to town, caught behind a double truck trailer hauling pigs. Pink, hairy eyes and snouts stuck out of open slats, the truck emitting a ripe aroma. While Kady exclaimed and felt sorry for the pigs, Sherry chafed at the delay. She hoped her mother would be up and prepared for this twelve-year-old invasion of her privacy.

There was only a bare hint of dawn in the eastern sky. This was the bitter time of the day, when steam rose eerily from chimneys and car batteries froze up, when depressing thoughts could overtake you, saturating your mind with blackness.

Someone had sent pornography to her child and now was tormenting her, chasing her down with a snowmobile. What would happen next? Would there be more unpleasant surprises, each more frightening than the last?

Sherry mentally planned her day. The first thing she would do, she decided, once she reached Timberline, would be to report the snowmobiler to the Sheriff's office. She should have done that right away, except she'd thought the driver merely another joyrider.

She had wasted so much time in futile questioning and in making assumptions!

They reached the curve by Dr. Frey's house, and automatically Sherry's glance slid toward the house with its big, attached garage and studio office. She'd be back here later in the day, for her appointment.

Her eyes stopped. Even before the sight fully registered on her brain, her breath caught, her pulse choking as if a scarf were tightened around her neck, strangling the blood supply to her arteries.

She slowed her car, her headlights picking up the burned-out wreck of what had once been Dr. Frey's office, all of it collapsed now into blackened and twisted pieces of wood and metal. Part of the house itself was still intact, but at least one room, the one nearest the garage, was badly damaged. Crisscross tracks across the yard and huge puddles of frozen water marked where the village fire truck had fought the blaze.

Horror flooded her. Dr. Frey!

"Mom?" Kady had seen it, too. "A fire, Mom—look at the fire."

"Oh, no," Sherry whispered. "Oh, no, oh, no."

It must have happened hours ago—last night. There wasn't even any smoke in the wreckage now; it was all absolutely still and dead. A corpse of a building where once there had been a haven, a place where Sherry had gone to be shriven of her guilt and doubt and fear.

She braked, her tires skidding on the snow-slick road, causing the vehicle to spin.

"Mom . . . it's all burned *up*," Kady said in horror.

As soon as the car stopped, Sherry yanked open her car door. She went running and stumbling across the welter of tire tracks and footprints. Details jumped out at her, a piece of cloth on the ground that might have come from Dr. Frey's couch, the coating of filth and ashes that stained the snow, trampled into it with hundreds of footprints.

She came to a halt at the place where the stairs to Dr. Frey's office once had been.

*Rubble.*

Unrecognizable hunks of wood and bits of blackened wiring and melted-down objects that made Sherry want to turn aside and vomit. Through a huge, cavernous, blackened opening she could see the wreckage of what once must have been a car parked in the garage below. Now it was twisted, the paint black and disfigured, upholstery shriveled. Even in the freezing temperature, the stench of burned plastic and cloth was sickening.

No one could have lived through this. Sherry stood breathing deeply, fighting nausea. Dr. Frey—where was Dr. Frey? Maybe she'd gotten out. Maybe

she and her husband hadn't been here during the
fire.

"Mom— Mom—" Kady pulled at her anxiously.

"Stand back," Sherry snapped. "It might be dangerous."

Kady's face was white, twisted with the fright of
a child who has stumbled upon ugly, adult reality.
"I was just *looking*. Do you think . . . Mom? Do you
think . . ." But Kady, seeing Sherry's expression,
closed her mouth.

"I don't know," Sherry said grimly. "Come on—
we'll go to the neighbor's."

But as it turned out, they didn't have to, for as
they started back to their car, a Chrysler LeBaron
came pulling erratically down the road. It turned
into the fire truck–rutted driveway, stopping with
a jerk, as if the driver was not fully comprehending
of what he did.

A man was at the wheel and Sherry recognized
Nanette's husband. When she had seen Bob Frey
once at the A & P store, Sherry had thought him a
good-looking man of fifty, in appearance resem-
bling Donald Sutherland. But Bob Frey was almost
unrecognizable now, his complexion yellow, the lips
almost blue. Even from a distance, the eyes had the
dark-ringed, blasted-away look of the bereaved.

Dr. Frey was dead, she had to be. Sherry did not
need an official announcement, one look at this dev-
astated man was more than enough. But how? How
had it happened?

Bob Frey made no effort to get out of his car
and go into the part of the house that still looked
livable. He simply sat, his arms crossed on the
steering wheel, head bent. Sherry knew she was intruding but some force set her walking toward the
car, her feet slipping on the frozen, grayish chunks
of water.

"Bob? Bob Frey?"

Sherry began to wonder if he had even heard her.

Then he lifted his head and stared at her, his expression dulled.

"Yes?"

"I'm sorry," Sherry choked. "I'm one of her patients. How—how did it happen? Does anyone know?"

Bob Frey shook his head. "Who knows? She used to burn candles up there. Or arson, they're looking for that, too. It could be anything. I've been at the funeral home." He swallowed, gazed at her with eyes that looked flayed and raw.

It wasn't right for anyone else to see this pain. "I'm so sorry," Sherry said.

"She died trying to get out of the window," Bob Frey suddenly said. "They found her hanging there, stuck in the window, she must have been alive through it all, she must have felt herself burning."

By the time they started to town again, it was light, the horizon washed with baby pink and lilac. A few clouds suggested more snow later in the day. Already cars were driving past the Frey home, gawkers out to see where a woman had burned to death. Sherry's hands shook as she held the steering wheel.

*Arson.*

Hartwick was not a village where such things happened. There had been no arson in town since—

But that was so long ago, Sherry told herself in a flux of nerves, remembering the fire Elton Powers had told her about, the fire set in Ray Innis's room.

Frightened, she pushed the thought away. She could really terrify herself if she tried—and there was Kady to think about, a badly shaken Kady who sat curled in a ball in the passenger seat, staring silently out of the window.

They reached her mother's house to find Margaret Smith already up, full of garrulous speculation about the fire. It seemed that Maida Thomas's son was a fireman who had helped to put out the blaze. The village "telegraph" had already been at work, far swifter than any TV news update.

Kady didn't want Sherry to leave, and at the last minute clung to her mother like a six-year-old, begging to go with her. "Take me out of school! Take me to Timberline with you! I'll work in the cafeteria line, I'll make hamburgers, Mom, I'll sell lift tickets. I can make change, I'm as good with money as Becky Trimble is!"

"Kady, you know I can't do that. It's a school day," Sherry said through stiff lips. She wondered if that was exactly what she *should* do, keep her daughter close to her, or even take her away somewhere. But where could they go, and how long must they stay? Must she lose her livelihood over this? She refused to allow a faceless person to turn her life into fear.

Anyway, it was only nerves that made her think Dr. Frey's death and the 1965 fire were connected.

"She'll be all right, dear," Margaret Smith assured her. "I'm going to make her some breakfast, we'll have Belgian waffles, I've bought a new waffle iron."

"I won't be able to eat," Kady said, huge blue eyes swimming in tears.

Sherry steeled herself. "Kady, Kadydid, you're going to be all right with Grandma, and I'll come by tonight and see you. You can see your friends every day and ride the bus with them, too."

Kady had always complained that none of her friends rode the same bus she did. Now her daughter sobbed as if her heart would break. "I don't care . . . I want you . . ."

"Now you just stop that right now," Margaret Smith said in a voice that Sherry remembered from her own childhood. "Just put that nasty fire right out of your mind, don't think about it, Kady. Just tell your mind to shut it off, turn it off, stop. You don't have to think about bad things."

"Mom—" Sherry began uneasily, not even sure what she wanted to say.

"She shouldn't be dwelling on things, Sherry, it isn't healthy. That's what I always told you. Just put the bad things away where they can't hurt you. Never think about them and pretty soon they won't exist at all."

# CHAPTER 23

At school, Kady heard the girls talking about the fire.

"And she was burned up to a crisp, you couldn't even recognize her face!" Heather Wycoff, who lived next door to the Freys, held court in the girls' locker room, flushed with importance.

"Oh, gross!" shrieked the other girls. They were changing into their gym shorts, milling around the crowded locker room that smelled of damp towels and chlorine bleach.

"It's true, my dad saw it," Heather insisted. "We heard the fire trucks and everything and my dad went down there. It was just a horrible sight, he said, she was just hanging out the window all burnt up. And her husband came back from town and drove in the driveway and saw her like that, and he went running up to the house. He was screaming and yelling just terrible, my dad said, and then the ambulance came and they had a hard time taking her away because she was so—"

"That *is* gross," Kady interrupted in a muffled voice, bending down to stuff her jeans in the bottom of the locker she shared with three others. She wiggled into her running shorts, pulling them up over her hips.

"Well, my dad knows the paramedics, and they said—"

"I don't care what they said," Kady snapped. "Why do you talk like that, Heather? You just love talking about bad things, don't you? The grosser the better."

The other girls giggled nervously.

"I don't," Heather said indignantly. "I can't help it if we live down the road from the Freys. I can't help it if my dad went down there, and, hey, I've got to walk right past there on my way back from the bus stop."

Kady grabbed her gym T-shirt and pulled it over her head, wishing she could stop Heather's voice. She felt sick just thinking about the burned wreckage, the horrible smell of ashes. She remembered meeting Nanette Frey several times, once at the drugstore, another time at Karpen's, buying some slacks. She had been just a middle-aged lady, but her eyes had been very blue, and she had told Kady about a ski trip she and her husband once made to Zermatt.

Kady couldn't believe that an ordinary person, a woman she herself had actually seen and talked to, could have turned into a charred, blackened—thing. Things like that didn't happen. Ever since that snowmobiler had chased her into the woods like she was an animal, she'd been having these scared feelings.

Like, maybe life was not all safe and good and kind, the way she'd been brought up to think it was.

Horrible things existed. They did happen to people just like her and her mother.

"Do you think their house is going to be haunted now?" asked one of the other girls, Erin Shuttle.

"Sure it is," Heather pronounced with authority. "No matter what they do to that place, whether they rebuild it or what, her ghost is going to be in there, crying and moaning and wandering around. That's what ghosts always do, ghosts don't know they're dead and that's why they're ghosts."

"There *aren't* ghosts," Kady said.

"There are, my dad saw one once when he was in England in the service, he said all those old castles over there are haunted, and once he—"

"Is that all you can talk about, your dad, your dad?"

"Sure, my dad. You haven't got a dad anymore, do you, Kady? Your folks got a divorce and now you're a broken family. And what I hear, your dad's got all kinds of women, he has affairs with women. Sick, that's what I think it is, having affairs is immoral, and your dad is—"

"My dad is better than your dad ever will be!" Kady cried. Tears starting in her eyes, she slammed her locker door shut, snapping the combination lock in place. She rushed out of the locker room, pushing her way past the girls who were gathered around Heather enjoying the excitement.

Why had she ever thought Heather was her friend? Heather didn't know what she was talking about. Her dad did have girlfriends, okay, Kady would admit that, but not affairs. "Affairs" were sinful, "affairs" were what the characters had on *Days of Our Lives* and *One Life to Live*.

She ran into the gym where a couple of girls sat on the bleachers, waiting for the teacher who was fussing with a tape player, selecting music for their aerobics unit. As she ran onto the polished floor, her shoes gave a loud squeak.

The teacher, Mrs. Weeks, looked up. She had an angular face wrinkled from years of daily summer golf games. "Kady Vincent, are you coming onto the gym floor in your street shoes?"

Kady looked down at her feet. "These are my Reeboks."

"They may well be, but they have been out in the mud and dirt and this is a brand-new gym; the taxpayers sunk a lot of money into this new gym floor. I don't think they'll appreciate you putting a lot of scratch marks on their floor. Go back in and get your gym shoes, Kady."

One of the girls giggled, and Kady felt her eyes moisten with tears again. "Reeboks are Reeboks," she said. "These are just like what I have in the locker. They're identical *twins*."

Mrs. Weeks finished with the tape player, and suddenly "Twist and Shout" blasted into the air, its rhythm echoed and reechoed by the acoustics of the gym. The teacher gestured with her thumb toward the locker room, indicating Kady was to go there. Then she turned to speak to one of the other girls, ignoring Kady.

Kady felt slapped and rejected, more so than if the teacher had spoken harshly to her. She wasn't even worth speaking to, she was just an annoyance.

She opened her mouth to say something defiant, then the words died in her throat. What good would it do? She'd end up in the principal's office, over a pair of stupid gym shoes. She had never sat in the principal's office in her life; in fact, next year she was going to be one of the office helpers, and answer phones.

Silently she went back to her locker, reopened it, took out her clean Reeboks, sat down, and yanked them on. Nobody paid any attention to her. Heather was in the bathroom area, and the rest of the girls were now hurrying past her toward the gym door, the topic of the fire completely forgotten.

Kady finished the laces, then slumped down on the bench, watching the others as they pushed and jostled to get out. Suddenly she felt about five years old than they were, weary with all of her knowledge. Dr. Frey. And the video, the naked girls who had been just the ages of her and her friends.

Bad things happened all the time, the realization came flooding in to her. They did happen to regular people and they happened to kids, too. And you didn't get any choice whatsoever.

Word of the fire had traveled to Timberline, and as Sherry got herself a doughnut from the cafeteria line she could hear her staff talk of nothing else.

"Her arms were stretched out the window," Becky Trimble was saying. "Just stretched out like a cry for help, they said, just a cry for help."

"Oh, *sick*," said Kimberley Waller, a chubby eighteen-year-old on her first job as cashier. "My dad drove past the house and it looked like a bomb hit it; he said he never seen anything that bad before; it looked like somebody set it to him."

"You mean set it on fire?" put in Bob Nisinby, the chair-lift operator, already in his outdoor gear.

"Yeah, why not?" questioned Kimberley. "Like, maybe somebody came around that house with a match and just broke in one of the windows and stuck the match in."

"They'd need an awful long match," scoffed Becky.

"Well, they got long fireplace matches, don't they? We got them at home, we use them all the time, they light up with this glowy stuff, it's s'posed to look pretty."

"Hey, a fire set with a match couldn't fry a person that quick," Becky said. "A match fire gives you time to get out. She was sealed *in*, she didn't have time to run out or she would of. I think it was gas. Someone just took a gas can and poured—"

"For God's *sake*," Sherry said, her throat tightening over the bite of doughnut she had taken. "Will you people stop? Nobody said there was arson, and until they do, I'm going to believe it was an accident. It's 8:55 by my watch. That means we have five minutes until the chair opens. Aren't you supposed to be selling tickets, Becky? And, Bob, you have five minutes, it'll take you that long to get down the hill."

"Yo," her lift operator said, draining his coffee.

As her staff dispersed, Sherry prowled restlessly around the table area, where skiers still lingered over hot cocoa. Brooding, she stopped to stare out at the wintry day. Then she decided the hell with it—Timberline could limp along for an hour without her, she needed to drive to Grayling and report the snowmobiler to the Sheriff's office.

Forty minutes later, she was sitting in Arrington's office, cradling what must be her fifth cup of coffee of the morning. Arrington, too, had a half-empty cup on his desktop and, by the masses of paperwork stacked in front of him, had already been working for hours. His dark-blond hair was rumpled, and he looked tired.

"This person has been harassing us on a snowmobile," she told him. "Buzzing past our windows, chasing Kady into the woods, scaring her, making me scared, too. In fact, I've taken my daughter to my mother's for a few days." She gave him Kady's version of what had happened.

"What sort of machine was he driving?"

"Kady didn't—she didn't remember. She was too scared really to look—we're not professional police people, Mr. Arrington."

Gray eyes studied her. "You didn't examine the tracks?"

"How could I? She didn't tell me right away. The snow filled most of them in. As for the time I saw him . . ." Embarrassed, Sherry let her voice trail away. She had not even looked at the track marks.

"Has he done any damage, other than trespassing? Made any threats of any kind? Actually physically touched you or your daughter?"

"No, of course he hasn't. Look, I know this seems like small potatoes to you. I mean, this isn't a murder or anything, but my daughter did receive those videos and now this is happening with the snowmobiler and to us it's important."

"You're not just a number to us." He gave her a dry, quick smile that crinkled the lines that fanned out from his eyes. "And we are working on the case—I've already notified the postal service and they have taken the tapes you gave me and the wrappers and they're analyzing them. They're also investigating RAM Productions. But the process takes time, Sherry, and now you are complaining about a snowmobiler."

She bristled. He was beginning to make her sound like a hysteric. "Maybe it's the same person!"

"Maybe; but we've been getting a bunch of snowmobile complaints this year. Kids trespassing on property, running over shrubbery, making noise, breaking into summer cottages, having parties in the woods, and so forth. Odds are they haven't specially selected you out, you're just a coincidental victim."

She ran her tongue over her lips. "Fine; then what are we supposed to do? We live out at Higgins Lake. By the time I call the Sheriff's car and it gets here, the person can be long gone. As for tracks, you know as well as I do that it's ridiculous to try to identify tracks. They're all about fifteen inches wide, the track design looks about the same."

He nodded. "If you'd like, I'll have a patrol car drive by your property. Meanwhile, if the guy comes back I do want you to avoid walking on the tracks or messing them up: I'll come out and look at them."

She knew he was doing that just to placate her. What was she to say: that this would do absolutely no good? He was trying anyway, and she was lucky to get that.

"Okay," she finally said, gathering up her purse.

"And I'd like to come out and talk to your daughter, see if there's anything going on we should know about."

"I told you, she's only twelve years old."

"It's procedure."

Chilled by the word, Sherry slumped in her chair and finally nodded. "But there isn't anything that Kady can tell you. She's just a normal seventh grader." She gave Arrington her mother's phone number and told him not to come until she could be there, too.

The rest of the day at work, Sherry did budgets and payroll. Try as she might, she could not push the sight of Dr. Frey's burned studio out of her mind. She struggled with tax tables and a calculator, and finally pushed them aside to stare out of her window. Poor Dr. Frey. How had it felt to burn alive, to feel your own skin blackening? The woman had become a human torch. *God.*

She shuddered. Maybe it was a betrayal of Nanette Frey, but she just could not think about the way she had died, it was too terrifying. She forced her thoughts into something she could handle better, the person who had been harassing them.

A business was more than just a form of income, she reflected, it was an eighteen-hour-a-day commitment. Mentally she damned the person who had disrupted their lives. Maybe that was what they really wanted—to terrify her so much that she abandoned her business or went bankrupt.

Maybe Dick was doing it, the thought occurred

to her. He'd been angry when the judge awarded
her the ski resort. But she still could not believe he
would have a part in this. She had lived with him
too long, she knew his flaws and they did not include tormenting his own child.

*I'm not going to let another person do this to me*,
she thought, squeezing her pen so hard that it
nearly jumped out of her fingers. *I just won't. I'll
protect my daughter and I'll take care of my business, too.*

At 4:00 Sherry left Timberline and drove to her
mother's, where she found Kady sprawled in the
guest bedroom, lying on the floor with her feet
propped up on the edge of the bed, a long telephone
cord trailing out behind her. The dresser top was
crowded with the items Kady had brought with her:
stacks of Sweet Valley High paperbacks, *Seventeen*
magazine, and several of the little Pound Puppies
she had received for Christmas.

Her daughter, engrossed in a long conversation
with Maura, barely looked up.

"Kady!"

The girl waved to her, giggling at something
Maura said.

"Kadydid—"

Sherry stood in the doorway. The last time she'd
seen her, Kady had been teary-eyed, begging to
work the cafeteria line so she could be at Sherry's
side. Now here she was, apparently absorbed in her
friends and not needing Sherry at all.

"Kady!"

" 'Bye, Maura." Kady hung up the telephone, getting to her feet in one graceful, fluid line of motion.
But as soon as Maura was off the line, Kady's expression drooped. "Hi, Mom. Are we going out for
pizza? Is that why you stopped by?"

"Pizza? Oh, Kady—"

Her daughter's face crumpled still further. With
a pang Sherry realized that Kady's skin looked un-

usually pale tonight, and there were subtle violet tinges under her eyes.

Sherry felt her heart tear, and immediately she abandoned any plans of going back to Timberline for the next two hours. "Okay, sweetheart, but I think Grandma is going to be disappointed. Anyway, you're going to have a caller; that's one reason I came by. I want you to talk to Detective Arrington."

"Who?"

"The detective who's working on our case."

"I don't want to," Kady said, her brow puckering.

What was it with twelve-year-olds, why were they so contrary, their personalities constantly shifting, their emotions always volatile? "Why not? He's trying to help us."

Kady scowled. "Because I'm *not* some police drama, Mom, and you're not either." Tears started to roll down her cheeks. "We don't belong with all those bad things, Mom, and I won't talk to him. I don't like him and I won't do it."

"But he's just trying to find out who that snowmobiler was, the one who's been terrifying you."

Kady stood rigid, her hands clenched in fists at her hips. She was almost as tall as Sherry and in this moment, Sherry could see the adult woman she would be. "I hate it!" she burst out. "Dr. Frey died and Heather laughed about her and said she was going to be a ghost, and I am *not* going to talk to that detective because I am *tired* of all of this, I don't want any more bad things, and that's *final*!"

Twenty minutes later, when Arrington arrived, Sherry could not shake her stubborn daughter, and so she had to go down to her mother's sitting room, where Arrington sat in a needlepointed chair, staring at the gallery of photographs on the wall.

She told him Kady refused to talk to him.

"I know you can make her, I know that's your

prerogative, but I'd rather you didn't. She's had a lot of hurt recently. Our divorce is barely final, and those videos scared her. Now this snowmobiler, and the fire out at Dr. Frey's— She was with me when we drove past it, and it really shook her up. I'll talk to her myself and tell you what she says."

He nodded. "I understand. But, Sherry, I want you to realize something. We don't know who this guy is and we don't know what he's going to do. Some of these sex offenders can be pretty kinky and ugly. They fantasize, only their fantasies would make us sick. Don't leave your daughter alone. Not even for a minute."

He hadn't spoken to her this vehemently before. Sherry took a step backward, her throat tightening with alarm.

"There's something I didn't tell you, Sherry. This afternoon I got a call from the FBI. They did find out a couple things about that outfit that made the videos, RAM Productions."

"Yes?" Her heart was hammering. "What about them?"

"They operate out of Mexico. Someplace near Ensenada, we think. They kidnap young wetback girls, illegal aliens trying to get to this country; they drug them and force them into sexual acts. Make the videos, smuggle them to the United States, sell them."

She forced back her shock, so intense that she felt it reverberate in her chest. "But the girls in those videos, they weren't all Mexican."

Arrington spoke in a low, tight voice. "I believe, Sherry, that they are now also making videotapes here in the United States. We don't know where, or who, or anything about it. But one girl on the tape has been identified as a thirteen-year-old from Sarasota, Florida. She'd been missing for three weeks."

Sherry tried to imagine a mother identifying her daughter on video, seeing the degradation in full, hideous color. You would always be haunted by that nightmare, you would never recuperate. Even the idea of it caused her muscles to go weak.

"And this girl . . . was she found . . . alive?"

"She's never been found, Sherry. I'm sorry."

# CHAPTER 24

Dr. Frey's memorial service on Wednesday was a draining experience, with Bob Frey so chalky-faced that Sherry thought he was going to pass out. Her remains, ironically, had been cremated, and Frey said he was going to scatter the ashes in the Adirondacks, where he and Nanette had first met.

The sparse group of out-of-town relatives, a sister and several friends, seemed stunned and disbelieving. There seemed to be no children: apparently the Freys were childless, as Sherry had surmised. Sherry was relieved when the service was finally over, and she could escape to her car.

Dusk had already settled, and wind blew from the north, picking up surface snow and swirling it across the road. Still in a bleak mood, she switched on her car radio and fiddled with the dial until she found an Anne Murray tune. The Canadian singer's voice filled the car with cool, sweet harmony, driving away the worst of the funeral and death thoughts.

Driving back out from town, Sherry was forced to pass Dr. Frey's again. She tried not to look. Still, her eyes seemed to swivel toward the left without her volition. The sight of the burned-out garage and office was still a shocker.

Startled, she saw that Bob Frey's car was parked at the end of the driveway. He must have just pulled in. Wavering lights showed in the windows of the house, as if he were in there using a flashlight. The electricity was out, she realized, and would be until the house was repaired. What would he do? Sell and get out? She knew she certainly would. And why hadn't he gone to a motel?

Anne Murray sang of love and sorrow. Passing around the next curve, the shivers that had overtaken her at the sight of the house began to abate a little and Sherry lifted her foot from the gas pedal. She remembered Dr. Frey's phone message and wondered what it had been about. Kady had said "important." Too important to wait until their next session?

Mentally Sherry began replaying her last telephone conversation with Dr. Frey.

*We have to learn to trust, Sherry. Trust in our feelings and our instincts.*

A pause, the sound of ringing in the background, a bell.

*Sorry to interrupt, but I have a patient arriving. Call me again if you have any more problems . . .*

Another patient.

Someone else . . . Could that possibly be significant?

Another patient and then Dr. Frey had phoned again later, saying it was important. Sherry's hands tightened on the wheel, her mind worrying at the riddle. Could those two things be connected? Could

Dr. Frey have wanted to tell her something about *the other patient?*

She found herself slowing the car, her mind jumping around with possibilities. She and Dr. Frey had talked about the stuff she'd found in the Dietz's attic. Then the patient. Then the phone message.

*No*, she told herself. *You're being ridiculous. She wouldn't have talked to me about another patient— would she?*

She pulled into the driveway of a farmhouse and turned around, heading her car back toward the Freys'.

She parked at the end of the driveway behind Bob's car. Immediately after she pulled to a stop, trepidation seized her. Bob Frey was a man in shock, in deep mourning. He'd just come from his wife's funeral. She'd be intruding in the worst way.

*But a child is at stake here*, she told herself, and steeled herself to get out of the car. *And she would have wanted me to help Kady, that was why she called, I know it was.*

Arctic wind flapped at the dark gray skirt she wore, penetrating through layers of wool and polyester slip. She made her way up the drive, her tall dress boots slipping on icy patches. She rang the bell, and then she remembered that the electricity was out.

She banged on the door with her gloved fist, and finally he answered it, staring at her in surprise.

"Mrs. Vincent?" She didn't register with him. She could have been an encyclopedia salesman, not someone who had attended his wife's funeral only an hour ago. He wore a ski parka over his dark suit, a scarf around his neck. His breath steamed out in white clouds from his mouth, and Sherry realized that he was still very dazed.

"I came to see how you are," she told him, "and to be honest, I came to ask you some things. My daughter is in danger, Mr. Frey, she has been targeted by a sex offender, and I think there might be a clue here."

He shook his head heavily. "I don't know what I can do. I have office hours, if you want to come in next week . . . Call my secretary."

He started to close the door, and Sherry lunged forward. "No! Please! I know this is inconvenient, but please!"

"What?"

"This isn't a legal matter. Your wife called me the night she died. She had something she wanted to tell me. She told my daughter it was very important."

"I still don't know what I can do. She's dead. I wasn't privy to the matters from her practice, we kept that completely separate. I'm trying to find her papers and then I'm moving to a motel." He moved to close the door again, his eyes bleary from crying and lack of sleep.

"Please! You must let me in! You have to talk to me," Sherry pleaded. "Just for a few minutes, I beg of you. I have a twelve-year-old daughter. She's a beautiful girl, she's my only child. Your wife had something to tell me, she called me at 11:00 at night, and I have to find out why."

Reluctantly the man stepped aside to let her in. "Watch it," he said. "Don't trip on anything. All I've got is a flashlight. And it's cold as hell in here, all the pipes have frozen, it's going to take months to repair this house. I'm going to put it on the market," he added bitterly.

"I'm sorry," she said.

"You were at the funeral, weren't you?"

"Yes." Sherry stood awkwardly, looking around. The living room had been heavily smoke damaged, the carpet soaked with water that had frozen to ice. The home would require major rebuilding. She wondered who would want to buy a house in which a woman had burned to death.

"I'm collecting her papers," Bob Frey explained. "She had a fireproof safe and some of them are still partially intact."

Sherry launched into the story of the videotapes and Ray Innis's materials she had found in the attic boxes. As she spoke, Frey's face lost some of its grieflike mask, and he began to follow her story.

At last he said, "So what is it you want, Mrs. Vincent?"

"I don't know. No, I do know— I want to look at her case files."

He sighed. "You know I can't allow it. Legally and ethically those case records are not for public consumption. I'm sorry, I can't hand them over."

"Please, I just want to look at them. There is a ring of child pornographers—there are missing children—the things they do to little girls are vile."

"Mrs. Vincent, I can't deal with it right now."

"Later, then?"

"Now you'd better leave. I have to finish packing up the papers for the insurance people. Good-bye, Mrs. Vincent."

Sherry found herself on the doorstep again, the wind surging at her exposed cheeks and face. She started toward her car, then her resolve hardened. Bob Frey was here to collect papers and he'd already said there had been a fireproof safe. He couldn't possibly stay in that heatless, dark house tonight, so he'd have to be leaving fairly soon.

She started her motor, switching the heat to high. She would come back tonight, after he'd left. She intended to look at those case records for herself.

A February moon lit the sky. The air was incredibly thin and crisp, its clarity revealing stars like flung zircons. The Milky Way was a glowing slash written with a laser sword.

Sherry kept glancing at the moon as she drove, hoping that by some miracle of luck, some clouds would blow up and shield the cool glow. But no such luck. It was too cold for there to be any clouds, and the night lay spread before her, surrealistic in its stark contrasts.

She kept to the speed limit, in case there should be a Sheriff's car anywhere near. The closer she got to the Freys' house, the more this felt like the beginning of disaster. But as her speedometer clocked another two miles, she forced herself to relax. Who was there around to see her? She had driven eight miles now and had not passed a single car. Nearly all the homes she passed were dark. On weeknights, Hartwick residents went to bed early.

*He would have let me look if he hadn't been so upset*, a voice said inside her, and then she hushed it. That was a cheap rationalization. The truth was, what she was doing was illegal and she knew it. She had no right to go to the Freys' home, to pry among their possessions. It would be called looting. She could go to jail if she were caught.

She drove down the final hill and there was the half-burned house, separated from its nearest neighbors by about a quarter mile in each direction. She would have as much privacy here as if she were in the center of the Arctic tundra.

Still, her pulse pounding sickly in her throat, she almost floored the accelerator to speed on past, knowing that was what any sensible woman would do. But then as she neared the house, she tapped the brakes and switched off her car headlights.

The night immediately rolled over her, radiant with stars, a white moonlight palpable as wine. Every outline seemed unnaturally crisp. Trees were frozen individual spires, crystal holiday decorations. She got out of her car, her boots squeaking in the snow.

Something inside her car motor snapped as the motor cooled. Sherry jumped, her heart speeding up. She could hear the wind, and something banging in the wreckage of Dr. Frey's office.

*Bang, bang, bang.*

Sherry forced herself to walk up the drive, retracing the route she had always used to visit her therapist.

She stood surveying the wrecked end of the house, its blackness cavernous and dangerous. The garage-studio had partly collapsed in on itself, but brick walls remained on three sides, tumbled with wreckage. The staircase she had used to climb to Dr. Frey's office was gone, a few blackened shards of wood protruding crazily from the brick. The place seemed thick with death, the very ruins vibrating with psychic fear.

Any case records would have been burned.

Still, Bob Frey had said there had been a fireproof safe. Sherry remembered going through an office catalog once and finding a fireproof safe listed. It had been small, about the size of a medium cardboard box, and was listed as weighing eighty-one pounds. It had been proof against flames of 1,700 degrees up to an hour.

Sherry shone her flashlight in the rubble, searching for anything that resembled the picture in the catalog. The beam flashed eerily among the wreckage, creating shadows that lunged and jumped among the fallen beams and other objects. She aimed the beam into nooks and crannies, feeling as if she were excavating a mass grave.

She located what appeared to be a door, half tumbled now, leaning crazily. There were dark objects underneath about the size of steel cabinets. Stepping cautiously through the wreckage she picked her way closer. As she did so, her foot caught on a piece of pipe, and the section of pipe snapped up and hit her on the calf.

It was as if something alive in the wreckage had reached up to strike her.

Sherry jumped, stifling a cry and nearly dropping the flashlight. This was like the eleven o'clock movie. Any minute now there would be giant rats crawling out of the debris, or aliens from another universe. Or maybe there would be a ghost, the specter of Nanette Frey, staggering toward her, burnt black, arms outstretched in a cry for help.

She pressed her teeth into her lip to hold back a scream. She was going to have to get thoughts like that out of her head! Otherwise she'd never have the nerve to finish this. Nervously she cocked her head, listening for sounds outside. But all she could hear was her own ragged breathing, and tiny sounds coming from the wreckage as it settled.

*Get on with it*, she ordered herself. *Either find what you're looking for or leave.*

Cautiously she edged farther into the rubble, watching her footing with almost paranoid caution. She could trip on something here—cut herself—send things falling down on herself. Almost immediately her flashlight beam located a blackened box that appeared to have been tilted on its side, lid opened.

The safe. But obviously Frey would have gotten here first and Sherry doubted any papers would remain.

Still, she climbed over beams and other junk, finally reaching the safe. Squatting, she aimed the light directly inside, finding, as she'd expected, only a few scraps of paper. She sank back, disappointed. No papers here, and even if there had been, they would have been items like passports, wills, and insurance papers.

Stepping backward, hearing the crunch of debris under her boots, she bumped into a stack of something dark that seemed to disintegrate under her touch, breaking up into friable, ashlike pieces. Case records! But burned almost beyond recognition.

Her breath coming in puffs, she prodded at the stack with the head of the flashlight, creating a little storm of black fragments.

*Damn*, she thought. It was hopeless; how could anyone read these? And even if they could be read, how could she possibly know which case record Dr. Frey had wanted to discuss with her? Or even if it had been a case file at all?

Balancing herself on the precarious footing, Sherry felt herself sag with frustration. She'd risked being arrested as a trespasser for a pile of blackened ashes. What would she say if she were caught, how would she explain this? Did she fancy herself some kind of intrepid female TV detective, off to solve the case on her own?

She wasn't intrepid. She was a very ordinary woman who had no business here at 3:30 A.M. on property that didn't belong to her.

She kicked at the charred lump, watching as it fell apart. Something flashed gray-white at its center, and with a leap of her heart Sherry realized that there were still some intact materials. She knelt and, the light in her left hand, began carefully pulling apart the onionlike layers of charred paper.

There—there were the unburned pieces; somehow they had been protected by the sheer bulk of the other papers that surrounded them. But a mess, just bits and scraps. She sloughed away the ash and began flaking away layers of the paper on which fragments of writing could be read.

*Patient seems agitated about the extramarital affair she is* . . . read one truncated scrap in Dr. Frey's beautifully looped writing.

She deciphered another as: *his homosexuality is*

*a source of . . .* And a third: *incestuous thoughts torment . . .*

Sherry shuddered, feeling as if she had lifted a rock on the ugliest secrets of Hartwick, the dark side of humanity right here in her town. Did she know any of these people? Pass them every day on the road? Did any of them ski at Timberline?

She strained to read another scrap, her eyes suddenly stopping on the name *Carole*.

*Carole admits to unremitting jealousy about other women . . . fantasies of destroying the women she envies, in particular . . . Miss Michigan title . . .*

In her shock, Sherry almost dropped the flashlight.

Carole! Was she a client of Dr. Frey's? But then her surprise seeped away. Hadn't she really known, somewhere deep inside, that Carole envied her for her looks? Chance remarks . . . that sometimes bitter, slashing wit . . . Even Judy remembered the party celebrating Sherry's title when Carole got drunk and refused to come out of the bedroom.

*Fantasies of destroying the women she envies.*

But no, Sherry told herself, tightening her grip on the light. Everyone had fantasies, it was normal and natural, she had them herself, secret mind-pictures she wouldn't really want anyone else to know. She'd told a few of them to Dr. Frey, but just because she had the thoughts didn't mean she intended or even wanted to carry them out.

She froze. There was a noise outside the house.

A snowmobile motor.

Sherry's heart gave an enormous, guilty thump. She heard another motor sound, and then more of them, six, seven, she wasn't sure. She froze where she was, shivering like a caught animal. Her car was parked outside! Her light flashing in the wreckage! Anyone would know there was someone here.

Kids, it had to be kids. The ones Arrington had told her about, who broke into cottages and held wild parties. They were here, they'd been out joyriding and wanted to see the site where a woman had died. What should she do? Freeze here in the ruins, wait them out, hope they'd roar their motors someplace else and be gone? Or try to make it back to her car?

They would be annoying but probably harmless—or would they? The gang instinct, she thought raggedly.

Instinctively she gathered up the lump of paper and shoved it into the fireproof safe, slamming the lid as far shut as it would go. She switched off the light and crawled toward the edge of the wall where the garage door once had been. She was a sitting duck here in the wreckage, which was surely what had drawn them here in the first place. She'd be safer outdoors.

The motors revved louder; they were in the yard now, gathered in a circle, only feet away from her car, lights glaring, six machines and their riders. Sherry swallowed back her panic. Surely these people weren't the snowmobiler who had terrorized Kady, they couldn't be. They were in a group, he had been alone.

Pinned in the shadow of a pine tree, its branches denuded of snow by the action of a fire hose, she waited tensely. Had they come here to gawk at the house? To poke through the wreckage?

Then she saw something metallic fly in an arc, landing on the snow. A beer can. She wanted to laugh with relief. Just a gang of kids out for some fun.

She ran through the snow, using the large pines for cover. She reached her car, jumped in, started the motor. Someone shouted. She was nervous, her foot on the accelerator heavy, and as she backed out she swerved within inches of a big Arctic Cat. Her tires spun, caught snow, spun again.

Then she was on the road. She drove away, glancing behind her in her rearview mirror. Snowmobile headlights lit up the Frey house like some neolithic monument, dark figures passing back and forth in front of the light.

# CHAPTER 25

The sun had sunk below the rooftop of the ginger-bread house across the street from Grandma's, backlighting its chimney with a golden shine, like that of the metallic paint in Kady's old paint box. Kady glanced impatiently at the inching rays. If Grandma didn't hurry—

"I'm just going to run across the street," Margaret Smith said for the fifth time. She puttered over to the small closet that was crammed with the coats and jackets of twenty years and smelled of pot-pourri spice bags. "I want to have tea with Maida, we always have tea and coffee cake on Thursdays, and I can see you from her front window so all you have to do is wave."

"Okay." Kady yawned and sighed, turning a page in her math textbook, which had wrong answers scrawled in pencil by the last owner of the book.

"Now, mind, Kady, I don't want you answering the door. And if any telephone calls come for me,

I'll only be an hour, or you can tell them to call me over at Maida's. Oh, maybe I shouldn't go at all," her grandmother equivocated, this also for the fifth time.

"I'll be okay." Kady sighed.

"Well . . . What are you going to do while I'm gone? Are you going to finish that math assignment?"

Kady already had it done. "Yup, all one hundred problems."

"Are you sure? You don't look like you're concentrating very much to me."

"I'm concentrating," Kady said, giving her grandmother a big, wide false grin.

"Okay . . . Oh, dear, have I forgotten anything? Let's see . . . oh! I made some pumpkin bread! I forgot about that, it's in the fridge . . ." She scurried off to the kitchen, while Kady wriggled with impatience.

She stretched out on the couch, flopping her arms down the sides toward the floor. Living at her grandmother's wasn't anything like visiting. Grandma kept asking her questions, supervising every little thing she did, as if she were too young to know how to do her own homework, or put her dishes in the dishwasher.

Last night Grandma had insisted on taking her out to the Holiday Inn, the two of them sitting in a big booth all dressed up, Grandma in a blue dress made of some slippery material, herself in a skirt and sweater that she particularly hated, because the sweater itched. Trying not to squirm and scratch, Kady had endured a long monologue from her grandmother on how Brooke Shields had made it in modeling.

"Remember, I'll be *right* across the street, right within call," Margaret fretted, returning to shrug on the coat she had selected, a soft blue suede with wide, matching belt. "Forty steps away."

"No problem," Kady said with her face buried in her math book. As soon as she heard the front door close, she flipped the book shut and tossed it on the floor. This was getting boring. Grandma hardly let her out at all. She was virtually a prisoner.

Kady wriggled off the couch and loped over to the front window, where she watched her grandmother enter the house across the street where Maida Thomas lived. As soon as the door safely closed, she trotted to the guest room, where she turned her radio up real loud, to Grayling's rock station. Then she hurried to the closet and grabbed her powder blue ski jacket, zipping it up tightly.

Thank God. She and Maura were going to go downtown and window-shop—which, really, meant walk up and down the street looking in the store windows and giggling a lot, glancing sideways at the passing cars to see if there were boys in them.

Kady was proud of the fact that they often got whistled at by boys as big as sixteen and seventeen years old. It was a game to see if they could get whistled at. Of course, they didn't ever *talk* to the boys; Kady knew her mother would kill her if she did that. But it felt safe to walk up and down the street with Maura.

She slipped out the back way, being certain to leave the door unlocked so she could get in again. Grandma'd probably be over at Maida's more than an hour—they would talk and talk, about boring things like how Medicare hadn't paid their check, or how to make carrot salad, or that terrible Finney family that had two girls on ADC.

The small alley behind the house was deserted. Once, Grandma said, there'd been stables back here, but now the stables were just sheds or garages. A new wheeled garbage can on a cart waited at Grandma's back steps, its lid capped with a neat round of snow.

Kady took deep breaths of cold air. Another

thing, Grandma kept her house so hot that Kady was sweating all the time. Her boots crunching, she started down the alley toward the corner. It was only one block to Maura's from here, and four blocks to downtown; she could easily be back before Grandma even finished her tea.

She loped rapidly along sidewalks that had been shoveled by residents with varying degrees of thoroughness. Some had been done with snow throwers and were wide and full of wheel tracks. Others, shoveled by hand, consisted of tortuous paths about eighteen inches wide, along which she had to pick her way. Old Lady Hennessey hadn't done her walk at all, so she had just a path of footprints.

Three or four cars passed her as she made her way down the block, but none of the cars contained boys, and Kady didn't bother to look twice. She was anxious to see Maura for another reason, too. George Michael was doing a concert at the Palace in Auburn Hills, near Detroit, and Maura's cousin, who lived in Dearborn, had promised to get them tickets. So Kady and Maura had to figure out how to convince Maura's mother or Sherry to drive them down.

Another car clacked past, snow tires splatting out chunks of snow. Something made Kady glance more sharply at this one. The driver wore snowmobile gear, a hood pulled up so it hid most of his face.

Weird, she thought. Most people didn't wear their hood or hat in the car, not if they had their heaters on, it'd be too hot. Suddenly Kady felt uneasy. The afternoon was settling down to a winter twilight, a few house lights beginning to switch on. It was getting dark quicker than Kady thought—Grandma's fault for fussing so much and not being ready to leave!

Then, quickly, Kady dismissed the trill of fear she'd felt. She was in *Hartwick*, with people all around her, this was town, not their house way out on the lake, where their neighbors were summer people and seldom there.

Besides, she was almost to the corner where she was supposed to meet Maura, and the two of them together would be safer than anything. Anyway, she rationalized still further, her mother had said she could be with her friends, so she wasn't really doing anything wrong.

She reached the corner of Birch and Poplar. Maura hadn't arrived yet, but a big, black Labrador retriever with a graying muzzle was sniffing around some bushes there on the corner, so Kady stopped to pet the old dog and rub its smooth fur.

"Hey, guy," she murmured to the animal, extending her hand as she had been taught, so it could sniff her scent. "What's your name, guy? Do you live around here? Are you a nice guy, are you nice? Are you a good boy?"

She waited ten minutes, playing with the Lab, throwing it sticks, and watching it wallow heavily through the snow, rooting in the whiteness with its muzzle. It lost half the sticks she threw it. Glancing at her watch, she was puzzled. Maybe Maura's mother hadn't let her out. Or maybe Maura got a phone call.

The dog wandered off, and Kady paced up and down for a while, trampling a path in the snow. Lights were going on all over. It was getting darker by the minute, and colder, too. It occurred to her that Grandma really wasn't supposed to have left her alone like this.

Well, but she was still safe, this was a populated street, there were people inside all these houses, and it was no big deal. Kady decided, however, that it would be politic to start home, and she began trotting up the sidewalk again, jogging fast to keep warm.

Only one car passed her as she ran toward Grandma's. Maybe it was one of the same ones she'd seen before, Kady couldn't remember. Anyway, all cars looked alike at night, and it was definitely night now; she'd played too long with the dog, and what if Grandma returned before she got home?

She was out of breath and a little scared by the time she reached the alley, but she was still telling herself it was safe. This wasn't the woods, or a house way out along a deserted road, this was town. Bad things didn't happen to people in town. She turned into the alley, stumbling over an uneven spot in the snow crust.

The alley didn't seem as friendly as it had when she left. Shadows from several garages now stretched across, a pit of blackness along which she'd better hurry if she wanted to get in the house okay. Now she wished she hadn't left the house. Why had she? Just to show Grandma—and her mother, too—that she wasn't a baby.

Something caught her boot tip. Another ice crust that she'd missed seeing in the dark. Kady tripped forward, letting out a nervous cry that was more like a sob. She landed on her knees, hands splayed in the snow. That was when she heard something move out of the shadows.

She looked up and saw a black snowmobile suit. A gloved hand yanked at her, pulling her up out of the snow. Kady started to scream and then the chilly leather of a glove clamped over her mouth, blocking off her voice and most of her air. The glove smelled of dirt and fuel oil, nearly gagging her.

Terrified, Kady reverted to instinct. She struggled wildly, kicking at the bulk behind her. It was the snowmobiler, the man she'd seen in the car!

Adrenaline jolted through her like an electric shock.

She didn't think. She couldn't. She was all terror, all kick, her strength four times normal, augmented by fear chemicals that zapped through her veins like a shot of strong drugs. She wrenched her face away from the glove, biting through the leather. She panted and sobbed, twisting like a wild animal. She even managed a short, high scream.

Nobody heard her. This was the alley, and people were all indoors, watching the 5:00 news. Or maybe they thought it was just kids horsing around.

He bent her and turned her, crushing her toward his chest so that her nose was buried in slippery fabric, her neck nearly breaking from the unnatural angle to which he pushed it. *No*, her brain screamed. She butted her head into the stomach area, biting savagely with her teeth, cutting her lip on a zipper.

Then she heard a scratchy, tearing sound and suddenly something was being bound across her lips.

Tape! Tight tape!

Her mouth was being encircled, pressured, and Kady gasped in terror, able to draw in air only through her nose. Her nostrils pinched as they tried desperately to suck in more air. She was being dragged toward a car parked at the other end of the alley with its lights out. It must have been there all the time.

She was all animal. All hate. She dropped to the ground and tried to roll away, roll under the car so he couldn't catch her. But he grabbed her first and threw his weight on top of her. Arms racked out in front of her, he had her wrists handcuffed before she even knew it was done.

He threw her in the backseat of the car.

At work, Sherry glanced at her watch and interrupted a discussion she was having with two members of the Ski Patrol, and went to the phone to call Kady. The phone rang eight or nine times, and just as Sherry was about to hang up, Margaret answered.

"Hi, Mom, how's it going?"

"Oh, just fine. Your daughter is in her room listening to that loud music she likes; aren't you worried she'll damage her eardrums? I've read that loud music really damages kids' ears; we're going to have a whole generation of kids who can't hear."

"Well, tell her to turn it down then."

"Oh, I will. I just wanted to let her have a little pleasure. She's been good, Sherry, I'm not saying she hasn't, but I think she's homesick. Grandma doesn't do things the way Mother would, I guess."

Her mother sounded just slightly breathless, as if she had been down in the basement or outdoors when the phone had rung. "Are you sure she's in her room?" something made Sherry ask.

"Of course I'm sure," Margaret responded huffily. "The music is blasting out of there, Sherry, you've got yourself a regular teenager on your hands, is all I can say. How long are you going to want her to stay here?"

"I'm not sure."

"Not that I don't want her, of course. But Maida and I were planning to take a trip down to the Bahamas. We've already got reservations for March fifth."

"March fifth?" Sherry sighed. "You didn't tell me you were going on a trip, Mom."

"Well, I didn't actually know until today. Maida belongs to one of these travel clubs through the AAA, and they get real cheap rates by going places at the last minute, you know, when people have canceled. The price is based on double occupancy, Sherry, and you know how hard it is to find people who want to travel with you—they say they'll do it and then they cancel out at the last minute . . ."

Her mother still sounded breathless, and again

Sherry felt the odd tick in the back of her head, as if everything were not quite right. "Mom. Let me talk to Kady for a sec, will you?"

"Oh, all right." There was a clatter as the phone was laid down. Sherry held onto the receiver, gazing out her office window where knots of skiers could be seen gathered, taking off skis or locking them in the racks.

Her eyes glazed past the familiar sight, focused on her own thoughts. She hadn't been able to get back to the Frey house again. Last night when she'd driven past, the young snowmobilers had been gathered in front of a huge bonfire they had made in the middle of the Frey lawn. Beer cans were scattered all over the snow. The place must hold a macabre fascination for them, she realized, but she was angry at the desecration of Dr. Frey's home.

When she got home she had almost called the Sheriff's Department, but common sense stopped her just in time. She didn't want patrol cars over there because she wanted to go back herself.

Her mother was back on the wire, her voice sounding more breathless. "Sherry—Sherry, she's not in her room!"

"She's not? Then where is she?"

"I don't know . . . I looked in the bathroom, too, and the kitchen, and . . . hold on while I go upstairs, maybe she went up the back stairs to where the roomers are."

Another rattle as the phone was flung down. Sherry clung to the receiver, feeling perspiration sheen her forehead. That rambunctious little rascal, she thought. What had she done now? One December afternoon last year, she had caught her daughter climbing out on Margaret's roof dressed in a Santa Claus costume she had found in a drawer. Another time Kady tried to make peanut brittle and set the pan on fire.

*This is just another of her escapades*, Sherry told herself, forcing herself to relax.

Why wasn't her mother back on the line? What was keeping her? Without realizing she was doing it, she wiped her forehead, then the back of her neck where sweat had begun to collect. Kady. My God, if anything ever happened to her—

The receiver banged again and suddenly her mother's terrified voice screeched across the wire. *"She's gone, Sherry! She's not here! She's not here!"*

Sherry felt her insides clench and twist, as if her heart wanted to separate itself from her body. "But she has to be there!"

"She's not. I looked everywhere. I even looked outside—she's not here! Oh, Sherry," her mother's shaky voice continued. "I did a bad thing, I did a terrible thing, I went across the street to see Maida, I was only gone for an hour—"

"You did what?" Sherry shouted.

Rattled, her mother began talking fast, in phrases that ran into one another. "—Maida and I were planning the trip—she was doing her math, Sherry, she was right here—on the couch—she said she had one hundred problems—she had Pepsi after school—God, Sherry—"

"Mother," Sherry pleaded. "She probably went over to Maura's. I'll hang up and you call over to Maura's and see if she's there. I'm coming over. I'll be there in about fifteen minutes."

"Oh, God," wailed Margaret.

"Call Maura's house," Sherry ordered.

"This is my fault, I just ran across the street, I could see her from the *window*, I could *wave* to her— Sherry, I have a feeling, I have an awful feeling, just this awful feeling—"

Sherry felt a cold, icy ball form in the center of her. "Will you just call Maura's? Will you just call her?"

\* \* \*

She ran to her car and jumped in, her hands shaking so badly that she could not get the car in reverse, and had to stop, focus her eyes on the indicator, and position the arrow again. She could hear the ragged rhythm of her breath.

My God, Kady. She would die if anything happened to her child. She wouldn't even want to live.

A group of skiers were headed toward their cars, kids about seventeen years old, laughing, horse-playing, pushing one another. Sherry backed her Toyota out, swerving too close, so that one of the boys had to jump back. He banged on the fender of her car, making Sherry jump convulsively.

She floorboarded the car out of the lot, her tires skidding crazily as she twisted onto the access road. It was a fifteen-minute drive to town; there were hills, curves, and one caution light. She drove at seventy-five the entire distance, narrowly avoiding going into a ditch near the trailer park just outside the village.

*That's it*, she told herself. *Have an accident. Total the car, put yourself in the hospital. You can lie in bed in a body cast and wonder what happened to her.*

She managed to slow down and with this deliberate effort came a measure of calmness. Why was she hurrying so fast? She was allowing her mother's hysteria to infect her. Probably Kady had sneaked out of the house while Grandma was across the street and had gone down to Maura's.

But Kady knew she wasn't supposed to go out alone!

Suddenly Sherry felt a wave of anger at her daughter so intense she was shaking. Kady *knew* about the snowmobiler, she knew that was why she was at Grandma's in the first place. Why had she been so stupid? Couldn't she think ahead? Wherever she was, when Sherry caught up with her, she was going to ground her daughter for a month. No

TV, no phone calls, no pizza, no Sweet Valley High books.

By the time she turned into her mother's street, she had passed out of her anger and was coldly calm again. She noted as she drove up the street that it all looked very ordinary, an older street lined with oaks and elms, greenish lights of TV sets flickering in windows. Middle America, she thought, Mom and Pop and *Country Time* Lemonade.

She pulled into Margaret's driveway that connected through to the alley. Her mother came running out of the front door. Margaret wore a blue housecoat and her face was distorted with anxiety.

"She's not at Maura's! Maura got grounded for talking back! Maura doesn't know where she is! She tried to call Kady but her mother was on the line and she couldn't use the phone. Oh, Sherry—"

The cold, dreadful calm that had taken possession of Sherry still prevailed. Carefully she got out of the car, remembering to flick off her lights and remove the key from the ignition. She walked up onto the porch, looking at her mother standing shivering in her housecoat, on the verge of weeping.

"We'll go in the house and call Maura again," Sherry said. "And we'll call Heather and Kelly and Tracy—all of her girlfriends."

# CHAPTER 26

Kady lay as still as she could, trying to calm her breathing so that she wouldn't need so much air, so that she wouldn't suffocate on the tape that bound her mouth shut.

Her heart was trip-hammering with fright.

Where was he taking her? What was he going to do with her?

The tape was all over her mouth and chin and even on part of her nose, blocking the air. It wound all the way around her head, catching up her hair, so that when she twisted her head the hair pulled. It gave her a horrible claustrophobic feeling, like when a boy pushed you down under the water at Higgins Lake and held you with his legs so you couldn't swim up.

She began to cry, felt herself start, and then with a spurt of panic realized that if she cried she would probably die. Because when you cried your nose made mucus, and if she got any mucus in her nose right now, anything that interfered with her taking big, long breaths, she wouldn't be able to get enough air to keep her alive.

The car took a couple of turns, bouncing her around. All she could see from here was a dark seat back and the shape of the driver's head, encased in a hood that gave him a shapeless, scary look, like Darth Vader seen from behind. He had not said one word to her.

Where were they going? Even fighting to breathe as she was, Kady glimpsed the yellow flashes of a blinker light, and knew they must be on M-72. She felt the steady hum of the car wheels that indicated they were on a blacktop road.

Right now that didn't matter as much as breathing. She fought the trapped feeling the tape gave her. When the car stopped she'd try to make a noise—she'd hum or something—and maybe the man would loosen the tape. But then she remembered the brutal way he'd yanked her off the ground and she knew that he might not. In fact, he might not even care if she breathed at all.

He might just stop the car and throw her out. She'd seen that once in a movie on TV, a woman tossed out of a car like an old rag doll. For the first time Kady became aware of the spreading wet stain at the crotch of her jeans. She'd wet herself again, just a little. But this time it didn't seem as important. She lay still and frozen, concentrating on nothing but breathing.

She couldn't cry.

She must not.

Suddenly the car lurched again and Kady, lying on the backseat, could tell by the way the tires bounced that they had turned off the blacktop and onto a dirt road, one with lots of potholes and ruts and icy patches like their own driveway. Her heart sank. They must be getting near to where they were going.

The road must be long, because they drove and drove. Kady heard the tires wallow in snow, and once the wheels spun and she wondered if they were going to get stuck. Where was he taking her? And what would happen when they finally arrived? What would the man do to her?

Because she knew he was going to do something.

The videotape she had played on the VCR had drummed that into Kady's mind. A picture began to play in her head, of a man pushing a girl across a tabletop, forcing her to spread the cheeks of her buttocks with her own hands. The obscene picture kept flashing in Kady's mind like a movie frame gone bad. The lunging thrusts of the man, the girl's thin, rigid body.

*No*, Kady prayed, trying to breathe. *Oh, please, no.*

As the car continued to bounce along the track, struggling in the deep snow, Kady felt increased terror and helplessness. Any minute now they'd get to where they were going, and he would pull her out of the car. Then he'd start hurting her like the girls in the video.

Suddenly, just as she'd feared, the car pulled to a stop. Kady instantly panicked, rolling over, outstretched hands scrabbling for the door handle. But before she could push open the door he was already opening it. He dragged her out and dumped her in the snow.

Kady landed facedown, her nose digging into cold, crystal flakes. With a panicky roll, she twisted over on her back. She was in a woods someplace—she could see the shapes of snow-laden trees, big pines. Her kidnapper loomed over her. He wore a bulky, black, full-length snowmobile suit, its hood pulled up over his head. Beneath that a yellow ski mask was particularly horrible, for it had black, knitted bands around the eye holes, giving him the crudely drawn look of a Saturday morning cartoon.

Kady couldn't see his eyes at all. They were deep in shadow within the eye openings, increasing the shock of terror. Still, it was as if the hooded figure were inspecting her, assessing her.

Kady stared back, her handcuffed hands held awkwardly in front of her. She was careful not to whimper, because every instinct told her that might provoke him. She felt sure that he wanted her to be afraid—that he even liked it.

But she couldn't hold the gaze of a . . . a mask. Looking away, she darted her eyes from side to side, trying to figure out exactly where she was. It was too dark to see much. There was an impression of trees—lots of pine trees, some of them spruces. A couple of cabins made of logs. There was maybe a big shed, but none of it was distinct in the dark, and none of it looked familiar.

With the length of time they'd driven, she could be anywhere between home and West Branch. The realization caused a hollow terror to press into the center of her. Horrified, Kady realized she had started to cry, and desperately she sniffed back tears, fighting the constrictions of the tape.

He was still staring at her! Kady's mind struggled with it. Maybe he wasn't going to hurt her after all. Maybe he was thinking about letting her go. But then he lunged at her and dragged her up again, yanking her by the elbow. Nearly breaking her arm, he sent her half running, half falling toward one of the cabins.

Set off-balance by the handcuffs, she fell forward on her face again, burning her nose on ice crystals. He was right behind her, pulling at her, forcing her up. He shoved her in the center of her back, indicating the way she should go.

They reached one of the cabins, a structure that

even in the dark Kady could see was peeling and uninhabited. Wooden trim around its small windows was falling off in places, everything dusted with snow. Huge, six-foot snowdrifts had banked up along the side of it that faced the prevailing wind.

He yanked open a door and pushed her inside. A cold, clammy odor greeted her, the smell of a place that hadn't been used in a long time, of old wood and mildew, rotten cloth and spiderwebs.

Despair gave Kady courage. She twisted away from him and kicked out as hard as she could, with legs strengthened from a lifetime of skiing and swimming. She heard his surprised grunt and saw him stagger off-balance.

She kicked again, but the effort nearly strangled her, requiring so much air, and she felt a wave of dizziness, black specks dancing in front of her eyes.

He gave another grunt and swung his fist, hitting her across the side of her face. Kady moaned with pain and terror. She fell to her knees. He hit her again, the sound exploding in her eardrums.

Kady went limp, only half aware as he pulled her up some stairs—horrible stairs, their surface filthy with spiderwebs and the droppings of some small animal. At the top of the stairs he dropped her while he stopped and fumbled with a trapdoor at the top. He switched on a flashlight he pulled out of a pocket and dragged her into an attic room.

Shadows flashed on bare, slanting roof-walls. Kady's jaw felt swollen and she tasted blood in her mouth. She swallowed its hot saltiness, the pain sharpening her senses again.

The swinging arc of the flashlight lit up the space around her. She was in a small attic that obviously hadn't been used in years, flooring missing in places to reveal ancient insulation, dirt, and fragments of junk. There was an old ticking mattress in one corner, eaten with holes that revealed tangles of stuffing. Junk crowded one wall, rows of old garden tools.

Images coursed through Kady's mind, pictures from the tapes, horrifyingly vivid.

And then he threw her down on the mattress.

# CHAPTER 27

Sherry's icy calm continued. She felt it surround her like the lucite in which hermit crabs and seashells were often enclosed, protecting her from the raw agony that otherwise would be hers.

She performed the necessary tasks. She telephoned a long list of Kady's girlfriends, learning, as she'd known she would, that no one had seen Kady since school.

She drove over to Maura's and confronted the frightened girl again. In front of Sherry and Mrs. Camrack, Maura admitted that she and Kady had planned to meet on the corner, then walk downtown.

"But why? The stores were closing, Maura—why would you and Kady want to do that?"

Maura hung her head, glancing guiltily at her mother.

"Answer her," snapped Susan Camrack.

"We . . . we . . . boys," the girl finally whispered.

"What do you mean, boys?"

"We were just going to . . . boys drive up and down Main Street . . . You know . . ." Maura explained. "And then Ma and me got in an argument . . . she said I had to stay in my room."

Mrs. Camrack nodded affirmation.

Sherry left the Camracks', feeling as if all of her worst nightmares had come true. Kady had left for her rendezvous with Maura on the street corner and something had happened to her. In desperation she drove to the corner, got out of her car and walked around. The snow was crisscrossed with footprints and dog tracks but that meant nothing—these streets were full of children and dogs.

She drove up and down the two blocks of downtown, from the drugstore to the 7-Eleven. She rang doorbells, asking about her daughter, if anyone had seen her on the corner. A wizened retiree named Mrs. Hennessey said she had glanced out her living-room window and seen a girl in a blue ski jacket walk past. It had happened "in the middle of *Cheers*." This was a rerun which came on at 5:00.

Other than that, no one had heard or seen anything.

Beginning to panic, Sherry drove back to her mother's house and called Mike Arrington.

Within fifteen minutes, Arrington stood on her mother's doorstep, his forelock of blond hair looking rumpled. He wore the same blue ski jacket she had seen before, and it was unzipped and careless as if he had just thrown it on. He wore no gloves.

"How long has she been missing?" he questioned her even before he had stepped inside.

"Two hours," Sherry said.

"Are you sure she's not with one of her friends?"

"I'm sure! I wouldn't have called you if I wasn't!" Her composure almost broke and was not helped by the sight of Margaret Smith, who entered the living room still in her housecoat, her face sunken in with anxiety, dried tear streaks marking a path through her makeup.

"She's gone," Margaret wailed, "and it's my fault, I'm the one who left her alone, I'm to blame for this—" Her voice rose in waves of histrionic self-pity. Sherry stared at her. The tone of voice was all too familiar; that was the way her mother had sounded during the Ray Innis incident, crying and issuing orders, carrying on to everyone from the school principal to Sherry herself.

"Mom," she said. "Please." She began explaining to Arrington what had happened, outlining her own search.

"You haven't overlooked a girlfriend? Maybe a slumber party?"

"I wish I had." Sherry felt that the nakedness of her distress might interfere with this; she put a hand up to cover her eyes.

She heard his voice go on, drilling, almost hectoring in its tone, no time for nuances. "What was she wearing?"

"I—I don't know."

"Oh, those blue jeans," Margaret Smith fluttered. "A little sweater, I think pale yellow, with a little white turtleneck underneath. The sweater had a white bug embroidered on it."

Pathetic details that somehow made it feel as if Kady were lost forever. Sherry locked her muscles into rigidity to stop their trembling.

"Her jacket?"

"A blue ski jacket, pastel blue, she got it for Christmas. It's got a Timberline ski pass hanging from the zipper. She's wearing gloves, I think, and a white wool hat I loaned her. She lost her new hat, these kids, they—" Margaret stopped, appalled; for a second she had forgotten.

Arrington moved restlessly, obviously anxious to

get going. He was scowling now and looked very truculent, but Sherry knew it was all a shell. This bothered the detective and he was too macho to reveal it.

"I'll put out an APB right away. With an adult, we'd have to wait forty-eight hours, but Kady's just a child and you've already had troubles—I'm going to move sooner. Sherry, I want you to go back home and wait there, answer the telephone, see what kind of phone calls you get. Mrs. Smith, you stay here and do the same thing."

While Margaret fussed over a tabletop, selecting a silver-framed picture of Kady to give him, Sherry looked deep into the man's eyes, seeking out anything that might be there, any knowledge or evidence that all of this might be hopeless, that her daughter might already be lying dead somewhere, frozen in the snow. Her stomach was cramped from anxiety, the tube of her throat so tight she could hardly swallow.

Kady could already be dead by now.

She could be a corpse, her beautiful dark hair matted with blood.

*No.* It hadn't happened that way. Because surely she would know if her child were dead, there would be a psychological connection, surely something would tell her. Her thoughts slid away again, focusing on the thick, wiry look of Arrington's eyelashes, the blackness of his pupils amid the gray musculature of the eye.

"Did you hear me?" Arrington repeated. "I said you should go home."

"I— All right," she said, realizing she'd stared for too long. My God, what was happening to her? She didn't even recognize her thinking right now, she felt shell-shocked, as if she'd gone through the worst battle of Vietnam.

"Can you drive?" Arrington was asking.

"Of course I can drive!"

"You look woozy."

"I'm fine."

"I'll send a car for you," the detective announced.

"No, please, I'm all *right*." Determinedly, Sherry took her jacket off the back of a chair where she had left it, and dug in her purse for her car keys. She and Mike Arrington started out the door at the same time, colliding. He caught her elbow, and then patted her back, doing it with the awkward touch of a man who isn't used to doing much comforting.

"We'll get her," he said, "Don't you worry."

At home, Sherry paced the house. It was a hollow cavern, a mausoleum, without Kady. She felt numb, disconnected, her blood skittering in her veins in tiny jumps. She switched on the outdoor floodlights out of a nervous need to push the black night away. Their light bathed the pine trees in stark fluorescence, turning them into stage props. Beyond the reach of the light, the woods were masses of black. Her outdoor thermometer nailed to a tree trunk showed the temperature at one degree below zero. It would be ten below by morning.

She wandered into the kitchen, seeing the clutter of dishes beside the sink that she hadn't had time to put in the dishwasher. She began loading the KitchenAid, jumping back as a glass inexplicably dropped from her hand and crashed to the floor.

She picked up the glass, saw there was a triangle-shaped break, and started to cry. She leaned into the Formica, her hands splayed over her face, and let the tears burn down her cheeks. Whoever said it felt good to cry? These tears were hot chemicals generated by a churning agony. It had all come true, her worst fear, as if somehow Fate had come digging into her mind to pull out that which terrified her above all else.

And here she was relegated to an empty house,

condemned to pace its floors and look out of its windows at a pitiless winter night. Where was Kady now? Was she somewhere indoors where it was warm? If she was outdoors, did she have her jacket on?

Sherry had lived in the north all her life. The realities of cold weather were as familiar to her as putting on her boots. You needed the right clothes to survive ten-degrees-below-zero weather. You layered your clothes to trap warmth in each layer. Polypropylene long underwear could literally save your life. Mittens, not gloves, were a necessity, and it was best to curl your fingers together inside to create more body warmth. A ski mask would shield your face from freezing, and you did your breathing inside the mask, where your own heat warmed the air you took in.

And you had to keep moving. Inactivity, even for fifteen or twenty minutes, could start your own personal chill-down.

*Dear God*, she prayed. *Let her be warm, let her be wearing her jacket, let her still be alive. I'll do anything. I don't deserve this, I can't take this pain.*

She wandered the house, feeling lost. Four times she went over to the telephone and picked up the receiver, listening for a dial tone to make sure her line hadn't gone dead. She didn't go in Kady's room. She was afraid the sight of Kady's rock collection, her dog-eared teen romance books, her *Little House on the Prairie* set, her lamp shaped like a doll, her lineup of Raisin figures, baby Pound Puppies, and other childish treasures would make her sob uncontrollably.

She glanced at her watch. Only an hour had passed. My God, this night was going to be endless. She couldn't just stay here doing nothing, she would be broken by morning.

But Arrington had told her to stay here and wait for calls.

Kady might try to call.

Restless guilt tormented her. She went back into the kitchen to make scrambled eggs, but stopped after a minute, leaving the eggs sitting on the counter, uncracked. She got out some Fantastik and began to clean the appliances, then remembered that Kady had made most of the fingerprints on the refrigerator, and dropped her cloth in midwipe.

The phone stayed silent, and all around her the house creaked, the furnace blower and refrigerator motor adding their whir and hum to the light framework of sounds that were a part of any winter house at night. For the first time Sherry noticed that the kitchen wall clock made a tiny popping sound as the second hand progressed. She went over and pulled it off the wall, silencing it.

She had to do something or she was going to go mad.

At the small, cluttered desk at the far end of the kitchen, where Sherry made out bills and kept a wicker basket full of pizza coupons and junk mail, she found a pad of paper and a pen. She decided to make a list of everything she knew about the Innis case, everything that might have a bearing, even things that made no sense.

*Ray Innis*, she wrote first. *Hate.*

Then: *What if he is here in Hartwick? Right now? Would I even recognize him? He would be old now.*

*Judy, Carole, me*, she wrote. *All involved in seventh grade case.*

*Judy was raped. Maybe Carole.*

*Carole was angry because I asked questions.*

*Carole was jealous of me because I was Miss Michigan.*

*Carole was in therapy with Dr. Frey.*

*Don't women and men look alike dressed in snowmobile suits?*

The wind picked up, rattling a pine branch against one of the kitchen windows. The intrusion scattered Sherry's thoughts. She sat for a minute trying to gather them. Judy and Carole owned snowmobiles, but then, so did nearly everyone else she knew; even Timberline possessed two of the snow vehicles.

She stopped writing again and sat for a long time, listening to the wind and the sound of the furnace blower. What good was all of this? She could write and write, but it was still only conjecture, she didn't have any hard facts, only hunches and maybes. It seemed she was close to some vital realization, but as soon as she tried to focus, the secret slipped away.

But she did still have one of the videotapes, she remembered with a sudden jump of her heart. She had hidden it in the garage away from Kady. She hurried out to the garage to get it, tasting the frigid bite of the air even inside the garage.

She took the video out of the barbecue mitt where she had hidden it, and laid it on the counter to thaw. Even lying there it seemed black and menacing to her, as if plastic could be imbued with evil.

She waited fifteen minutes, then carried the tape into the TV room and fed it into the VCR. Flickering dots and lights filled the screen, as before, and then the title: *Nymphets*. Sherry shook her head, vaguely remembering a novel about an older man who had lusted after young girls: *nymphets* had been his name for them. It had been a best-seller when Sherry was in high school. *Lolita*.

She steeled herself as the first scene began, and this time instead of seeing nakedness and ejaculating penises, she looked at the girls. Many were Caucasian and had a look about them of suburban children who had been well nourished and cared for. One little girl had a fall of straight blond hair with an expensive, beauty-salon cut.

Another child had a large bruise on her hip and red marks on her wrists.

Scenes flickered past, embodying every sexual act that Sherry had ever read about, except that these had an added strangeness because of the largeness of the men contrasted with the dainty immaturity of the children. Not only were the men large in terms of their sexual apparatus, but also their physical size. Two-hundred-pound men forcing themselves on little girls of seventy and eighty pounds.

Sherry began to gag, sour vomit swelling up, but savagely she swallowed it back and forced herself to continue watching. The scenes unfolded, plotless, rife with evil. A man ejaculating on a child's stomach. A little girl being anally raped with a soda bottle. She almost couldn't go on. Then she saw it, a scene with a child cowering on a mattress, both frail wrists chained to a wall, as a naked man approached her.

Sherry sat frozen, realization thudding through her. Of course. The girl with the red mark on her wrist—and this girl. They kidnapped the children and hid them away, cuffed and chained, until they were needed.

She switched off the set without bothering to rewind.

*One*, she thought. Kady had been kidnapped by the people who made the videos and was going to be used for another tape.

*Two.* Someone intended to imitate the acts on the tapes, using Kady as those girls had been used.

*Three.*

But her mind was already reeling. She fell back onto the corduroy couch, a headache hammering at her temples. Whatever the scenario, she thought, whether this was connected with Ray Innis or not, there was a good chance that if Kady wasn't dead yet, then she was being imprisoned somewhere, waiting to be raped and used.

Sherry tried to phone Arrington, but was told he was not there. She started to leave a message and then changed her mind. She was a person of action, she was not going to wait here in this empty house when she could be doing something, however small, to bring her daughter back.

She had no answering machine, but she did have call forwarding, and she punched in the code and her mother's number. Let Margaret do the passive waiting and agonizing; she deserved it after leaving Kady alone to be taken.

She changed to outdoor gear: polypropylene underwear, turtleneck, wool sweater, warm-up pants over her jeans, jacket, hat, scarf, ski mask, and thick, padded leather ski gloves. Then she was in her car, speeding toward town again, taking the curves on M-72 with more caution this time; she could not afford an automobile accident.

Darkness and Sherry's mood made the village seem sinister, a collection of squat, one- and two-story dwellings behind whose lit windows any depravity could be happening.

This time when she drove up Carole's street, she found Carole's house dark except for one dim light glowing somewhere in the interior of the house. Her headlights ignited the reflectors of several snowmobiles parked by the carport—the same ones she'd seen before. Sherry eyed them. Dressed in a snowmobile suit a person's sex could not be distinguished. Could it be *Carole* who had buzzed her home late at night, who had chased Kady in the woods? Could Kady be *here*, locked in an upstairs room?

She stared at the vacant house, which gave no answers. Sherry cursed under her breath: Carole was either out or at work.

She took a chance and drove to Grayling, parking in the hospital lot and hurrying into the lobby. A guard, pacing inside the double doors, eyed her with sexual interest.

She went inside. The desk usually manned by volunteers was deserted, visiting hours over. Like a thousand other waiting rooms, this one smelled of tired people and despair. A nasal voice on a PA system called for a Dr. Boyer.

Sherry found a phone booth and called Carole's usual station.

The nurse who answered the phone sounded harried.

"Can I speak to Carole Hamner, please?"

"She's not here yet. She's working the midnight shift today."

"This is Sherry Vincent, it's a family emergency. I need to speak with Carole. When she arrives, would you tell her I'm in the lobby? I just need to talk with her for a minute."

The lights in the lobby had been dimmed. Sherry found a seat and began leafing through a badly dog-eared copy of *Better Homes and Gardens* that showed summer gardens, the masses of gold, pink, fuchsia, and white in sharp contrast to the bitter winter wind that blew outside the hospital, rattling the windows. Last summer she and Kady had planted impatiens under the overhang near the garage. Kady had been thrilled with the pink, frivolous, nodding blossoms. Now summer was a lifetime ago, a different world ago.

Ten minutes later Carole appeared in the lobby, still dressed in coat and boots, her legs encased in white nylon uniform pants.

Sherry stood up as Carole walked toward her, a stranger, a woman she didn't really know at all. A woman who had harbored resentment toward her all these years, who had been secretly seeing the same therapist as she, who had hated her. Who had probably never been her real friend, not since childhood anyway.

"Sherry? Jesus, what are you doing here? I only have a couple of minutes break—are you all right? You look positively white."

"Kady's gone," Sherry said simply.

"What? What do you mean, gone?"

"I mean just that, she's gone. She was at my mother's house and she left to go and meet Maura, but Maura got grounded, and Kady never came back."

Carole stopped where she was, her chin tilted alertly, a tension in the way she carried herself. "She's probably at one of her friends' houses, Sherry, haven't you called all her girlfriends?"

Despair hardened Sherry's voice. "I've done all that, I've called them all, I've driven through town, I've called the Sheriff's Department, I've made it official. I need to talk to you."

Carole looked nervous. "Me? Well, I'll do anything I can to help, Sherry, you know I will."

A woman crossed the lobby on her way to the elevator. In her sixties, she looked bent and beaten, a visitor allowed open privileges because the patient was desperately near death. That was the kind of night it was. A night in which people died. Sherry shuddered, looking away.

"Do you use your snowmobiles often?" She threw out the question.

"Did you come all the way here to ask me that?" Carole stared at Sherry. "Sure, I have three of them, they were my father's. I think I've used them twice this winter. The Ski-Doo needs a tune-up, it's not running right. Sherry? Why are you looking at me like that? What's wrong with you tonight?"

Sherry searched for a good way to say it, a way that sounded in control and not querulous and paranoid. She found none.

"You've always hated me."

"What?"

"I said you hate me, don't you?"

Carole's round cheeks flushed red underneath the layer of rust-shaded blush she wore. "What are you talking about?"

The tight cord that controlled Sherry's emotions began to fray. "I *know*, Carole. I went to Dr. Frey's house—I looked through the wreckage. I saw that you were one of her cases. I saw part of your case record; I saw what she wrote."

She saw Carole recoil, her hands fly protectively to cover her breasts.

"You went there?"

"Yes."

Carole shook her head. "Sherry, are you crazy? You went there and you *read her case records*? How could you do that?"

"I did it because I had to, because Kady is at stake. Because I have to find out who was sending her those videotapes, who's been terrifying us with their snowmobile."

Carole gave a hard, short laugh. "And you think *I* did it, is that it?"

"Maybe. I don't know. Did you?"

They faced each other like enemies. Sherry felt the hostility radiating from this woman who had been as much a part of her world as the woods and trees.

"Sure I hated you," Carole finally drawled, digging her hands into the pockets of her blue down coat and slouching defiantly on one hip. "You had it all, Sherry—you had every goddamned thing I ever wanted. You were the prettiest girl in school; God, you were ten times prettier than anyone else, and you didn't care about that, did you? You really didn't *care*. You lived in some fucking ivory tower. You sent puppy-love letters to Ray Innis and got us in that mess and then after it was all over, your mother pulled you back home and you never knew how the rest of us suffered, did you? You really didn't. *And you never even asked.*"

Sherry stared, shocked at the hoarse genuine feeling in Carole's voice. She opened her mouth to say something but Carole went on, as if a plug had been pulled, releasing a cistern of dammed-up hate.

"And then, Glen Dietz. God, I loved him. I would have walked to hell and back for him, but he never looked at me, not until after you dumped him, and then it was only a revenge screw, it never meant anything. But you threw him away, didn't you? You broke your engagement and drove him out of town so no one else could have him."

Her whole life twisted inside out and distorted, like the exploits of a soap-opera character. "Carole, I—"

"After *that*," Carole mocked, "you entered the Miss Michigan pageant because your *mother made you*. What a crock, Sherry, you did it because you wanted it just as bad as the other girls. I saw you, I saw your picture in the paper, you were crying when you won. You were doing exactly what every other bitch beauty queen does when she wins!"

Sherry couldn't remember crying at all. It was so twisted, so unfair! She nearly shouted her reply. "You're a liar, Carole! I was only twenty-one! I didn't know what it was all about!"

Lights flamed in Carole's eyes. "Yeah, you were twenty-one and arrogant as hell, because you weighed one hundred fifteen fucking pounds and I weighed one fifty-five. Don't you remember the bikinis you wore then? So little and fancy and ruffled? While I wore black one-pieces with fucking *skirts*!"

Sherry took a step backward, stunned at the pus-like poison of these resentments, spewed out before her.

Carole went on, "And then you married Dick. Well, let me tell you something, Sherry Vincent! I had my revenge on you! I had it and I'm still having it!"

"W-what do you mean?"

"You can guess, can't you?" Carole sneered. "I was the promiscuous one of us, wasn't I? I was the one who slept around, I had gonorrhea twice, did you know that? Well, let me tell you, cookie, *I gave gonorrhea to your husband.*"

"What?" Sherry reeled backward, stunned.

"I was the one, you bitch! I did it, I knew I had it and I hoped he'd get it, I hoped and prayed he'd transmit it to you!"

Sherry was sickened, both at the revelation and the change in Carole. Gone was the Rubenesque, exuberant, raffish, and sensual nurse who wore her affairs like badges. Here was a woman rotten with hate, a woman who glared at her with burning blue eyes.

"Then *you* were the snowmobiler, weren't you?" Sherry asked quietly. "*You* sent the tapes. You bought them somewhere in a porn shop and you sent them to her. How could you?"

Carole didn't seem to hear her. "I'm still putting it to you, Sherry, *dear.* Do you want to know how? Well, I'll tell you how. I've got Glen Dietz again. I've had him in my bed eight times since he's come back to Hartwick; I've done everything to him but pee on his stomach, and maybe I'll do that, too. You thought he was interested in you, didn't you? Well, *I'm* the one who's having him. *Me!* Don't you believe me?" Carole asked as Sherry reacted with a small cry.

Sherry felt her mind dip and swim under the impact of this shock. She thought of Glen, his aura of sexuality, his confidence, the way he had spoken to her, touched her. And all the time he had been having Carole. How dirty, how disgusting, and suddenly how believable. Glen was exactly the sort of person who would go after two women at once. Somehow she had always known it.

"I believe you," she said, her voice cracking.

Another nurse came squeaking across the lobby, pushing a cart before her laden with medications, staring at them curiously. Carole leaned forward and lowered her voice. "No, I didn't send the videos," she hissed. "But I wish I did. Oh, Jesus fucking Christ, *I wish I did.*"

# CHAPTER 28

After the last sounds of the car died away into the distance, Kady huddled herself into a ball, her handcuffed hands awkwardly stretched in front of her, palms facing. She leaned her face on her forearms, tears spurting to her eyes despite all her resolve to stop them.

She tried not to think about what he had done to her, the way he had stripped off her jeans and panties and prodded a hard finger into her opening, then attempted to insert the flashlight into her, while Kady writhed and screamed. Then he had turned her over and began roughly pawing at her buttocks. Just as a terrible pain began to split her, there was a sound from outdoors.

Snowmobile motors. A bunch of them, their motors whining between the trees, as they joyrode in the woods. *He* had abruptly stopped what he was doing, as if the sounds scared him, and then, hastily, he looped a short chain through her cuffs and chained her to a ring set in one of the roof beams that supported the slanting wall.

Suddenly he was gone, taking the flashlight with him, leaving her chained in the attic in the dark.

Kady fought panic. It was so *dark*. Once, Kady had visited Tampa, Florida, with her parents on vacation. She could still remember the night sky, a grayish pink from all the neon lights. Here in northern Michigan they were hundreds of miles away from any big city that would create light reflections. This was real blackness, as thick as if ink had been sprayed on her eyelids, blinding her.

She stretched out her hand, hearing the clank of the chain that fastened her to the wall. Losing control, she dissolved into shuddering tears that shook her body and hurt her chest.

She cried and trembled for long minutes, but finally exhaustion turned her sobs into long gasps and then hiccups. At last a minute passed, then two, in which she wasn't crying at all. The darkness still pressed all around her, smotheringly black.

Experimentally she pulled at the chain, trying to see how far she could move. It took about thirty seconds to pace out her range of movement. A couple of steps backward and to each side. It was tighter than a dog chain. She could stand up, walk a couple of steps, or she could sit or lie down—but always her hands were stretched out in front of her toward the ring set into the wall.

She was twelve years old, and she was trapped here like a dog, waiting for *him* to come back and finish what he started. Something so awful that Kady had no words for the splitting, violating agony.

What was she going to do?

Trembling, she assessed her situation. The tape still blocked off her breathing, so that every breath was an effort. The side of her face throbbed painfully. There were other sore places all up and down her body from where she had fought him. Her . . . private place was sore. But Kady didn't think she was bleeding much, and she knew that a few black-and-blue marks weren't going to kill her.

Cold would.

Kady had skied days as cold as ten below zero. She knew how the cold, in just ten minutes or less, crept into your gloves, stinging your fingers, making them burn, the sensation agonizing. How it penetrated through the fabric of your ski pants and froze your legs. Cold even inserted itself into your nostrils like icicles. It made your eyeballs feel chilled and glassy.

Finally it started you shivering. First you'd tremble just a little. Gradually the shivers would grow more violent, until finally you were shaking so hard your teeth chattered, and you nearly bit your tongue. After that—but Kady had never stayed outdoors past that point.

She'd heard of people who had, though. Only two winters ago a couple of seventeen-year-olds from Hartwick had been out necking in the boy's car and had run down the battery. It had been two below zero, with a windchill factor of fifty below. They got out and started walking toward town. The boy, Brent Fishman, only made it two miles. The girl, Kim Bender, reached town, her face so frozen she couldn't talk. Later they found the boy lying under a pine, already frozen solid. Kim lost part of her nose and four toes, and the family had to move to Detroit so she could get plastic surgery.

This old cabin, closed up for years, couldn't possibly have a furnace, Kady realized. It would be as cold in here as it was outdoors. And the night hadn't even reached its coldest point yet. It could drop to ten below zero.

Anxiously Kady assessed the clothes she had on. Her hat had fallen off in the car, and she didn't know where her gloves were. Her jeans and panties were at her knees. Manipulating her cuffed hands, she managed to wiggle the jeans back up over her hips. If she leaned forward, she could even fasten the snap.

There. He had left her ski jacket alone, thank God, and she still had that, with its pull-out hood, to keep her warm on top. But somehow that was not much solace. *He* was going to come back—she knew he was. Kady knew she would never forget the slimy, crawly, scary violation of that hand between her legs if she lived to be 109. To be helpless—to be at the mercy of someone like that—to not be able to *stop* that hand—

Her lips started to tremble again, and she bit down on them hard, wincing as her teeth caught an area that had been made raw by the tape. A thought struck her. Maybe this wasn't really real. Maybe this was just some scary nightmare caused by eating too much pepperoni. Any minute now, she'd wake up and she'd be in her bed, cozy in the warm sheets and blankets, with her night light safely glowing.

But as soon as she finished the thought, she knew it was only a trick of her mind. Her stomach, anus, and crotch hurt too much for it not to be real, the metal handcuffs cutting into the tender, exposed flesh of her wrists.

Oh, it was real, all right. What was she going to do? Flaring her nostrils to breathe, she took in needlelike breaths of frigid air. She wriggled her hands, trying to get more comfortable.

Then she realized. Her hands were in *front* of her. She'd already pulled up her jeans. That meant she could bring her head down to her fingers.

Concentrating, she began the painful job of peeling away the tape that had been wound around and around her head, gluing her mouth, hair, and skin in its grip. The tape was slick in texture, like the tough strapping tape that was used to send packages in the mail.

The edges didn't want to come. Desperately she felt along the length of the tape, searching for the bumpy area that would indicate an end. Finally at the back of her head, she found it.

She gave a tug and heard the sticky sound as the tape peeled away. For a minute it didn't hurt and then the tape found hair that had been caught. A million pinpricks pierced her skull. Tears of pain sprang to her eyes. She had peeled a bandage off her forearm once, and it had been agony as it literally ripped out a hundred blond hairs by their roots. This was much worse.

Whimpering under her breath, saying, "Ouch, ouch, ouch, ow, ow," she kept pulling.

Then, in one huge yank, she grabbed off the rest of the tape and flung it out into the blackness. She heard a little scrape as it landed somewhere on bare flooring.

Kady sagged to the floor dizzily. Blackness lapped around her so thick it was like being in grape jelly. She lay still, pulling in great, deep breaths of icy air that tasted of dust. After a minute, she felt almost a euphoria. She'd done it, she'd got the tape off and no one had helped her. For a while she just breathed, no thoughts in her head, nothing there but the joyous animal awareness of her own lungs, sweetly expanding.

Then she heard a rustle. It came from somewhere in the impenetrably black depths of the old attic, a small-animal, furtive sound as something changed its position, maybe brushed up against something.

Kady froze.

*Rats* was her first terrified thought. Maybe rats made a nest here in the attic. Unconsciously she jerked at the cuffs, the metal fraying the already raw places on her wrist bone. *Rats!*

But then she expelled the gasp of air she'd taken,

relaxing her arms again. There could be an animal living up here but it didn't have to be a rat. Raccoons lived in chimneys and garages all the time, and birds got into places, too, and made nests. Or chipmunks. Even owls or squirrels.

She crouched very still, listening to see if she heard the scurrying sound again. But now there was nothing, except for tiny sounds in the flooring, as pieces of wood creaked and reacted to the cold. The silence was as smothering as the dark, so thick that she wanted to cry out, talk, bang on the floor, anything to fill up the vacancy with noise.

Memories flashed into her mind like movie frames. The ski mask with its yellow-rimmed eye holes that stared eerily. The metal ring on the belt of the snowmobile suit, cinched tightly. Gloves that tasted of oil and dirt. And the incredibly horrible feel of hands pushing apart her legs . . .

She felt tears begin again, and she blinked them away savagely. What was she, a baby blubbering in the dark, afraid to be alone, whimpering and whining for her mommy to come?

Maybe no one was *going* to come.

No one could hear her cry. No one cared if she was crying. And crying was useless, it wasn't going to get her out of here.

She had never had such a hard thought before, and it scared her with its grown-upness. Fresh shivers rippled up her back, seeming to emanate from her thighs and crotch where he had touched her. She huddled herself into a ball, managing to get her knees up between her forearms, so that she was as compact as possible. Her fingers were beginning to feel icy, and the skin on her face was icy, too.

This was like being locked up in a freezer, Kady reflected bleakly. This must be how steaks felt, or hamburger patties, tucked away in the ice. Only . . . this was a lot colder than any freezer.

How cold would it get by morning?

* * *

An hour later, Kady knew she was in serious trouble. What had begun as tiny, rippling shivers now had progressed to big shakes that rattled her teeth. She tried huddling in a ball; she tried jumping up and down, she scrunched up close to the wall so that she could retract her hands a few inches inside the sleeves of her jacket. And still she shivered.

The darkness played tricks on her, seeming to pulse in and out like a billowing black cloth. She blinked her eyes open and then shut—but it was just as black with her eyes squeezed shut as it was with them bolt open. Maybe it was the dark, maybe the cold, but waves of sleepiness had begun to wash over her, almost powerless to resist. Three times she caught herself nodding forward, and straightened her head with a jerk.

If she fell asleep now, she might die.

Anxiously, she shifted around again, repeating all the keep-warm movements she'd done before. How long did it take a person to freeze to death? Kady's mind worried at the question, picturing her mother putting a big T-bone steak in the freezer of their refrigerator. If you pulled the steak out after an hour, it wouldn't be frozen solid yet. But the top layer of the meat would be full of ice crystals.

Panic was like a spear, stabbing her chest.

But a steak wasn't alive! She wasn't a steak! She wasn't meant to be locked away like this, what was she going to do? Kady had been brought up to believe that there was always something you could *do* about things. You might cry, you might complain, it might be really hard, but you could *do* something.

Now everything she'd tried hadn't worked. She didn't even know what time it was anymore—it felt like she'd been here all night, but Kady had the horrible feeling that not very much time might have passed at all. What if she'd only been here a couple of hours? It had been, what? About 6:00 when she'd come back to the alley. The car ride had taken about half an hour, she guessed. So ... maybe it was only 8:30.

Eight-thirty at night was early, the cold hadn't really begun to drop yet, the way it would by dawn. And if it was zero now, it could easily drop ten or even fifteen more degrees. Kady knew, because she always looked at the outdoor thermometer nailed to the tree by the garage, which could be seen from her bedroom window.

*Mom.* The coziness of their TV room, both of them laughing at *Bill Cosby* with bowls of microwave popcorn in their laps. Sadness and longing swept violently over her. She almost gave in to it, but something at the last minute saved her. If she gave in and cried and became a baby, then she was going to die, because she'd be crying too hard to help herself.

*I am not going to cry*, she vowed. *I am not a little crying baby.*

She knew she might not be discovered missing for a while. She'd deliberately left the radio on so Grandma would think she was in her room, and Grandma might very well have come home, called in to her, then switched on the TV for her regular night's viewing. Maybe Grandma didn't even know she was gone yet!

Struggling against adult despair, Kady got to her feet again and began to pace, like a dog paces at the end of its chain. It was hard pacing in the dark because she couldn't see where to put her feet, and the floorboards were uneven, some of them raised as much as a half inch over others. If only she had a blanket, or a quilt, or even some old newspapers to pull over herself!

But she was in an attic, a voice inside her head reminded her. Weren't attics stuffed with old things? Wasn't that why people used them in the first place? Suddenly the video player in her head switched on again, flashing scenes at her: the wild, swinging arc of the flashlight as the black-suited figure dragged her upstairs. Shadows that leaped and jumped. Glimpses of some things that looked like old shovels, or big pieces of wood. He'd been dragging her toward—

A mattress.

She stood still, replaying the image of the mattress, seen in brief seconds before she'd been hurled down on it. Old. Stained. Covered with a kind of thin striped, ugly cloth that Kady bet was about forty years old. And this mattress hadn't been thick, like the mattress on Kady's own bed at home, filled with nice, solid innersprings and support. This one was thin, only three or four inches thick, leaking soggy, rotted, ratty-looking stuffing. In fact, Kady wondered if rats, or at least mice, had been making their nests in the stuffing.

But where *was* the mattress now? Was it close enough to reach? Her sense of direction was gone, and the inky darkness made it as if she were blindfolded. Still, hope flared in her. *If* the mattress was close enough to reach, she could pull it over and use it to keep warm. Folded in half, pulled over and around herself, it would be like a tent or an igloo, trapping her body heat inside. She could stay alive a long time if she had that mattress.

*Once when she was eight she and her mom had built an igloo out of snow, carefully packing each block and stacking them in a circle, just the way it showed in one of Kady's library books. They'd even packed the crevices with snow, and left an air vent at the top. They'd gone inside and had a picnic and found themselves actually getting hot in there. Amazed, Kady had had to take off her jacket.*

Her heart racing, she paced the floor with a purpose now. But try as she might, moving her right foot in front of her to scrape its surface, she couldn't locate anything except floorboards and some pieces of grit or junk. With a sudden inspiration, she lay back down again, stretching herself out so that she could achieve the longest reach from the chain.

Why couldn't she see? Why did it have to be so dark! She felt suspended in a vat of black paint, and only the tough texture of the floor let her know she was in a place and not just floating.

Slowly, agonizingly slowly, she made a sweep of the area where she was, exploring with her stretched-out boot toe, then moving over a few inches and repeating the movement.

Nothing.

Kady was ready to cry from disappointment. How could this be happening? There wasn't anything she could reach! Nothing except dirt and dust balls! What happened if she grew thirsty? What if she had to go to the bathroom? What if she kept on shivering until—

She clamped down on her lower lip with her teeth, cutting off a sob. Maybe she hadn't searched *everything*. It was so dark, she couldn't see where she'd been, maybe she'd missed something.

So she started over again. Lying down like a person trying to rescue someone on the ice, probing with her foot for any object. This time she decided to start from the wall to her right. She reached with her foot, probed empty space, then moved a few feet and repeated the motion. Edged her stomach along, her face inches away from what must surely be the most horribly dirty and disgusting floor in the world. She could smell awful things on it— maybe bird poop, even, or the droppings from the little animal she'd heard earlier.

She had circled around a long ways now, but since she couldn't see, she didn't know how far she'd come. Surely she must be ready to hit the wall on the other side by now. Trying not to breathe the smell of the floor, she continued to work, and then, abruptly, her toe tip hit something solid.

Something that felt cushiony—something covered with cloth.

The mattress.

But her boot tip barely touched it.

# CHAPTER 29

Sherry left the hospital and drove through town, barely aware of stopping at the blinker light, of turning right onto Hartwick's main street lined with stores. Almost everything was closed now except the Shell station on the corner. She felt strange; her pulse alternately racing and dragging, clammy perspiration damp on her face and underneath her ski sweater, despite the coldness of the night.

Kady missing, maybe locked away somewhere waiting to be raped or worse.

*But not dead*, her mind said firmly. *She is not dead because I don't feel her being dead, there would be an emptiness, I'd know. I know I'd know.*

Her mind flicked from one thought, one horror, to another, unable to settle or concentrate.

Carole. She had slept with Dick—given him the case of venereal disease that had been the final, cutting blade that severed their marriage. Now, apparently, she was also sleeping with Glen Dietz, the act one of revenge, rather than any desire, passion, or love. At least that was what Sherry had concluded from Carole's hissed spasm of hatred.

How could Carole hate her that much?

Was being Miss Michigan really so hurtful to someone else?

Or did Carole's enmity date even further back, to seventh grade, when Sherry had unwittingly set in motion a whole string of events that would affect Carole and Judy to this day? *They* had been raped, she had not. Their suffering had been great in comparison to hers, which had been relatively minor. And, as Carole had shouted at her, she hadn't even cared enough to ask.

The two blocks sped past her, and automatically Sherry's eyes searched each storefront, each empty parking space, each alley between buildings, each passing car, of which there were four. She saw no pedestrians, except for a man leaving the drugstore hurriedly for the warm shelter of his car. No tall young girl, extravagantly pretty, in a powder blue ski jacket with a Timberline ski tag.

Her thoughts segued again. *Was* she uncaring, unfeeling, arrogant, as Carole had accused? *Had* she flaunted her prettiness, or had her arrogance been merely that of any healthy and good-looking, self-absorbed twenty-one-year-old?

*I never meant to hurt anyone*, she thought, sudden tears brimming to her eyes. She reached the corner of Main and McKinley in a blur of kaleidoscopic, rainbow lights and had to sit there for a minute until her vision cleared. Snow had begun to fall again, but the flakes were hard little pellets, compressed by cold. They flurried downward, danced and bounced by the wind. It seemed as if they were eternally in winter, as if there could be no other condition.

Sherry felt sick, alone, fearful, and angry. Had

Carole lied? Memories flashed into her head, times when Carole had "gotten even" with one or another of their friends, telling creative lies they had all giggled about. (*"I told her I saw Frank over in Traverse City with this girl in a strapless sundress. She believed it, what a kick."*)

Maybe Carole hadn't slept with Glen, or Dick either—but Carole had thought that the lies would hurt Sherry. She considered it. Carole was capable of such a vicious fabrication. But up until this time Carole hadn't harmed anyone physically. She'd been promiscuous, she'd gossiped, sometimes unkindly, but did that make her a kidnapper and killer?

Besides, Carole worked as a pediatrics nurse. Whatever her faults, she loved children. Carole wouldn't hurt Kady. She wasn't a child molester, she was cruel only with words. Sherry would stake her life on it.

*And Kady's too?* an inner voice mocked her.

Sherry turned back toward her mother's house. This was too much—she didn't have the heart for figuring out Carole's motives. She would go there and call Mike Arrington, tell him what she had learned about Carole, let him decide.

Back at her mother's, she found cars parked in the driveway and every light in the house burning. The living room was filled with people making notations on torn-out pages of the county telephone book, talking urgently, or hand-printing posters that said, *Have You Seen This Girl?*

Walking in, Sherry was struck by the sight of that poster as if by a blow with a heavy plastic ski boot. She actually staggered backward, her abdominal muscles tightening, cutting off her breath. Her daughter was turning into a milk-carton child, one of those poor, hopeless waifs who existed only on cardboard and in police files; who would never be found.

*No*, she wanted to scream. *No, please, God—not that.*

People were staring at her, Maida Thomas, Augusta McClurg, others from her mother's gossipy, active social set. Even Joelle Hartman, her mother's boarder, looked up from the poster she was making with a black felt pen. Joelle's mouth hung open; here was Sherry, a bona fide Victim of Tragedy.

A moment of embarrassment for everyone; was she going to fall apart? What did you say? In answer, Sherry found herself curving her mouth into what might pass for a frozen, defiant smile.

"Hi, everyone. Thanks for your help."

There were murmurs and several people came up to hug her.

"Hello, Sherry," her mother greeted her hurriedly. "We've formed a calling chain."

"A what?"

"Yes—everyone is calling twenty others and asking them to call twenty others—we can cover the whole county in a couple of hours. We've marked pages in the phone book of people we know. Do you want to call too? We've got plenty."

Sherry stared at her mother in dulled amazement. When she had left, Margaret had been disheveled and shocked, her hair unkempt, wearing the blue housecoat she usually wore only to put on makeup. Now here she was, handsome in a pair of gray wool slacks with long, intarsia-knit sweater, her eyes bright and snapping with zest as she directed this informal citizen search.

"Well, Sherry?" Margaret asked briskly. "We can't use this phone, you know, we have to keep it open for incoming phone calls, but you could go across to Maida's, she's got an extra phone line she had put in to Martin's room last year."

Martin was Maida's forty-year-old, painfully shy son who worked as a mail carrier.

"We're trying to call everyone in the county. We're asking them all to look everywhere they can. Otherwise I don't see how the Sheriff's Department can cover the area. This county is just too big and they haven't got nearly enough cars, it's a crime."

Sherry hesitated. Making telephone calls like charity solicitations, while her daughter waited somewhere, cold and terrified! But what else was there to do? Making phone calls was certainly a lot better than uselessly driving through town.

"All right," she said, accepting the torn-out page. She added, "Has Detective Arrington called?"

"Yes, once. We're supposed to call back if we think of anything. You haven't thought of anything, have you, Sherry?"

"I don't know."

"Well, if you have you'd better call him. This is your child who's missing, Sherry; we can't afford any 'I don't knows,' we have to follow everything up."

A tone of voice Sherry recognized from the past. She felt a flare of resentment. Taking her mother aside, she whispered, "*You* left her alone, Mom. I know you're trying to make it up, but don't you lecture me. I *know* she's missing. No one needs to inform me of that."

Her mother recoiled, her cheeks reddening in hurt, and several of the ladies in the room looked shocked. Sherry pressed her lips together, her eyes watering again. These people were trying to help. What was she trying to do, alienate them? She and Kady couldn't afford to have any enemies right now.

"Sorry," she mumbled. She backed out of the room and wearily walked across the street to Maida's, where all the lights were also on, and a plump lady Sherry recognized as Laura MacPhee, Hartwick's part-time librarian, was busily talking on the extension in Maida's kitchen.

Sherry walked into the son's room. Pudgy and

introverted, he was Hartwick's resident sci-fi fan, and bookshelves on three walls bulged with paper-backs with titles like *Dragon's Pawn* and *The Wizard of Whitechapel*.

She picked up the page she had been given, which covered the letter *T*, from Taback, Edwin to Turner Chiropractic. Some of the names had been underlined in pencil, presumably those people known to her mother's circle. She dialed the first name, *Tabor, B. E.*

"Yes?" answered the voice, that of a middle-aged female, cozy sounding. A TV set blared in the background; someone was switching channels.

How did you word it, what did you say that was drained sufficiently of emotion so that you wouldn't begin bawling? "This is Sherry Vincent," Sherry began in a monotone.

"Oh, yes, Margaret Smith's girl. I know your mother from Tuesday Bridge Club."

"I'm calling because my daughter is missing, and we're hoping . . ."

Numbly she finished, barely aware of what she said. There was a surprised silence.

"You don't mean . . . Margaret's little grand-daughter, that really pretty girl, the one who's going to be a model?"

"Yes, that one."

The woman kept her on the line for ten minutes, exclaiming in shock, asking questions, pouring out sympathy, wanting to know all the details. Sherry endured it, feeling as if this were some new kind of psychological torture. Maybe her mother was right. Hartwick was a small village, why not use that small-townness? But she hadn't bargained on the effort it took, the courage to bare herself like this. She felt helpless and futile, talking on the telephone when she could be out doing something.

She made twelve or fifteen more calls, mostly to women. Each promised to get on the line and make more calls. Many volunteered husbands or sons to man search parties, and Sherry told them her mother was organizing that, too.

She hung up from the last call and sat for several minutes staring blindly down at the torn-out page. The people of Hartwick were good folk, willing and innocent. But there was hardly any serious crime in Hartwick. People rarely locked their car doors, and many homeowners didn't lock up, either. If you weren't going to be home for Halloween, you could leave candy on your doorstep, and at the end of the evening, you'd still have Hershey's Kisses left.

If you weren't used to crime, or to looking for crime, could you even notice the small details that might point to a lost girl?

Depressed, she focused her eyes on the last underlined name, which was next to the large-type notation for the law firm of Turner and Frey. This must be Bob Frey's law firm, she remembered, Nanette's husband. He had refused to let her look at his wife's case records, but that was before Kady was missing.

Would he be more cooperative now? Sherry doubted it. She remembered the sodden black mass she'd hurriedly tossed into the old safe, and wondered if it contained anything readable—or anything that would pertain now.

Her thoughts were interrupted by the ringing of the phone, and she snatched up the receiver. "Yes?"

"It's Mike Arrington. Your mother gave me this number." He sounded annoyed with her. "I thought I told you to stay at your house in case your daughter calls over there."

"I have call forwarding. I coded in my mother's number. I can't just sit home and passively wait," she snapped.

"But that's what a kidnapper would expect—if there's going to be any calls for ransom you have to be there to receive them. You're not at your mother's either."

She felt a wave of hot anger. "Well, I'm right across the street trying to use the phone. Ransom? What ransom? We're not going to get a ransom call and you know it as well as I do. They have Kady somewhere, they're keeping her tied up, and they're going to do something terrible to her if we don't hurry!"

"Hey," he said. "What makes you think they've got her tied up?"

"Because I played back one of those videotapes. That's what they do to these young girls—that's their method, what is it you detectives call it? Their M.O."

"Calm down," he said. "We know all that, Sherry, we played the tapes, too. Look, why don't you go home and try to get a little rest? I'll keep in touch with you there; I'll let you know everything that's going on, I promise."

"I won't sit around and do nothing!"

"Well, you're going to have to. You—"

"Anyway," she interrupted, "I went to see Carole Hamner. She was—" She stopped, suddenly unsure of herself. Yes, Carole could have sent the videos, she was sophisticated enough to know about pornography outlets, and she owned three snowmobiles ... but were those things enough to incriminate? All she had was Carole's hate and the hissed denial: *No, I didn't send the videos. But I wish I did. Oh, Jesus fucking Christ, I wish I did.*

"Yes?" the detective prompted.

"She—we argued. She said she hates me, she always has, ever since—since I was Miss Michigan. She said some nasty things. She said she wished she'd sent me the videos."

"Jealousy," he said. "But we'll talk to her, see what's happening." Sherry could tell by the sound of his voice that he discounted this lead, and she

supposed she did, too. She just could not picture
Carole Hamner kidnapping Kady.

"Anything else?" Arrington asked crisply, sounding very official and busy. In the background she
heard telephones ringing and harried male voices,
someone cursing.

"No," she said.

"Where can we reach you then? At your mother's?"

"She'll get me a message," Sherry heard herself
say belligerently. She realized as she hung up that
she'd been clenching the receiver so hard that her
knuckles hurt. And she'd done another thing, too;
she'd committed herself to doing something more
than phone calls.

But what?

She dialed her mother. Glancing at her watch she
saw that two hours had passed, it was now after
2:00 in the morning. Impatiently she waited for her
mother to pick up.

*What if Kady's at Timberline?* The thought leaped
into her head, igniting electricity that sped along
her muscles, galvanizing them.

"Hello?" came her mother's familiar tone,
sounding a little tired now, a little stressed.

"It's me. I'm going to drive out to Timberline,"
she said. "Take a look around out there."

"At this hour?"

"Why not at this hour? Mom, I have to do something, I can't just sit here on the phone, it's not
enough, I have to be doing more. Maybe she's at
Timberline. Maybe—" Her heart leaped. "Maybe
she went skiing and fell down somewhere, maybe
she's lying in the woods with a broken leg."

"Sherry!"

"Well, she could be. They sweep the slopes, the
Ski Patrol, but maybe she's there and they missed
her. I've got to go, Mom." And she clicked off. As

she ran out of the house she was zipping her ski
jacket, pulling the wool hat over her head.

The lodge at Timberline was lit with its regular
night floodlights, stranded at one end of the empty
parking lot. Sherry pulled into the lot, marked with
tire tracks of all the skiers who had used it during
the day. A dropped scarf lying on one of the snowbanks fluttered in the wind.

She doused her headlights, darkness instantly
swallowing up her car. As she got out, an icy wind
swirled at her, washing her face with cold, penetrating up the passages of her nostrils and down
her throat. It was the kind of wind that burned, like
dry ice. She knew it would be a killer wind for anyone who had to be in it for very long without jacket
or proper clothes.

She walked over to the scarf and picked it up. It
was made of some dark, tartanlike wool plaid with
fringed edges and she had never seen it before. She
stuffed it in her pocket, then stood still in the parking lot, listening for sounds.

Pine branches, heavily crusted with snow, moved
against each other, and there were the plopping
falls of chunks of snow whose delicate balance had
been unsettled by the wind. Distantly came the
whine of a big truck somewhere on M-72, hell-bent
for home.

She could hear her own breathing, and the slip-
page as the ski tag she wore was blown by the wind
to rub against the fabric of her jacket.

But other than that, nothing but the cold hush of
the winter night. No human sounds at all, and certainly not the muffled cries for help of a skier
downed and freezing somewhere in the woods.

Sherry felt a wave of real doubt. Ski Patrol always "swept" the slopes before the chair lifts
closed. They skied trails looking for injured victims
and observed for signs that skiers might have taken

off alone into the woods. Anyway, Kady certainly knew better than to ski alone. She had grown up around skiing and knew the dangers.

She walked across the parking lot toward the building, fumbling for her master key, already swept with the growing certainty that her daughter could not be here. The idea had been only a trick of her desperate mind, groping for anything, no matter how faint, that could offer hope.

She walked in. A night light by the ticket window glowed eerily, creating heavy blocks of shadows down the long room filled with trestle tables, framed ski posters decorating the paneled walls. She flicked on the main light, and the room seemed to jump at her, like the stage set of a ski lodge before any actors arrive.

In her own office, she switched on the master floodlights, the ones they used for night skiing. She opened her locker, found a flashlight, put on her boots, and carried her skis out through the back door to the edge of the hill. Wind bit at her face. Automatically she clicked the metal plates at her boot tips into the bindings of the skis. She pulled on a ski mask and zipped her jacket. The chair lift wasn't running but she could herringbone up the hills; she had done it before many times.

The lodge was at the crest of one of the rounded hills that—thousands of years ago—had once been a sand dune, created by the glaciers and by wind over an ancient great lake. Sherry stood narrowing her eyes at the run that had been cut through the trees. Snow glowed dimly. On either side were the woods, where kids sometimes spontaneously made trails or created their own ski jumps.

Was Kady out there somewhere, sprawled face-down in a snowdrift under one of those pines, unable to move or crawl because of the pain of a fractured femur?

She stood listening again, hearing nothing but the night, and then she called out her daughter's name. "Kady! *Kady! Ka-deeeeee!*"

No answer: had she expected one? She called again, hearing the way her voice hoarsened. Then she kicked off and began skiing down the first slope, making long traverses from side to side so that she could inspect the recesses of the trees. Stopping three or four times, she cried out Kady's name again.

It wasn't until her legs were shaking with the effort of climbing the hills and her fingers were numb inside her ski gloves that she admitted that Kady wasn't out there. She stood by the silent chair lift, seeing a ghost there of a pretty four-year-old who had to hop upward in order to slide onto the chair.

At last tears streamed from her eyes and she let them come, until her sobs rang out on the vacant slopes and echoed among the cruel trees. Was this somehow her own fault, had she created the events that had telescoped into other events, that became secrets and hatred and lust, and somehow ended up at her own door, and Kady's innocence?

But she, the young Sherry, had been only twelve years old. A child, innocent too. She hadn't *meant* to set anything in motion. She hadn't known she'd done so and could not have stopped events from turning anyway.

There were no answers, she realized with a deep stab that cut into the lining of her heart. All she could do was go back to her mother's, try to wait the night out, try to wait for news.

# CHAPTER 30

Kady lay flat on her stomach on the floor, too mad and frustrated to feel despair. There it was—the mattress she needed to keep warm—and it was so close she could nudge it with her boot. But she couldn't get a good hooking grip on it, enough to drag it toward her.

She couldn't believe she could be this close to the mattress and not be close enough to get it. She shouted out her anger—"*Oh, shit!*" And then again: "*Shit!*"

Then Kady opened her lips and sucked in a deep breath of the biting attic air. She hadn't stretched hard enough, that was it. She hadn't tried as hard as she could. She was being a baby, feeling sorry for herself, getting ready to blubber again.

Lying flat, digging her chin and nose into the floor, she began stretching herself, pulling on her arms until she could feel things popping in her wrists, and the steel cuff cut into her skin. She humped and wriggled backward, stretching the ligaments of her arms and sides, extracting every inch of space she could. And all the while she was tap-tapping with her boot tip trying to get a good enough grip on the old mattress to drag it toward her.

Her efforts hiked her jacket, pulling up her sweater, and slivers from the floor stabbed her bare stomach like little picks.

*Why couldn't she be taller?*

Over and over, she touched, but her boot was too clumsy to hook into the material, and she began to be afraid that her efforts would only push the bulky mattress away beyond her reach. Finally she sank onto the floor, panting with the effort. Already she was getting so cold she could barely suppress her shivering. She *had* to get the mattress.

With her nose against the floor, she shut her eyes and prayed. *God, help me get the mattress and help me get out of here. I'm sorry we didn't go to church more. If you let me out of here I'll go to Maura's Sunday school with her. I'll pray every night.*

*I really mean that, God,* she added.

She lay there for a few seconds, feeling the cold from the floor creep into her naked stomach with inexorable thoroughness. The cold wasn't something you could beg to, or reason with, it didn't care what you said or did, it didn't care if you died. If only she wasn't wearing her thick boots with the hard toes that didn't give any flexibility. If only she had on her Reeboks. Their rubberlike front tip would give her a lot more traction.

Unconsciously she wiggled her toes inside her boots, feeling the familiar sensation of her socks rubbing against the inner pile lining. Even her toes were cold now. They—

Her toes. Bare feet.

Almost laughing, Kady scrambled up, crawling close to the wall again so there'd be enough chain length to work. Sitting, she managed to untie her right boot. She stripped off the wool ski sock, carefully tucking it inside the boot so she could find it again. She'd have to hurry—she didn't have much time—but this might work.

Again she was on her stomach, again stretching and pulling full length, torturing her wrists against the steel cuffs, extending her bare right foot as far as she could into the blackness. There. She felt the mattress. And this time her right big toe could hook into the fabric.

Grunting with effort, she hooked her toe forward and felt the cloth move a little. She tried again. There was a reluctant sliding sound and Kady repositioned her toe, this time managing to sink it into one of the many holes in the ticking. The hole acted as a handle. On her hands and knees now, her toe sunk in the stuffing, she dragged the mattress up toward the wall.

Then she had it, she was half kneeling on its foul, lumpy bulk. Laughing, Kady used both feet to kick it forward, to a place where she could reach it with her hands.

Kady's fingers were stiff when she pulled the ski sock and boot on again, her toes burning with cold.

Inside the crude tent she'd made for herself, the thin mattress arched over her head so that she had to stay curled in an uncomfortable ball, her body heat warmed up the enclosure.

She tried to sleep. Her body, battered and sore, cried out for rest. Her wrists had begun to throb, and putting her face close to her wrists and extending her tongue, Kady had tasted blood. The slivers embedded in her stomach gave pricky stabs every time she moved. And there were other sorenesses, too, at her hip, her rear end, and along her jawline where he had slugged her.

Curled in a fetal ball, she tried to relax. But a

mass of the coarse mattress stuffing protruded near
her face, her body heat bringing out its stench of
rot and mildew and mouse droppings. Maybe there
were even mice living inside the mattress. Revulsion shuddered through her, and she fought the im-
pulse to kick the vile-smelling mattress away.

If there were any mice, she soothed herself, all
the pulling and tugging had scared them and they'd
run out. Anyway, no matter how gross and horrible
the mattress was, it did create a nice little warm
space for her, and that was what counted.

In the morning she'd—

Sleep stole toward her, fuzzing her thought, and
then she was adrift in fragmented dreams, from
which she woke several times, giving high, sharp,
agonized cries.

Dawn crept into the attic, lighting the air almost
imperceptibly from pitch-black to deepest gray,
then pearl gray, then pearl. Kady stirred and mumbled to herself.

Pressure on her bladder was what finally woke
her. She moved jerkily, her muscles cramped from
having hunched in a ball all night. She opened her
eyes, seeing the grayed, striped ticking with its
myriad of unmentionable stains. A hunk of equally
gray stuffing hung in front of her eyes, dotted with
little specks that looked like dried-up bugs.

She jerked her face away from it. She had to
pee—and she had to pee badly.

Kady pushed away the edge of the thin mattress
like a chipmunk coming out of its burrow. She
blinked her eyes in shock. Two spiderwebbed windows, one at each end of a thirty-foot enclosure, let
in the diffused light of a gray, bitter winter morning. One of the windows had been broken, glass lit-
tering the floor, and that was why it was so cold in
here. Snow had drifted up on the floorboards.

She bit her lip in dismay. The flooring was a filthy

gray, crusted with dirt and gobs of dark gray spiderwebs. There were cavities between some floorboards, filled with dark stuff. Visible were roof beams made of old logs that still showed ax marks on them. Leaning against the opposite wall were some old rakes and pitchforks, their wooden handles weather-beaten and splintered, and a big, rusty hammer.

Her eyes focused on more signs of human occupancy—old tin cans, lids sticking up, had been tossed in a pile. Another pile held unidentifiable scraps of clothing, a curled-up leather shoe, and a couple of old whiskey bottles. A pillow had been torn into by some animal and was now sodden with age, bleared by dust.

A bum or hippie had slept up here one summer, probably on the very mattress she now wrapped around herself.

Seeing the remains of another person's stay seemed to people the attic with ghosts. Kady stirred again, trying to clamp down on her urinary muscles. She knew she was going to have to go to the bathroom whether she liked it or not. Humiliation surged over her. She was just going to have to squat down and pee on the floor, like a dog in a pen.

Daintily she moved away from the mattress and circled on the short length of chain until she was as close to the wall as she could get. Here, she saw, there was a break in the floorboards where a knothole had caused a partial splintering away. Edging close to the wall to give slack in the chain, she managed to get her jeans down. Positioning herself, she was just able to squat over the hole.

Bleakly she listened to the sound of her own stream, and smelled her own urine. She could go to the bathroom here, she could endure the stink, but what was she going to do about something to drink and eat? She was already hungry, her mouth dry from thirst.

There wasn't any food up here, and the old whiskey bottles—even if she could get to them—had been empty for about ten years. Although there were huge snowdrifts outside the cabin—she'd seen them last night—that did her no good at all. She could not drink snow if she couldn't reach it.

She moved back toward the mattress and crawled within its protection again, dragging it back over herself, nesting carefully to keep herself warm.

The morning—was it Friday?—passed interminably slowly. Once Kady heard a pack of snowmobiles go roaring through the property—two or three of them at least—but no one heard her shouts. She had to lie there listening to the motors fade into the distance again, tears stinging her eyes.

She didn't even know what time it was. She wasn't wearing a watch, and even the sun wasn't any help. Narrowing her eyes to stare out of the broken window, she could tell that it was one of those grim, cloudy pale winter days when light comes from every direction, and the sun is invisible.

She inspected the chain that fastened her, looking for a weak link that she could pull apart. But the chain was a heavy-duty one, with thick, small links. As for the ring that held it to the beam, that was sunk in solidly. Kady spent some time kicking at it, trying to jar it loose. But it seemed to her there was no give to the wood at all.

Odd thoughts, grisly ones, tormented her. Like, she remembered reading in the *Free Press* about a fifteen-year-old girl who had been raped, then her rapist had cut off both her arms at the forearms. That girl had had to go through the rest of her life with no arms. How did she manage it? How did she eat, get dressed, go to the bathroom? How did you read a book with no hands?

Thinking about that other girl caused fingers of

fear to scuttle at the edges of Kady's mind, bringing with them dark suggestions of vileness. Images she was afraid to think, fears she was afraid to name. *He* would be coming back. What would he do to *her*?

Nervously, she shifted positions under the mattress, unable to deal with a reality so stark.

She twisted her mind to another thought. Like— how thirsty she was. She would give anything for a tall, fresh glass of orange juice mixed with banana that had been whipped in the blender. Or one of the mugs of hot cocoa they made at Timberline, thick and chocolaty, with dollops of melty white marshmallow on top. Or maybe just a glass of the incredibly cold, clear water that came from the taps in their house, served in the cut-crystal glasses that Sherry saved for "company."

She swallowed, salivating, angry at herself because she knew she was only making it worse. She wondered if they knew she was missing yet. Had her mother gone to the Sheriff's office, to that young-looking detective she'd talked to before, Arrington? Probably! Probably they had all the patrol cars in the county searching for her by now, which would be very exciting, something to tell the girls at school, better than any story that Heather Wycoff ever made up.

Then Kady slumped against the mattress, stifling the spurt of hope she'd felt. Tears wobbled on the edges of her lids, ready to fall. She blinked them down, angry at herself for crying again. There were old cabins all through the area, hunting lodges, fishing shacks, forgotten places people hardly ever used. Miles and miles of state forest. Thousands of empty summer cabins and lake homes.

What if her rescuers had no idea of where to start looking? No idea at all?

# CHAPTER 31

Arrington telephoned three times, to find out if there had been any ransom calls. Known sex offenders were being questioned, Kady's school friends and teachers had been questioned again, and officers were searching for Dick Vincent who was not at home at his A-frame near Lake Ossineke.

"Maybe he's with one of his women," Sherry suggested tiredly.

"Do you know their names? Where they live?"

"Me? He doesn't exactly keep me informed. I know he had a ski instructor he was seeing—and last week I saw him pick up a woman in a bar in Traverse City. Dick likes variety. Long weekends, that sort of thing. And he usually picks women out of town, so there won't be gossip."

"Is there anyone who might know who he's with or where he is?"

Sherry thought. Like many men, Dick hadn't had close male friends. There'd been some sailing buddies, though, members of the boat club. She named several, adding, "But Dick couldn't have had anything to do with this."

"He's the father, isn't he? Fathers have been known to kidnap their own children. Did you ever argue about custody? About who she should live with?"

"That's not a factor. He didn't want her living with him," Sherry said, her voice still scratchy from all the shouting she had done on the cold slopes of Timberline. "He wanted the bachelor life, and a child would be a real impediment. Please, do you have any other leads, anything? It's— She's been gone hours now. Anything could have happened."

"We're doing the best we can."

"*I want her back.*"

"Sherry, we've called in men to work double shifts, we are working on this, we're combing five counties."

Her voice rose. "What if she's been taken farther away than that? What if she's in the trunk of some car on I-75 somewhere, what if she is two hundred miles away by now, what if she—"

"We've thought of all that" came his reply, thinned by the telephone wires. "Try to stay calm, Sherry, it won't help things if you're upset. We're doing our best, and I need you as our center, the place where she can call."

*He thinks I'm hysterical*, she thought, compelling herself to say good-bye quietly and hang up. It was so late now—she felt groggy with weariness.

"What did he say?" Margaret demanded.

"Nothing new. They're trying to find Dick, that's all."

"Dick is an unfeeling bastard," her mother said, the venom in her voice surprising Sherry.

They continued to work. Sherry estimated the telephone chain had contacted maybe 4000 people, if all the callees had made other calls. The phone kept ringing—friends, neighbors, employees from Timberline who had heard. Some wanted to join a search party; others wanted to know if they had investigated Rialto Perry, a local Alzheimer's victim, if they had put a roadblock on M-72, if Kady might have hitchhiked to Grayling and taken a Greyhound bus.

By 2:30 A.M. Margaret's kitchen counter was littered with dirty coffee cups and soda cans. The phone calls had thinned to only one or two a half hour. Maida Thomas was still making posters, pasting on old snapshots of Kady. Maida was a game old soul, Sherry had to admit; seventy-two years old and willing to stay up most of the night.

"You should go home, Maida," Sherry said, touched. "You've been great but there's not much we can do now until morning."

"I couldn't sleep anyway," the older woman said.

So they continued to work, leaving in shifts to tack posters to telephone poles and trees, and duplicate more flyers on the copier in the lobby of the post office, which the postmaster had reopened so they could use the machine. But by 4:00 even Maida was flagging, and Margaret had already slumped full length on the living-room sofa.

Gazing down at her sleeping mother, Sherry felt a rush of almost-forgiveness. This was Hartwick, after all, a village where you could leave your door unlocked. To Margaret, being able to wave from the opposite window was contact, not desertion. Who would suppose you could walk across the street and a child would be gone?

She stretched out on a love seat and put her stockinged feet up, pillowing her head on the armrest. Her muscles sagged, her body releasing its built-up tension, and she went into a trancelike, semisleep state, still dimly aware of noises in the room, the sounds made by Maida as she cut, pasted, and glued.

The sounds grew more distant, as if she heard them from the bottom of a hundred-foot well, and then someone put a cover on the well and she was in the dark, falling still further, gold foam sparking around her, falling faster and faster, out of control—

She awoke suddenly to find herself sitting up. Maida Thomas was shaking her. "Sherry! Sherry! You were screaming."

She shook her head, feeling disoriented. "What? Did anything happen? Did the phone ring?"

"No, nothing's happened, your mother is snoring. Go back to sleep, Sherry, it's only five-thirty."

"Oh." Sherry groaned and lay back down, shifting her legs that ached from being cramped onto the small love seat. She closed her eyes and was falling again, this time wearing a black snowmobile suit trimmed with zippers that had teeth that glittered like miniature rows of razor points.

Then she landed on a snow-covered ski slope, but instead of skiers, there were dozens of snowmobiles, roaring and zigzagging, nearly hitting her, while she stood in the middle of them screaming out Kady's name.

The ringing of the telephone battered across her consciousness like the Gestapo thumping on the door. She struggled out of the dream, adrenaline jumping through her like a sickening jolt of drugs. Maida had picked up the phone.

"It's for you, Sherry."

"Me?" Sherry tried to acclimate herself. Her heart was still pounding. She blinked her eyes, trying to force the lids open. It must be morning, for pale light penetrated her mother's Nottingham lace curtains.

She stumbled over to pick up the phone from the whatnot table where her mother kept it.

"Hello?" she croaked.

"Sherry, I've just heard about Kady." It was Glen

Dietz, his voice sounding deep, male, and healthy with morning energy. "Is there anything I can do?"

Sherry hung onto the phone, as a dozen feelings swirled through her, none of them forgiving. "I don't know."

"Are you bearing up all right? You sound terrible."

"Of course I'm not bearing up all right," she snapped. "What did you expect, that I'd be all bright and bouncing around, full of good cheer because my child is missing? Anyway, who told you? Was it somebody we both know?"

"What do you mean?"

She heard her voice turn spiteful. "Maybe it was Carole, maybe she's the one who called. I understand you and Carole are on the best of terms—even better than best."

There was a silence. "What are you talking about?"

"*Carole,*" Sherry burst out. Then she caught herself and bit off the rest of the sentence. God, she sounded just like a jealous wife. She didn't have any rights to Glen, she didn't even want any. He and Carole could do what they wanted, when they wanted, and it was not her concern. Except that she still felt betrayed because Carole had tried to hurt her.

"What?" Glen said. "Come again? What're you trying to say?"

"Never mind, it's not my business, is it?"

"*What* isn't your business? What's wrong with you?" Glen's voice hardened. "Look, Sherry, I'll tell you how I found out about Kady. Some Sheriff's officers were over here again, asking more questions, asking if I knew anything about it or knew anyone who knew. Does that satisfy you? I'm sorry I ever took those pictures of her. It's sure opened me up to a lot of shit I don't need."

"I'm sorry," she said.

"I don't know anything about Kady and if I did I'd tell you, Sherry. I thought she was a great kid. Bright and pretty and unspoiled. Look, what can I do?"

Across the room Margaret was waking up, with the stiff morning movements of an arthritis sufferer. In the thin morning light Sherry's mother looked haggard, her face a network of pouches and wrinkles. Sherry saw her look around as if in shock to find herself on the couch.

"Answer me one question," Sherry said to Glen.

"Yes, what?"

"*Have* you been seeing Carole Hamner?"

"Why do you want to know that?"

"Because I need to know," she cried. "Have you, Glen? This isn't just an idle question, it has to do with Kady, it has to do with her being missing."

She heard him breathe over the wire, and there was a burst of the tiny, tinny ghost voices that sometimes haunt telephone lines. "Yes, she called me a couple of times. So what, Sherry? We went to high school together for God's sake. She called to welcome me back to Hartwick, and she came in and got a portrait taken, too."

Sherry lowered her voice, turning away so the others could not hear. "Did you sleep with her?"

"Hey." Glen sounded angry. "What kind of a question is that? Sherry, look, I called and offered to help you look for Kady, I'll help any way I can, I owe you that. But I'm not going to be grilled about my personal life. Do you want me to come over? We can ask around, go door to door, drive through town—"

He had evaded her question, refused to answer it. As he had every right to do, she reflected. She had violated his privacy, and he owed nothing to her. "We've already got people doing that," she said dully. "But thanks anyway."

* * *

Somehow it had become Friday. Sherry spent the day helping to coordinate search teams, who were traversing the state forest and other large tracts of woodland on snowmobiles and cross-country skis, looking for (she knew) a dead body. She refused to allow herself to consider that they would find one.

The phone constantly rang in a flood of queries, crank calls, and sympathy calls. Sherry answered each ring with a horrible leap of her heart that subsided when the caller turned out to be a member of her Timberline Ski Patrol, or Emmy Weibull, the Mayor's wife. Reporters from the *Hartwick Voice*, *Detroit News* and *Detroit Free Press*, Channels 4 and 7, were already writing stories about "the town that cared."

Sherry tried to emotionally disengage herself from it all. If she behaved normally, if she didn't fall apart, then nothing truly bad was going to happen, it would all be just a matter of being patient, and praying.

Maura Camrack arrived on Margaret's doorstep to sob that she wished it were her, that if she had met Kady on the corner as she was supposed to, none of it would have happened.

"It wasn't your fault, Maura," Sherry said, hugging the crying twelve-year-old.

"But it was! I didn't mean ... She's my *best friend*," Maura wept.

Sherry pulled the girl close, breathing in the scent of fragrant young hair so much like her own daughter's. "It's okay," she kept whispering, and nearly broke. She was relieved when Mrs. Camrack came hurrying up the walk and took her daughter in tow, apologizing for the interruption.

"It's all right," said Sherry.

"Are you sure? Oh!" Susan Camrack rubbed at red eyes and Sherry realized she was not the only one put under strain; the whole town was feeling it now. In Hartwick if one person hurt, others did, too. No life existed without touching a network of others.

Gray morning faded into afternoon. Some hidden strength or stubbornness anesthetized Sherry from total despair. With 4000 pairs of eyes and ears—more by now, the whole state knew Kady was missing—there was still a chance. All she had to do was believe that, and Kady would come home.

Mike Arrington stopped by and Sherry did not even have to ask him how the case was going, she could tell by the drained, exhausted look on his face that nothing new had happened.

They stood looking at each other, both of them too exhausted to stay on ceremony. Sherry's courage ebbed. "The chances are getting less, aren't they?" she whispered. "With each hour, they get less."

"Don't think that way."

"But I'm right, aren't I?"

He hesitated. She could tell he hadn't had any sleep, his cheeks were stubbled and his hair looked darker, lanker. His lips were cracked from the cold. "No, dammit," he said, "we've got, what, 3000, 4000 people out there, we've got posters everywhere, TV crews, everybody in the state knows she's gone now. We're going to find her."

"Oh, God," she said, swaying toward him.

"We'll find her," he repeated.

In the attic, Kady waited out the day in her mattress shelter. Again, she had heard snowmobile motors, again she had screamed desperately, but the machines had not come close. And even then, how were they going to hear her with the motors running?

She was cold but not unbearably so, troubled by occasional bouts of shivering. The slivers on her stomach had begun to infect, and alternately itched and burned. Her cheek felt black and blue where he had hit her, her lip was sore, the skin on her wrist bone scabbed raw. But the worst was, she was incredibly thirsty.

The inside of her mouth felt like the chamois rag her mother used on the car, and it seemed to her that her tongue was stiff and wrinkly. She kept swallowing, trying to get more saliva to her mouth. The thought of the snow, lying outside the cabin by the ton, was maddening. If she had a handful, she could shove the cold stuff in her mouth, let the heat of her mouth melt it.

She heard the rustling several times, and finally, after she'd been sitting huddled in the mattress very quietly for a long time, there was another delicate rustle. Then it emerged: a raccoon with glossy fur, an adorable mask over its face, and snappy black button eyes.

Kady sat motionless. She held her breath as the raccoon ambled toward the opening where the stairs were, gave a hop downward and was gone. She felt a stab of disappointment and desertion. It was probably going out to raid people's garbage cans. Maybe it was even a mother raccoon, pregnant with babies, like the one that had lived in their own garage several years ago. They had lured it out with leftover pizza.

Her eyes watered thinking of home. What was her mother doing right now? Would she be mad that Kady had left Grandma's and gone to meet Maura? Kady knew she deserved to be grounded. But she didn't care, if only she could go home and sit in their own TV room watching *Bill Cosby*, with their striped Hudson's Bay blanket pulled over her knees, safe and warm and protected.

She moistened dry lips. She hadn't had anything to drink since yesterday after school when she'd drunk a can of Pepsi. How many hours ago was that? About twenty-four, she figured, but it was so hard to tell without a watch. The fighting and crying and worrying had used up all the moisture inside her, she guessed, and now she was thirstier than she had ever been in her entire life.

She felt that she would give anything for one crystal glass full to the brim with sparkling tap water. Or a frothy root beer float from the A & W, with vanilla ice cream. She was hungry, too, but being thirsty was what really scared her.

How long could she live without anything to drink?

Suppose *he* just left her here tied up and never came back to get her? That was what a very mean, big boy would do if he got too scared at the awfulness of something he'd done. Just run away and forget about it. Leave her here handcuffed to the wall until she died.

The thought chilled her even more than the wind whistling through the hole in the attic window. She pictured herself a clean, white skeleton still dressed in her blue ski jacket and jeans, lying up here for years and years. Kady shuddered and made pushing motions with her hands, rejecting the mind-picture.

It couldn't happen! It wasn't going to happen! She was Kady Ann Vincent, she was going to grow up and become a children's doctor. She was going to move out to Aspen, Colorado, and live in a house right at the foot of Ajax Mountain, where she would train to be an Olympic slalom racer.

She was getting another attack of the shivers, her teeth chattering so badly she nearly bit her tongue. She didn't know which was worse—to pray he'd *never* come back, or to pray he'd come back and give her a drink and take her out of the handcuffs.

Restlessly, she thrust the vile-smelling ticking aside and got to her feet. To keep warm, she paced back and forth on the end of the chain, then began to jump up and down in place, pretending she was jumping an invisible rope. Her wrists hurt worse when she jumped, but the pain made Kady feel more awake, more alert. It made her think harder about how to escape.

She had to make her plans for when he came back.

Somehow, she'd have to make him unlock the handcuffs.

Next, she'd have to squirm away from him, get away somehow, and run out of the cabin.

Then she would run through the snow and into the woods, darting through the trees so fast he couldn't catch her. She'd keep running until she found a house with a telephone, or some cars on a road, and she'd ask for help. The people would telephone the Sheriff and the Sheriff would call her mother and Sherry would come and get her.

Kady stopped jumping, because breathing with her mouth open was making her thirstier. She stood still for a minute, the brave plans gradually fading and dissolving under the pressure of reality. He might not unlock her at all, because it would be easier to do things to her if she was still handcuffed. If he did unlock her, she was weak from thirst and hunger, and she was only a girl, and she might not be able to roll away fast enough. And even if she did try to run through the woods, he might have a snowmobile, he could follow her.

*No*, she told herself. *It won't be like that. I won't let it be. I'll fight. I'll fight hard. Those girls on the videotape, they didn't fight hard enough; I bet they just cried and felt sorry for themselves and didn't fight to get away. I'm different.*

She peered toward the end of the attic where the broken window gave a view of white sky and treetops. A few specky snowflakes were coming down, some of them drifting inside the attic itself. Even as she watched, their speed and velocity seemed to increase. Was it getting a little darker?

Hadn't the sky faded to a slightly deeper shade of gray?

She pulled as far as she could to the end of her chain, straining to see. Yes. Those were snow clouds, it was already late afternoon and it was going to snow, it would probably snow all night.

Her throat constricted, her heart thumping in slow, thick beats.

Snow.

It would cover everything with inches of white; it would cover up the rough road that led into these old cabins, blocking access to any car. It would smooth over all the footprints and tire tracks. Everything would look flat and white. Even the snowmobiles wouldn't find her then.

There would be no clue, no trace, that Kady Ann Vincent had ever been here at all.

# CHAPTER 32

By 7:00 Saturday it was snowing thickly, the blizzard gathering momentum. When volunteers came in to Margaret's to grab a cup of hot coffee and a plateful of food, white flakes dotted their hats and shoulders and stuck in beards and mustaches. Margaret's carpet became soaked with snow people had tracked in.

Sherry had not believed they could know so many people, or that so many others besides herself could be so anxious. The phone had rung nonstop. She had begun to accumulate an odd collection of gifts—stuffed animals for Kady, an envelope full of savings bonds (from Maida), a bottle half full of Valium, a book called *When Bad Things Happen to Good People*, and already a grocery sack full of cards, many from people she did not even know. One was a hate letter informing her she was being punished by God for divorcing her husband.

"Look, Sherry," her mother said. "Buddy brought

today's *News*. You're in it, honey. You're on the front page again."

She thrust the state edition at Sherry. Slowly Sherry took it. Despite an odd protectiveness of the town that had concealed this for a day, the papers had finally realized who she was. Now a black-and-white photograph of a beauty queen with an armload of roses dominated the top half of the front page.

A headline blazoned out pathos. *Former Miss Michigan Says "I Want My Little Girl Back," Brave Mother Won't Give Up, Say Small-Town Neighbors.*

Sherry studied the grainy reproduction, feeling as if it had been taken of someone completely different from herself. The picture in every way depicted a stereotypical beauty queen entranced with her own accomplishment. The wide smile was straight off a runway. The face was smooth and young and porelessly plastic, lips perfectly outlined with lipstick, the expression exactly right, like the features painted on a Barbie Doll.

This was herself? This was Sherry Smith, the girl who had had such a struggle with her mother, the girl that Carole Hamner had hated for her beauty? Whose husband had philandered shamelessly and given her gonorrhea?

"Isn't it pretty?" Margaret was saying. "Oh, Sherry, they haven't printed that picture in so long, I'd forgotten how nice you looked. I wish they'd used color, though. They didn't use color in the *News* back when you were crowned."

Sherry scowled, thinking that in spite of everything, her mother could still find a part of herself to enjoy this publicity. How could she have grown up in such an atmosphere, raised by such a woman? Had there been some kind of infection in her upbringing, had they somehow passed it on to Kady? Was Kady now paying the price?

She shook her head, thrusting the paper away.

The snow had brought on a mood of deep depression and she knew she was getting dangerously close to falling apart. She'd barely slept in days, and last night, although she'd grabbed five hours, it had been more nightmare than sleep. How long could a person push herself without cracking?

She was so tired of waiting! It was debilitating her, trying to keep up a brave front when she didn't feel brave, forcing herself to push away the emotions she really felt. She wasn't going to be able to do that successfully for very long. Something had to happen soon. It had to.

With a wild rush of sadness and longing, she wished for Dr. Frey. She guessed maybe part of her had loved Nanette, because Nanette had given her a penlight that she could shine into the depths of her soul, illuminating blocks of problems but also revealing something else. She had strength. Real strength that would not let her down.

Margaret had taken the *News* and spread it out on the couch, and was reading the cover story avidly, following its continuation on the back pages of section one. "Sherry! Listen. *An entire town has rallied around the loss of a beautiful twelve-year-old residents say was slated for a modeling career in New York. Kady Ann Vincent was scheduled to meet with officials at the Wilhelmina Modeling Agency in New York when—*"

"She was not scheduled," Sherry said.

"Well . . . It wouldn't have hurt anything just to talk."

"She did not have an appointment. Who told them that? You know I didn't want her to go. Why do the papers jump on everything and sensationalize it?"

"But I'm just trying to read you this—"

"I don't care, I don't want to hear it, they make it sound all wrong." Sherry jumped to her feet and began to pace back and forth with quick, hard steps.

"I don't think it sounds that wrong, Sherry, they're just trying to make the story a little bit interesting, and it may even help when Kady gets back. Remember the little Cichan girl, the one who survived that airline crash? What was her name, Cordelia? Cecilia? She got all kinds of recognition and if her family hadn't hidden her away, she would have—"

"This is not a media event!" Sherry shouted. "Mom, I can't believe you're really talking like this. I can't *believe* you. I'm going out for a while. I have to get out of here, I can't take this anymore."

"But, Sherry—"

"I'm going *out*. You can answer the phone; I've had it."

"But, Sherry, where are you going, if anyone asks? If that Arrington man calls? I should know because if I have to contact you—"

"*Out*," Sherry snapped.

On the porch, she breathed in great gulps of frigid air, while the wind whipped through the Victorian latticework at the far end of the porch, spraying her with snow. Around the porch light, snowflakes formed a forty-five-degree angle in a ceaseless pattern. Down the street someone was running a snowblower, hoping to get a start on the six or seven inches that were sure to fall.

Someone had parked too close to Sherry's car, and she had to rock it back and forth, making sharp, tight turns, before she could finally get out. "*Oh, shit*," she muttered angrily. "*Oh, fuck shit shit.*"

She drove straight through town. She had decided to drive by and see if Arrington was in his office. She was tired of phone conversations, she would talk to him in person; she would even stand with her head bent into his chest, and let him put his arm around her if he wanted to do so, because right now she felt like sagging, giving in and crying, being held.

This was too hard to do alone anymore. She needed someone, if only for a few minutes, to whom she could let go.

The expressway had been plowed and salted, but snow already covered it with several fresh inches. Snow spangled in front of her headlights. She passed several cars spun off the road, and a Spartan Stores truck was jackknifed at a ramp, flares glowing pink.

She skidded on the exit and had to fight the wheel, crawling sideways for what seemed an interminable length of time. There was an AAA wrecker in front of the Sheriff's Department as she pulled up, hauling a motorist out of a ditch. In this kind of weather you would wait four or more hours for a tow.

She squeezed into the lot behind the truck and parked.

Sherry trudged up a flight of stairs to the office Arrington used, to be told by a pudgy man with a brown, drooping mustache that the detective was out.

She experienced a wave of disappointment so strong she almost cried right then and there. She'd been counting on seeing him—counting on the hug. Maybe he'd been brusque on the phone, but it was only because he cared as much as she did, and she needed to be with him for just a minute or two.

"Sorry, he's been working practically right around the clock, Mrs. Vincent," the man said, recognizing her.

"But don't you know where he's gone?"

"Probably home. Sorry."

"Where—where does he live?"

"I can't give that out."

Tears sprang to her eyes. "But I need to talk to him!"

"Sorry, it's policy, we don't give out home addresses."

She turned on her heel and walked out, feeling a rush of anger that she knew was childish; he had been working twenty-four hours a day, he probably had gone home to sleep; he would be no good to Kady if he was too exhausted to make decisions. Her own emotions were starting to fray, she was too tired to keep them in check much longer.

On the way back to the expressway, she passed a cafe, its windows lit up, steamy from the heat inside. Silhouettes of patrons inside were hunched at a counter over coffee. Her mouth suddenly watered; she hadn't been able to eat since Kady had been taken. A place like that would have hamburgers with cottage fries, thick slices of apple pie swimming in tart juice, coffee so hot it burned the tongue.

She didn't stop. She left Grayling, pointing her car stubbornly into the face of the snow-filled wind, damned if she was going to give up yet, or take comfort when Kady was somewhere out there, full of terror.

Back on I-75, she tried to decide what to do next. She couldn't go back to Margaret's again, at least not yet. There must be something more effective for her to do than just wait.

She wondered if she should stop at Dick's again, just to see if he was back. She felt reasonably certain that Dick was with a woman; he was what she had once seen described in a book as a "sexual varietist." She wondered if he even knew that Kady was missing. Didn't he read the papers? Maybe he'd been in bed the entire past two days, screwing his brains out.

She really thought she hated him for being so callous. His daughter was gone and he couldn't even be found.

The road that went into town took her past the Freys', and Sherry took her foot off the accelerator, slowing the car. The house looked shrouded tonight, its cavernous black burned area softened with drifting white. The house seemed to mock her with its secrets. How had Dr. Frey died? Was it really just an accident of a burning candle, or had it been arson?

She remembered the case records she had found, compressed into a nearly indecipherable mass. She had pushed most of them back into the fireproof safe.

Were any of the papers readable at all? She doubted it. Anyway, what did finding a case record prove? This wasn't the dark ages anymore, plenty of people went to see a therapist and there was no crime in it.

Still, she pulled to a stop a hundred feet down the road and began to back up. No doubt the Fire Department had gone through the rubble, sifting out any possible clues. But maybe they didn't know what to look for. Maybe they'd been careless. And tonight she saw no gang of snowmobilers to scare her away.

The Freys' drive was unplowed but previous tire tracks had left a flattened area lengthy enough to park in. Sherry had just gotten out of her car and started toward the house, however, when she was startled to see headlights on the road, headlights that came to a halt just behind her own car.

"Hey!" a man called out.

My God, it was Bob Frey. Sherry jumped guiltily. She hadn't done anything yet—she had only parked in the drive. Still, she felt as if she had been caught breaking and entering. Which, she supposed, was exactly what she planned to do.

"Hi," she said, deciding to brazen it out.

"I saw you coming off the expressway, I was right behind you, I recognized your car."

"Yes, I was in Grayling."

He got out of his car and came up to her, steam pluming out of his mouth, a Russian-type Astrakhan hat pulled down over his ears. He looked even more haggard than before, puffy, dark circles bagging under his eyes.

"Your daughter," Bob Frey said. "One of my clients called me, about her being missing. My God, I'm sorry. I've been thinking about her ever since, thinking about what you said to me." He paced about in the snow, almost as if angry with her for putting him in this position.

"Yes?"

"I don't know what the hell to tell you. I told the Sheriff's Department that all the case records were burned, and that even if they hadn't been, they were going to have to get a warrant before I turned them over."

She lifted her chin and stared him straight in the eye. "I'll tell you something," she said. "I've already been picking through the wreckage here. I came at night and I found some bits and pieces that hadn't been burned, and that's why I'm here right now. I was going to look for more."

"What? That's trespassing!"

"My little girl is missing, Mr. Frey, do you know what that means? Some horrible child molester has done this, I'm sure of it. She's being kept locked up somewhere. Maybe she's already been raped by now." Sherry's voice quivered. "Maybe they are planning to kill her."

"You don't know that."

"I do know it! We received obscene videotapes, Mr. Frey; it was all spelled out!"

He was staring at her, his mouth open. Sherry went on in a rush, "You can tell the Sheriff to get his warrant, you can tell me to stay away from your house, but if I thought there was really something here, you couldn't keep me out. You'd have to have this place guarded twenty-four hours a day, and even then you'd better have guns and dogs, because *my little girl is more important to me than any damn search warrant and dammit I don't see how you can be so callous!"*

She was shaking and she knew she'd been yelling at more than just Frey. He looked at her, then stared away across a vacant field where snow swirled, beginning to mound into drifts.

"I *have* been thinking about you."

"Oh, well, that's wonderful! I hope you've been thinking about Kady, too, because she's the one who needs someone to think about her. She is twelve years old. She weighs one hundred ten pounds. She is five feet seven, that's pretty tall for a girl of that age, and she has—blue eyes—and her hair is—"

She stopped just in time to spare herself from breaking down in front of him.

"I saw her picture in town," Bob Frey said. "Look, Mrs. Vincent, I'm not an inhuman monster. You say you've looked through the wreckage, well, I don't think you found much, did you?"

"No," she choked.

"Well, I've been back here to the house, too," he told her. "I feel like there are a lot of unfinished things here. And I found some pieces of case records that weren't destroyed by the fire. They were lying outdoors, they were in the snow, maybe the explosions blew them out."

She stared at him. *"You mean you might have found something?"*

"I was in Grayling making copies of them, trying to decide whether to take them to the police or not. There is one record in particular— But I don't know."

He turned away, and Sherry chased after him,

damning his fussiness and uncertainty. "Please!" she panted. "If you've found something you *have* to share it with me! Please! You might not have had a daughter but you can understand my feelings, can't you? My little girl deserves a chance to live!"

"I know that."

"Please! Jesus, who are you lawyers, anyway, with all your sanctimonious legality? Lawyers don't care whose side they're on, as long as someone pays them money. Everybody knows that, that's why lawyers are so hated. We are not talking about *lawsuits* here, we are talking about a child. A child's life!"

"Your child's life may have nothing to do with these case folders I've found. The two may be totally irrelevant."

"They may, and they may not be. Do you want me to go to the Sheriff's office with this? If you want a warrant, I'll get one. I'll get Judge Waters to sign it, I know him, he and his family have ski passes at Timberline. I'll call him right now, dammit! I'll drive over there, I'll cry and I'll beg and I'll get that warrant!"

"Okay," he said.

"What?"

"It's in the car," he told her curtly over his shoulder.

She waited, stunned, while he went to the parked LeBaron and pulled a box out of the front seat. He stood holding it possessively. Sherry wondered wildly if it contained her own case record, and if he had read it.

"She was so careful to be confidential," Bob Frey said. "This town is a hotbed of gossip, she used to tell me. Not only did patients tell her their own secrets, they told her other people's, too. She said it was a terrible responsibility. She said it bothered her, being the repository of other people's—"

"Please," Sherry begged. "Oh, please show them to me."

His hesitation seemed to go on endlessly, but the wind was buffeting at both of them, and finally Frey motioned to her to slide into the front seat of his car. They slammed the doors and were enclosed together, the interior of the vehicle still holding a fading warmth from the heater Frey had had turned on. He switched on the motor and the vents began producing more heat again.

Slowly he pressed the levers that opened the case. She realized that he was almost enjoying this, that he was at a point where he wallowed in tragedy, unable to let it go. She wondered if she would be like that. You never knew what you would be like until something happened to you.

"Actually, there were six different bits of case files," he told her pedantically. "Whatever she was working on, probably a very small percentage of her total caseload."

"What kind of case records?"

"Most of them were of no interest, they belonged to minor neurotics or alcoholics, I presume. Not all the sheets I recovered had names on them or identifying material of any kind. But one of the records . . . well, when you read it you'll see what I mean."

He handed it over. It was a plain sheet of typing paper, one end seared by smoke and partly torn. The name at the top, Sherry saw to her intense astonishment, was Leonard Gray.

Disappointment burned through her like a grass fire. "But I don't even know him!"

"Read it," Frey said.

Now that she was this close to something, a real clue, Sherry's hands suddenly began to shake. She looked at the paper again. She saw that about three quarters of a page of case notes had been written in Nanette Frey's even and legible script.

Apparently Leonard Gray had been seen for six

visits. The first one had taken place on November 12, shortly after he had arrived in Hartwick. *Patient appears to be a very depressed, mildly overweight man in his mid fifties who says that since he underwent surgery for a cancerous growth in his throat, he has been bothered by obsessive thoughts of suicide.*

Sherry looked up. "But I don't understand. This is just— What does this man have to do with Kady?"

"I told you, read it."

She was too anxious to read the case record word for word, so her eyes skipped on. ... *is secretive about his past ... broke down and cried ...* She forced herself to slow down. *The patient slipped and referred to himself by another name, Bob.*

She looked up. "He didn't come to her under his own name?"

"It's common when people have information they are afraid will get out, and they are afraid the therapist might talk."

"But if the name is false ... then how can we know who it really is?"

"We can't. However, she did confide a few things to me about her patients, without mentioning names, of course," Frey told her. "She said she was sure one patient was using an assumed name. She saw him one day driving out of Timberline, that ski resort you run. When he saw her he ducked his head and turned the other way."

"Oh. But who was he? Bob? Bob is such a common name." She was very let down. This wasn't going to lead anywhere—why had he wasted her time and hope?

"Maybe he skis at Timberline. Or works there."

"Maybe ..." She reread the notations, trying to think who at Timberline was in his fifties, mildly overweight, maybe with a husky voice, and named Bob. Suddenly a thrumming sick feeling began in the center of her chest. She knew ...

Bob Nisinby, of course. Her chair-lift operator.

She was about to say so when Frey reached into the pocket of his jacket and produced another sheet of the paper written in the same script she recognized as Nanette's.

"This was stapled to that other sheet," he said. "I didn't want anyone stumbling on this material and making any connections, so I took the two sheets apart. But I think you should read it, Mrs. Vincent."

Her hands shaking, Sherry took the faded, crumpled sheet. It described Leonard Gray's seventh visit. Apparently the man had arrived late at night and had had what Nanette described as a "clinical breakthrough." Volumes of material had come pouring out, a confession.

The phrases were dry, clinical, boiled free of emotion, but still there was a sort of concentrated horror projected by that very compactness. She read every word, unable to believe, and then she read the sheet again. By the time she finished, her head was pounding as if someone had inserted a sharpened stick into her brainpan.

One paragraph in particular seared her.

*Patient complains of many sexual thoughts about young girls. He states that in his lifetime he has molested more than 350 children.*

# CHAPTER 33

Nighttime again.

Kady had started to cough. It was a sharp, hard, painful cough unlike any other she had experienced before, although her mother said she'd had croup as a baby and had barked like a seal. This cough seemed to take over her whole chest, bending her double, feeling as if there were giant zippers in the center of her, pulling her chest apart.

She couldn't seem to stay warm.

She huddled under her mattress-padding cover, with difficulty managing to pull its edges a bit closer. She was lucky *he* had handcuffed her with her hands in front, she knew. She could at least use her hands a little bit, and if she had not been able to, she would have frozen to death by now. She coughed again, shifting restlessly. It was snowing fairly thickly now, she could tell by the amount of snow that blew in through the broken window and onto the floor. Frigid air swirled past her, thrusting icy fingers inside the mattress shelter. It grabbed the small amount of body heat she had been able to accumulate, twirling it away, dissipating it in the rest of the attic.

It was because the wind had shifted direction, she thought in despair. Before, she'd been somewhat sheltered. Now she wasn't. Now even the mattress and the ski jacket she wore weren't going to be enough to keep her from exposure. And she hadn't had anything to eat or drink, which had weakened her.

The cough tore through her chest again, like Brillo pads rubbing against her bronchial tubes. What if she had pneumonia? Kady's Grandpa Smith had died of pneumonia brought on after ice-fishing on Higgins Lake.

Her skin felt funny, too. Partly hot, partly cold, and all of it, the entire length of her, achy. Kady squirmed forward to create slack in the chain that would permit her to touch her own stomach. Where she'd gotten the slivers was sore and festering. One wound in particular felt hot and hard, as tight as a marble. She wanted to dig into it with her fingernails and pull it out, rid herself of the pain.

She must have an infection.

Oh, boy, she thought, she had everything. What if she was freezing to death and had an infection and had pneumonia and was dying of thirst, too, all at once? She twisted again, clenching her chattering teeth before she bit her tongue. Shivering was a defense of the body, she'd learned in science class. It was supposed to shake you around and warm you up, that's why you did it. But when you shivered, it was a bad sign, too. Because it meant your body was losing heat at a rapid rate . . .

Another cough tore out of her. She let it come, and when it was done she leaned forward, hanging her head over her bent knees, the strength and resolve pouring out of her like water through a child's beach sieve.

They had to come for her soon, or she wasn't going to last very much longer.

The realization chilled through her, colder than any blizzard wind.

She could actually die up here, handcuffed to a ring bolt in a dirty, horrible, deserted attic where nobody ever came except camping-out hippies and raccoons. She had better start praying that *he* came back, because if he didn't, she wasn't going to make it. No matter what he did to her, even if he put his hand between her legs again, even if he did more than that, even if he hurt her, as long as he didn't kill her it was still better than dying.

Tears flooded her eyes, using up more of her precious body moisture. She thought again about the girls on the videotape, the look in their eyes of both horror and acceptance. She could understand them now, in a way she hadn't been able to before.

You would do anything to avoid dying, Kady realized with a sinking heart. That was why those girls had done those things, and she'd bet they would have done more things, too, if they'd been asked to do them, because dying was the scariest thing in the world, especially when you were locked all alone in an attic in the dark.

*Mom*, she wept to herself.

*And my dad, and Grandma, and Maura and all my friends—*

She seemed to see them all, gathered in the main room at the Timberline Lodge, where she'd had nothing but happy times. They were silhouetted under soft, warm light, the air scented with the good smells of the kitchen. Her mother wore the blue ski sweater Kady loved best, the one with leaping deer woven in a line across the front. Grandma wore the blue dust-coat she used in the house when there wasn't company, and her father was wearing the yellow ragg knit sweater Kady had given him for Christmas.

Dick Vincent sat sandwiched between Kady and Sherry, one arm around each. He pulled his two women close, saying that he was going to move back in with her mother and they were going to be a family again.

Her mother looked up, smiling, and then the fantasy faded. Kady heard the sound of a snowmobile motor somewhere outside—a noise that began as a distant insect hum and gradually grew louder and louder.

One snowmobile. Not a group, as there had been before but just one.

*What if it was him?*

The noise grew in volume, so loud it could have been in the attic with her. Kady's body actually hurt with the pressure of crouching so still. She was like a little wild deer, frozen in a thicket of trees, hearing the boot treads of the hunter. For it was the hunter. She felt it deep to the center of her. Nobody rode this deep into the woods by themselves on a snowmobile; it wasn't safe, you could get all kinds of engine trouble or injuries.

The motor revved loudly and then—suddenly—it stopped. He had switched off the motor. Wet silence dropped on the woods like a cornice of snow, punctuated by the sound of wind whistling across the jagged window glass.

Then . . . nothing.

No boots crunching in the snow.

Nothing at all except the wind, and her own terrified heartbeat. Seconds ticked past, enlarging and lengthening until Kady had counted to one hundred two times, then three, then four. Then she was too scared to count anymore. She just cowered in the dark, fighting a cough that threatened to erupt through her lung passages again.

She buried her face in her jacket sleeve. She

couldn't cough! She mustn't let him hear her! He must be sitting down there on his snowmobile in the falling snow, trying to decide what to do about her, whether to come up and hurt her, or go away again and leave her.

*Please*, she prayed. *Don't let him come up here.*

A step crunched in the snow. There was another hesitant step and a third, as if he had started toward the cabin but was still trying to make up his mind. Kady strained to hear. Was something clinking?

Yes, something metal, maybe he was getting an object off the snowmobile, something he'd brought with him.

Frissons of anxiety raised the hair follicles on her scalp. *What? What would he have been carrying with him? Something horrible, she'd bet. Something awful that he would use to do things to her with.*

She was so scared her heart seemed to stop. If he came up here, he would rape her and then he would kill her. The terrible certainty surged through her. She was only a twelve-year-old girl and she was going to die! Just like this, there wasn't going to be anything else for her but this.

She breathed in gasps, sinking her teeth into her lower lip, so that she wouldn't cough. Instinctively she knew that if she made any sound at all, if she indicated her presence by any means, it would be the trigger that would bring him up the stairs to her.

More sounds.

Snow, crunching.

A wood-on-wood noise as the cabin door was pulled open.

Another hollow sound as something was set down on the bare wood floor.

What? What was he setting down?

More silence, long, nerve-wracking, until Kady

thought she would scream with the tension of it. Her senses were so attuned to him that she felt as if she could almost think with his mind. He was downstairs now, he was *inside the cabin* and he was thinking, trying to decide something. Through a knothole in the floor a suggestion of yellow flashed; he must have a flashlight with him.

Any second now he'd be climbing the steep, dirty staircase; he'd shine the light on her like the raccoon they'd caught in their garage that time, and she'd stare back, the flashlight making her eyes yellow.

She swallowed dryly, her tongue sticking to the papery skin of her upper palate. She tried to think. Yes. As soon as he came up, she'd sit up and smile at him, use the smile that Grandma said was going to make her a million dollars someday in New York. Maybe that would make him think it was okay to unlock her handcuffs.

Kady figured rapidly, as the silence from downstairs seemed to envelop the whole attic like a deadly miasma, that was exactly what she would do. He had put her here because of *sex*, because of stuff that men like him did to little girls. That was what he wanted of her. That was why she was here. So . . . all she had to do was make him think she was going to let him do those things.

Let him think it long enough for her to roll away from him and throw herself toward the stairs, run down them, run out into the snow . . .

More silence, stretching on and on.

She tried to imagine his thoughts, fear forcing her into an effort that sickened her with its glimpse of adult bestiality. She imagined him torn—agonized—horribly distressed and scared.

She felt almost a psychic wave, a sensation of being in his body, thinking his thoughts, feeling the horror and indecision that spread through him now like acid. He had gone too far. There wasn't any way to turn back the clock and pretend it had never happened, because she was *here*. She was in the attic, she was chained to the wall, he couldn't undo that, could not make it go away.

If he came up here and unlocked her, what was he to do, put her in the car and take her back home to her mother? How could he do that? The Sheriff's office would be after him—all the officers, all the police cars, all the people—they'd all know what he'd done.

If only she wasn't up here now.

If only he hadn't done it.

If only he could start over again.

Kady gasped, feeling as if she'd opened a window and stared into a black, empty, yawning, terrifying hole.

She heard another scrape and clink. The sound was terrifying because she didn't know what it meant, she couldn't imagine the purpose of it.

At last came the sound she had dreaded hearing for three days now—the sound of his boots on the stair treads. Shuffle, shuffle—he moved more slowly than she'd thought he would, as if he still could not decide. And there was another sound, too, Kady realized, with a flash of pure horror.

The sound of liquid being poured.

The ploppy sound of the sides of a metal container burping as liquid came out through its opening.

He was pouring something on the stairs, Kady realized with an explosion of fear. *What liquid?* came the horrid question.

And then the answer came with the whiff of an odor that began drifting up to her, a smell oily and sharp, mechanical, sickening and familiar.

*Gasoline.*

# CHAPTER 34

Sherry stared at Bob Frey, shock thrumming through her. She glanced down at the paper he had handed her and read it again, as if perhaps she might have made a mistake the first time. But she had not. The words were still there, in Dr. Frey's handwriting, unmistakable in their meaning.

*He states that in his lifetime he has molested more than 350 children.*

She was icy cold, as if she had suddenly walked into a crypt. Her thoughts tumbled at wild tangents. This was why Dr. Frey had been trying to get in touch with her! The man had arrived late at night, had dumped this incredible story on her, and Dr. Frey had telephoned.

Her mind hesitated on the verge of a terrible knowledge like a precipice that gave way to a thousand-foot drop.

*Was Bob Nisinby, who had been running her chair lift for half a season, was he really Ray Innis?*

"Are you all right?" she heard Bob Frey ask.

"I— Yes, I'm fine."

"I have some Valium with me, I could give you some."

"No. I—I don't want any. I—" Pictures segued through her head, little girls, classrooms full of children. My God, 350 little girls could fill an entire grade school, and all of them . . . all of them had been . . .

She leaned forward, feeling a wave of dizziness and nausea.

Frey fumbled in his jacket pocket and brought out a drugstore bottle, uncapping its lid and shaking out a capsule into his palm. "Here, this is what the doctor gave me, you can swallow one without water. They fuzz your brain a little, relax you, and you don't care as much anymore. I know it's only temporary but you need something. Here. Take one."

She pushed his hand away, gathering her purse. "I have to go now," she blurted, and pushed open the car door.

"Mrs. Vincent!" he called after her. "Mrs. Vincent, where are you going? Are you going to call the—"

She was already in her own car, slamming its door. She didn't even hear him.

She drove in a frenzy, fighting waves of nausea that seemed to flow over her and subside, so that once she thought she was actually going to have to pull over to the side of the road and vomit. But gradually the nausea passed, leaving behind it a fierce anger. Bob Nisinby—Ray Innis—whoever he was—had been in *her employ*. He must be the one who had sent Kady the videotapes. And he was also Ray Innis, the man who had molested her, Judy, and Carole.

Had he also taken Kady? Did he even now have

her locked away in his home, tied up and waiting to be victimized?

Then, despite her fright and anger, she felt a rush of cold sanity and doubt. She had no proof—not really—nothing more than a piece of paper in Dr. Frey's handwriting.

She tried to picture how it would have been. Innis left Hartwick years ago under a cloud of scandal. Unable to get a teaching job, he'd drifted from place to place, taking jobs in ski or resort areas. He continued to seduce children, unable or unwilling to stop, addicted to the "high" it gave him. And always, he brooded about Hartwick. The town that had humiliated him, fired him, burned his living quarters, exposed him for what he was.

Cancer of the throat had stricken him. Guilt grew, along with increasing thoughts of suicide. He heard about the job at Timberline (Sherry had advertised in the Denver newspapers). It was a perfect vehicle for him to return, and he learned after he arrived that there was an added embellishment—by some irony of fate, Sherry had a young daughter. Prey for him, the exact age and type he preferred sexually.

Of course, Sherry had not recognized her former seducer. Why would she? Innis had been in his early thirties when she'd seen him last, handsome and black-haired. Now here he was, in his fifties, forty pounds heavier, bearded, his complexion damaged from years of sun exposure, his hairline receding. To complete the final metamorphosis, surgery on his vocal cords and subsequent radiation therapy treatments had probably changed the timbre of his voice.

Her thoughts jumped rapidly about as she tried to decide what to do. She had to call Arrington, of course—but he was at home, unreachable. And where was Bob Nisinby now? With a horrid thrill Sherry realized that he was at Timberline, running the chair lift for night skiing. He would be working until 11:00 tonight.

*If* he was Ray Innis.

What if he was not? She had jumped to a lot of conclusions, she realized. Dr. Frey had seen someone leave Timberline who she suspected was using a false name for treatment. It might not necessarily be Bob Nisinby. And even if it was, that was not enough to prove that Nisinby was Innis. Even the fact that Nisinby claimed to have molested 350 children did not automatically make him her former seventh grade teacher.

Disturbed people led strange inner lives. Suppose Nisinby had only had bad *thoughts*, what if he never actually carried them out? What if he only told Dr. Frey his thoughts, rather than actual deeds? The man was her employee. The ski area where he formerly worked had given him good recommendations. Nothing had been said to Sherry to indicate in any way that Bob Nisinby had a problem.

Or, maybe it had been another Bob who Dr. Frey had seen leaving Timberline. "Bob" was a very common name, especially in the age group of men in their fifties. "Bob" could have been one of dozens of well-to-do men who used the resort including, Sherry realized, several of her own neighbors such as Bob Engleson, even Bob Frey.

She decided that she could not call Arrington or anyone else at the Sheriff's Department until she had more solid proof. If she were to accuse her own employee of sexual deviation and kidnapping, without very solid proof, Nisinby could file a lawsuit against her that would ruin her. To pay damages she would have to sell Timberline, and even a settlement out of court would destroy her.

No, she was going to have to find out for herself.

As she turned onto the county road that led to the ski resort, a salt truck was making a U-turn from the opposite lane, lights flashing. Ahead of her was a car with a ski rack on the trunk, carrying four pairs of skis. They were obviously headed toward Timberline to take advantage of the snow. There would be plenty of work for Nisinby tonight—he couldn't possibly leave and go home until after 11:00.

The clock on the dashboard of her car said 8:33. That left her two and a half hours.

When Sherry pulled into the lot at Timberline she saw that the lot was three-quarters full of cars. Even last week, she would have been pleased at this evidence of profits. Now she couldn't have cared less. She drove around the lot searching for a space, cursing the little clock that already said 8:41.

At the door of the lodge she collided with Glen Dietz.

"Hey, Sherry. Your mother told me you might come here."

"Glen!" He looked like an ad for *Ski* magazine, wearing a blue racing-type ski jacket with inserts of yellow, ski gloves and a matching knit hat stuffed carelessly in his pocket. She stepped back in surprise and some annoyance. This was the last thing she needed! She guessed a part of her *had* been attracted to Glen; she'd be lying to herself if she said it was not true. But his sojourn with Carole had repelled her.

She continued in through the door, saying to him over her shoulder, "Sorry . . . I came here to pick up something . . . You'll have to excuse me, Glen."

Ignoring him she rushed inside, heading toward her office, where she kept her employee files with personal information on every person who worked for her. She went to her file cabinet, yanking out the middle drawer to search for the Nisinby folder.

"Sherry? Have you found something? What are you doing?" He had come into the office behind her, the feel of his presence an actual physical sensation, even though he was not touching her.

"Never mind," she said.

"Hey, come on, I'm your friend, I care."

"Glen . . . not now." She flipped through folder labels that seemed to be out of alphabetical order.

"You don't think I care about you, do you? That's why you brush me away like this. You think that Carole— She is just a pushy woman, Sherry. I suppose she's got a crush on me, but I don't have any control over that. Why do you think I came to Hartwick? Sure, I wanted to live in the country again, I wanted a simpler life, but I could have chosen to do that in a hundred other places. I came here because of you, Sherry."

"Oh, God."

"My mother wrote and said you'd gotten a divorce, she said you were free. I decided to take a chance."

"Glen—could we talk later? I'm busy with something."

He would not take the excuse. "I don't want to talk later. There's something in me that never stopped loving you, Sherry. I always compared other women to you. I always fell for tall brunettes, did you know that? Brunettes with athletic ability. Models . . . women I photographed. But they weren't you. They didn't have your life, your courage, Sherry. They weren't like—"

She had stopped listening. She found the Nisinby folder and pulled it out, opening it to the application form the man had filled out when he first applied for the job. The address was Box 28, Smith Road, Lake Ossineke. A country road that went through state forest land, a twenty-minute drive from here in good weather. Who knew how long in a blizzard? And the side roads wouldn't be plowed until last, and there could be considerable drifting by now.

She pictured herself driving down Smith Road in a blizzard.

*Damn*, she thought. There was a possibility she'd get stuck. She would need help to push her car, and she could not count on the help of neighbors. There would not be any. There was little but trees out there. And what if she needed help with Kady? Her child was not a baby anymore, but weighed as much as some grown women.

Glen's voice caught her attention again. "You're going somewhere, aren't you? You've got a lead on your little girl, don't you?"

She turned and looked at him. Glen's new car had front-wheel drive, he was male, with male strength, he was available, he wanted to help, and he did not work at Timberline. She could not possibly ask one of her male employees to accompany her tonight; what if Bob Nisinby turned out to be the wrong man and the employee talked? She would have to put aside her disgust at Glen's behavior. She had to move now, there was no more time to waste.

"Can I trust you to keep a secret?" she said to Glen.

"What kind of secret? Sherry, I'll do anything for you. Don't you know that?"

She reached out to touch his arm lightly. "We have to drive someplace, and we have to hurry."

Lake Ossineke was more a mailing address than a village—a collection of shabby homes strung around the perimeter of a small, muddy lake, one end of which was unusable because of a dead forest of pine tree trunks and stumps that rose out of the water, making the water dangerous for swimmers and water-skiers. Summer people seldom bought here, although the lake was reputed to have excellent fishing. Running off the lake like spokes were several secondary roads, on which small hunting cabins had been built a generation ago.

If anything the snow had worsened. Glen had to put his headlights on low beam and slow to a crawl. In the passenger seat, Sherry fidgeted nervously, her foot automatically braking and accelerating on air. Ugly possibilities tormented her. They could be discovered by Nisinby and charged with breaking and entering, jailed as felons, unable to search anymore because they would be incarcerated.

Or they could find Kady, dead. But her mind pushed that one away. She refused to allow herself to imagine the negative, in case thinking might make it real.

They reached Smith Road and turned left, driving into a welter of wind-driven snow that nearly obscured the road sign. Glen had downshifted, and the tires bucked along a road surface that consisted of five inches of fluffy new snow, and about six inches of hard-pack.

They were like a bickering husband and wife.

"Careful!" Sherry couldn't help backseat driving. "Don't veer to the edge, Glen, you might spin into a ditch."

"We do have snow in New York, you know."

"But not like this—not so wild."

Glen snapped, "Just let me drive."

Sherry peered into the spinning snow. Thickets of trees grew right to the road's edge, so thick and convoluted with small shrubs and scrub pines that it was nearly impenetrable. All of it now was drenched with snow, like some sort of winter jungle. Her heart sank. On roads like this, the few homes were built back from the road as much as a quarter mile. The only sign of such a dwelling might be a trail cut into the trees or a leaning mailbox.

"See anything?" Glen asked.

"We have to look for a mailbox—dammit, some of these mailboxes are twenty years old. And they could be half covered in snow."

She thought she would jump out of her skin from

agony and tension. They didn't have much time and the snow was delaying them. All at once she hated the snow—she could have jumped out of the car and run screaming down the road, cursing God and nature for blocking her like this, for wrecking things. If Kady died because of this blizzard—

"There!" she cried, jerking against the seat belt with such force that it hurt her hip bone. "There's a mailbox! Stop! There's one!"

As Glen slowed the car, Sherry pushed open the car door, skidding out onto the road. Snow pocked her face, stabbing her with needles of ice. She ran over to the box, slipping in the snow and nearly falling to her knees. The mailbox itself was just visible; it was a miracle she had seen it. It leaned at an angle, so coated with snow it might have been painted.

She batted with her gloves at the white, clearing it away. It looked like faded paint but it was too dark to see.

"Shine your headlights!" she shouted to Glen.

Glen backed up and turned the car, focusing the high beams on the mailbox. Sherry now saw some faded letters that might be an E, or was that a B? *Bead* was what it looked like. And numbers that might be a 2 and an 8, or was it another 2? This mailbox must be fifteen, eighteen years old.

Tears sprang to her eyes. Nisinby was renting, so the name on the mailbox would not be his. And the numbers were so blurry it was anybody's guess what they said.

Oh, they had to hurry, they were wasting time like this, the snow thickening with every minute. They could not afford to find themselves stuck in Nisinby's driveway when he arrived home from work. Desperation dried the saliva in her mouth, tasting sour under her tongue. She'd never done anything like this before; she was about to commit a criminal act.

She knew she'd commit any criminal act for Kady, and pay her time in jail, too.

"Well?" Glen leaned his head out of the car window. "Is it the one, Sherry? Can you tell?"

Sherry took a gamble and decided that the number that looked like a 28 actually was. "I think so! Come on, let's try— Oh, Jesus, I can't stand this, I feel like I'm in the nine o'clock movie." She jumped back in the car, her jacket and jeans coated in snow, her boots filmed with snow all the way to their tops. She pointed down the narrow trail that cut through the middle of jack pines and trash trees. "Let's go. Let's do it, Glen. Oh, Lord, I'm scared."

Suddenly reality seemed to be overwhelmingly close.

If they were to find Kady's body here—

What would she do, how would she bear it? She would never be the same again. Her whole life would be divided in two from this moment on, into before and after she found Kady. She would go on living but life would be empty for her, it would be sucked dry of all meaning or joy, and she knew she would grieve forever, as long as she drew breath. She would never recuperate.

*God*, she prayed. *God, please. Please let her be safe. I don't want to go on without her.*

Glen nosed his car between the trees. The trail wound several times, curving deeper into the snowy tangle, but it had obviously been plowed regularly, for there were plow banks on each side. Sherry took that as a good sign. Someone, at least, lived here.

It was perhaps a third of a mile when they saw the cabin, set in a small clearing that was ringed with hundred-year-old, huge stumps, raddled and rotting now, what was left from the fabulous pine forest that once had covered this land. The stumps were about twenty feet apart, plastered with snow, ugly and jagged and ghostly.

"Nobody's home," Sherry said, staring at the

cabin. It was a one-story structure built fifty or sixty years ago. It had that hutlike look common to cabins from that era, and the roof was badly in need of new shingles.

"Look," Glen said, pointing to the cabin wall. Camouflaged by snow, a snowmobile was parked there, covered in plastic sheeting that blended in with the drifts. A snow shovel leaned against the wall, and now Sherry noticed barbed-wire fencing that had been built to protect garbage from being raided by wild animals.

They got out of the car and waded through the snow up to the porch. Glen tried the door but it was locked. It was the kind with a window in it.

"Break in," Sherry said hoarsely. "Break that window in the door and you can reach in and turn the doorknob."

He hesitated. "Are you sure you want to do this?"

"I'm sure. Hurry!"

"This is breaking and entering."

"I don't care what it is. He'll think kids did it. Hurry!" she begged. "Or I'll do it."

"Okay." Glen picked up the snow shovel and bashed in the window.

# CHAPTER 35

Sherry fumbled for the light switch. It flicked on, illuminating a typically northern Michigan cabin of a generation ago. The inner walls were made of logs between which gray caulking showed, the floor carpeted with a grimy blue shag that looked as if men in work boots had been walking over it for the past ten years. There was an antlered deer head on the wall, and two or three stuffed fish. Old magazines were stacked on the floor and on tabletops: *Field and Stream, Fly Fisherman, Michigan Outdoors.* Crusted cooking pans had been left on a table unwashed, and a green plastic garbage can was being used as a trash receptacle.

"Oh, God, how do we know this is the right place?" Sherry groaned. She was getting a crawly, uneasy feeling, the sensation of having walked into the lair of a complete stranger. Even the smell was alien, disgusting: a combination of oniony cooking odors, garbage, ancient wood, dirty carpet, and, soaked deep into the cheap nylon of the carpet, the doggy odor of some long-departed pet.

"We'd better make double sure," Glen said, going over to one of the magazine stacks to look for a mailing label. Meanwhile Sherry went to a small pine desk that was shoved up against one wall. Its surface was covered with a litter of old *Reader's Digest*s and *Publishers Clearing House* contest envelopes, beer cans, and assorted junk mail. She pulled out the top desk drawer, finding it stuffed full of old masking tape, screwdrivers, washers, jar lids, matchbooks. Crammed in with the junk was a wad of rent receipts made out in the name of Bob Nisinby.

She stepped back from the desk, sick excitement clenching her stomach muscles.

They *were* in the right place. This stinking bachelor pad was where Nisinby lived. She swallowed back a sudden surge of sour acid. The very smell was making her sick, disgust rippling through her. All the garbage . . . the filthy shag, its variegated blue nylon strands a travesty of beauty . . .

"I found a *Michigan Outdoors* with his name on it," Glen announced.

"He lives here. I found a rent receipt."

Proof, Sherry was thinking. They still needed proof. She bent over the desk, already searching the other drawers, her hands shaking so badly that the bottom drawer stuck and she had to yank on it. The double-deep drawer moved heavily, and when it was open, she discovered why. It held several old shoe boxes, dog-eared and nearly ready to fall apart.

The sight chilled her, making her think of the boxes she had found in the attic.

"Glen," she whispered. "I think . . . I think . . ."

She lifted one of the shoe boxes out, its cover gone soggy from humidity and years of handling. She pulled off the lid. Inside were several dozen letters penned in girlish handwriting on school notebook paper. But dominating these, filling the rest of the box to bulging, were more than one hundred Polaroid snapshots.

"Pictures," Sherry choked. "Oh, Glen . . ."

She picked one up. It showed a little girl about ten, posing in a bikini bottom for the camera, her hip jutted to one side in imitation of a model in *Glamour*. Her immature chest showed only nipples, no sign of breasts at all.

"He's discovered the Polaroid camera," Glen said, taking one of the pictures and holding it up to the light.

Sherry's voice thickened. "But did he take Kady, that's the question, my God, Glen, has he got her somewhere?"

"We won't know till we look. I'd say the chances are pretty damn good, though, wouldn't you? I mean, the guy has been involved with, what did you tell me? Three hundred fifty kids? How many child molesters do you think a town like Hartwick has, Sherry? He did it. You know and I know that he did it."

Sherry wanted to cry out, *No, I don't know that he did it! I don't want anyone to have done it! I want my child, I want my little girl back!* She felt a growing sense of unreality. Surely this wasn't happening, she and Glen prowling the home of a stranger. The very air seemed filthy, the smell of cooking and dog and old carpet nauseating.

"Are you okay?" Glen said, taking her arm.

"Yes, I— Oh, God, Glen." She sagged into him, leaning her face against the slick, waterproof fabric of his ski jacket. "I can't take this—I'm not brave—I just want her back." Sobs tore out of her as painful as if her heart were being shredded inch by inch.

Glen held her, one hand pressing into the center of her back as if to offer solid support, and the more strength she felt come from him, the harder Sherry cried. She'd been living under such terror for so long— How long was this nightmare going to keep up? She couldn't stand much more of this. She was living in hell right now. This was actually hell.

"Sherry, baby, please—it'll be okay, I swear it . . ." Glen murmured things and Sherry fought to bring her sobs under control. She realized that Glen was actually rocking her back and forth, and for a few seconds she allowed herself to give in to the sensation of being safe and sheltered and protected.

Then she forced herself to pull away, jamming at her eyes with her fists, smearing away the tears, angry at herself for her weakness. She didn't have time to cry. Her daughter needed her. She fumbled in her pocket for a tissue and blew her nose.

"Are you better now?"

"Yes," she said hoarsely.

"Then come on, Sherry, I hate to be cruel about it but you're going to have to cry later. We're cutting this pretty fine."

They began searching the cabin. There wasn't much room to hide a person; the place did not have closets. The tiny kitchen had oilcloth tacked over open shelves stuffed with ancient, carbon-caked pans. Bending to peer underneath the filthy sink, Sherry felt a surge of the nausea that affected her when she was afraid.

She stood clinging to the old, plastic-covered counter, fighting not to throw up. Glen came out of the utility area that held an oil furnace and small water heater and slid his arm around her.

"Don't fall apart again," he warned.

"I'm not falling apart! I'm fine!" she snapped.

"The guy's a real crud, isn't he? I can't believe this place. A garbage can for his wastebasket. That's convenience—you can lug it right outdoors, you don't have to mess around."

Sherry pulled away and started for the bedroom,

small and dark with its log walls, the bed half-made with a soiled green blanket. Clothes hung on hooks, many of them workmen's coveralls or flannel shirts Sherry remembered having seen Bob Nisinby wear. She could not bring herself to touch anything. She felt that if the hanging sleeve of one of those nappy plaid shirts touched her, she would scream.

There was an old pine wardrobe stuffed with fish-ermen's gear and more clothes. Sherry stood back while Glen pushed the clothes aside. No Kady. The clothes smelled of old wool and sweat.

"Under the bed," Glen commanded, pulling up the edge of the blanket.

They peered underneath, seeing nothing but dust and more of the shoe boxes. "She isn't here," Sherry said, straightening up. Bitter emotions poured through her. "I don't see how she could fit under that bed anyway. Those horrible shoe boxes barely fit." She felt a rush of anger at Glen she knew was unfair: it was hardly Glen's fault. Her eyes stung. "She's just not here!"

"We'd better check outside," Glen said.

Sherry nodded, unable to speak. If Kady were outside, then what they would be searching for would be signs of her death, indications that a body had been buried—either that, or maybe a shed or other structure where she could be being kept.

They went outside again, their boots crunching on the broken glass from the window.

"Jesus," Glen said as the wind came tearing to-ward them. He pulled the gloves out of his pocket and put them on, and Sherry zipped her jacket, feeling a chill that had nothing to do with the bliz-zard.

It was so . . . *lost* out here. All around them was the tangled wilderness of trees, the jagged, ghostly stumps, the ceaseless snow that already was drift-ing up one side of the old cabin halfway up to its roofline. It seemed as cold and cruel a setting as any Mars landscape. Sherry stifled a sob. No, it couldn't be true, it was not possible that her Kady could be lying somewhere near here.

"Flashlight," Glen said, walking to his car. While she waited for him, she pulled down her cap and put on her own gloves. Already her fingertips stung from chill, icy pain shooting up through her nails.

He came back swinging the light, which made an eerie, snow-streaked yellow cone in the dark. They started near the porch, wading through drifts that came above their boot tops. It was hopeless, Sherry thought; snow had obliterated footprints and carved out smooth, white, sculpted mounds. The blizzard was in command here, not human beings.

They tramped the snow, wading through deep parts, searching with their feet for lumpy areas beneath the white, or signs that the underlying crust might have been disturbed. Sherry knew that they were wasting their time. When they were finished here they would call Arrington, and in half an hour this place would be swarming with cars and men. Meanwhile, she wanted to look first. Sherry still believed in the psychic cord that connected her to her child.

"Come on," Glen called at her through the wind. "There's a fence over at the back—it looks relatively new."

"What?" she shouted back.

"I said there's a fence and it looks new—and I think I saw a shed back by the stumps."

She followed the flashing beam of his light, leaning forward into the blizzard wind. The fence surrounded a dog run that obviously had not been used in a long time. The shed was old, made of weathered barn wood, with cracks between the boards, sagging crazily on its foundation and about to fall down. Snow had drifted up along its western side, plastered to the boards. The door was locked with a combination lock, but Glen kicked in three of the boards, and they shone the light inside at a collection of machinery that looked as if it had once been used in a small tool and die shop.

"Shit," Glen said, thumping with his glove on the side of the shed. His jacket looked lumpy, the pockets stuffed full, and she noticed he was not wearing his hat. *Men*, she thought. Too proud to admit they might be cold. She realized that her mind was jumping around, focusing on the trivial.

"Kady's not out here," she said.

"Then where is she? Dammit, Sherry, he's got her somewhere—where could he have put her? In the woods somewhere?" Glen made a sweeping gesture that took in the snow-burdened trees fading into darkness and snow.

"No."

"Then where? She's somewhere, Sherry, and he knows where."

Sherry said, "I'll have to call Arrington. He's at home but they'll give me the number, I'll make them. I saw a phone in the cabin, we'll just have to call from here."

They had gotten as far as the porch steps when they heard the sound of a car motor and snow tires. Bob Nisinby's Chevy Blazer materialized out of the thickening blizzard. Nisinby pulled up behind Glen's car and parked. The man jumped down and started toward them, clad in the heavy-duty army surplus coverall that he wore to run the chair lift.

"It's him," Sherry groaned.

"Let me talk."

"Tell him we had car trouble—we needed to use the phone—"

The bearded man approached them, bent over in the wind. "Mrs. Vincent! What are you doing here?"

he asked his employer in obvious surprise as he drew close. "I came up the road, I saw the tracks, I didn't know who could be here."

"We needed a phone, you know how these roads are," Glen said. "We'll pay for the window."

The porch was partially sheltered from the worst of the wind. Sherry drew close to the log wall of the cabin, feeling a jolting sense of déjà vu. Here was her chair-lift operator, clad in the familiar khaki stained with oil and grease from working on the bull wheel, a sight she had seen nearly ninety times so far this season. Yet now he had leaped out of familiar context, abruptly so alien that she took a backward step, unable to breathe.

*Ray Innis.*

Despite the loose hood pulled partly up over his head, she could recognize him now, something about the eyes and the set of the mouth and chin that had not changed despite the years, the beard, and forty added pounds.

She was filled with such revulsion that she had to clench her fists.

*"You,"* she blurted.

Frightened, the man looked from her to Glen and back, his eyes traveling to the broken window, then to her again. He coughed. "I . . . I didn't feel good," he said. "I'm coming down with a flu bug or something, so I left work early, there was only another half hour of night skiing left anyway so I didn't think you'd mind. We shut down the number two chair."

Did he think she was angry because he left work early?

Glen tugged at her arm, trying to pull her toward the car, but Sherry stood her ground. "That's not why I'm here."

"I didn't think you'd mind," Nisinby repeated.

Sherry was breathing fast, her mind struggling to reconcile this, the juxtaposition of the man she knew as her chair-lift operator with the man who had sexually molested her. This, this was the handsome young teacher who she had written love letters and yearned over, the man who had caressed her by the river, his voice murmuring in her ear, the same blandishments that still spoke in her dreams.

*Ray Innis,* her mind kept screaming. *This is Ray Innis.*

"Sherry." Glen tried to urge her toward the car.

"No. I want to talk to him. Let go of me." She shook Glen's hand off. She was possessed by a devouring need, like a train hurtling toward a destination, unable to stop. Ray Innis had affected her entire life for years and she hadn't even known it. He had lurked in her unconsciousness like something evil.

"Mrs. Vincent?" Nisinby was saying.

Her voice was strong and accusing. "You knew me as Sherry."

He stared at her, fear radiating from him like heat from the old quartz heater he kept in the bathroom.

"No. Please." He looked around like a hunted animal, wind buffeting the khaki suit, his complexion suddenly gone waxy. Sherry might have felt sorry for him if the situation had not been what it was.

*"I want my little girl."*

"Your little ..." Nisinby's mouth worked, his tongue extending to moisten his lips. "I don't have ... do you think that I ... Oh, God ..." He gave up, staring at her again helplessly as if she were a snake about to strike.

"Her name is Kady," Sherry said clearly. "I'm looking for my daughter and I think you have something to do with her, don't you, Ray Innis?" She emphasized the name and was rewarded by Nisinby's lunging backward a few feet as if she had attempted to hit him.

"No," he muttered.

"I *know* who you are!" Sherry shouted, anger flooding her. "*You* were the one—in seventh grade! You molested me and Judy and Carole! You took them down to the river and raped them, didn't you?"

He looked down at the snow, his posture and attitude that of a beaten and discouraged man. He appeared more dazed than guilty, a pathetic sight rather than a frightening one. His lips moved several times before the words would come out.

"I . . . It wasn't like that. Not rape . . ."

"What was it then?" she shouted. "We were twelve years old! Twelve, does that mean anything to you? We were babies, we didn't know what anything meant, you used us, you victimized us, how could you? How could you have done such a terrible thing? And now Kady— She is innocent! Do you know what innocent is, can you even guess? She—"

"Yes, I know what innocence is," the man said hoarsely. "And I've seen your girl, your little Kady— She is perfect. She's so . . . like a rosebud . . . so beautiful. I would never hurt her, I've never hurt anyone ever, I wouldn't . . ." To her horror, Nisinby began to cry, his mouth awry like a clown mask.

"I don't feel sorry for you," she grated. "You took away my little girl, didn't you? You have her hidden somewhere. I want her back. I want her now."

"Sherry—" Glen began.

"*I want her now.*"

Nisinby shook his head, ugly tears running down his cheeks, freezing in the wind. "I don't have her. I never had her. I never even talked to her. I saw her pictures downtown in that store window but that's all. Please . . ."

Something about the way he said it, so passive
and helpless, not aggressive at all, shook Sherry's
sense of belief. This was Ray Innis, yes, but . . .

He seemed too weak and scared to have kidnapped a strong twelve-year-old girl. She looked
away from him, fighting her emotions. A horrible
doubt assailed her. Was it possible, remotely possible, that Nisinby was not the one? That he'd had
nothing to do with this? Oh, God! What was she
going to do? Every second could count. Kady could
even now be on the verge of death, crying, calling
out for her—

"Why did you decide to come to Hartwick then?"
she demanded.

"Because I saw your ad . . . I wanted to start
over," he told her in a strangled voice. "Please, Mrs.
Vincent—I didn't mean—I had cancer surgery last
fall, it changed me, have you ever lived with something like that hanging over your head? I don't
know why I came back. It just happened."

Sherry stared at him, fighting to read his expression. Nisinby just did not seem violent, and even
the pictures they had found in the shoe box were
not violence-oriented. There had even been a flirty,
teasing quality about many of the Polaroids as if
the girls themselves had cooperated. Such a contrast to the pornographic videos she'd been sent,
with their raw and obscene violence. She remembered the soft, murmuring voice of her dreams, and
even the way Nisinby had referred to Kady as a
"rosebud."

"The fire," she said at random. "What about
that?"

Nisinby looked confused. "I didn't set it. I don't
know who did. I was coming back to my room
when I saw her, I thought she did it but I never
said anything, I didn't even have time to finish
packing. Those women were after me like a pack

of bloodhounds. Your mother would have had my balls."

She stared at him, realizing he was not referring to the fire at Dr. Frey's, but the earlier fire, the one that had nearly burned down Glen's mother's house. She felt a choked, thick feeling in her throat and saw that Glen, too, had tensed beside her.

"What do you mean, 'she'? Who did you see running away?"

"The little blond one, the chubby one, little Carole."

*"Carole?"*

"Yes, I'm sure it was her, they were all after me, they were talking about cutting my balls off, your mother was the worst one, I had to just leave— They said I'd never teach again, they'd write every school district in the country, and they meant it, too . . ."

But Sherry had heard only the name *Carole*. Her pulse pounded as her mind raced over what Nisinby had just said. It seemed to have implications leading to other implications, like waves fanning out after a stone is tossed into the lake. Carole, too, had had a case record at Dr. Frey's!

*What if Carole had been the one to send the videos, and set fire to Dr. Frey's office?* It was an astonishing thought, one that seemed to roll through her mind with the force of a tidal wave.

Carole, who hated her.

Carole, who might have hated Kady, too, for her youth and supple slimness and beauty.

Carole, whose father had died three years ago, leaving her three snowmobiles and—the tidal wave kept washing, rocking her with its force—*and also leaving her an old canoe resort, the very resort near which, twenty-four years ago at the river, Ray Innis had—*

She clutched at Glen's arm. "Glen! Oh, God, Glen—"

"I have a problem," Nisinby babbled. "I tried, I

went to get counseling, I did try. I finally told her. She said I could get better. I never meant harm, I loved them, can't you see? I never hurt them, I never tried to hurt them. I'm not that way. I was a teacher, I loved kids, I love kids—"

"GLEN!" Sherry shouted. "I think I know! I think I know where Kady is!"

# CHAPTER 36

The narrow road seemed even darker, more snowy, than when they had entered, snow cutting visibility down to only yards.

"Faster!" Sherry urged, beside herself with fear. "Can't you drive any faster than this, Glen?"

"Not on this road, it's too slippery. As it is, I can't see, we're liable to get stuck, and we never should have come down here in this snow. Sherry," he added, "don't you think you're going off half cocked about this? What makes you think Kady is over at Carole's father's old canoe livery?"

"Because *Carole* has private access to it! Glen, I really think she is there. That snowmobiler, the one who was bothering us. Why did he have to be a man? Why couldn't he have been a woman? All those suits look alike . . . And I know Carole hated me because she told me she did, she told me, Glen, she *admitted* it."

"But why would she set fire to Dr. Frey's house?"

"Dr. Frey had her case record! Dr. Frey knew her secrets, Glen! This town is just full of secrets."

He manipulated the steering wheel, headlights meeting a wall of snowflakes. "Fuck," he swore. "Fuck this damn weather. Shit!" he exclaimed as the wheels spun over some obstacle under the snow. "I'm going to take you back to town, Sherry, if we can get there. I'll take you over to your mother's, and you can call Arrington, have him come out and pick up Nisinby. Search his place, give it the once-over."

She was so impatient she was on the edge of her seat, almost bouncing up and down with urgency. "Back to *town*? Glen! Kady could be at that old canoe place right now, right this very minute!"

They were at the mouth of the driveway now, and Glen accelerated, knowing if he stopped the car it would become mired in the snow. He was a good enough driver, Sherry had to admit, although she itched to be at the wheel herself. It felt passive and helpless to be a passenger now.

"You're spinning your wheels, Sherry," Glen said. "Carole Hamner didn't take Kady, she's a nurse, for God's sake. A pediatrics nurse. She loves kids, she works her butt off around kids every day."

"You're just saying that because you screwed her!" Sherry lashed out. "You don't want to believe it. Well, you weren't there when she was spewing out all her hate toward me, she really does hate me, I'm telling you the truth."

Glen looked at her. "Maybe you're the one who hates her."

"What?"

"Wasn't she the one who had the affair with Dick? The one that broke up your marriage?"

How had he known that except from Carole? Sherry stiffened, glaring at his profile. "But I didn't know she was the one, all I knew was that Dick had gonorrhea, I didn't know who he got it from! I didn't find that out until this week when Carole told me."

"And you hated hearing that, didn't you? It really boiled your blood, didn't it? All those years Dick treated you like dirt, having successions of women, always another one, not even bothering to hide it, but you never thought he'd choose one of your oldest friends, did you? You hated both of them."

"Glen!" she cried. "My God, you're twisting things . . . Are you saying that I would accuse Carole of kidnapping Kody just because she had an affair with my husband? You think I'd do that?"

"I do think you're overreacting."

"I am *not* overreacting."

"Aren't you? You cried twice while we were in that cabin and you're about to cry again now, I can hear it in your voice. Sherry, Sherry. It's been a long, rough haul for you. To meet that man again after all these years, anybody would be climbing out of their skin. It's understandable."

Who did he think he was, her shrink? Sherry drew a shaking breath. "*I am not upset.* I just want to do this, that's all."

Snow flacked the windshield of the car and swept in runneling streams across the snow ahead of them as if sprayed from a garden-hose nozzle.

"It's the middle of a blizzard, Sherry. We'll be lucky to get back to town without ending up in a ditch. We'll call Arrington when we get back, and that'll be it. Are you going to put Carole in jeopardy for nothing more than hysteria? You haven't got one ounce of solid proof about her."

Sherry slumped back in the passenger seat, feeling her head hit the neck rest. She started to speak, then closed her mouth. Was Glen right? *Was* she aiming conscious or unconscious hostility toward Carole? *Was* she "spinning her wheels," heading them both on a fruitless errand in the middle of the worst blizzard to hit the area in several years?

She felt her nervous energy drain away, as if someone had pulled out a stopper. She was so tired. Seeing Ray Innis—Bob Nisinby—had really sapped her strength. Anyway, maybe in the time they'd been gone there had been a phone call. Maybe Kady had already been found and now was eating pizza and wondering where her mother was.

They rode in silence, the enclosed space of the car forcing intimacy on them.

"I'm sorry I said those things," Glen said as they turned onto the Ossineke cutoff. "But you are so overwrought, Sherry. How much sleep have you had? A couple of hours? You just are not thinking very straight."

She thought about going back to her mother's. There would be a pot of hot coffee, plenty of tuna fish and chicken casseroles with cracker-crumb crusts. There would be Margaret's anxiety and Maida's brusque sympathy and other people to urge her to go in the guest bedroom and rest.

In the guest bedroom would be the bed Kady had slept in while she was visiting Margaret, her clothing and books still scattered on the dresser. Jeans, sweaters, the issue of *Seventeen* she had been reading, still opened to a page on "Major Makeup Mistakes."

That magazine still had Kady's fingerprints on its pages. The very oils from her skin would still be visible if someone were to dust them with fingerprint powder. If Kady never came back, those minute traces of her would soon be the only living traces, and then the magazine would grow old and be thrown away and even her fingerprints would be gone.

"*No*," Sherry blurted.

"No, what? What are you talking about? I

thought it was settled. You need some coffee, for God's sake, and maybe a sedative."

"I don't need anything except my daughter. And I am *not* going to go back to my mother's and passively wait until I am told that she is dead. I am going to keep on searching for her with every ounce of energy I have, every drop of blood in my body, and I don't *care* if it's a wild-goose chase. I don't *care* if it is useless and futile, and I don't care if Carole is falsely accused. *This is not the time to think of Carole's feelings*. When we get to M-72, Glen, turn toward the river."

He looked at her, and then he nodded. "*Okay*. Blizzard and all."

"Dammit, do you want me to drive? I will. Pull over and give me the wheel."

"I will drive."

White was all around them, snow contained in the air like dots in suspension, as if half the flakes never fell but just swirled endlessly. Sherry looked out the passenger window and thought that this blizzard would knock out the whole state. Highways, airports.

They reached a little convenience store/gas station located near Lake Ossineke, and Sherry made Glen pull in so she could use the outdoor phone. Snow whipped into her face, and she had to turn away from the wind to dial.

"Sheriff's Department? I want to talk to Mike Arrington."

"Could you hold please?" The female dispatcher's voice sounded far away, thinned by cold, the connection rattling with static.

Sherry waited on hold, hunched over the awkward little phone box that was no more than a shelf barely concealed from the elements. She could turn and see Glen's car, windshield wipers going against the snow. Glen was staring straight ahead, his face grim-looking.

"Arrington's office" came the reply at last.

"I need to speak to Detective Arrington," she began, her voice tense with hurry. "This is Sherry Vincent."

"He's out of the office, I'll have him call you."

"Please. It's important. It's *very important*," she emphasized. "Tell him I'm going out to Carole Hamner's father's old canoe resort near Sturgeon Road. That's Sturgeon Road, tell him to come right away—" Crackles burst along the wire like tiny sparklers. "Did you hear me? I'm driving out there. It's about Carole. He'll know what I mean."

She hung up and ran back to the car again, bringing in swirls of snow and wind as she jumped inside. "Drive to Sturgeon Road," she said. "You know it? Just past the road to Lewiston, near town?"

"Hell, yes. I grew up here, Sherry, if you'll remember."

Then they were on the road again, the car almost swimming through puffs of drifted white. The road blended with the snow, white-on-white.

"Jesus fucking Christ!" Glen kept swearing as he peered ahead, and Sherry tensed herself for the stomach-dropping thump that would mean they had skidded into a ditch. Her mind raced with calculations. The roads were too snowy, she needed a snowmobile. But where could she get one now? Timberline was miles out of the way . . . *Dick*. Her ex-husband owned several, and they would pass his place on the way to Sturgeon Road.

Ten minutes later they floundered into the snow-covered road that led to the A-frame subdivision. Disoriented in the pervading whiteness, Glen drove too close to the edge of the road and the car hit a snow-covered object, probably a large stone that was being used as a mailbox guard.

"Watch it!" she shouted, too late.

Glen cursed, spinning the rear tires. But the rock was thrust under the car body, immobilizing it. Sherry grabbed the ignition key and pulled it out, picking up Glen's flashlight off the seat. "Come on— I know where Dick keeps his keys and stuff. We'll borrow his Ski-Doo."

They ran through the heavy snow. The group of summer A-frames were totally deserted, no lights showing from any of them, not even Dick's. Wind had sculpted the snowdrifts between them into swirled, fantastic waves, through which they broke with their footprints, human destroyers in a world of white.

To Sherry's vast relief, the Ski-Doo was parked behind Dick's A-frame, and it was only a matter of a few minutes to dig in the snow, find the extra door key he habitually kept under a backdoor mat, track into the dark cottage, and go to the old smokeless tobacco tin where he stored an assortment of boat, locker, house, snowmobile, and other keys.

*Bastard*, Sherry thought, when an old Swedish calendar fell down from behind the tobacco tin, featuring pictures of lean-buttocked men pushing huge, red penises into blond women with yellow pubic hair.

Then they were outdoors and she was inserting the key in the Ski-Doo's electric ignition, praying it would start. There was a cloud of smoke, the motor revving obediently.

"We don't even know if this thing has gas," Glen said, bending to peer at the window gauge.

"Oh, great!" Sherry cried, and went wildly rummaging and kicking in the snowbank near the Ski-Doo until she had located a five-gallon gas can. It was only a third full. She cursed Dick for his carelessness and feverishly poured in all of the gas, the fumes dissipating in the wind.

"I'll drive," Glen said, starting toward the machine.

"No, I will." She was suddenly incensed by the balky, macho expression that had appeared on Glen's face. Was he going to pull male ego on her now, when every second counted? If she didn't need a man along she would leave him right here, let him call a wrecker from Dick's house or stay here until the snow stopped.

"Sherry—"

"For God's sake, I've been driving these things for fifteen years and you've been in New York riding in taxicabs! Don't give me a hard time, Glen, I need your help, not a stupid argument over who's going to drive! Get on behind me. Hold on to the bars and keep your feet on the running board—when we turn, lean with me, and if you see any bumps coming, prepare yourself. Have you got anything for your face? Goggles, anything?"

Glen fumbled in his pocket and brought out what looked like a folded ski hat. Sherry didn't wait for him to put it on. "Get on," she ordered. "We're going."

The Ski-Doo's motor filled Sherry's ears, the sound wet, hollow, roaring, hungry, exciting. The trail that led back to the old canoe resort had been used several times this winter by cars or snowmobiles, Sherry could tell by the feel of the trail beneath them. But now the snowmobile headlights revealed only white, surrounded on each side by the ever-present forest.

Goggles over her eyes to protect them from windchill and the sting of snow, Sherry pushed the machine to its top speed. Snow rooster-tailed out behind them in great plumes. It created a wild, exhilarating sensation almost like flying. No wonder so many people drove the machines for sport. It was an untrammeled feeling, as powerful as piloting a great jet. You soared through snow, wind beating at your face and body, you were beyond the elements, you practically *were* the wind.

An old wood-burned sign, nailed to a pine and nearly obliterated with snow, flashed past them. *Hamner Canoe Livery and Resort*.

But it was only a flash in Sherry's vision and then they had sailed past it, snow kicking up an incredible trail behind them.

She sensed a dip in the trail ahead, nearly totally concealed by the snow. She rose up on bent knees. The machine bucked and lunged beneath them, nearly throwing them off. Glen's hands dug into her waist but he threw his weight with hers, and then they were on the straight again, the motor roaring in their ears.

It was nearly a mile back, coming from this direction, although she, Judy, and Carole had used the river path in 1965. Sherry squeezed the throttle, coaxing every ounce of speed out of the Ski-Doo. She hadn't raced in years. If it were not for the situation, she could almost enjoy this.

Then there was another sign, broken in two but both halves still nailed to the tree. The road took an abrupt hook to the right. Sherry slowed the machine, leaning into the turn.

And they were there.

She stopped the Ski-Doo, the hair follicles on her back and neck rising up with the sudden, sharp sense of *having arrived*. They were so far back in the woods that the great, snow-covered forest seemed to have a presence, the trees living and almost conscious.

A scattering of log cabins grew out of the white, more shapes than anything real. One of them was only a roof supported by log poles, the shelter where the canoes had been stacked one atop the other on racks. The last canoe had been pulled out of the river here fifteen years ago, after Carole's father had his stroke. The river was invisible now, though. It would be thick ice, coated with white.

She felt an urgency somewhere deep in the center of her brain.

Glenn stirred behind her. "Jesus, there's nothing here," he said in her ear. "Look." He gestured toward the desolate scene, the scattering of cabins half buried in drifts. "No footprints, nothing. This place hasn't been used in years."

The woods and snow seemed to prove him right, the feel of the place hollow. Had she been wrong? Sherry wondered. Not a sound except for the wind. It was derelict here, almost ghostly now. The place mocked her for her foolishness. She had broken into two houses, stolen a snowmobile, all to come here to the dead center of winter.

"I don't know," she said stubbornly.

"What do you mean you don't know?" Glen burst out. "What do you *want*? What are you trying to prove here? No one's been here in days, weeks, maybe years. Listen—can you hear a shingle flapping in the wind? Carole wouldn't bring Kady here—she didn't bring anyone here. Better not idle that motor too long," he added. "We don't want to run out of gas. Talk about deserted . . . It'd take us hours to get out of here on foot."

Sherry lifted her leg over the saddle of the machine and stepped a few paces into knee-deep snow. The urgency, the sense of being *close*, still possessed her.

Glen was right. If there were tracks, the snow covered them.

"I'm just going to take a turn through," she said, turning back to the snowmobile.

This time they didn't speed, she just floated the machine over the distance between the cabins.

There were six of them, scattered over four or five acres, some almost buried under spruces that had been planted fifty years ago and now were huge, dwarfing the cabins. There was also what passed for a main lodge, with an ancient Coke machine still positioned in front, rust-pitted.

It looked unutterably lonely and cold.

"Have you seen enough?" Glen asked.

"I don't know. I want to go through the cabins."

"Oh, Jesus, are we supposed to break into them, too? What, six cabins, a lodge, a canoe shed, we should get some kind of medal for quantity." The rest of Glen's words were half blown away by the wind.

"What?" Sherry shouted. She turned off the snow-mobile so she could hear him.

"I said, if Carole did kill Kady, she wouldn't put her in a cabin, for God's sake. She'd bury her. In the woods where we'd never find her."

The world seemed to tilt under Sherry, sliding her toward its edge. *Dead.* That was why Glen didn't want her to come back here, why he thought all of this was hopeless. He thought her child was dead.

Sherry's breath caught.

Glen didn't believe that Kady was alive anymore. Maybe no one really did, maybe that was why everyone at her mother's had avoided looking directly at her, had lingered in the house as little as possible, why even her mother seemed abrupt.

Sherry's eyes glazed with tears that she had to blink away immediately before the wind iced them. She sucked in air, but it held no oxygen. Waves beat forward and back in her head, breaking on the shores of her agony.

*Dead.*

*Kady dead. Lying in the fetal position, frozen solid under the snow, not to be found until spring or maybe never.*

A dark, cowardly panic crashed in on her. She

had to get out of here! She didn't want to be the one to find her baby dead. They could not ask that of her. She needed to get back to her mother's. At least it would be light there, and there would be the smells of coffee and pasta, and the sound of voices. If she did not leave here soon, she would start screaming and crying in front of Glen. She would expose her private torture, and she couldn't stand that.

Then a sound cut across the snow.

A sound that was not wind, not a shingle knocking against an old, rotting, snow-covered roof.

It was a human voice, thin, high-pitched, and desperate.

*"Help! Oh, please, help me."*

Kady.

# CHAPTER 37

"*Kady!*" Sherry screamed, looking wildly around; the cry had seemed to float out of the driving flakes, without direction. She began running toward the nearest cabin, stumbling in the deep snow.

"Glen!" she screamed. "It's Kady! *Kady!*" She fell forward and picked herself up, snow stinging the bare skin on her face that wasn't covered by the goggles. She flung the goggles away.

"*Kady! Kady!*" She was laughing and sobbing. "Oh, where are you, baby?"

The cabin was one of the bigger ones, probably a prime choice for the tourists who had rented here by the week in the fifties and sixties. Lumps protruding from the snow indicated the shapes of an old picnic table and a homemade fieldstone barbecue. Spruces rustled, sheltering the lee side of the cabin from the worst of the snow, although she could see part of a huge drift piled at the other end, nearly halfway up the wall.

"Mom?" came the muffled, urgent call.

Sherry ran up to the old cabin door screaming behind her for Glen. She yanked at the handle and it gave immediately, nearly causing her to fall backward. She rushed into the cabin and stopped short. The interior was intensely dark, a pool of blackness unrelieved by the slight glow that seemed to shimmer from the snowstorm.

Her nostrils sucked in air, and she smelled something acridly familiar. *Gasoline.* The place smelled as if it had been saturated with it, fumes rising up from bare wooden floor. Sherry stumbled over something that sounded metal and was probably the gas can.

"KADY!" she screamed.

"Up here . . ." Her daughter's cry sounded weak and remote. "Upstairs in the attic. Mom . . ."

Sherry remembered Glen's flashlight—somehow she'd had the sense to stick it in her jacket pocket. She pulled it out and almost turned it on, but then remembered the gas fumes and didn't. What if there was a spark? Did flashlights emit tiny sparks when the batteries were used? She could not take the chance.

She heard Glen's boots behind her. The floor was obviously bare wood and probably dirty as hell. She imagined the cabin was much like the one Bob Nisinby lived in. Her grandfather had also owned one for hunting when Sherry was a child. Three cramped rooms, a staircase that led to a dormer attic with trapdoor.

"Glen. We've got to find the stairs. There's gas, it's all over everywhere, *don't light a match.* Oh, God!" She cried out as she tripped on something, maybe an abandoned chair. It was disorienting to be in such dense darkness. She felt as if the log walls were leaning toward her, ready to crash in, and the smell of gas was nauseating.

Why had the gas been poured, what did it mean?

It was as if someone had intended to burn down the cabin, then stopped at the last minute.

Had Carole done that? Did she hate Sherry that much? But she couldn't think of it now, she was crashing through the first room, groping blindly for a staircase. It was like one of the games of Blindman's Buff she and Judy and Carole had played as children, where you were terrified as you tripped into things, afraid to rip off the mask because that meant you were chicken. Unseen barriers yawned at her. She waved her hands in front of her, criss crossing the air with her hands.

The air stank of gas.

She bumped into a doorjamb, hitting her forehead on the molding with such force that she reeled backward, groaning. She was sure her forehead must be bleeding.

"Sherry?" Glen said out of the darkness.

"I hit my head on a door." Sherry was on the raw edge of adrenaline. "Glen, help me look for the stairs. I just need to find the stairs—"

She heard him crashing behind her, but she was the one who plunged forward into the dark, feeling ahead with her hands. Finally her foot hit the bottom tread of a staircase. The gasoline odor was prevalent here, too, and the stair treads actually felt greasy under her feet.

They had been soaked.

*Oh, no,* Sherry thought as she started to climb. The walls were dripping with disgusting spiderwebs. Had Carole put Kady up here and then intended to burn the whole cabin down with her in it, so nobody would ever know what had happened to her? She felt a wave of horror and anger. It was a miracle the match hadn't been lit. Carole's training as a nurse had rendered her unable, after all, to kill a child.

She felt her way up the staircase with her hands, Glen behind her, only a few steps below. The stairs were covered with crud and dirt. She jabbed her fingertip into a nailhead, the pain surprisingly intense. Glen bumped into her.

"A nail," she panted.

"Go on," he said. "Go on up then."

She reached the top. There was a trapdoor, she discovered, splintery and warped. It felt rough under her fingertips. She struggled to see in the masklike darkness, but could not. This felt like being at the bottom of a well with the lid pushed on tight. Claustrophobia pushed through her. She fought the urge to scream, panic, and run.

"Go on," Glen ordered. "Push the door up. I'm right behind, I'll try to help."

Sherry shoved at the uneven wood. It shifted and creaked, and she threw her weight behind her arms and shoved it on over. It slammed loudly on the upper attic floor.

"Mom, Mom, Mom, Mom," Kady sobbed. "Mom . . . I'm over here . . . under the mattress. I'm against the wall, I'm chained."

Sherry flew to the sound of her child's voice, handing the flashlight to Glen and just running. She tripped over something soft and padded, and lifted it aside. Kady was underneath. Sweet, soft, warm Kady, the feel of her ski jacket achingly familiar.

Sherry tried to scoop her child up, but something gripped Kady and held her fastened down. She crushed her daughter to her, burying her face in the tangled hair that smelled of cold and snow and dirt. She kissed her over and over. Cried shamelessly, kissed her, wept again. It was the most intense feeling of her life, far more sharply emotional than the moment of giving birth.

"Oh, God, oh, Kadydid . . ."

Their tears mingled together. Sherry held her child until the first raw emotions were spent. Gradually reality seeped in. They were in a deserted log cabin in the middle of a blizzard, the floor soaked with gasoline. They had to get out of here.

In the darkness she felt for Kady's hands, located the chill metal of the handcuffs, and followed with her fingers to the chain, which ran into a ring bolt in a beam. Horrified, she felt the ring. Her child had been chained here like an animal. If the gas had been ignited she would have had no possible chance to escape.

*Damn Carole*, she thought. *How could she have done this? How could she?*

"Glen," she called. "Glen, she's handcuffed here! We've got to get her loose. Over here . . . straight ahead . . . Oh, God, it's so damn dark up here."

She heard him over by the trapdoor. Kady coughed hollowly. "I'm thirsty," her daughter husked. "Nothing to drink . . . and it was so cold . . . Mom, he put gas on the stairs, he poured out gas. Then he went away."

"I know, baby, I know. We'll get you out of here right now. Glen!" Sherry called. "Over here, we've got to get these handcuffs off. We'll have to get this bolt out, or else saw through the chain. You don't suppose there's any tools around here, do you?"

"The wall," Kady whispered. "I saw some. Over by the other wall."

Glen said something and suddenly the flashlight beam played on them, spotlighting them both. Apparently it was okay to use a light because the attic did not blow up. Sherry stared down at her child in horror. The girl's wrist was raw and scabbed with dried blood in which particles of filth and mattress stuffing clung as if glued. The sleeve of Kady's new powder blue ski jacket was as begrimed as that of a bag lady.

But it was her daughter's face that gave her the biggest shock. A puffy red bruise disfigured half Kady's cheek, extending from her chin up to her blackened eye. More dirt was embedded in her skin, and filthy particles of mattress stuffing clung to her skin and even to her eyelashes.

"I l-look horrible," Kady croaked through trembling lips that were cracked and scabbed. "And I've got splinters in my stomach and they hurt awful."

Sherry felt such a wave of intense anger, she thought she would cry out. "We'll take you to the doctor, baby, as soon as we get you out. Glen, shine the light around the attic, I want to look for something to get her loose with."

The beam flickered and moved, and then Kady's thin, high scream cut through the air like a stiletto.

*"Mom, Mom, Mom! It's him, it's him!"*
"Who, Kady?"

The panic in Kady's voice was absolutely genuine. "The mask! The ski mask, the black eyes! That's what he wore! Mom!"

Sherry turned to look at Glen. Despite her entreaties, he had not moved from the top of the stairs, and now stood looking at them with what she'd thought was a ski hat pulled all the way down his face. The dim illumination from the flashlight coupled with the black trim around the mask's eye holes gave him an eerie mannequin look.

"Kady, it's just the bad light in here, and that mask. Glen, why don't you take off the—"

*"It's him!"* Kady keened. Her eyes blazed in her battered and bruised face. "Him! He took off my pants! He put tape on my mouth so I couldn't breathe! He threw me on the floor! He put me up here, he put the chains on me!" She hurled herself at Sherry, stopped cruelly by the short length of chain.

Was it true? Could it possibly be? Sherry stared at Glen, a hollow crevasse opening up in the center of her breast bone. He still had not taken off the ski mask even when it frightened the girl. He hadn't moved or denied it, just stood with the flashlight, training it on them.

My God.

"GLEN!" she screamed.

And still he said nothing, not denying the accusation.

She stared at the man she had known since grade school, who had been her fiancé, with whom, sixteen years ago, she had engaged in hot, panting necking sessions, with whom she had laughed, quarreled, and danced. Glen had given her an engagement ring embedded in an ice cube in her Pepsi glass. If she had married him, Glen would have been Kady's father.

Now he kept the mask on as if he wanted to hide from her.

She screamed, "Take that mask off!"

Glen said nothing. Did nothing. The flashlight beam wavered only a little, while Kady cowered away from the brilliant exposure of its beam, sobbing softly.

"GLEN!"

The mask made him inhuman, alien, monstrous, and Sherry's mind tumbled down horrible paths, remembering vile scenes in which young girls had been tortured and forced to have sex with men, dogs, bottles, dildos. Glen had been a part of that— how much a part she was terrified to find out. Had he only bought the videos or had he been a part of their actual filming?

Glen had to be the snowmobiler. Yes, he had buzzed their home, frightened poor Kady in the woods, terrifying her so violently that she had lost control of her bladder. Had he set fire to Dr. Frey's house, too?

*The fire at Dr. Frey's.*

If Glen had done that . . .

Then he must have poured the gasoline here, too. He must have decided there was no way to return her alive without risking identification. So he saturated the place with gas, planning to destroy the evidence of his crime in one big blaze.

Sherry would bet anything there was a book of matches or a cigarette lighter in Glen's pocket right now, waiting to be used.

Why hadn't he lit the fire yet?

Fear, she realized.

There must still be pockets of decency in Glen that had made him hesitate. Which gave her a chance to talk to him . . . persuade him . . .

"Glen, I know it must have been hard for you," she began in a voice that struggled to be even. "But it can still be okay. Why don't you just turn around and leave? You can have the snowmobile. Go now, go tonight, go back to New York. We'll say we never saw you here. Kady never saw who took her, she never saw the face. If we refuse to testify they can never convict you."

Kady was a limp bundle on the attic floor, her face gritted into the floorboards, manacled arms stretched out like an Auschwitz victim.

"Before you leave, do you have a key to the handcuffs?" Sherry asked.

"No," Glen said heavily.

"But you have to! You—"

"I threw it out of the car."

Sherry shivered violently. Despite the chill in the attic, sweat had drenched her body. "Please, I do have to get her loose, she's been up here for days, she's been injured, she needs a doctor."

"Thirsty," Kady sobbed.

The beam moved a few inches, focusing on Sherry. She squinted into its glare. "You wanted to come here," Glen said in a monotone. "I told you not to. I tried to take you to your mother's and you wouldn't go. You made this happen."

"*You* made it happen! *You!*" Then she stopped, horrified at her own outburst. She had to calm him, not upset him. Oh, God— She still couldn't believe this. Glen Dietz.

The blank yellow face in its ski mask accused her. "It would have been all right if you hadn't interfered, Sherry. It would have been fine. I would have disposed of everything; I would have disposed of it all."

*Disposed.*

Sherry listened in horror, realizing he was telling her he had intended to burn the cabin with Kady in it if she hadn't insisted on coming here now. He still intended to burn it. That was why he blocked her exit and why he refused to take off the mask; he did not want them to see his face now.

Oh, Jesus, he was psychotic. All along she'd sensed some wrongness in him, something skewed.

"Why Kady?" she whispered. "Why my child?"

The ski mask turned as if Glen's eyes were glancing nervously about the attic, finding no place to land. "Beauty is a tormentor," he muttered. "It mocks and is cruel."

"What?"

"I wanted it flamed in the ash."

Sherry stared, moistening her lips. It didn't even make sense to her.

"Dr. Frey? Did you hurt her? Did you set the fire at her office, Glen?"

His head swung from side to side.

"Glen!" Sherry screamed. "Answer me, Glen!"

Silence. Then: "She had my case file."

"She had your—" Sherry felt her insides swoop emptily. "Do you mean that *you*—"

He said it sullenly. "I went to see her in New York two years ago, I didn't use my real name. I talked about Hartwick, but I didn't know she was going to come here, the bitch. She must have liked the stuff I told her, can you believe it? She must have thought Hartwick was a great place to live."

Glen began rambling on, a confused account of a

man he had met, and filmmaking, and people not paying him for his work. Apparently he had participated in the filming of the obscene videos, then had quarreled with the producers and had quit.

"They were charlatans!" he burst out. "Assholes! Using my talent on their shit and then refusing to pay—and then the police, they were being investigated, I had to get out. I'd won prizes, I was a top photographer, I didn't want to go to prison."

Sherry tried to absorb this, horror raising the hackles on her skin.

"I made a mistake," Glen went on, his voice sounding choky. "Guilt. I don't know. I'd gotten too far in, I was afraid those people wouldn't let me out, they were—they would kill for anything. I knew I was fucked up, messed up. That's why I went to see that bitch psychologist. But it didn't help. She wanted me to give myself up, sign myself into a mental hospital. A HOSPITAL!" Glen suddenly screamed. "*I would never go to a hospital. Hospitals are for loonies. They give shock therapy.*"

It was eerie, the screaming in the dark attic, with only one narrow beam of flashlight that jumped wildly. Kady whimpered, and Sherry drew back, too, her heart thudding.

"And then when I came to Hartwick I saw her at the A & P," Glen said in the monotone again, as if the scream had never occurred. "I nearly crapped my pants. The damn psychologist, right here in Hartwick . . ."

"And that's why you set the fire?" Sherry felt sick. "Because you saw her here?"

His voice rose. "She had my case record! She had everything! She was going to put two and two together! Sooner or later she was going to run into me again and remember that other name— I had to do it, Sherry, I had to!"

She was silent for a minute, reeling under the implications of all this. "But . . . if you wanted to start over again, why did you send my daughter those videotapes?"

"TO SHOW HER," Glen shouted again in that eerie animal cry. "Beauty! It's hard and killing—she needed to see. I pictured her watching—it turned me on, Sherry! I wanted her to watch everything first, I wanted to prepare her—"

His voice droned on, rising and falling, weaving in and out of a confused litany that included herself, Carole, and Judy. Something about a summer day, and a boy fishing in a small boat on the river, drifting downstream. Realization began to dawn slowly on Sherry.

"*I saw you,*" Glen cried. "*By the river, I saw you! I saw them!*"

"You were . . . you were there?"

Glen's voice grew thick, excited. "I saw him do it, I saw him touch you . . . God, God . . . it got me so excited I kept coming back. I came to the river every day. Hoping to see more. I saw him do it to Carole, I saw her white skin and her opening, and him . . . I saw it all . . . *I wanted to do it too.*"

Sherry felt sickened to the core. Glen, a twelve-year-old boy with his sexual orientation just developing, he had watched young girls being raped and this had been a catalyst. After that, just like Ray Innis, he needed young girls to experience sexual pleasure. Grown women didn't turn him on. That was really why he had broken their engagement. Perhaps he had really hated Sherry for her expectations that he would behave as a sexually normal male . . .

A thought occurred to her. "But what about the fire at your house? Ray Innis said he saw Carole running away."

"Sure, she was running away. I tried to touch her. I wanted to do what Mr. Innis did. She yelled at me and slapped me and said she'd go and tell my mother! She was just the kind of fat bitch who would. I hated her! I hated all of you! I went back to the house. *He* was just packing, carrying stuff out to his car. I went and got a can of gas out of the garage and I poured it in his room.''

Sherry pulled her thoughts away from Glen's psychotic ramblings, nervously wondering what he planned to do, and how she could get over to the tools along the wall. She'd glimpsed a thick-headed hammer, and thought she might be able to use it to knock away the ring bolt.

But how could she? He had them pinned under the flashlight beam as surely as if it were a gun. She couldn't even attack him with the hammer. All he had to do was pull a match out of his pocket and drop it on the gasoline-soaked stairs . . .

She herself might run, but Kady was helpless, chained.

She fought to think. Glen couldn't toss the match while he was still in the attic, because then he would trap himself in the fire, too. So he would have to wait until he went outside. Toss something safely from a distance.

Unless, of course, he wanted to burn up, too, and was suicidal as well as a murderer.

She would have to hope that he was not. Because she had only one slim hope. If he turned and left her alone in the attic for a few minutes, she could rush over and smash the wall ring with the big ball peen–type hammer. Then she and Kady would just have to take their chances jumping out the window. There was a big snowdrift on that side of the cabin, Sherry remembered, and it would cushion them.

If, if, and if, she thought despairingly.

But he did intend to burn them. It was written in his body language, in the way he would not reveal himself, in the tense spread of his feet, and the way he targeted them with the damn flashlight beam.

He stepped backward toward the trapdoor, the light still trained on them. Sherry's heart felt as if it would punch its way out of her mouth. He was leaving. It was going to happen.

"Leave us the flashlight," she begged. "Please— leave it. All I ask . . . just a light. It's so dark up here, Glen. Kady is afraid of the dark."

Why would he care about that, she wondered despairingly, if he was going to burn them alive? As she said it, her eyes darted to the wall again, measuring the exact location of the big hammer. If he took the light she would have only seconds to dart for it in the dark, and she must not allow herself to become turned around.

"Please, Glen, the light."

He ignored her plea. He flashed the beam down to where the steps met the attic floor, so he himself could see to go down. As he did this, all the shadows in the attic shifted massively, looming like giants. Kady gave a little scream. Sherry waited rigidly, her pulse beating in her neck. She must time this just right; if she rushed to the hammer too soon, Glen would know, he might panic or start the fire now. Or he might even try to kill them in some other way; did he have a gun or knife? She realized in panic she hadn't even thought of that.

Shadows merged and throbbed as Glen descended the stairs, his head still above floor level. He was probably bending to see the steps. Sherry surmised, and not looking at her—anyway, she could wait no longer, she had to use the last bit of light. The wall where the tools were was already falling in blackness now, as impenetrable as funeral draping.

Lifting her feet, praying she would not stumble on an obstacle, Sherry ran toward the last dimness, to where her memory said the hammer was. Suddenly the remaining light doused. Inky blackness flooded in like an enormous wave. Sherry nearly sobbed from frustration as she dived in the direction of the hammer, her clutching hands meeting nothing but the roughened plank underside of the sloping roof.

God, God, she'd missed.

She could hear Glen walking across the cabin. She scrabbled along the wall in the dark, frantically searching for the hammer. Something hit her across the face with a sharp crack that brought tears of pain to her eyes. She gave a little indrawn scream; it was the hoe.

Down below, floorboards creaked as Glen found his way to the outer door. Sherry's hands closed on something cold and blunt: the head of the hammer. She grasped it and went skidding across in the dark again, back to where Kady was.

"Mom, are you going to—?"

"Hush!" she snapped.

Suddenly she tripped on Kady's outstretched legs, invisible in the dark, and went flying. The hammer fell out in front of her, rolling away into impenetrable darkness with a horribly loud crash.

"Mom?" Kady said, frightened.

Sherry dived after it, searching ahead of her on the floor, slivers entering her palms like tiny scalpels. *Where was it? Where the hell was it?* She'd been stupid—she hadn't positioned Kady in her head, she'd tripped, and now that hammer was lost somewhere in the dark, and those few seconds she'd lost could cost them their lives.

Maybe he wouldn't light the match right away. He'd been nervous before, maybe he would need a few minutes to work up his nerve, and in that time she could use the hammer—

She threw herself flat on the floor, doing a full body search—arms, hands, even legs scrabbling on floorboards searching for the hard, cold length of the hammer. Glen would hear her, of course. What if he came back upstairs?

Desperately Sherry probed the darkness. Had it rolled somewhere? How could a hammer that big and heavy roll anywhere? Glen was now leaving the cabin; she heard the outer door creak and then slam shut. He was locking them in here. God. He was really going to do it. Would he throw a burning rag through a window, wrapped around a rock? Make a little firebomb?

Her fingers closed on something cold.

She gripped the hammer and hurled herself across the floor again, finding Kady in the dark, traveling up her daughter's prone body with her hands until she reached the outstretched arms, and the handcuffed wrists, traveling beyond that to the chain that reached to the ring in the wall.

The damn ring. In the dark she could not see. She was going to have to hit the ring blind.

The sound of breaking glass crashed around them—a sound that came from below—and then another noise that roared and swooshed and cracked and exploded all at once. He had done it.

"MOM!" Kady screamed.

Sherry screamed, too, and threw herself toward the ring in the wall. She was going to have to anchor it with her left hand, hit with her right. Already there was smoke in the attic and dull red light flickered between the floorboards. They only had seconds; this cabin was old, its wood dried by age, and the gasoline had been all over the first floor and steps.

Desperately she lifted the hammer and pounded toward her left hand with all her strength. The head of the hammer scraped along the slant of the wall, jamming sideways into the ring and Sherry's knuckles. The pain was unbelievable; she was sure she had broken her knuckles. Sobbing, she lifted the hammer and slammed it down again.

This blow hit the ring solidly.

*"Mom!"* Kady screamed. *"The fire's coming up*

*here, it's coming through the floor, it's coming through the floor!"*

Sherry didn't even look. Red light suffused the attic. She saw that she had pounded the ring sideways like a nail that is pounded in by a novice. All she'd accomplished was to flatten the ring, not loosen it at all. Heat pressed around them, growing hotter and more virulent with each breath they took, and already the air swirled with thick, choking smoke.

"Up!" she gasped. "Kady, get closer to the wall. I'm going to have to smash the chain."

*"Hurry!"* Kady yelled. *"Oh, hurry, hurry, I don't want to burn, Mom, we're going to burn up, oh, hurry, hurry—"*

The other side of the attic was burning, the flames alive with shooting tongues of red and blue, flames that traveled slantwise toward them. Only seconds, Sherry thought frantically as she lifted the hammer with both hands. That was all they had. Then the flames would be on them, and Kady was hopelessly trapped, she'd be a pig in a barbecue pit—

She brought down the hammer with a smash.

The chain didn't break.

"MOM! MOM! MOM!" Kady was hysterical. *"The fire! The fire!"*

"Lie still!" Sherry shouted. "Don't move the damn chain."

She smashed it again. The metal links bounced under the blow, skittering. Something in Sherry snapped, and she attacked the chain in a frenzy, smashing and smashing with strength she had not known she possessed. Again. Again. Battering. Pulverizing. Her whole lifetime behind each blow: love, frustration, fear, terror.

"I can move!" Kady screamed. "Mom, stop— I can move—"

It was Kady who dragged at her now, Kady somehow pulling her away from the tongues of flame, pulling her toward the far window, the one that was broken. Sherry shed the sick weakness that had briefly descended on her and grabbed her daughter by her outstretched, still-cuffed wrists.

They got to the window, flames pursuing them, hot breath and damnation and licking smoke. The window was small, just barely big enough for a slim person—big enough for Kady. Viciously Sherry punched at it with her fists, breaking away the rest of the glass. Heat pushed at her back like a living thing.

They looked out. Snow glowed phosphorescently.

"I can't jump!" yelled Kady.

"It's snow down there!" Sherry screamed back and she lifted her child as you would a puppy, by scruff of neck and seat of pants, shoving and twisting when Kady's shoulders would not fit, and sailed her 110-pound daughter through the aperture.

"MOM!" Kady screamed into the wind, and then she fell face forward into the night and Sherry felt an agonized clenching of her chest and wondered if she was going to die of a heart attack before the fire got her. Kady sailing into air—and what if the snowdrift wasn't deep enough?

*Better than dying of fire*, her mind clicked the thought, and then she felt hot breath behind her.

She turned. The fire had reached all the way across the attic, covering the place where she and Kady had struggled with the chain, the old mattress curling and blackened and red-devoured like a special effect in some midnight movie.

Sherry's heart dropped like a stone in her chest. Frantically she turned toward the window again. Its frame was too small to fit her shoulders.

God, she couldn't get out.

She was going to burn here, right by the window, just like Dr. Frey.

Thoughts ribboned in her head like computer

tape. This was it, did it hurt to burn alive? There wasn't time for her to die of smoke inhalation, her clothes and hair were going to flame alight, and then—

She grabbed the wooden window frame and shook it. If the frame were gone, there'd be room for her to get out. The wood was old and the frame rattled a little, and desperately Sherry threw her weight on it, in a frenzy now, battering her shoulder against rotted old wood that had been installed in the 1920s. The right side of the frame cracked and Sherry threw herself at it, using her body as a battering ram, feeling the agony as her shoulder blade cracked.

"MOM!" Kady screamed from somewhere below, and then the right side of the frame splintered away. Sherry stripped off her ski jacket to make her bulk smaller, the flames behind her grasping it with red tongues even as she aimed herself into the aperture, shoulders at an angle.

Either she got through or she didn't. Either she fit or she didn't.

She wriggled and shoved herself, pain arcing through her shoulder, and for what seemed an eternity she hung there, crying in terror and anger that this could be happening to her, and then she braced her hands on the outside log wall, and pushed with every ounce of strength.

And suddenly she was free.

Falling forward, falling into white.

# EPILOGUE

"Mom? Are you ready yet? Are you ready?" Kady's excited voice drifted into the bathroom where Sherry was just toweling after her shower, the room thick with steam. It still hurt a little to use her left hand, but the doctors said there'd be no lasting damage. She would even be able to type, if she chose.

"Am I ready? Not unless I plan to go draped in a towel. Are *you* ready, that's the question. You need to be sure your carry-on is packed, and are your good shoes in the bag? And a book for the airplane, and some gum, and—"

"—and two new Sweet Valley High books," Kady finished, bursting into the bathroom. Kady wore a lavender sweatshirt and stone-washed jeans, her mop of black curls glossy. Not a trace remained on her face of the huge, ugly bruise that had marred it only six weeks previously. She was beautiful again, her peach-milk skin glowing with the health that comes from a winter of almost daily skiing.

The snow base that had covered Timberline, sometimes to a depth of three feet, had melted to dotted patches of icy slush, ending the ski season for another year. Now moist April winds tantalized with aromas of new grass and wet earth. They had Super-Saver tickets to New York. They were booked to see *Cats*, and Sherry planned to take Kady to the top of the Empire State Building, Radio City Music Hall, shopping along Fifth Avenue, to Chinatown and all the other touristy spots.

One thing they would *not* do was visit a modeling agency.

Sherry had been absolutely adamant to Margaret about that. Her daughter was not going to be pushed into the marketing of adult sexuality, which was what a modeling career was all about. In fact, Sherry was secretly pleased that Kady's orthodontist had discovered an overbite. Kady was going to need braces.

She would need to wear them for two years.

While she had wires locked onto her teeth, and a bite plate, she wouldn't be a sex object, she would live like other girls her age, pretty and leggy and toothy, just another giggly teen. When the braces came off, Kady would be two years older, better able to face the constant pressure her beauty was going to inflict.

Maybe she would handle it better than Sherry had done. Maybe she would be able to face it directly, and not deny it by living in boots and never wearing makeup.

Kady's new therapist had suggested the trip—a warm, brown-eyed woman with a new Ph.D. from the University of Michigan, whose office was in an office building just completed on the outskirts of Grayling. She was helping Kady to vent her feelings about her horrible experience, to talk out what happened with Glen Dietz in a way that Sherry, at twelve, had never been allowed to do.

Sherry was hopeful her daughter would get out of this without any permanent scars. As for herself—

She stared at her reflection in the mirror. Her own face looked back at her, made misty and haloed by steam. Her eyes had a softer look in them, a hint of confidence that had not been there before. She was different now. Stronger, although she wasn't yet quite sure how, or what this would mean to her. She had battled her own demons. She had fought for herself and her child, *she had survived*.

There was a trial ahead—a trial at which both she and Kady would have to appear as witnesses, although Kady's testimony would take place in the judge's chambers. Glen had been declared medically able to stand trial. He was facing a hell of his own, for in fleeing Sheriff's officers on Dick's snowmobile, Glen had accidentally run the machine into a tangle of snow fencing and barbed wire that someone had dumped as trash in the woods.

He had fallen with outstretched arms, and both arms had been so severely lacerated that the right one had to be amputated at the elbow, and two of the fingers on his left hand were severed as well. Doctors had sewn them back on, but Glen would have very little real use of the fingers.

In prison, Glen would have to struggle with a handicap. He had molested a child and would be at the very bottom of the prison pecking order, Sherry had been informed. There was nothing inmates hated more than a child molester, and his fellow prisoners would see that Glen paid in full.

*What goes around comes around*, Sherry thought with a stab of feeling that almost approached pity, but was not. Glen had named names in the child-porn ring, and there were going to be many more convictions. Bodies of eight young girls had al-

ready been uncovered, and the case had made national headlines.

As for Bob Nisinby, who had been Ray Innis, he
had driven away in his Blazer that blizzard night
and his whereabouts were unknown. Sherry realized he might try to molest more little girls, but he
had sought help once; perhaps he would again. She
could not control that. She had notified Arrington,
and that was all she could do.

She did not think he would be back to haunt her
dreams.

Kady had run out of the bathroom, and now she
was in the hall, calling excitedly. "Mom—hurry,
will you? You're not even dressed yet and I hear a
car in the driveway, I think he's here! I think Mike
is here!"

Oh, yes— Detective Mike Arrington was going to
drive them to Midland to the airport. Sherry wasn't
ready to date anyone, she didn't know how long it
would be before she was. Mike Arrington was
younger than she, comfortably outdoorsy, and, even
though he'd grown up in East Detroit, he fit Hartwick and Hartwick fit him.

Maybe—

"Mom, will you get *dressed*?" Kady called. "We
need to close your suitcase and we can't do it until
your deodorant and toothpaste and all that stuff is
inside it, and— *Oh!*"

"What is it, Kadydid?"

"He's brought us flowers, Mom! They're all
wrapped up in green flower-shop paper! He's crazy,
it's this huge bouquet, how are we ever going to
carry it on the *plane*?"

Sherry smiled. She didn't know how they'd carry
the flowers. Maybe they'd each wear one in their
hair. They deserved to wear flowers.

"In a minute," she called to her beautiful daughter, dropping the towel and beginning to get
dressed.